Mermaid Confidential

A NOVEL

Tim Dorsey

WILLIAM MORROW

An Imprint of HarperCollins*Publishers*

MERMAID CONFIDENTIAL. Copyright © 2022 by Tim Dorsey. All rights reserved. Printed in the United States of America. No part of this book may be used or reproduced in any manner whatsoever without written permission except in the case of brief quotations embodied in critical articles and reviews. For information, address HarperCollins Publishers, 195 Broadway, New York, NY 10007.

HarperCollins books may be purchased for educational, business, or sales promotional use. For information, please email the Special Markets Department at SPsales@harpercollins.com.

FIRST EDITION

Library of Congress Cataloging-in-Publication Data

Names: Dorsey, Tim, author.
Title: Mermaid confidential : a novel / Tim Dorsey.
Description: First edition. | New York, NY : William Morrow, [2022] |
    Series: Serge storms ; 25
Identifiers: LCCN 2021033574 (print) | LCCN 2021033575 (ebook) | ISBN
    9780062967534 (hardback) | ISBN 9780063211285 (large print edition) |
    ISBN 9780062967558 (ebook)
Classification: LCC PS3554.O719 M47 2022 (print) | LCC PS3554.O719
    (ebook) | DDC 813/.54--dc23
LC record available at https://lccn.loc.gov/2021033574
LC ebook record available at https://lccn.loc.gov/2021033575

ISBN 978-0-06-296753-4

22 23 24 25 26 LSC 10 9 8 7 6 5 4 3 2 1

For Steve Hearn

MERMAID CONFIDENTIAL

Prologue

The tourists crashed through the sheriff's blockade so they wouldn't miss the rumrunner special at a popular tiki bar.

Obviously it was Florida. But sometimes even that needs to be explained.

"Let me explain," Serge told Coleman. "Remember the hurricane last week? . . ."

. . . Earlier that day, precisely two hours before the deputies would see their white-and-orange barricades explode in splinters and land in the mangroves on the approach to the Overseas Highway. Fifty miles north, an aqua 1973 Ford Galaxie sat at a curb in the Little Haiti section of Miami, featuring block after block of sun-scorched strip malls that were all boarded up except for the jujitsu studios, immigration law offices, and wholesale outlets for all your discount voodoo needs.

Coleman pointed out the window. "There's a naked guy running down the sidewalk with a sword."

"I'm sure he has his reasons," said Serge. "Try to stay focused."

"What were we talking about?"

"The hurricane last week," said Serge. "After each storm blows through, the authorities set up checkpoints between the mainland and the Keys to keep out looters, looky-loos and others with unwelcome manners. The blockades only allow in emergency workers and bona fide residents. The beach bars are the first to open because they're more essential to the locals than electric service. A while later, after the lights come back on and the streets are cleared of coconuts, the sheriff removes the barricades for the tourists to stampede back in like herds of wildebeest on the plains of Mozambique after spotting the cheetahs."

"But Serge, how do the cops tell the residents from the tourists?"

"By that." Serge aimed a finger at a yellow decal in the corner of his windshield. "It's an official Monroe County hurricane re-entry sticker."

"But we don't live down there."

"I know," said Serge. "It's not an official sticker. It's counterfeit."

"Counterfeit stickers?"

Serge grinned large and rubbed his palms in delight. "This next fact is so nectar-of-Florida that I grooved on it a whole day when I first heard. You see, the Keys are like crack, and the addictive high is so powerful that tourists can't handle the withdrawal after a storm. They'll do almost anything to get in early and hit the watering holes on the shore. So a couple years back, some cats in Miami began cranking out counterfeit decals and selling them in alleys for twenty bucks."

"No way," said Coleman. "You're shitting me again."

"Look it up. Just type the search term 'Florida Keys counterfeit sticker,' and it will fill pages."

"Typing sounds like work," said Coleman. "I'll just agree with you."

"Anyway, that's why we're here."

"Where's here?"

Serge swept an arm at the view out the windshield: a vacant lot next to an abandoned British double-decker bus. An unusual concentration of sports cars sat parked in the dirt.

"There's a line of people waiting in that field," said Coleman. "What's going on?"

"The Miami shadow economy," said Serge. "I need to buy a counterfeit sticker."

"But you already have one."

Serge shook his head. "Here's another totally true Florida factoid that spins my propeller: The *Miami Herald* just reported that deputies at the checkpoints discovered the scam and, at last count, have confiscated more than two hundred bogus decals. The TV stations showed a huge pile of the crumpled little yellow suckers on a table at a press conference."

At the far end of the field, a Jamaican man in a green-and-yellow knit cap conducted fleet commerce. He stuck another Andrew Jackson in his fanny pack. ". . . And here's your decal—"

"Chiz!"

The Jamaican looked up. "Oh, hey, Serge. How's it hanging?"

"I need another sticker."

"Different car?"

Serge pointed back. "No, same one, but I wanted to see if you'd upgraded your decals. The cops are onto the old stickers like mine."

"Jesus! Keep your voice down." Chiz pulled him aside by the arm and whispered: "These tourists just got here and haven't heard the news. I'm trying to dump my supply and relocate to Little Nicaragua."

"Then Godspeed." Serge gave Chiz a complicated handshake and headed back to his car.

Coleman pointed across the street at a cloud of white feathers. "Two dudes are wrestling over a live chicken."

"Coleman, we've been here a million times, and you still haven't learned to filter," said Serge. "On the streets of Miami, there's more noise than signal."

An hour later, the Galaxie took the final exit off the Florida Turnpike and rolled into Florida City, the last trace of civilization on the southern tip of the mainland.

Coleman rolled a fatty in his lap. "How are we getting back into the Keys if your sticker's counterfeit?"

"That's what Walmart's for."

"Walmart?"

"One of their supercenters," said Serge. "Strategically located in the strip of chain motels, fast-food joints and gas stations before society gives way to eighteen miles of treacherous mangrove jungle between the mainland and the bridge to Key Largo. The last chance to stock up at bargain rates and wide selection before you're trapped by the sea all around and forced to purchase overpriced lamps made of seashells."

The muscle car pulled into the monster shopping center. Coleman pointed behind them. "The Walmart's back there."

"We're not going to Walmart," said Serge. "All the real action is in the parking lot."

Coleman stared out the window as they drove down rows of vehicles. "There's a bunch of people just wandering around and not getting in cars."

"Another of Florida's shadow economies," said Serge. "If you couldn't score a counterfeit sticker in Miami, this is the other way back into the Keys during the current lockdown."

"Why are so many of them wearing backpacks?"

"Stealth camping."

"What's that?"

"A huge under-the-radar phenomenon," said Serge, turning a corner and scanning the scene with keen eyes. "A tight-knit community that utilizes websites, bulletin boards and Internet videos to share the safest places to illegally sleep in your car or in the woods, which is no small trick in this state with all the 'No Overnight Parking' signs. This section of Florida City is the most popular spot before jumping off to the Keys, because the supercenter is open twenty-four hours, which gives cover to the unauthorized vehicles. You'll never notice the stealth campers until you hear about them, and then you realize they're everywhere in plain sight. See those people spilling out of that van rubbing their eyes?"

Coleman looked the other way. "Why are the campers going car to car, looking at windshields?"

"Trying to find hurricane re-entry stickers for Keys residents who drove up here to shop after taking a baseball bat to all their seashell lamps."

"What good does that do?"

"The shadow economy I mentioned," said Serge. "They wait for the car's owner to return from the store, and the haggling begins like an open-air seafood market in Morocco. Most of the campers offer money for rides or even for the sticker itself, because residents can always show their driver's license if they don't have a decal."

"You said 'most'?"

"The rest get ugly."

"I'm seeing a deal right now," said Coleman. "Those two dudes are handing over cash and throwing backpacks in a trunk."

"Re-entry stickers are recession-proof."

"So this is how we're getting back to the Keys?"

"Yes and no. I prefer trying to pinch pennies first—" Serge cut himself off and slowed to a crawl down the next row of cars.

"What is it?"

"Those two guys checking windshields up on the left."

"I don't see them."

"Because they just crouched down next to that Camaro," said Serge. "The car's owner is returning."

"She's placing shopping bags in the back seat," said Coleman. "Now she's— Holy shit! One of them just grabbed her! He's forcing her into the passenger seat, and the other got behind the wheel! Jesus! They're kidnapping her just to get to the Keys?"

"That's the ugly part," said Serge. "It's been done before. Just check any search—"

"I know," said Coleman. "Typing."

The Camaro screeched backward out of its spot and took off. Serge hit the gas. "Let's have fun."

The Galaxie followed at an unsuspicious distance through the rest of Florida City, then down into the mangroves and the causeways to Key Largo.

"Serge," said Coleman, "I hate to bring this up, but you never got a new sticker back at the parking lot. You still just have the old counterfeit one."

"Remember I mentioned pinching pennies? Everything's falling into place."

The Galaxie maintained a steady separation behind the Camaro. Five miles passed without incident, then ten, twelve . . . traffic began slowing until Serge was right on the Camaro's bumper.

Mile marker 112.5.

Traffic inched forward toward the cluster of sheriff's cars and wooden barricades. Deputies leaned to check for stickers. A few cars were allowed through, but the lion's share made pissed-off U-turns and headed back to the mainland.

Finally, it was the Camaro's turn. A deputy examined the decal. All was in order.

"Serge, what's taking so long? Why aren't they moving?"

"My guess is the deputy picked up a vibe from the female passenger," said Serge. "Hard to hide that kind of stress."

The deputy walked back to a portable tent that served as the checkpoint's command post. He talked to his colleagues, pointing back at the car. One of them got on a radio, and three other deputies headed toward the vehicle.

"Wait for it . . ." said Serge. "Wait for it . . . Now!"

Suddenly, the Camaro's tires squealed with a plume of smoke, and the barricades shattered. The deputies reversed course, sprinting back to their cruisers and taking off after the vehicle with the full ceremony of lights and sirens.

When the checkpoint was finally empty, Serge casually applied the gas and rolled through unmolested, counterfeit sticker and all.

Coleman cracked a beer. "You planned this, didn't you?"

"Me?"

The Galaxie eventually crossed the bridge to Key Largo at mile marker 107. Serge looked off to his right and slammed the brakes with both feet until the Galaxie squiggled to a stop on the shoulder. Coleman stuck out his tongue to catch the spilled beer dripping down his face. "Why'd you do that?"

Serge threw the Ford in reverse and backed up in the breakdown lane. "I saw a sleeping bag at the edge of the brush."

"You tired?"

"No, one of the kidnappers had it on his backpack." Serge stopped the car and jumped out. "There it is."

"Pinching pennies again?" asked Coleman.

"I don't want the sleeping bag," said Serge. "These guys must have had a rare flash of logic and let the woman go because they knew there'd be another roadblock around the bend organized especially for them after the deputies radioed ahead. The kidnappers headed out on foot into the mangroves and might actually get away. After what they did to that poor woman, I must deputize myself."

"The bat light went on for you again?"

"Coleman, I'll need you to drive the car and meet me three miles up the road. How much drinking have you done today?"

"That was just my first beer because I've been working on my pot responsibilities."

"I guess that's a *little* better." Serge headed toward a break in the mangroves. "Just drive slow."

"Slow is the only way to drive on weed," said Coleman. "Sometimes eight miles an hour feels like eighty. Sometimes it feels like I'm driving backwards."

"I'll need to forget I heard that." Serge took a couple steps toward the brush, stopped and closed his eyes. "I can't forget I heard that . . . Coleman, you're benched. Throw me the keys."

"You got it."

Serge caught them on the fly and disappeared into the dense shore vegetation . . .

. . . An hour later, Coleman was out cold in the passenger seat, bubbles forming on his lips with each breath. He was dreaming. It was a pleasant dream about sleeping in a car on the side of the road. Then he woke up: "Ahhhh! Now I'm confused." He looked out the window. "Why is the car moving?" He looked the other way at Serge behind the wheel. "You're back?"

"That's why the car's moving," said Serge. "Any other scenario with the car in gear would be less good."

Coleman yawned and cracked a wake-up beer. "So how did it go out there?"

"Can't complain."

They rounded the western bend, and U.S. Highway 1 straightened out on Key Largo proper. Two minutes later, they approached an empty lot next to the historic Caribbean Club, where deputies with guns drawn pulled a wiggling tarp off of two hogtied backpackers.

Coleman chugged the dregs of a beer and rested his head back with a smile. "People aren't kidding when they brag about the Keys."

"What more could you ask for?" said Serge. "Island life and fighting crime."

A FEW WEEKS LATER

The toilet seat was painted a Day-Glo orange.

It hung vertically from a tall PVC pole. The lettering on the seat celebrated some people named Katie and Jared, who apparently were married in 2014. The pole rose from salt water.

The water went down four feet, which was the depth of the tide at this hour in Toilet Seat Cut, a convenient but shallow channel along the north side of Plantation Key that allowed boaters to avoid the longer route up to Cowpens Cut while traversing Florida Bay one island down from Key Largo.

Near the wedding toilet seat was another, marking a graduation, then one for a birthday: 50 SHITTY YEARS. The white poles and their rainbow-painted seats marked the channel to prevent boaters from running aground in the seagrass and marl. More and more poles had been added over the years until it was practically a picket fence. Most had pithy bathroom-themed slogans: SITTING PRETTY; POTTYING IN THE KEYS; EAU DE TOILETTE; SOME SINK, SOME FLOAT; AINT TAKIN NO MO CRAP. One green seat had teeth and eyes to look like an alligator.

It was a Keys thing. It was also a mystery. Nobody seemed to know how the tradition had begun, only that it was the logical thing to do at this latitude. Finally, a few years back, some long-time residents came forward with a rumor: In 1960 Hurricane Donna had raked the Keys, airmailing debris throughout the mangroves. A broken-off toilet seat finished its flight by landing on a nail sticking out of a channel marker, and a man named Vernon Lamp got out his paintbrush. Sure, why not?

Today, nearly three hundred toilet seats form an almost solid row along the channel. It is a source of local pride. It can be seen from space.

Another spark of regional esteem are the giant charter fishing boats, with their tall gleaming metal towers, that sail out of sight into the Gulf Stream for tournament-size game fish. The boats are like the hood ornaments of the Upper Keys.

But there is another less gaudy kind of fishing in these islands: back country. Small, shallow-drafting skiffs head out the other way, into the labyrinth of mangrove flats in Florida Bay, where purists stalk silently to finesse some of the smaller but most elusive fish that constitute the "grand slam."

"I've almost completed my grand slam!" barked a customer's voice as his special deck-gripping sneakers stomped down the dock on Plantation Key.

The fishing guide looked up from where he was kneeling next to the livewells, pouring a pail of bait. "You must be A.J."

"All my life." The fisherman climbed aboard with the smile of perpetual hope. "I've already caught bonefish and permit on my last trips. Just need a silver king now to finish the slam."

The fishing guide, by the name of Slick, felt it was best for business if he didn't mention that an official slam needed to be accomplished within twenty-four hours. "I'm sure I can put you on a tarpon. Then you'll have an official slam."

The guide sized A.J. up as a big tipper, since he was a walking billboard for all-new, top-shelf purchases stocked at the World Wide Sportsman megastore up the street, from the designer shorts to the ventilated angler's shirt, long-brim hat with neck cover for the sun, and thousand-dollar spinning reel outfit. He also chose not to mention that the fly-casting shirt didn't match his gear. "Where you from?"

"South America. But I have a seasonal place off the Old Road on the ocean side."

Damn, the guide thought, those were the most expensive

properties on the island. No wonder he could afford all the new gear. Slick untied the line to the dock, and off they went. "Ever been to our cut?"

"I usually fish Upper Matecumbe."

"Then it'll be a surprise." Slick throttled up onto a plane across the bay.

Fifteen minutes later, A.J. scratched his head as it rotated in bewilderment. "What's with all the toilet seats on the channel markers?"

"Surprise," said the guide. "That's our cut."

Soon after, the motor was still, and Slick stood on a small platform over the engine. He was holding a long pole that silently pushed its way along the bottom so the fish wouldn't be spooked. They neared the edge of an unnamed mangrove island on the falling tide.

"We're here," said Slick. "You mentioned tarpon on the phone, so I filled the livewells with silver-dollar blue crabs. Just hook them through the edge of the top shell. Also, attach a bobber a foot or two up the line."

"Why?"

"So they'll stay suspended in the fish's line of sight. Otherwise, they'll drop right to the bottom." From his elevated platform, Slick scanned the shallow water with polarized glasses, which allowed his eyes to penetrate the brightly reflecting surface like X-ray vision. "There's one now. That fin on direct bearing off the bow. Lead him to the left."

A.J. cast, and it went just about as Slick had expected. Way off target, and too high, with a clumsy, loud *plunk* that sent the tarpon for deeper water.

"That was a perfect cast," said Slick. "You can't figure fish. Give it another try . . ."

. . . And so went the rest of the morning and into the afternoon, until the mangrove roots were tall in the water and the tide was all wrong.

A.J. reeled in another small bait crab that had died on a fool's errand. "Are you sure this is the best spot?"

"The tide's perfect here," said Slick, digging the end of his pole into the seagrass.

The sun continued tracking west, and the diligent, tedious pursuit of success became simply tedious. White heron, ibis and egrets stood erect on patches of exposed sand, as if enjoying the spectacle of futility. A.J. pulled off his cap and wiped sweat. He reached into a cooler of melting ice for a Sprite.

Nearby, someone else swept perspiration off his forehead. He was standing close to the shore of an upcoming island, concealed in the mangroves with binoculars and a cell phone.

"What am I doing wrong?" asked A.J.

"You're doing great," said Slick. "The tide's down, so slide that bobber closer to the hook."

The fun had drained out of the day, and now A.J. cast with the enthusiasm of a chore.

But as they say, even a blind pig finds the occasional acorn. Suddenly, A.J.'s rod almost jerked out of his hands. The line zipped through the water, spraying droplets, and a majestic silver fish launched into the air. "I hooked one! I can't believe it!"

Slick was even more surprised. "Less drag!" yelled the guide. "Give him line or he'll snap it."

A.J. did as told, and the show continued, the tarpon splashing and leaping over and over with its trademark airborne twists, trying to throw the hook.

"He's tiring," said the guide, poling closer. "Be patient on the reel."

It took a full half hour, but the respectable eighty-pounder eventually lay still and spent in the water next to the boat, its gills gasping. A.J. grabbed the gloves and tools to raise the fish for a photo before the release.

"Easy, so you don't drop him." Slick grabbed a cheap camera and climbed back up the platform over the Mercury engine.

A.J. strained to raise the tarpon next to his side, then turned and posed with his biggest smile of the day. "Take my picture!"

Instead, the guide quickly glanced toward shore and dove off the platform behind the skiff.

"What the hell are you doing?" A.J. unthinkingly dropped his arm, and the fish was back in the water.

Behind a canopy of mangroves, a ruddy finger pressed a button on a cell phone. Back on the boat, a radio receiver picked up a signal. It was attached to the fuel tank. A small explosive charge did its thing, and the tank's gasoline vapor did the rest.

The blast blew the motor clean off the stern and sent A.J. spinning skyward, unnaturally, like a rigid mannequin, engulfed in the fireball. The skiff had already begun burning down to the water line as A.J. splashed back into the flats. Then, anticlimactically, slivers of flaming wreckage fluttered down and sizzled themselves out in the water surrounding the charred corpse.

The emancipated tarpon swam away, thinking, *What the fuck was that about?*

Part One

Chapter 1

Down below, a puffy blanket of bright sugar-white clouds stretched to the horizon.

The Learjet continued due north on its three-hour journey. It was the kind of private jet favored by corporate boards for business travel, but this one had been converted into an expensive toy. The regular seating was replaced by a wet bar, big-screen TV, lounge chairs and a spacious couch that was often used as a bed, and not for sleeping.

The jet dropped through the clouds, revealing an emerald ocean. Ahead in the distance, a long ribbon of archipelago extended west to east across the horizon.

The lone passenger stared down from his window at the tiny charter boats, as he did on all these trips. He subconsciously thought: *What kind of fish are they catching? Should I take up the sport? What type of shoes are required?* From habit, upon approach to shore, he got up and poured himself two fingers of Diplomatico Venezuelan rum from a green sea-glass bottle. Then he joined the pilots up front for the view out the cockpit windows.

He was the kind of man who didn't require many words. You entered his proximity and automatically became alert. It was nothing he did. No soulless gaze in his eyes. Not even an expression. You just *knew*.

The pilot on the left glanced over his shoulder. "I was wondering when you were going to join us, Mr. Benz. You come up here every time."

"I like the view."

Mr. Benz had jagged facial features but soft skin, which left people uncertain upon first meeting and not knowing why. His perfectly-in-place coal-black hair matched his black Parisian suit with a maroon necktie cinched all the way up. It somewhat hid his fit frame. He didn't need for people to know he was muscular because everyone already knew he had more than enough such people on his payroll. The pilots wondered why he never loosened his tie on these flights and got comfortable, but they didn't ask. It was the Benz way, like how Frank Sinatra never sat down after dressing for a performance, because it might wrinkle his pants.

Through the cockpit's windows, the previously indistinct ribbon on the distant horizon began to take shape in two distinct categories: bridges and land. To the east, the ancient Long Key Viaduct; to the west, the unmistakable Seven Mile Bridge over Moser Channel. And on the far ends of those spans, barely discernible at this range, the islands of the Upper and Lower Florida Keys. Straight ahead in the middle were, well, the Middle Keys: a collection of isles, separated by creeks, that fit together like jigsaw pieces. Grassy Key, Fat Deer Key, Crawl Key, Vaca Key and the other lesser cays. Most visitors don't know these names, just that the city of Marathon encompasses most of them at this halfway point on the hundred-plus-mile Overseas Highway to Key West.

Mr. Benz leaned over the pilots' shoulders as the control tower came into view. It was a decent-sized runway of eight thousand smooth feet. Time and again, there were some regularly scheduled commercial flights: short-haul passenger planes called puddle jumpers. But demand was dependably undependable, and now it was just these private customers in Lears.

As the plane dropped below a thousand feet, the pilots and Mr. Benz glanced down at a solitary residence, alone at sea on its private island—a circular piece of land barely bigger than the house—surrounded by an equally circular breakwater of large boulders that created a kind of moat. There was a helicopter pad. Another stray thought in Benz's head: *I need one of those.*

The plane touched down without incident and taxied across the runway, past rows of other small jets, empty, moored with taut lines along the edge of the tarmac. The Lear rolled to a stop, and a staircase flipped down from its side onto the pavement. U.S. Customs officials came out to meet the plane. It was a perfunctory inspection. They knew the owner well and, given the nature of his work, there was no chance anything would be out of order. The brief bureaucracy ended, and Benz trotted away from the plane. The back door of a stretch limo was already held open by an assistant. Others on the Benz team were waiting inside the vehicle. The chauffeur pulled out of the airport's gates and turned east onto the Overseas Highway.

Nobody would speak until Benz did, and they knew he wouldn't speak soon because his face was at the side window, just like every other time when he first arrived on one of these visits, watching this other world go by.

He loved Marathon.

The name came from the "marathon" of night-and-day labor of the workers constructing Henry Flagler's railroad to Key West at the beginning of the twentieth century. Today, Marathon was about as urban as the Keys got. Besides the airport, there was a smattering of chain supermarkets, drug and hardware stores, Hampton and Holiday Inns. As the limo continued on, the density became less so. Benz's face drew closer to the window as they passed a stretch of old mom-and-pop-style motels. Whitewashed and trimmed in yellow, tangerine, pink, pale blue. Roadside signs with words like *Lime Tree, Seashell, Siesta, Bay, Rainbow Bend,* some in neon, some just painted, some with no signs at all. They sat on the ocean. The beaches were full of light and space, dotted with coconut palms. Lying around the patches of washed-ashore seaweed were a few plastic pails, Frisbees, badminton rackets, volleyball nets, inflatable rafts, swim noodles and a single dubious rowboat that was just left on the sand because who was going to take it?

They came to what Benz had been awaiting. The bridges. Longer and longer as they headed east, past the tiny span connecting Duck Key to the highway. Unobstructed views of water so vibrant, across a palette from jade to aquamarine, that even if you had never done drugs you began getting high.

Benz slipped under a wave of calm euphoria as he watched a fly-fisher cast from the bow of his skiff toward the shadow of a bonefish.

Screeeeeeech!

Benz tumbled violently onto the floor of the limo.

"What the hell!"

Everyone else in the rear of the limo swung into a frenzy of terrified motion. "Let me help you up!" "Are you all right?" "We don't know what happened!" "Must have been that asshole chauffeur!"

"Get your hands off me! Jesus! I'm not a child!" Benz brushed off the sleeves of his jacket as he retook his seat. He glared toward the chauffeur. "What on earth's going on up there?"

"I don't know . . ." The chauffeur gestured out the windshield at the taillights of a Dodge Ram towing a pop-up camper. "All the traffic just suddenly stopped. Not my fault."

Benz rolled down the back window and stuck his head out,

taking stock of the endless, stationary line of more taillights on sedans, convertibles, trucks, boat trailers, RVs and motorcycles, gently curving down off the bridge, onto the next island, around a bend and out of sight.

"How fast are we going?" demanded Benz.

The driver sheepishly looked down at the speedometer. "Uh, zero."

"Fantastic!" Benz fell back in his seat with a sigh. "Anyone have an idea what this holdup's about?"

Any resident of the Keys could have told him, and the answer would have been this: Anything.

It was an accepted part of the lifestyle. There was just one road, U.S. Highway 1, connecting the islands from mile marker 107 in Key Largo to the end in Key West. And any problem on that road—the slightest problem—brought a shit-stop to the whole program. Could be a fender bender, a big rock falling off a dump truck, even traffic cops helping a parking lot empty out from a school or church or one of the art fairs or music fests or something called the Nautical Flea Market. Didn't matter; everyone's day planner went out the window.

And here's another thing about the Keys: In most of the popular tourist destinations in other sections of the country, the locals live apart from the big attractions. But here, where many of the islands barely stretch a hundred yards from the big road, the two worlds exist simultaneously and congruently, and often collide. The locals are called conchs.

So when traffic becomes still life, like a painting of a fruit basket, tourists huff and curse as they feel precious vacation time draining out of their bodies like blood itself. The conchs, on the other hand, from decades of experience that has altered their DNA, emotionally plan for the unplanned: "No problemo. We get to live in the Keys, after all. Just ride with the tide and go with the flow." Which means getting out the blender. Their only impatience is with others' impatience.

The limo crawled along toward the apron of the bridge. The chauffeur glanced up in the rearview. "Excuse me, Mr. Benz . . ."

A snap: "What!"

"Uh, I think I know what's going on."

"Oh, you do?"

A nod. "It's Presidents Day weekend."

"What's that supposed to mean? . . ."

Again, any local could have told you: An unhinged *Days of Wine and Roses* descent into madness of a three-day holiday weekend, tourists enthusiastically throwing themselves into the hope of untold titillations. Then they're shocked to find themselves like this, vacationing in a stationary car on a bridge, going through the third bag of Doritos.

The conchs know better. There's nothing to see out there on the highway but heartbreak, so they prepare for each three-dayer as if it's an approaching hurricane, emptying the liquor stores and hunkering down far from the road with sacks of iced shrimp, weed and tunes. In the Keys, there is a spike in the birth rate nine months after each holiday weekend.

Back in the limo, Benz pounded his armrest and checked his wristwatch. "It's taken two hours to go ten miles. And now we're not even moving again! This can't just be the holiday!"

"I think there's also a bad accident," said the driver.

"How do you know?" Benz stuck his head out the back window once more. "I don't see anything."

The chauffeur pointed up through the windshield. "The helicopter just took off."

"What's a helicopter got to do with it?"

"Whenever there's a serious smash-up in this part of the Keys, the ambulance races from the wreck site to Coral Shores High School."

"What can the school do?" asked Benz.

"They have a football field, where the medevac helicopters land to fly the victims to trauma centers in Miami."

"Just great," said Benz.

"At least the helicopter's gone," said the driver. "They're that much closer to clearing the road . . ."

It was after nightfall when they finally reached Islamorada in the Upper Keys at mile marker 74, getting close. But not close enough at this speed. Traffic was moving better, which meant ten miles an hour. The chauffeur, though, had a secret plan . . .

FIFTY MILES AWAY

An aqua 1973 Ford Galaxie sped across the new Bahia Honda Bridge.

Coleman hung out the passenger window, retching. Then came back inside.

Serge sighed and looked over from the steering wheel. "You do realize you'll be cleaning the side of the car at the next gas station."

"It was worth it." He wiped his mouth with the back of his arm and popped another Schlitz.

Serge did a double take at his compadre. "Wait, you're a genius!"

"I am?" said Coleman.

Serge nodded hard. "You just gave me a brainstorm!" He slapped the dashboard. "I'm going to start a service to rival Uber and Lyft."

"I don't know," said Coleman. "They're pretty big outfits."

"All I need is the slightest edge, and you just gave it to me," said Serge. "Most people don't realize that down in the fine print of the terms of agreement, there's a hundred-dollar penalty for throwing up in a car. My company's motto? 'Puke for free!'"

"I'd sign up."

"You're my target market."

A few miles later, the Galaxie passed a venerable motel.

"Serge, why is that place called the Sugarloaf Lodge?"

"Because we're on Sugarloaf Key." Serge pulled over and leaned across Coleman with his camera. *Click, click, click.* "Named for the type of pineapples that were farmed all over this place back in the old days. I'm totally down with fields of pineapples. They give me hope. Then Henry Flagler built his Overseas Railroad, creating an affordable sea route for the ports in Key West to import much cheaper Cuban pineapples, and my hope was zapped. But wait! Then came the passage of the Volstead Act and Prohibition. Hidden coves in the mangroves all up and down the Keys became popular smuggling destinations for rumrunners."

"That gives *me* hope," said Coleman.

The Galaxie pulled back onto the highway.

"Serge, why do you have your hand up to the side of your face like that?"

"Because we're passing the turnoff to Bat Tower Road. I can't look." A grimace gripped his face. "The bat tower was a failed attempt in the twenties to establish a bat colony here to feast on the plague of native mosquitoes and open the island to real estate development. Or at least that's what the real estate people told everyone, and when all the bats flew away, the locals said, 'I saw that one coming,' and they went back to their mosquitoes. But the remaining wooden tower became a magnificent monument to futile strangeness that lasted almost a century, until Hurricane Irma knocked it down in 2017." A single tear rolled down his cheek. "I need to keep my hand up to block my view of the heartache and resist negative urges."

"Urges?"

"Shortly after it fell, I drove out here to pay my respects, but the locals had barricaded the end of the road and access to the site," said Serge. "They wanted to prevent tourists from swarming and taking pieces of the tower for souvenir relics like the bones of saints until there would just be a bat-tower-shaped depression in the sand. Maybe they were hoping for an Internet fund-raising campaign to upright it. Whatever the case, I'm glad they blocked the road because I wanted to get a souvenir and never would have forgiven myself. Well, not *never*. I'm big on forgiveness."

"What if they don't put the tower back up?" asked Coleman.

"In that case, I'll just have to fill that hole in my heart by going to Fantasy Fest in Key West, where some noble keepers of the flame have built a parade float with a replica bat tower, complete with monster-size bats and mosquitoes circling it," said Serge. "What other chamber of commerce in America encourages parades that include giant mosquitoes? That says integrity."

They crossed the Sugarloaf Channel Bridge to the Saddlebunch Keys and Big Coppitt. Serge made a left onto Boca Chica Road, winding south toward the Atlantic.

"Aren't we going to the Hemingway house again?" asked Coleman.

Serge shook his head. "Change of plans. We have a new mission."

"What's that?"

"I'm perfecting the Art of Slowing Down."

"Slowing down?"

"At my rate of velocity, it might have to be Operation Pump the Brakes. But whatever the nomenclature, it's about the simple things, like leisurely traveling the old roads. I've done some introspection, and all these years we've been going too fast. We need to dial it down and relax." Serge nodded firmly and swilled a travel mug of cold coffee. "My mission is a total counteroffensive against the passage of Time, because damn if Time isn't getting all up in our shit and kicking our collective ass. It's the existential threat of the ages. And by 'existential threat,' I don't mean how that term is misused constantly by TV commentators who don't even know its definition as Kierkegaard conceived it, the role of the individual to breathe meaning into life. And while I'm on the topic, ever notice how one cable commentator will use a phrase, and then all the others latch onto it for a month and beat the living piss out of it? 'Suck all the oxygen out of the room,' 'at the end of the day,' 'the view from thirty thousand feet,' 'the budget cuts are an existential threat to the sewage plant.' Wrong. An existential threat is a philosophy professor with a flamethrower."

"I still don't know what exis—what that word means," said Coleman.

"Let me put it in terms you can easily grasp. Remember that childhood song, 'Row, Row, Row Your Boat'?"

"One of my favorites," said Coleman. "'Life is butter dream.'"

"No, Coleman. Not 'butter' dream. 'But a' dream."

"But I like butter," said Coleman. "I think my version's better."

"Fuck it. Onward," said Serge. "The new mission starts by getting bone-deep into the old roads. All over Florida, there are roads that used to be the big thoroughfares, until population and traffic got too intense. They were replaced by new highways, sometimes just yards away, and the old roads are now snapshots frozen in time of the way we used to be. We're currently on the trail of one of the most famous: U.S. Highway 1, from Maine to Mile Zero, or rather the remnants of the former highway before they paved the super-wide new version." The small two-lane street swung gently west through a modest fishing neighborhood, then over the tiny bridge at Geiger Creek. "It's hard to believe now, but this narrow ribbon of pavement used to be the island's version of U.S. 1. Can you dig it?"

Suddenly, there was a tremendous roar overhead, and Coleman looked up out the windshield. "What the hell was that?"

"Probably an F-16," said Serge. "We're on Boca Chica Key, home of the Naval Air Station. U.S. 1 now sweeps by on its north side, but this old route still hugs the southern shore right along the water."

The Galaxie pulled over and stopped behind a giant concrete barricade next to a fence topped with barbed wire at the edge of the airfield. RESTRICTED AREA. NO TRESPASSING. U.S. PROPERTY.

"Looks like we're screwed," said Coleman.

"No, we're not," said Serge. "Those signs just mean don't climb the fence, and the road runs *outside* it, on that narrow sliver of land between the fence and the surf. These barricades here are only to stop cars, because in a few hundred yards the pavement collapses into the sea, and they don't want to be constantly pulling convertibles out of the drink. But you're allowed to walk the road. In my case it's mandatory."

"Why?"

"Because driving slower isn't enough." They exited the vehicle. "We need to get out on foot to extend our lives even further. Let's chill out and take a stroll—"

Bam! Bam! Bam!

Serge spun. "What the hell was that?"

Coleman pointed. "The dude you put in the trunk."

"Son of a bitch! He's speeding up time!" Serge popped the lid and swung a tire iron down until the captive was still again. "Is wanting to relax too much to ask? Or am I just crazy?"

Chapter 2

THE UPPER KEYS

Islamorada is Spanish for "purple island." It is actually four islands, incorporated into the city by the same name, plus other outlying keys, but we'll get to them later. Islamorada, as observed briefly by passing motorists, seems to have been the victim of nuclear fallout, because it's full of really giant shit. A giant mutant conch shell stands outside the Theater of the Sea roadside attraction. A giant lobster threatens traffic outside the Rain Barrel souvenir and fashion village. A giant shark sits in front of Mangrove Mike's diner, and the popular Lorelei bar features a giant plywood mermaid waving at traffic. These had been sources of idle amusement for Mr. Benz near the end of previous drives, but not now.

The chauffeur crossed the bridge at Snake Creek near mile 86 and reached the easternmost of Islamorada's main islands, Plantation Key. He made a couple of quick turns to the south.

"What are you doing?" asked Benz. "We never go this way."

"Because we've never been stuck in this much traffic," said the driver. "I know a shortcut."

It was a locals' trick. State Road 4A, or the "Old Road," as they call it, used to be the main highway before it was replaced by the new one running parallel just to the north. What's left of it exists in short bursts here and there that the residents know by heart. So whenever traffic becomes a hair-pulling test of sanity, the conchs detour and zip by on the narrow Old Road, passing the rest of the nearby vehicles as if they're standing still, which they are.

The limo entered a stretch of the Old Road known as Millionaires Row. The only clues it was even there were the few heavily wooded and easily overlooked security gates leading up modest gravel driveways that twisted and vanished into the jungle. What made it so renowned locally was the mind-numbing amount of acreage. In the Keys, where a postage stamp of land costs a fortune, all of these properties had ridiculous footprints of real estate, stretching all the way from their unassuming beginnings near the road, through the overhanging gumbo-limbos and rubber trees and banyans, until a bright view of sun and sand finally opened up at this secret row of Xanadus on the ocean.

The expanses of land provided maximum privacy, and nobody ever saw the mansions except the offshore fishermen and kayakers, and even they didn't get the full picture. Unless you were flying above in an airplane, you never would have guessed that halfway up this string of properties, in the middle of the strangling woods, sat a baffling number of tennis courts. Why? "My neighbor's got one. I need one." Several of the tennis courts went unused, and the jungle had begun to reclaim them. The tourists back on U.S. 1 ate Doritos.

The reason for the phenomenon of "the Row" was history. Plantation Key got its name from the farms that principally grew pineapples in the late 1800s, much like Sugarloaf Key. Then the pineapple gig tanked, and the land was chopped up in subdivision frenzy, as is known to happen in Florida, until someone said,

"Whoa! There are some rich northerners who will pay even more for larger intact parcels! Stop chopping!"

They called it Pearl City.

And here's where history gets tricky. They say that truth is the first casualty of war. It's also the first casualty of the real estate business. For example, a home described as "cozy" is Martin Sheen's bamboo cage in *Apocalypse Now,* and "lots of light" means it's next to a prison. Similarly, nothing is certain about Pearl City. It came into being around 1900 and, from a distance—say, New York City—the sparkling name conjured images of an equally shimmering paradise. Then they visited Pearl City and hit the kind of withering heat, humidity, and insects that make people snap and run naked into the sea.

The original development is gone now, and historians alternately describe it as legendary or lost. Even its exact location has become clouded by the title search of time. Today, no signs or markers are left, and almost no locals have ever heard of it. But now and then, the occasional real estate agent still touts "Pearl City" in flowery listings for homes that may or may not be in the right place.

Then there's the dispute over the name itself. At least three documented stories are floating around: Someone once found a record-sized pearl in a conch shell and showed it all over town, which was the source of much celebration and people getting laid. Or some local residents simply heard rumors of a big pearl, probably started by a real estate agent. The last story is that it was never literally about a pearl, but simply a figure of speech, when some forgotten footnote of a person famously proclaimed, "This place is a real pearl"—probably another real estate agent, right after he told his assistant, "They're starting to ask too many questions about that fake pearl, and we've already painted the signs. I'm shifting the narrative."

Nobody knows for sure. Realtors are the natural enemy of history.

Millionaires Row eventually came into existence and thrived until it became a seismic understatement. On each end of the Row are side streets with small plots of land and modest-sized homes crammed together. And *those* places now go for north of a million. If you want to buy into the Row, get out a scientific calculator . . .

The stretch limo containing Mr. Benz entered a portion of the Old Road that was densely wooded right up to the street on both sides, creating a narrow corridor and blocking all view of anything else. The traffic jam from which they'd escaped might as well have been in Georgia. The limo approached a security gate shrouded in banana trees. The chauffeur spoke into the intercom and they were buzzed in. The limo began a slow, winding journey through the woods as if searching for a lost Aztec temple, passing a vine-choked tennis court, until the sky finally appeared above through the canopy of branches, and they arrived at a post-modern fortress, all white and right angles, a configuration of interconnecting cubes with lots of glass blocks and wire railings. One of the cubes hung precariously over a corner of the building, facing the ocean. The glass was bulletproof.

Rows of burning tiki torches surrounded the circular drive out front, where a trio of men in suits continued making their appointed rounds. You couldn't see the military-grade weapons hidden under their jackets, but the overall context told you they were there.

One of the men opened the mansion's brushed-metal front door for Mr. Benz. Inside, a much different staff in white uniforms stopped whatever they were doing and stood obediently. Benz didn't make eye contact as he started up the floating staircase of high-impact acrylic.

Mr. Benz's first name was Mercado, but his armed staff referred to him as Mercedes. Because it was anti-clever. It wasn't remotely meant as an insult, but they still never used the nickname within his earshot. Nobody but his father and brother was allowed to use his other nickname, Sonny.

Benz reached the top of the staircase and stood in the doorway of the master bedroom. Conserving space meant everything in the Keys, and here it meant nothing. The bedroom was that cube jutting out toward the ocean, and it had the square footage of an entire house. Except most of it was deliberately unused. Minimalism. The floor was white marble, and the bed sat tastefully elevated on a foot-high island against the far wall. Outside the back window, something else was elevated: one of those "infinity" swimming pools where the water pours over the edges into an unseen reservoir. Later, after the moon had risen, it would appear as if the pool were emptying directly into the ocean.

An old man was in the bed, holding a remote control. He lowered the volume on a flat-screen as Benz approached. Someone else in a white uniform stepped back demurely from the other side of the bed. She was holding a blood-pressure gauge.

Benz climbed up onto the bed's island and took the old man's hand. "Papa, how are you feeling?"

"Dammit, I'm fine. I can still run circles around most of you, but now everyone treats me like a baby with whooping cough."

"Yes, I'm sure you're fine," said Benz. "I just want to make sure you stay that way . . . What are the doctors saying?"

"Doctors don't know shit." The old man turned the volume back up with the remote. "You've heard the saying: Fifty percent of all physicians graduated in the bottom half of their class."

Benz glanced toward the screen. "*Andy Griffith* again?"

"I like the old American TV."

"Is the nurse—"

"Sonny," said the old man, "you can stay as long as you don't talk about my health."

Benz paused. "How is everything else?"

The old man set the remote down and turned sideways. "You have got to do something about the fucking food! No hot sauce? No salt? It's ridiculous!"

"The doctor says they aren't good for your health."

"We're going backwards now." The old man gestured dismissively toward an untouched dinner tray on his nightstand. "I need something with taste! Is that too much to ask?"

"No, it's not," said Benz. "I'll look into it."

"Speaking of looking into it, how's that business matter?"

"The last thing you need to worry about is business—"

"Can't you just give me a straight answer?"

"It's not good," said Benz. "It's the newer generation. Trying to make their mark."

"Fuck them making their mark!" said the old man. "We have order. A way of doing things. They'll get their chance if they respect that."

"We've got a meeting set up."

"Jesus! Like I need another war!" said the old man. "Do I have to come back down there myself?"

"No, my brother's taking care of it, Papa . . . *Papa?*"

The old man had dozed off, and Benz lightly shook his hand. "Papa?"

"What?" asked the old man, opening his eyes.

"You scared me," said Benz. "You just fell asleep a moment."

"How long have you been standing there?"

"Papa, I said you only fell asleep a moment."

"Who let you in here? Who are you!"

"Papa, it's Sonny."

"No, you're not! Sonny's a little boy!"

Then he was asleep again.

Benz stared at the floor a few seconds before looking up at the nurse, still quiet on the other side of the bed.

"Try to do something about his food."

She nodded a single time, and Benz went back downstairs. He stopped and tried to uncoil from the day's menu of frustrations.

Some of his men from the limo were waiting inside the front door. Their expressions asked a silent question: *What do you want us to do?*

"First thing tomorrow," said Benz, "get some cement trucks in here."

BOCA CHICA

Coleman peeked over Serge's shoulder into the trunk. "Is he dead?"

"Not yet. I'm just slowing his life down by helping him relax." Serge tossed the tire iron back in the trunk and slammed the lid. "Follow me . . ."

Serge led Coleman through a break in the barricades and began hiking. "I'm often in such a rush to compress as much into every single day that I go too fast. Zooming along in whatever car I've got at the moment. Fast is bad. Walking forces you to slow down. Let's walk faster."

"Hold up," said Coleman.

"And walking the state's old roads puts things in perspective. You notice all kinds of things in the grass and on the shoulders that you'd never see from a speeding vehicle. It's an exercise in contemporary archaeology. There's the expected assortment of trash, from the beer cans to scratch-off lottery tickets, but then there's the weird stuff, like dentures, Ping-Pong balls and Christmas sweaters for poodles. What kind of lives are going on out there?"

Coleman looked down. "There's a used condom."

"That's exactly what I'm talking about," said Serge. "When I'm road-walking, I see an inexplicable volume of condoms. What the hell is the backstory there? It obviously didn't just get dropped where it was put into play. Maybe, like, some guy was walking along, and he thinks: 'It's been nagging at me. I know I'm forgetting something, but what could it possibly be? Hmmm . . .' And he walks some more. 'Oh yeah, I forgot to take that off.' And he reaches down in his pants"—Serge pointed at the ground—"and here we are."

"You really think so?"

"Given the current state of dystopia, I'm not ruling anything out. Anyway, that's why I like to walk."

"To see condoms?"

"In part. Life has a big spice rack," said Serge. "And lucky for us we're in the Keys, where along many stretches of old roads, they're constructing the official heritage trail that will soon connect the entire length of the islands."

"Why are you stopping?"

"To groove on it." Serge placed his hands on his hips. "Check it out: This tiny little road is right up against the fence of the military base, and right up against the other side, a wall of boulders piled along the pavement where it now drops off to a thin tendril of sand and the ocean."

Coleman stepped forward. "Someone spray-painted a creepy eyeball on one of the boulders."

"And someone else painted a giant alligator head in the middle of the road that can be seen from satellites," said Serge. "I know because I checked Google Earth. Also, this spot is the precise location of a fabulous word-of-mouth Keys ritual."

"Which is?"

Serge pointed north through the fence. "Look over there."

"What is it?"

"We're right at the end of the runway. Locals come out here all the time to watch the military jets take off right over their heads."

"There's one now." Coleman cupped his hands to fire up a roach and rapid-fire toked. "Okay, I'm ready. There's a giant iguana lying on top of the barbed wire."

"It wants to see the takeoff."

The jet picked up speed and noise.

"You're right, it's coming straight toward us."

Serge rubbed his hands with high friction. "This is going to be so excellent!"

"It's deafening." Coleman covered his ears. "It looks like it's not going to take off."

"That's the best part," Serge shouted over the roar. "It always looks like its going to cream you until the last second. Don't you love it?"

"No!" yelled Coleman, covering his eyes and peeking between fingers. "It's not going to take off!"

"Here we go!"

"Ahhhhhhhhhhhhhh!"

As Serge predicted, the jet was almost to the fence when the wheels left the tarmac and it screamed over their heads. They both spun toward the ocean and placed their hands atop the boulders, watching the plane bank to the west.

"That was trippy." Coleman looked down over the rocks at the narrow strip of sand below. "Serge, there's a nude guy down there lying on his back watching the takeoff."

"It's the Keys."

They resumed walking.

Soon, the pair arrived at the edge of the airfield's fence. The end of the road crumbled down into the beach and ocean.

Coleman turned around.

"Where are you going?" asked Serge.

"There's no more road. We have to head back."

"Ah, but how wrong you are," said Serge. "Our journey has just begun."

Serge started climbing down to the sand, but Coleman beat him by tumbling.

"Will you stop fooling around?" Serge jerked a thumb over his shoulder. "We're on our way to Red's place."

"What's that?"

"The full name is Red's End of the World." Serge stepped through seaweed. "It's going to blow your mind. Another word-of-mouth gem."

"Is this even a trail?" said Coleman.

"Not remotely." Serge wove his way through trees and branches and back to the sand. "This is strictly wildcat hiking with lots of natural obstacles, where you often must plot your own course, detouring out into the water or bushwhacking upland. It's a long hike requiring local geographic expertise. You really have to want to get where we're going."

Coleman tugged the back of his pal's shirt and whispered. "Serge, there's a naked woman out in the water, and more naked people up in the brush, just like that guy back by the runway. And two more are cooking lunch in a campfire."

"This is also a clothing-optional zone."

"Cool."

Serge had the GPS going on his cell phone. "I hate to pollute the natural experience with electronic shit, but this is essential to finding Red's."

"I still don't know what this Red's place is."

"Better if it's a surprise."

They crossed another serpentine expanse of the ad hoc trail.

"There's a guy coming toward us," said Coleman. "He's naked, too, but holding a folding lawn chair in front of him."

"He respects our opt-in clothing lifestyle."

They all nodded as they passed.

"What's that way up ahead?" asked Coleman.

"We're arriving at Red's."

"I still can't make it out."

They finally were right on top of it, and Serge crawled through, followed by Coleman. "What the hell?"

Serge stood up on the other side. "Welcome to Red's." He pointed at a plaque. "Years ago, a man known simply as Red, 1948 to 2015 R.I.P., began building a primitive beach house by hand out of limestone blocks and driftwood, and he kept going like a maniac until we have this. We just crawled through the living room, and if you noticed on the way, the bedroom was off the foyer. Also that little garden meditation area, and various pyramids of smaller blocks, God knows why. It was all so solidly constructed that we could wiggle through that hole in the rocks to the fortified back room and probably ride out a tropical storm." He turned another way. "Someone, maybe Red, painted that sign, 'Know Thyself.'"

"Check out all these cool decorations," said Coleman. "There's this crazy totem pole."

"And other stuff was made from recycled beach trash," said Serge. "Crab-trap floats and milk jugs. Wind chimes crafted from bottles and nautical rope. I even think people have been adding new stuff recently. See, that's the coolest thing about Red's End of the World: All these years since he died and it's still here. Nobody messes with it, from the authorities to the nudists. People in these parts respect individuality, including the guy who added that plaque in his memory."

"I dig it," said Coleman. "But is Red's place even legal?"

"Not remotely, no permits or deeds, just a fierce spirit of liberty." Serge spread his arms wide. "Generally speaking, in other locales, the powers that be like to shut down any sign of individuality, even if it's harmless."

"Why's that?"

"Because it's in their DNA: 'We realize you're not hurting anyone, but you know the rules. Nothing bizarre. We've worked hard to provide you with many other culturally narcotic options. Please comply and move along to the nearest Olive Garden.'"

Coleman fired up another fatty. "That sucks."

"Indeed it does. That's why I love these spots in the Keys." An upturned palm swept from the ocean to the intricate pile of driftwood. "This is one of those rare ends of the line, so remote and annoyingly inconvenient to get to that The Man can't be bothered to mess with uncharted offshoots of home-building and naked people."

Coleman puffed the thumb-thick joint as they began the long

trek back to the car. "So Operation Pump the Brakes is all about a lot of walking to nowhere?"

Serge shook his head. "Nowhere Walking is just the tip of the berg. At the core of my mission is a massive notion about Florida that I've been pondering forever, but I was always moving too fast to get my arms around it. Now that I'm pumping the brakes, I finally have the opportunity. And it will definitely slow us down."

"You've got to let me know!"

"Not yet," said Serge.

Coleman looked down, forlorn. "I *knoooow.* I'll have to wait for another surprise."

"But one so fantastic that it will be worth the excruciation. I'll give you a hint: It's a major segment of our state's population for which Florida's known far and wide. And it's long past due that we immerse ourselves with these people and learn their ways. Want to guess who it is?"

"Sure, I'll take a stab." Coleman sucked in a mondo hit. "Is it those rival gangs of guys in Miami who steal used vegetable oil from vats in alleys behind restaurants and sell it to those other guys who make something else? What is it?"

"Biodiesel fuel," said Serge. "Points for imagination, parting gifts for accuracy."

"Guess I'll just have to wait." Coleman continued to puff the big spliff with gusto. "Getting a bit roasted here, blah-blah-blah, doodly-doodly-do, wocka-wocka-wocka-wocka-wocka . . ."

"Mr. Pac-Man," said Serge, "I think you bought the strain of weed again that makes you verbally incontinent. Try focusing on the visual cues around you . . ."

". . . Naked people, ass, more naked people, boobs"—eventually climbing back up the washed-out end of old U.S. 1. Three jets in a row took off ahead of them into the crisp, cloudless sky.

"Iguana," said Coleman, "creepy eyeball . . ."

"Now try to focus on walking," said Serge. "You're getting your swerve on again."

"Giant alligator head . . ."

They came to the end of the hike, squeezing themselves back through the barricade and reaching the Galaxie.

"Ah, the simple joys of walking," Serge said with a deep inhale.

Coleman arrived. "Beer bottle, Styrofoam cup, Red Bull, cigarette butts . . ."

Banging from the trunk resumed.

"Condom . . ."

Chapter 3

MARATHON

Traffic on the Overseas Highway was at a standstill as a Learjet from South America approached the airport.

Mercado Benz looked down out the window again at that curious little house alone at sea with its own helicopter pad and a circular breakwater of boulders. Then he went up to the cockpit as usual for the view.

The jet landed and taxied to a stop, and the chocks went under the wheels. Benz trotted down the staircase.

Some of his men were waiting once more, holding a door open for him. But this time it wasn't a limo. It was a Sikorsky luxury helicopter. Specifically the S-76C model used by the royal family.

The chopper lifted off slowly, reaching a few hundred feet before tilting forward and picking up speed. It flew slightly offshore parallel to the highway.

Mr. Benz's face was at one of the windows. He yelled up toward the pilots: "Can you fly closer to the beach?"

"Sure. But why?"

"Just humor me."

The pilot shrugged and swung the copter a few degrees north before straightening out again. "How's that?"

"Perfect," said Benz. He grinned spitefully as he watched the aircraft's shadow race up U.S. 1 over the roofs of the vehicles crawling like slugs after a warm rain. He reclined in his leather seat and smiled even wider. "Absolutely perfect."

Thirty miles later, the chopper's shadow crossed the bridge at Snake Creek, then onto Plantation Key. A few miles ahead, another chopper took off from the football field at Coral Shores High School and made a beeline for a Miami hospital.

Benz's Sikorsky soon slowed to a hover before descending toward the island. Mercado looked down at the rooftop of a postmodern compound with an infinity pool, then something new on the beach. "Best money I've ever spent."

It was a slower descent than usual because of wind gusts off the open seas on both sides of the threadlike island. But the chopper's pilot had over a thousand hours, and he kept the bird steadily on target toward the black X below, as if docking a lunar module.

The X was in the middle of Benz's latest and most satisfying project. He had gotten the idea subconsciously from that offshore home south of Marathon, and again, quite consciously, when he noticed one behind a neighbor's house on the Row. That's why he'd called in the cement mixers during his last trip to the States, and paid a serious bonus so they'd get moving like a military campaign.

The chopper dropped its retractable landing gear before touching down ever so gently on the newest and arguably largest private helicopter pad in all the Keys. Benz ducked his head as he jumped out beneath the slowing blades and jogged toward the mansion.

Mercado bounded up the floating staircase with a new verve in his step. He walked into a guest bedroom for a private update from his most trusted lieutenant. They were interrupted. The flat-screen was on extra loud: "*Bar-ney!...*"

Benz entered the master bedroom and smiled at his father. "*Andy Griffith* again?"

His father promptly clicked off the set with unexpected anger. "What in the name of Jesus, Mary and all the saints was all that fuckery back home I just heard about?"

"Uh, I told you we'd take care of it," said Benz, off balance in a way that only his father could make him. "No need for you to worry about business."

"No need to worry about business?" The old man smashed the remote control against a wall, and Mercado pretended that a battery had not hit him in the eye. "Now I have to worry more than ever!"

"We were only following your advice," said Benz. "These new guys just wouldn't listen to reason. No respect for the old order."

"Your so-called meeting was a goddamn bloodbath. Now there's no order at all!" The old man's head fell back on the pillow. "My phone's been ringing nonstop from all the police chiefs and judges we have down there on the payroll. They say there's no way they can stand by us after this. It was just too high-profile! And the newspapers go nuts over gory photos like that!"

"It can be fixed . . ."

"Front page! Every front page!" The father slammed a palm onto his mattress. "Those pictures almost made *me* squeamish! How did that one guy end up in so many pieces?"

Benz lowered his head. "We have fancier weapons now. I'm sorry I disappointed you, Papa."

The old man flicked his wrist. "No disappointment, Sonny. You've always made me very proud. Your brother, too. It simply boils my blood how these new guys operate."

"We'll stay on top of it," said Benz.

The old man just sighed and picked up one of the five remaining remote controls on the bed next to him. He clicked a button.

Benz looked at a blank screen on the wall. "Why did you just turn off *Andy Griffith*?"

"I've seen all the episodes on this channel," said the old man. "Sometimes twice."

"I can get you a box set."

"What's that?"

"All the episodes on discs."

"No, what's *that*?" The old man pointed.

Mercado looked down at his chest. "Just my tie clip."

"Why does it have a *B* on it?"

"In honor of the family name."

"What family name?"

"Benz, Papa."

"You're not in the family. And why did you call me Papa?"

"Papa, it's me, Sonny."

"Sonny is small." Then the old man began looking around for the remote control that was still in his hand.

The nurse on the other side of the bed stepped forward. "I apologize for interrupting, but I have to give him his medicine now. It's important that he stays on schedule."

"Do what you have to," said Benz.

The nurse propped up the old man's head with an extra pillow. She removed five different tablets from one of those plastic organizers that is needed when the number of prescriptions requires logistics. Then she reached for a glass of water from her medical table.

The first tablet was placed near his lips. "It's time for your medicine again."

"Those damn pills! Somebody's getting rich somewhere," said the old man. "And they make me gag!"

"You need to drink enough water." Then playfully: "Is this one of your grumpy days? As soon as you take these, I've got a yummy lunch for you."

"Hot sauce?"

"Applesauce."

"Blech!"

"Please open your mouth."

He reluctantly complied.

She went through the rote procedure—*gag, gag, gag*—and held the glass to his mouth. "There now." She smiled. "That wasn't so bad."

"Maybe from where you're standing . . ."

"Papa," said Benz.

"You *keep* calling me Papa." Then he was asleep again.

Mercado looked up at the nurse. "He seemed fine six months ago. How often does he get like this?"

"Actually, he's sharp as a tack most of the time." The nurse snapped a compartment closed on the pill organizer. The lid had a *W*. It was Wednesday. "But a few months ago he starting having these brief slips."

"Will any of those pills fix it?" asked Benz.

"A bit, but they can only do so much."

"Then do something else."

"Mr. Benz," said the nurse, "it's not that bad now, but it's progressive. And irreversible."

"There has to be something."

"Medicine-wise, we're doing everything," said the nurse. "But there are some other techniques."

"Techniques?"

"Like the TV shows he watches. Keeps his mind engaged. I've tried to get him to do puzzles or the crosswords, but he hates those worse than the food."

"What else?"

"Conversation is good, too."

"Okay, that's positive," said Benz. "You talk to him all the time."

She paused and pursed her lips. "He needs company."

"You're great company."

She shook her head. "I've been doing this more than twenty years, and I've seen it over and over. Your father and I talk, very friendly. But he needs *company* company."

"What's that mean?"

"Someone he can relate to, things in common. Baseball, business, love of art, anything," said the nurse. "The patients I've seen do the best when they have company where the conversation rolls nonstop, jumping from topic to topic. Laughter helps. But the most beneficial are old stories and memories, like catching a fish, going camping, learning to drive."

"Where do I find someone like that?"

"There, I can't help you."

Benz took it all in with a sigh. "Thanks for telling me this. I'll put my head to it."

"Any time." Something caught her eye. "He's waking up." The nurse grabbed a mobile radio and called down to the kitchen.

Soon, another member of the home-care staff arrived with a tray of food. The nurse slid a hospital-style table over his stomach and set the tray down. "Here you go. Lunchtime."

There was a bowl of mild sodium-free chili, half a ham sandwich cut diagonally, and the applesauce, plus one of those small elementary-school boxes of milk.

The old man surveyed it all like a collection of turds.

"Thanks again," Benz told the nurse. "Now if you don't mind, I'd like to have some private time with my father."

"No problem." She left and closed the door.

"Papa . . ."

"This guy with the Papa thing again. Who are you?"

"Papa, look what I brought." Mercado reached into one of his jacket pockets and produced a bottle of hot sauce with a skull on the label.

"Oooo!" The old man scooched himself up on the pillows. "Give me that!"

Mercado handed it over and smiled for the first time all day. "Bet that chili will now hit the spot."

The old man uncapped the bottle and poured it on the apple-sauce.

Mercado frowned. "I'll let you eat and be back later." He headed down the stairs.

The crew in black suits were waiting in the foyer for whatever was next. They were perplexed as Benz said something uncharacteristically undisciplined.

"I need to go to a bar."

One of the crew nodded. "I'll go get the car."

"No, I said I *needed* to go to a bar. Not that I was actually going."

"I don't get it."

Benz waved an arm toward the front of the house. "Have you forgotten about all that insane traffic? And we can't exactly take the helicopter."

Another member of the crew quietly raised a hand. He was one of the armed guards permanently stationed at the mansion to protect Benz's father. "Sir, I have an idea. There are a bunch of nice places I've discovered from living down here. They're not too far."

"Didn't you hear me about the goddamn traffic?"

"That's the best part," said the guard. "You don't have to go out on the highway. They're all off the Old Road, hidden from the tourists just up around the bend toward the creek. That's why the locals love 'em. There's the Old Tavernier Restaurant if you want fancy, and an excellent breakfast joint called Made 2 Order, which is obviously closed, and farther up a couple dockside places like the Mar Bar and a joint that serves seafood rolls. They also rent paddleboards."

"I don't want a paddleboard!" said Benz. "I want a drink!"

"We'll get the car . . ."

A deafening roar as another Navy jet took off for a training run over the Gulf of Mexico.

Serge stood on the Old Road behind the trunk of the Galaxie, glancing around suspiciously as the banging resumed.

Coleman stumbled and fell against the fender. "Tell me what this guy did."

"You were there."

"Tell me again."

Serge inserted a key and peeked inside. "You know how tiresome this gets? . . . *Alllll* right, from the top. Geez, it was just yesterday afternoon . . ."

Yesterday afternoon.

The 1973 Galaxie headed across Stock Island and then the Cow Key Channel Bridge onto "the Rock," which would be Key West.

"Serge, what do you think of my new look?" Coleman's vision was partially obstructed because he was wearing those novelty springy eyeballs.

Serge turned sideways. "It's definitely you."

Coleman looked down at a to-go cup of rum and Coke in his right hand. "Except they keep getting in my drink when I try to take a sip. It makes it impossible."

"Then stop wearing them."

Coleman threw the novelty on the floorboard. "You have a solution for everything."

"Stay sharp," said Serge. "We have work to do."

"Work?" said Coleman. "I thought you told me we were going to Duval Street. That means party!"

"Oh, it will be a party all right. Just not the kind you're thinking of."

"What other kind is there?"

"I have to do another favor for Diego in Miami."

"A favor?" Coleman frowned. "Can't it wait? We're in Key West. Par-tay!"

Serge shook his head. "He's the one loaning us this car and says we can keep it another month if we help him out. Plus it's the right thing to do."

"What kind of favor?"

"A friend of his had some trouble," said Serge. "See, here's the thing: Tourists unfamiliar with Florida have no idea how much shit they have to guard against. You've got violent predators targeting rental cars at gunpoint, strong-arm robbers putting visitors in the hospital, time-share people. Shoot, I know all this stuff and even I have trouble keeping up."

"So which problem was it this time?" asked Coleman.

"Manipulative credit card charges," said Serge. "Example: You know how pizza places slip menus under motel doors? So you order a supreme meat-lover's for twenty-five dollars and get charged for three. It's the perfect crime. Most people don't check their credit card statements, and the pizza people simply give refunds to the ones that do. It happened to a friend of mine, except he hadn't left his motel yet when he noticed the charge, and he goes in person to the pizza parlor to complain he was triple-charged, and the owner immediately—and I'm talking immediately—says, 'That was a mistake. We'll fix it right now. Would you like a soda while waiting?' I mean, where the hell do you ever get customer service like that, saying you were overcharged, and they don't even check their records and start handing out free beverages?"

"What if a customer complains to the police?" asked Coleman.

"Like I said, the perfect crime. 'The button got stuck on the credit card machine, and we had to keep pressing it to get it unstuck and thought the charge only went through a single time.'"

"Wait a minute," said Coleman. "We came all the way down here over two pizzas?"

"That was just to illustrate the principle," said Serge. "In certain tourist strips like Duval Street, it's an order of magnitude. There was a scam down here years back that became so bad and generated so many scandalous headlines that the city government ordered a savage crackdown bordering on martial law."

"What was it about?" asked Coleman.

"T-shirt shops," said Serge.

"T-shirts?" Coleman turned to Serge and pointed at his own chest. "I wore my favorite Key West shirt today because I knew we were coming here. See? 'Please tell your boobs to stop staring at my eyes.'"

"And yet the women aren't flocking," said Serge. "I'm stunned."

Coleman grinned and nodded. "It's just a matter of time." He drained the to-go cup. "But T-shirt shops like that are every other business on Duval. What could they do that was so bad?"

"First, they would only target people they suspected were visiting from Europe, because those would be the least likely victims to fly back across the Atlantic to testify. Then it was another plausibly deniable malfunction of a credit card machine, except, as I mentioned, an order of magnitude. This time it was the decimal button that allegedly got stuck. Someone would buy a couple of T-shirts that cost, say, $38.72, and then they get back to Copenhagen and see a charge for $3,872. I thought all that was in the rearview mirror, but apparently not. It just happened to one of Diego's friends. The store screens all its calls and they can't get through. No e-mail either. They've tried everything..."

... The standard rotation of Jimmy Buffett songs wafted out of the bars on Duval Street. All the visitors strolling down the sidewalk past the Bull & Whistle were cheerful. Except Serge. Characteristically focused, he turned into the doorway of one of the countless anonymous souvenir shops, striding with purpose past rows of banal shirts: IF IT'S NICE OUT, LEAVE IT OUT... IT WON'T LICK ITSELF.

He was almost to the employees-only door in the back of the store when a clerk ran up from behind. "Sir, you can't go in there."

"I need to speak to the owner," said Serge.

"He's not here. I'm the manager on duty. Maybe I can help."

Serge shook his head. "This is official. I'm trying to keep it as low-key as possible so the press won't find out. I'm sure the owner would appreciate me speaking to him confidentially."

Her expression changed. "Let me check to see if he's come back." She opened the door and went into the back room, and Serge followed her without invitation.

A stub of a man with the stub of a cigar in the corner of his mouth jumped to his feet. A Ukrainian named Dimitri. "What's the meaning of this! You can't just come back here!"

"Sir," said the clerk, "they're with the police." She turned to Serge. "What agency did you say you were with?"

"I didn't," said Serge, turning to Dimitri. "Normally this would be a grand theft investigation, but I think the decimal button on your credit card machine is just stuck. I'm sure we can work something out."

"Uh, Jessica," said the owner. "You can leave now. And close the door."

The ensuing conversation went downhill fast until Dimitri demanded to see a badge.

"Oh, I'm not with the police," said Serge.

"Then who are you?"

"A friend of an exchange student who was staying at the youth hostel on South Street," said Serge. "I'd like the money now, please."

"Get out of my store! Get out!"

"Since you're playing it that way, I'm guessing this wasn't a one-off. I'd like to see all your financial books, starting with credit card receipts from Europe."

"Get out!" Dimitri opened the top drawer of his desk and

grabbed a pistol. He aimed it between Serge's eyes. "Last chance to leave! I'll claim it was a robbery! I have friends down here!"

"I was hoping you'd say that," said Serge. "Until now, this was only about money. My car is parked in the alley just outside the back door of your office."

"What's that supposed to mean? . . ."

Back to the present:

Bam! Bam! Bam! "Let me out of this trunk!"

"Oh, I remember now," said Coleman.

"Good, because I need you to help me with something," said Serge. "Run down to the end of the runway and look over those boulders and tell me if that naked guy is still down on the beach."

"Can I walk instead of run?"

Serge threw his arms skyward. "Whatever! Just go!"

Coleman waddled off.

Serge looked down into the trunk. "Do you have friends like this? . . ."

. . . Ten minutes later, Coleman returned. "He's gone."

"Perfect." Serge had since gotten the captive out of the car and explained in convincing terms that he was a quick draw with the gun in his waistband, and any attempt to escape would be a very short race.

Serge picked up a small tote bag at his feet, then shoved the hostage's back. "Get moving. Head down that embankment toward the sand . . ."

. . . Twenty minutes later, another familiar scene, at least in Serge's world. Another "guest" fastened to the ground, spread-eagle on his back. The sand was too soft for regular tent stakes, so Serge used large corkscrew hurricane tie-downs, the kind used to keep small storage sheds from blowing away in winds up to 130 miles an hour.

Serge finished twisting the final huge screw in place. "There you go!" He patted the head of the duct-tape-gagged hostage and stood up. Then he grabbed his tote bag and unzipped it, removing a handheld digital device.

"What's that?" asked Coleman.

"A law enforcement tool," said Serge. "In this case, maximum enforcement."

"But why is the back of that thing-ding broken off and taped up? And that extra battery glued underneath?"

"Because I hacked it." Serge reached again in the bag and removed several long wires and a plastic box with all kinds of warning decals.

Coleman pulled a sweaty can of Pabst from a pocket in his cargo shorts and popped it. "Another of your science projects?"

"How'd you guess?" Serge wrapped the wires several times around one of his hands. "This one involves trigonometry and the physics of angles."

"Can you make it simple?"

"You've played pool?"

Coleman chugged half the can. "A million times."

Serge finished wrapping the wires. "Think of it like setting up a billiards shot. Eight ball, corner pocket, but the cue ball isn't straight on, so you shoot to clip it off the side. If the physics of billiards is intuitive enough in your bones, you hit the perfect angle and sink the shot." Serge grabbed the digital device and warning box. "Coleman, stay here and watch our friend." He began climbing back up to the road.

Coleman drained the rest of his beer and looked down at Dimitri with a crooked smile. "So, you like the Keys? . . ."

Another twenty minutes and Serge was finished. He called down to the beach. "Coleman, we're out of here! Grab my tote bag!"

Coleman reached for the nylon straps and grinned downward a last time. "Nice talking to you."

Chapter 4

THE OLD ROAD

A summoned stretch limo arrived with alacrity in the circular drive of a post-modern manse on Millionaires Row. Mercado and crew climbed in.

Minutes later, they were all seated on stools with drinks in front of them and a boating canal behind. Above them a couple hundred yards away—almost close enough to hear the rumble of tires—sat the short bridge over Tavernier Creek, which separated them from Key Largo. Some of the seawalls of the homes on the boating channel had underwater lights, like those in swimming pools. At night, they illuminated ripples in the water that rolled across the channel and reflected off the docks.

Some of the crew had paper umbrellas in their drinks, but Benz opted for a double of the bar's most expensive rum. Neat. His glass was mostly empty now, raising the crew's eyebrows.

The aide who knew him best and longest: "That stuff must really be good."

"I'm not drinking because I like it. This is medicine."

"What's the matter?"

"My father."

"Raffy?" The old man's proper name was Rafael, but he'd been tagged in school with Raffy, and he liked it.

Mercado idly swirled and sniffed his drink. "The nurse says he has something, and it doesn't look good. He's been forgetting who I am."

The aide decided to stop talking.

The rest of the dockside stools were filled with locals, even though it was a weeknight. Or rather afternoon, still during working hours. It was a Keys thing. Bermuda shorts, flip-flops, tropical shirts, fishing caps. The conversations were loud and rambling: Someone got busted for hitting her husband with a Jeep, the high school lost another close one, stand-up paddleboards were the new thing.

"Julie! Over here!"

A customer's head turned as another patron waved at her from his stool. "How's your dad?"

"Doing great," said Julie.

"Didn't he just get out of the hospital? . . ."

Benz held two fingers up to the bartender. She poured him another double. He put a hurt on it. The others in the crew began wondering if they'd have to keep Mercado out of some kind of upcoming trouble, but Benz was in a more introspective funk. Deeper into the drink, he turned his attention toward one particular conversation at the bar. He started clumsily piecing something together in his head. A few moments later, the rum sufficiently loosened his tongue.

"Excuse me," said Benz. "Did I hear your name was Julie?"

An attractive, mature woman in a Miami Dolphins jersey pivoted on the next stool. "Yes, it is. Do I know you?"

"Now you do," said Benz. "Just flew back into town today."

A chuckle. "You mean you flew into one of the airports, and then got stuck in our lovely traffic."

He shook his head. "Been there, done that. That's why this time I took the chopper to the family home."

"Where did you land?"

"At the home."

A look of confusion on her face. "What's the address?"

He told her, and Julie's head jerked back. "*You* live on the Row?"

"Actually, my father does," said Benz. "I just visit from time to time."

Julie noticed he was downing the stuff pretty good, but his demeanor was easy. He probably had his reasons. "What does your father do?"

"Retired. International exports." He upended his glass. "Didn't mean to eavesdrop, but your father was a fisherman, was it?"

"Big time." Julie sipped a fruity drink through a stirring straw. "*Charter* boat fisherman. The prices people paid to put them on a marlin." She whistled. "I was just a child and he always took me out when I wasn't in school. I learned all the knots, could rig any line, and was fixing motors by the time I was twelve . . . You've probably seen the signs that Islamorada here is the 'Sport Fishing Capital of the World,' but that's mainly chamber of commerce stuff."

"What? People don't catch fish?"

"No, they catch tons," said Julie. "It's just that they have to go out twenty miles or so to land the big ones. How are we any closer to that than the other islands?"

"So what's the reality?"

"We're more like the Charter Boat Capital of the World," said Julie.

"You mean those big boats with the super-tall towers that I see lined up at piers cheek by jowl?"

She nodded and sipped again. "Makes business sense. Put all the charter boats in one place, broadcast a slogan about a fishing capital, and beat out the rest of the Keys with their tiki-bar-based economy."

Eventually the alcohol began affecting Julie as well. She wasn't a big drinker, or even a small one, but her girlfriends had encouraged her to get out and have some fun for reasons to be discussed later. They were all there with her, occupying three stools on the other side, her wing girls. They had taken stock of their friend's new conversation partner and decided that Mercado wasn't too hard on the eyes. Plus the suit. He must be doing pretty good. They were silently rooting for her.

"Seen the city's signs with the tarpon on them?" asked Julie.

"Didn't really notice."

"The ones entering Islamorada say 'Welcome,' and ones leaving say 'Catch You Later.'"

"I guess that's clever."

"Maybe somewhere." Julie sucked the tiny straw.

"So what do you do?" asked Mercado.

"Take care of my father," said Julie.

"Yeah, I overheard them saying he just got out of the hospital." Mercado signaled the bartender again. Just one finger this time. "But what do you really do?"

"That's what I really do," said Julie.

"I don't understand."

"He didn't, like, just get out of the hospital this one time," said Julie. "It's an extended thing."

"So that's your full-time job? Nothing else? What about for enjoyment?"

"I volunteer."

"Where?"

"At a hospice. It also doubles as long-term care," said Julie. "Limited space in the Keys."

"That doesn't sound like fun."

"You'd be surprised," said Julie. "Dad lives at my place, but sleeps a lot. Also watches TV for hours. It lets me get out and see people."

"You mean the patients at your volunteer place?"

"They're a hoot! I read to some of them, but the others we just talk and talk."

"How long have you been doing this?"

Julie idly looked up at a sign, STONE CRAB CLAWS $3. "Oh, I'd say at least twenty years now. I got my first taste back in high school when community service was a requirement of the curriculum. The other kids hated it, but I actually started looking forward to my shifts. And it pays you back. You never look at your own so-called troubles the same again."

Mercado leaned back to glance around her down the bar. "Those women keep looking this way and smiling. You know them?"

"Oh." Julie quickly turned. "These are my friends from the care center, Bonnie, Tracy and Suze."

Each of the women smiled and waved in turn. Then they regrouped for a private conversation.

"They're volunteers, too?"

"No, on the paid staff." Julie absentmindedly twisted a napkin. "I used to be as well, but my hours are too irregular with Dad and all. Just going there is its own reward."

"But you must have done something else along the way. Career?"

"A great one," said Julie. "After high school, I became a deckhand. Growing up with Dad, it was second nature. And I got to stay in the Keys. If Dad wasn't going out a particular day, one of the other captains hired me."

"Sounds like you had a fantastic childhood."

"The best!"

"I'll bet you're hungry."

"I could eat something."

Mercado signaled the bartender, and soon two orders of stone crab arrived, with the butter, lemon slices and nutcrackers. "Three dollars *each*. Seems a bit much."

She began cracking the first claw like a pro. "It's a bargain.

Go to any restaurant in Miami and you'll come back singing a different tune."

Mercado tried cracking his own claw, and juice squirted on his lapel.

"Let me get that." She squeezed lemon onto a napkin and dabbed his coat. "And let me get this." She took his nutcracker and had the claw open in two seconds. "It can be tricky if you're not used to it."

Mercado dipped the supple white meat in butter and popped it in his mouth. "That *is* good . . . What's your father's name?"

"Ralph. Captain Ralph."

"And his last name must be Csonka."

She chewed her own bite. "Why would you say that?"

"The back of your jersey. The number thirty-nine and the name Csonka."

Julie dropped her nutcracker and searched his face. "Do you know anything at all about sports?"

"Sure, I love football. Know just about everything there is."

"Obviously you don't."

"Oh, I mean, it's what you call soccer," said Mercado. "I'm from South America."

"That explains it." She resumed cracking. "Larry Csonka's in the Hall of Fame. Bruising running back on the undefeated seventy-two Dolphins team. Most people like the quarterbacks best, but he was my favorite growing up. My family name is Cootehill."

"What's that?"

"Irish, like the town."

Deeper into afternoon, arguably evening now. Most of the daytime patrons had left. Julie's friends began checking the time on their cell phones but didn't want to interrupt.

"If you don't mind me asking," said Mercado, "how can you afford to take care of your dad at your place without a paying job?"

"Dad's money."

Mercado whistled. "Those fishing tourists really must have paid him well."

"Yes and no," said Julie. "He had a decent place down here, and I had an okay one. We turned his into a rental because you wouldn't believe the rates people are begging to pay. Then we moved into my place and live off that rent."

Mercado locked on her eyes. "I have a proposition."

Uh-oh, thought Julie. *Here we go again. Nice gentleman, polite chitchat without a hint of hitting on me. Then we always end up here.*

She wiped her hands thoroughly with the napkins because she had just decided she was done eating, despite the remaining claws. Julie took a deep breath and faced him. "Okay, what's this proposition?"

He leaned forward and whispered. Then he wrote a number on a napkin and slid it her way.

It was quiet at the bar for the longest time, except for a pelican dive-bombing a fish in the channel.

The proposition wasn't remotely what she expected. She looked down at the napkin and immediately up again. "Are you out of your mind?"

"Couldn't be more serious," said Mercado. "How did you get here tonight?"

"My friends drove me."

He looked over her shoulder again. "They're looking fidgety. Why don't you cut them loose and let me give you a ride? It'll give me some time to flesh this out more."

A ride offer? From a stranger in a bar? A couple hours after first sight? It was the equation of an automatic deal-breaker for many women. But Julie was a tough conch, confident handling herself. Oh, and there was the matter of her concealed-carry permit. Julie grabbed her purse, the one with the Walther nine-millimeter, and hitched the strap over her shoulder. She turned to tell her friends. "Girls? . . ."

Murmurs. *"Good luck." "Be careful." "Don't do anything I wouldn't."*

"Trust me. I've got this."

The girlfriends finally left and Julie got up from her stool. "Ready when you are."

They headed up a path to the parking lot as the sun began to set, and the day of surprises continued. Julie stopped at the sight of someone holding open the back door of a stretch limo.

"What's the matter?" asked Mercado. "Never been in a limo before?"

"Actually, no." She climbed in.

Most of the traffic on U.S. 1 was headed for Key West and by this hour had already passed through to reach the bars in time, considerably thinning the congestion. The limo drove several miles, over Snake Creek, onto Windley Key and past the giant roadside conch shell. Then onto Upper Matecumbe.

Julie pointed at a neon outline of a fish. "Coming up on the right, a little street just past the Blue Fin Inn and Key Lantern. Slow down or you'll miss it."

The chauffeur turned onto a street that was more like a path just wide enough for the limo. Mercado's face was at the window again as they slowly rolled through one of the funkiest and most eccentric enclaves in the Keys, which is no small achievement. On both sides, mobile homes crammed so closely together that you could practically reach out the front door of one and touch the next. Many were curved and silver. Airstreams. The residents seemed footloose and happy. All kinds of upbeat decorations. Wooden tiki gods, strands of colorful crab-trap floats, metal geckos painted psychedelic colors, old Florida license plates, smiley-face decals, makeshift wet bars of bamboo, a rusty sign for something called the Mermaid Lounge, out-of-season Christmas lights, and one of those signposts with arrows pointing all directions indicating mileage to various destinations, in this case states of mind: HAPPINESS, MORE HAPPINESS, SUPER HAPPINESS and so on.

"That's the one," said Julie.

The rest of the crew waited in the limo as Mercado got out and followed Julie past the happy signpost and up the steps of the Airstream with an American flag in the window.

Mercado scratched his head. "When you said 'home,' I was expecting a house."

Julie unlocked the door. "It's as home as home gets." No light inside except the blue glow of a TV in the back room.

Julie began creeping. "Be quiet in case he's asleep."

They reached the doorway. A stuffed mackerel looked down from a wall. It was about all that could fit in the bedroom besides a bed and the old tube television.

"Yep, his eyes are closed." They retreated silently to the kitchen nook.

"Have you given it more thought?"

"Yes," said Julie. "And it's not going to work out. I'm sorry."

"Fair enough. Just if you could think about it some more." Mercado reached in his pocket and pulled out a gold money clip with a scorpion on it. He quickly peeled off a grand and set it on the counter. "No strings attached."

"I can't accept that," said Julie.

"You can't say no."

"Excuse me," said Julie, "but I don't like to be given orders."

"What I mean is, you can't say no because it's not for you. It's for your father."

Mercado left the trailer, and the limo drove off.

BOCA CHICA

A half-dozen police cars with all the lights going were already on-site, with more arriving. But the concrete barricades to the derelict road behind the naval base prevented convenient access to the crime scene. So they had to walk.

There was the usual contingent of crime scene techs with evidence bags and cameras. Half were working up on the road and the rest down on the beach.

A sergeant stood in the sand and wiped his forehead. "Damn, that was a long walk."

A detective concentrated while jotting in his notebook. "Just be glad you're not him."

"I've seen some gruesome crime scenes in my years," said the sergeant. "This one is just weird."

The pair looked down again at the recently deceased, lying next to the surf with a giant coral boulder on his chest. It had a creepy eyeball painted on it.

A woman with the technical team strolled toward them on the beach and held up an evidence bag. "I think we've solved our mystery."

The detective looked up from his notebook at the clear bag. "What's that?"

"A decibel meter," said the woman. "The kind we use to enforce sound ordinances so nightclubs don't disturb neighbors."

The sergeant furrowed his eyebrows. "Why is the back all taped up? And an extra battery glued underneath?"

"Because our killer hacked it."

"Hacked?" asked the detective.

The woman nodded. "See these wires coming from under the tape? He hacked it to send out an electric signal from the extra battery through those wires. The threshold was set at a hundred fifty decibels. Almost nothing's that loud except—"

A naval combat jet took off over their heads, and the needle on the meter spiked well past the threshold.

"Then what?" asked the detective.

She pointed up toward the road. "We found traces of nitrate on that boulder wall. Probably a couple of small demolition charges from a construction site, but that's all it would take. Readily available on the black market. The killer was probably long gone when one of the jet takeoffs triggered the murder."

"But what about the sound of the explosion?" asked the sergeant. "They were taking a big risk. If a jet took off before they could get away, they might have been caught." His right arm pointed east down the Old Road. "It's a hell of a long walk back to the barricades and their car."

"That part was ingenious," said the woman. "Since the blast was triggered by a jet on takeoff, the plane would be directly overhead at a couple hundred feet. We just heard one. The roar of those engines' afterburners kicking in would drown out a whole building being blown up."

"One more question." The sergeant glanced over the rock wall down to the beach. "How did he know the boulder would land on the victim?"

"It was far from a sure thing," said the woman. "I'm guessing our killer plays a lot of billiards."

"I'm not following," said the detective.

"He lined up his shot," said the woman. "Placed the explosive charges at the desired angle, and physics did the rest, sinking the eight ball. Or in this case the eyeball."

Chapter 5

MILE MARKER 17

The wind picked up as clouds rolled in from the Gulf Stream. The deep-sea boats raced back to port after a short-notice small craft warning went out on the marine radios from the weather service's antenna on Tea Table Key.

A 1973 Galaxie sped east across Sugarloaf Key. Serge quickly rolled up his window as small but high-velocity raindrops began pelting the car. Another routine afternoon. "Coleman, roll yours up, too."

"Why?"

"The rain's coming sideways."

"So that's what's stinging my cheek," said Coleman. "I want it to stop."

"Then roll up your window!"

Coleman began cranking with one hand and chugging straight from a bottle of Captain Morgan with the other. He casually looked out the window at a venerable lodge sitting next to

Bat Tower Road. "Serge, tell me again about the rum-smuggling coves."

"The coves are everywhere down here, all up and down the islands," said Serge. "Because of their remoteness, geography and relative lawlessness, the Keys have a rich and unrivaled smuggling history. And it's not just rum. Earlier, there were Confederate frigates from the Bahamas running the Union blockade, then Prohibition, and later, bales of marijuana, Cuban refugee boats and cocaine."

"Wow, that's some history." *Glug, glug, glug.*

"History that continues today." They crossed the bridge to Cudjoe Key and Serge pointed up out the windshield. "See that small white tethered balloon in the sky?"

"Yeah, what is it?"

"A radar blimp that allows the feds to see over the horizon for drug boats," said Serge. "Affectionately nicknamed Fat Albert."

"They still need that thing?"

"Are you kidding?" said Serge. "Over the decades, they've been making so many arrests at sea that it doesn't even merit the front page. Just tiny news items buried inside next to Elks lodge spaghetti dinners. But I read them all."

"Give me an example."

"There are so many to choose from." Serge tapped his chin. "Okay, I got one, the first I read a long time ago, back in 1977. But it was such a tiny article that I'm sure they left out most of the details. I wonder what the full story was . . ."

1977

As the saying goes, "Red sky at night, sailor's delight; red sky at morning, sailors take warning."

This particular evening over the Gulf Stream, the sky was an ambiguous pink.

Four union auto workers from Detroit departed a three-hour Eastern Air Lines flight, and carried luggage through the Miami airport, because, in the age after the moon shot, someone still had yet to invent wheels for a suitcase.

But they were in top spirits because their dream plan that had been eighteen months in the making was finally unfolding. Great Lakes fishing is one thing, but the Florida brochures had put the proverbial hook in them, twenty-odd-mile adventures off-shore into the Straits of Florida. Over that wait time, they grew mesmerized by the promises of the slick brochures: giant, vibrant sailfish, in fidelity to their name, sailing out on the water and onto the fishermen's laps. Eighteen months. It had also taken that long to save the money. They were the exception to the charter captains' usual clientele, who tended toward college degrees: accountants, lawyers, insurance agents, dentists, literature majors who now worked for General Electric.

On the other hand, these just-arrived fender welders had all known each other since their high school football years in Pontiac, known all of each other's earlier crappy jobs since paperboy. And they knew they were punching above their weight class in their fishing-guide budget.

But the months of frugality was also that much more time to let the anticipation build for their vacation of a lifetime together. In the jet black of pre-predawn the next morning, they were *there,* pent up on the pier in Upper Matecumbe Key before the charter captain arrived. They huddled with their lunches and coffee thermoses, pacing behind an immaculate vessel. The name across the stern: JULIE.

On the dock behind the boat was a wooden sign, like the ones behind all the other fishing boats lined up in an impressive, stately row. This particular sign: CAPTAIN RALPH COOTEHILL.

Captain Ralph was anything but unpunctual.

"Morning, guys, seems like you're looking to grill some fare tonight from our waters."

"And how."

Ralph placed a skid-proof length of wood between the pier and the boat, and they climbed aboard. The sky began to lighten as the gang settled in and stowed gear and eagerly rummaged through their hooks and leaders. One of the guys held a lure in each hand, weighing the merits of feathers or no-frills plugs.

Headlights hit the pier as a white van with no windows rolled down the dock past them and stopped behind another charter boat four slips over. There were vague forms in motion at the stern, just like on most of the other vessels. The morning routine of the Matecumbe Keys.

Captain Ralph stopped to watch the van for a few moments longer than such an ordinary sight would demand. Then his attention went back to giving his customers the required Coast Guard instructions about life preservers and fire extinguishers. A customer blew steam off a cup of thermos coffee.

Someone else hopped aboard.

"Who's the little kid?" asked one of the auto workers.

"Julie, my daughter," said Captain Ralph, firing up the engines. "The boat's named after her. She'll be your deckhand today."

The fishermen raised eyebrows as they watched the young girl expertly unwind the braided nautical ropes from the dock cleats and push off, then leap over the water back onto the boat. The forty-foot, four-engine Merc center-console cruiser idled away from the pier. It planed up in a channel with green and orange markers.

They cleared the shallows, hugging the southern shore. Captain Ralph threw the throttle forward and it was full speed ahead. The sun was about to come up, under-lighting a conga line of clouds dancing down the horizon. The clouds were pink, uncommitted, like the night before.

The charter boat lost sight of land as the sun rose. There was a slight wind from the east and barely a chop, not bad for the twenty-mile mark. Captain Ralph reached six hundred feet of water and cut the engine, letting the boat drift.

"Okay, boys, let's see what you got in ya."

They didn't need to be told twice, readying their rods and staking out deck positions. All smiles and proudly wearing their purchases from a shopping spree the night before at the local mom-and-pop tackle shops. Straw hats and tarpon caps, long-sleeve wicking shirts, wraparound fishing sunglasses. On the back of a retro shirt: ZANE GREY LODGE.

Just one question: What was the deal with the little girl in their midst?

"Here, let me help you with that knot," said Julie. "Set the drag on the reel a little lighter." "Try this bomber lure." "A larger weight if you're going for deep stuff like bonita." Then she put her own line in the water.

The initial excitement gave way to perspiration. A straw hat came off and a brow was wiped.

"I got one!" Despite her size, Julie expertly reeled in an amber-jack.

The northerners were impressed. *Damn, she's not half bad.*

Fifteen minutes later. "I got another one!" She put a cobia in the boat.

The guys glanced at each other. *Okay, now she's getting too good.*

Captain Ralph put an arm around his daughter's shoulders and lowered his voice. "I'm very proud of you, Julie, but I think you should stop fishing for the day."

She glanced around at the auto welders, all looking back at her. "I understand," said the youth. "I'll go get some cold drinks for them." She went digging through a cooler.

"That's my girl."

Captain Ralph knew his fishing spots. Despite the slow start, the customers began getting strike after strike. They pulled out the nets and gaff hooks. First a yellow tuna, then a kingfish, a wahoo, a mackerel. Finally showtime: fighting fish leaping into the air, a bull dolphin followed by a sailfish. Shouts and laughter filled the boat, photos were taken, and the beer never tasted so good.

One of the fishermen had a radio. A song came on and he cranked it up.

"... *Wastin' away again in Margaritaville...*"

Another angler pointed at the portable radio. "What's that song?"

"You haven't heard it?" asked the first.

The second shook his head.

"I can't believe you don't know it," said the first. "Just came out, pretty good. Been playing all week."

The second just shrugged.

They paused for roast beef sandwiches. One of the rods left idle in its holder began letting out a serious amount of line, so fast that the unseen fish pulled the filament taut out of the sea, flinging a spray.

"It's a marlin! It's a marlin!"

Everyone gathered around the welder in a turquoise bucket hat. He strained and put his back into the battle, ten minutes, twenty, thirty. But the fish was finally tiring and getting near the boat.

When it was alongside, they all hung over for a view.

"Holy shit! It's at least fifteen feet!"

"At least!"

"And well over a thousand pounds!"

"I can use the winch," said Captain Ralph. "But the trouble. Release her?"

"Okay," said the angler. "Just get my picture first."

One of his buddies took the rod, and the proud tourist hung over the side near the marlin's head and smiled for the camera. *Click, click, click.*

They had just released the billfish, watching it gather strength as it swam away, when they began hearing a faint buzzing sound from the other direction.

They didn't even notice at first, but it quickly became too loud to be ignored. Everyone turned toward the east.

"What the heck's that?" asked an angler.

"It's a Grumman," said the captain. "One of those belly-landing seaplanes with pontoon struts under the wings."

"Isn't it flying a bit low? Is he trying to land?"

"Not this far from shore."

"Then what's he doing?"

"I have no idea," lied the captain. Because there was only one reason. It was trying to stay under the radar.

It would still be another decade before the Air Force would launch its so-called Fat Albert blimp from the station on Cudjoe, giving them those eyes over the horizon. For now, contraband pilots only had to worry about a chance spotting from a military jet.

The charter boat's passengers remained transfixed on the plane as it grew closer.

"Is that smoke?" asked an auto worker.

"Yes," said the captain. Okay, there was a second reason for uncharacteristic low altitude. The plane was in trouble. Ralph got on the ship-to-shore radio for the distress call. "Mayday, we have a Grumman losing altitude twenty miles due south of Windley Key . . ."

"What do you think's wrong?" asked a fisherman.

"That's definitely an engine," said Ralph.

"There's stuff coming out of it," said another. "It's hitting the water."

"They're trying to lose weight and climb," said the captain. "It's not working."

The seaplane continued chucking contents as the men in the fishing boat shielded their eyes from the sun, looking straight up as the doomed flight flew directly overhead at a few hundred feet.

There was a tremendous splash in the water behind them, but they paid it no mind, all eyes following the plane as it continued west, lower and lower. It was mere miles downrange when it finally slammed into the sea and broke apart.

"Should we do something?" asked a fisherman. "Maybe go over there and try to help?"

The captain shook his head. "Coast Guard rescue chopper's already on the way and will get there sooner."

"What's this?" asked the angler in the Zane Grey shirt, pointing off the starboard side. "Looks like it came off the plane."

Captain Ralph joined him at the railing and knew immediately. He'd heard the stories from some of the other captains back at the dock, seen their activity after dark and before dawn with the white vans, and convinced himself that it would never happen to him. Ralph had figured this day would never come, but now it was here, and he had a serious decision to make. And he had to make it quick.

"Julie, why don't you go down below for a little bit?"

"What's going on?"

"We'll talk later. Just listen to your dad for now."

Julie obediently went down below into the cabin without further discussion. Captain Ralph started the boat up, swung slowly to the east, and stopped.

One of his customers was pointing again. "Is that what I think it is?"

"Yes," said Ralph. "I have an important question for all of you."

"What is it?"

"How would you all like to fish for free today?"

"Sure, but there's got to be a catch."

"What's about to happen never happened." Ralph raised an eyebrow. "We got a deal?"

They understood and slowly began nodding in unison. "You got it." "What do we know?" "Free fishing is good."

"Okay then," said Ralph. "I'll need for you to give me a hand."

He extended the gaff over the side, snatching the giant bale of marijuana, and they all grabbed its canvas covering and heaved it on board. Then Ralph threw a tarp over it for good measure. "Julie, you can come out now."

There was no further mention of the inauspicious intermission the rest of the day on the fishing grounds, or on the way in. Just loud tall tales as the visitors got heavily into the beer.

Upon sight of land, Captain Ralph's heart suddenly began to race. A Marine Patrol boat approached. *What brainlessness have I done? I knew better. I am so fucked.*

Ralph was sure he was going into cardiac arrest until the officers on the patrol boat waved and sped right by without even slowing.

What just happened? But of course: Captain Ralph had the perfect cover. A bunch of half-drunk fishermen with a local captain. And a little girl.

"*. . . Wastin' away again in Margaritaville . . .*"

Back at the pier, the Michigan natives profusely thanked Ralph more than he'd ever been thanked before. Then they headed off, deciding what to do with all the extra scratch in their pockets from the full fishing-guide refund. The strippers that night would take that problem off their hands.

After they all waved a cordial goodbye, Captain Ralph drove his daughter back to their modest ranch house on Plantation Key.

"Julie, stay here. I have to go back to the dock."

"What is it?"

"Just remembered something," said her father. "I had a little hydraulic thing acting up out there, and want to check it out before I take the next group tomorrow."

"I didn't notice any hydraulic problem." She was already sharp enough around the boat that she would have seen the drops of purple-red translucent fluid.

"A minor thing, probably nothing." God, he hated lying to her. "But better safe than sorry."

"Can I come?" asked Julie. "I like to fix things."

"I know you do," he said, heading out the door. "But I'm tired and want to make this a quick trip. Like I said, probably nothing. Make sure to keep the doors locked. I shouldn't be long."

And off he went in a wood-paneled station wagon.

A couple of the other captains had their marine tool sets out, performing routine maintenance on their own boats. One of them waved at Ralph with a socket wrench when he arrived. Besides that, it was empty, dark and quiet.

These were the primitive times when phone booths were still the rage. One booth sat at the end of the dock near the Texaco gas pumps. Captain Ralph went inside and closed the glass door. He looked up at a phone number with a 305 area code scribbled in tiny numbers near the ceiling. Every charter captain knew about that number. Ralph took a deep breath. "Hoo boy. Here goes nothing." He stuck a dime in the phone and dialed the number. "Hello, I work down at the dock. . . . Yes. . . . Yes. . . . Twenty minutes? . . . It's slip number five—" The line went dead.

Ralph stared at the silent receiver a moment and hung up. To himself: "I hope you know what you're doing."

He climbed aboard his boat and got out a wrench set, over-acting the pretend mechanical work. He kept checking his watch with growing regret each passing minute. After nineteen rounds of the sweep second hand, headlights swept toward him. A white van with no windows stopped and three men got out. Two of them climbed onto the boat with silent efficiency. They pulled a tarp aside, grabbed the large canvas square and tossed it onto the dock, then into the van.

The third man approached the stern and handed Ralph an envelope. Then the van sped off. It had taken less than three minutes, without a single word. Ralph glanced around suspiciously.

Two other captains were watching and quickly turned away. They had been to the same rodeo before, several times in fact, but they both remembered that the first time had been hell on their nerves.

Captain Ralph Cootehill stood next to the wooden sign bearing his name, peeking inside the envelope—"Jesus"—and drove the station wagon back home.

Chapter 6

ISLAMORADA

Sneakers slapped the pavement on a narrow street hugged by tall vegetation right against the pavement. It was noon and quiet and pelicans glided through the sky with plans of their own.

Coleman intently scanned the ground. "I'm not seeing any condoms."

"Don't look so sad," said Serge. "There's a whole bigger world to walking than that. It's all about milking the precious few seconds that have been bestowed upon us to roam the planet." Serge pulled out his cell phone and snapped a photo down the road.

"Serge, you accidentally had your flash on."

"That was no accident." The phone went back in his pocket. "And I wasn't taking a photo. The purpose was just to make it flash."

"I don't get it."

"One of my newly patented techniques to trick my mind into stretching out life." They continued strolling past a narrow break in the woods with a modest gate and a gravel road that wound out of sight into the jungle. "If you took the entire fourteen-billion-year history of the universe and reduced it to a century, our lives would be like a flashbulb going off. *Foof!* That's it, fade to black."

"When you put it that way, it's kind of depressing."

"It's *insanely* depressing." Serge pulled out the camera again. "That's the key to the strategy, a variation on Einstein's theory of relativity. Thinking about frighteningly heavy shit stretches time. I'm terrifying myself to enjoy life." *Flash.*

They passed another isolated break in the woods, and Serge shook his wrist.

Coleman hit a furtive joint. "You got a new watch?"

"Not exactly. It *does* tell time, but that function's practically an afterthought. It's a Fitbit."

"What's that?"

"The newest techno craze to distract us from enjoying life." Serge continued shaking his wrist. "Back in the good ol' days, people just walked around getting fresh air. The joy came from the elegant simplicity. How could it be more complicated than that? Here's how: 'Can't I just walk around and smell flowers?' 'No, no, no, simple is over. Now you must monitor your heart rate, calories burned, oxygen saturation, elevation climbed, receive Internet notifications, listen to music, remotely control your thermostat. Please step away from the flowers.' 'Forget it. You've ruined walking for me. I'll just relax and take a nap.' 'No, no, no, you can't *just* take a nap. You need to monitor your sleep stages, restlessness and REM time, then as soon as you awaken, immediately log onto your computer to see your score against the competition.' So they fucked up sleeping, too."

"Then why'd you get one of those gadgets?"

"I want to be a man of my times. Plus, this thing pisses me off, which stretches out time and makes me happy." He stopped shaking his wrist and looked at the display. "Damn this thing!" He started shaking it again.

Coleman's joint was down to a roach. "What's the matter?"

"It's supposed to count my steps, but I know I've taken more than that," said Serge. "And then some unfair score goes up on my Internet Chart of Shame. That's how they get you. So you have to fight back." Serge resumed strolling as he aimed his phone at his watch. *Flash.* "Two can play at this game."

A hundred yards later, they passed a third tiny break in the woods, followed by another long patch of tangled overgrowth. Then another break.

"Where do the roads go behind those gates?" asked Coleman. "What's happening back there?"

"We're on another stretch of former U.S. 1, now called the Old Road, just a stone's throw from the new highway," said Serge. "Most people have no idea this is even here. But those security gates in the woods are like keyholes to another world. We're at what the locals call Millionaires Row, but that's in like 1960 dollars."

"Millionaires live back there?"

"In high style. Another of the Keys' hidden phenomena." Serge stopped to examine one of the nicer gates of verdigris wrought iron and walked up to peer between the bars. "These are some of the most accomplished people around. I can't even imagine what kind of rarefied sophistication is transpiring back there . . ."

. . . Down the gravel drive behind the verdigris gate, at a postmodern mansion, an old man secretly poured hot sauce on his lunch before the nurse could return. He clicked a TV remote control: "*Andy, Otis the drunk just fell through the plate glass at Floyd's barbershop again.*"

. . . Back on the road, Serge bent down next to the verdigris gate to smell a flower. The gate automatically opened, and a black stretch limo pulled out and turned toward Upper Matecumbe. Serge took another photo of his watch and headed back to where he'd left their car.

"Uh-oh."

"What is it?" asked Coleman.

"That flock of peacocks in the road," said Serge. "I've heard stories. If you're a local, you know all about the feral peacocks that populate the Old Road, and they don't move for anything, not even cars. Really shitty attitudes, giving you the hairy eyeball."

"They're creeping me out," said Coleman.

"Me too," said Serge. "And because of their beauty, most people don't realize that peacocks are assholes and attack for no reason! Plenty of news stories about zoo visits that went south for elementary school classes."

"They're blocking the street," said Coleman. "How do we get back to our car?"

"We must walk like peacocks while giving off a prison-yard bird vibe that we're too crazy to mess with. Come on."

Serge jerked his body from his legs to his neck, wiggling arms in the air like fluttering feathers and strutting funky past the flock. Coleman strutted behind him until they reached the car. They got in.

The '73 Galaxie remained parked.

"Why aren't we going?" asked Coleman.

"I'm ready to unveil the huge surprise I mentioned on our trip to Red's place."

"The core of our new mission?"

Serge nodded hard. "To truly slow down, we need to take a break from all our road-tripping and drop anchor."

"We're getting a boat?"

"No, I mean like a longer-term residence than a dive motel. I've always wanted to live in the Keys. I need to establish roots and stability."

"We're getting a house?"

"Not exactly." Serge reached under his seat for a pile of newspapers, real estate magazines and free shoppers. "I've given this a lot of thought, Coleman." He folded over a page in one of the newspapers' Classified section. "I don't want to constantly mow and pick up brown palm fronds. So my plan of attack nicely dove-tails into another classic slice of Florida culture that I've yet to experience, similar to when we hunkered down at that retirement park to learn the secrets of our senior citizens."

"You don't mean . . ."

"That's right." Serge started up the car. "We're going condo!"

The Galaxie arrived in Key Largo and pulled into the parking lot of a squat concrete square of a building with a low flat roof. Painted teal. A sign over the door indicated real estate was the current game plan. Business had picked up after the company planted a row of crotons out front.

"But, Serge, we don't have enough money to buy a place."

"Who said anything about buying?" Serge showed him the folded newspaper page. "The beauty of this operation takes into account that many Keys residences are second homes. Some are vacation rentals and others just have the storm shutters pulled closed and sit empty. We're taking advantage of that dynamic . . ."

Soon, they were sitting with big smiles across the desk from a real estate agent who dabbled in property management. The name tag on her blazer said GRETCHEN.

She smiled back. "So you're interested in a condominium?"

"Damn straight," said Serge. "It's the cornerstone of my new mission."

A confused pause. "What mission?"

"To slow life down." Serge pressed his right foot on an imaginary pedal. "I'm pumping the brakes."

"Oh, I get it," Gretchen said with a chuckle. "That's why a lot of people move down here: to kick back and live on island time. Mainland life can get so crazy."

"You have no idea." Serge pointed his phone down and clicked the shutter.

"Why are you taking a picture of my floor?"

"I wasn't taking a photo. It's all about the flash. More on that when we know each other better. What have you got for us?"

"A lot of great locations. Just depends on where you'd like to live."

"Really?" said Serge. "If I had my druthers, I'd pick Pearl City."

"You know about Pearl City?"

Serge shrugged. "I'm a history buff. And you're a real estate agent. Which means we should be in a big fight by this point, but I've learned to let it go. You know how Pearl City got its name?"

"Not really."

Serge reached into the file folder on his lap and handed pages across the desk. "Those are the three stories floating around. You don't have to read them now. Just hang on to it in case you have some explaining to do."

"I don't understand—"

"And what's all the fuss about pearls?" asked Serge. "They're supposed to be so great, but you know how they're formed? It happens when something goes awry with the health of a shellfish, like a parasite, foreign object or injury to the mantle tissue. How did *that* lead to jewelry? It's like if some sophisticated woman went to a cocktail party wearing a necklace of shiny gallstones."

Gretchen just stared.

"Enough of that," said Serge. "Condo!"

"Were you looking to own or rent?"

"Definitely own," said Serge. "But can we start on a lease with an option to buy? I'd like to give the place a shakedown cruise. That's especially important for a condo. There could be building maintenance issues, or the walls are too thin and you hear intercourse sounds all day. Have you ever been there? Jesus, the banging and screaming, and you involuntarily learn all the secret sex talk that your neighbors request of their partners to get off. Then every time you run into them in the hallway, you can think of nothing else. And if the sounds are especially loud while you're entertaining guests—*awkward* . . . Do you know what one of my neighbors liked to hear? 'You are a bad, bad girl and need—'"

"Uh, excuse me," said Gretchen.

"What?" said Serge. "I was going to clean up the language. I know proper etiquette in a business meeting like this. It just involved chocolate syrup and Ben Wa balls before she came. Please continue."

Gretchen maintained poise and grabbed her own file off the desk. "Great. Let me put together a list for us to tour. Meet back here after lunch? Say two?"

"We'll be here with bells." Serge stood and shook her hand. "Remember that Smokey Robinson song, 'Going to a Go-Go'?" He winked at Coleman and they began singing.

"Going to a con-do, everybody . . ."

". . . Going to a con-do, do-do-do . . ."

They jitterbugged out the door.

Chapter 7

TWO O'CLOCK

A '73 Galaxie sat in front of a real estate office in Key Largo. Serge had arrived a half hour early, brimming with anticipation, and spent the time idly ruminating: "Who was Ben Wa, anyway? Was he proud of his unique fame? Celebrated in his time with pats on the back as he walked down the street? Or did it go the other way: 'Jesus, everyone else can have one bad night at a party, but not me! I have to pass out in the bedroom, and all the guests find me with that stupid thing I rigged together, and now I have to leave town.'"

"Serge, are you sure about a condo?"

"Never been more sure of anything in my life."

"But I've heard horror stories about the condo commandos," said Coleman. "Fights breaking out at their meetings."

"Those are just the exceptions that prove the rule," said Serge. "Take any thousand random people walking around, and there are bound to be outbreaks of hullabaloo. And given all the condo association meetings in this state, I'd be more surprised if someone *didn't* get clobbered with a punch bowl."

Serge handed Coleman his smartphone. It displayed a screenshot.

"What's this?"

"I did some research on a few condos in the area and took the liberty of capturing the official minutes from recent meetings, just to get a taste of the fabulous culture we're about to enter."

Coleman slowly began reading aloud. "Let's see . . . There's something about a mysterious fish smell in a laundry room . . . They're having trouble matching the color of some chipped tile in the lobby . . . One person volunteered to make signs not to drop bottles down the trash chute, because broken glass was a growing problem . . . Someone else tracked a trail of drops that smelled like fish to the door of one unit, but the person denied it . . . Another woman said that non-residents trespassing in the pool were perturbing her . . . Serge? What does this all mean?"

"If the word 'perturb' comes into play, it means these mellow people have gotten a bad rap . . ."

The door of the office opened and Gretchen stepped out with a smile. She approached Serge's window. "Ready?"

"Lead us to mellowness."

The agent climbed into her silver Camaro, and the Galaxie followed her a few miles west, back across the bridge over Tavernier Creek. They slowed as they passed a sign: THE SEA GULLS.

The trio took the elevator to a unit on the sixth floor. Gretchen punched a code into the lockbox, and soon she was gesturing inside with the biggest smile yet. "You're just going to love—"

Serge abruptly brushed past her. "Where's the thermostat? I have to find the thermostat!"

"Uh, on the wall next to the closet for the air handler."

Serge's nose was an inch from the little box.

"Is everything okay?"

"No!" said Serge. "I mean, yes, this place is okay. I'm speaking in generalities. In Florida, air-conditioning is everything, and you would not believe the ordeals I've endured in motels, but fortunately I can now hack most of the chains' units. That's why when I'm on the road, the A/C is the first thing I check. And not just motels, but friends' houses, malls . . . Holy crap! We've only been here minutes, and the temperature has already jumped two degrees! The condenser must be defective!"

"I think it's fine." Gretchen pointed behind her. "I just left the door open. It's pretty hot outside."

"Oh, of course," said Serge, grabbing the sides of his head. "The stories I've seen in the news about what happens to female real estate agents showing places to dudes. Now you have to make sure the doors stay open so people can hear your screams, and even if it's too late, they can find the body quicker. Forget I said all that. This must be the kitchen . . ."

"Completely updated with glass-door cabinets and Italian marble counters," said Gretchen. "The side-by-side fridge is also the latest."

"*Ewwww,*" said Serge, holding his nose. "I won't waste your time. This is just too new."

"It's not nice?" asked the agent.

"No, it's very nice. But nice is bad." Serge pointed at the fridge with a digital display on the door.

"What exactly are you looking for?"

"Character," said Serge. "I'll know when I see it. Next place . . ."

A short drive to the next sign: POINCIANA LANDINGS.

Up the elevator again to another lockbox and another front door left open.

Serge emerged from the spacious master bath. "There's a Jacuzzi in there."

"I know," said Gretchen. "Isn't it great?"

"No," said Serge. "When I'm in the bathroom, it's all business."

Gretchen scratched her head. "What about the built-in wine rack?"

"Too French. Next place."

They drove past another sign: OCEAN POINTE.

Serge stood in the middle of the living room with folded arms. "Track lighting?"

"I take it that's bad?" asked Gretchen.

"A tragedy."

Next sign: THE EXCELSIOR.

Serge followed Gretchen inside. Through the walls: *Thud, thud, thud. "Yes! Yes! Don't stop! Faster! Faster! Screw me harder! Get the syrup! . . ."*

Serge's head slowly turned toward the agent. "I didn't say anything."

And so it continued the rest of the afternoon. "Too fancy," "Too pretentious," "Too much modern art," "Too— . . . I don't know, it's just too."

Gretchen sighed and checked her watch. "I don't know what to say. You've seen some of the nicest places from Tavernier to Lower Matecumbe. There are a few other properties I can show you, but I get the feeling your reaction's just going to be the same. If you could be a little more specific than just 'character.'"

"You know, old Florida Keys," said Serge. "Authentic, rustic, flawed, minor damage, salt-air rust and shabbiness that screams the place has a history. I want a fishing cabin in the sky."

"I've never had a request quite like that," said Gretchen. "Hmmm. Well, there is the one place, but I never show it because nobody wants it. In fact, none of the Realtors show it because they're afraid to hurt their reputations."

"What have we got to lose?" said Serge.

A few miles later, back on Plantation Key, they arrived at a stucco building that was painted in colors that hadn't been popular since the seventies, and they weren't that popular then, either. Brown, deli-mustard yellow and an off-salmon. A row of giant coquina boulders prevented drivers from plowing through the wild azaleas. A sign:

PELICAN BAY.

"You'll have to forgive me," said Gretchen, "but this needs to be the last stop of the afternoon. I've got work piling up back at the office."

"You've been more than generous with your time," said Serge. "Let's go on up. Fourth floor is it? . . ."

Gretchen had the opposite of hope as she extracted keys from the lockbox and opened up. Unlike at the other stops, she made no sales pitch as Serge strolled inside. Then something happened as if a switch was thrown. Serge began vibrating in place, then running around in pointless circles like a headless chicken. "I love it! I love it! I love it!"—disappearing into the bedroom—"Still loving it!"—then into the bathroom—"I haven't seen seafoam tiles like this in decades because everyone else hates them, but not me! I love 'em! And the sink! And the banana-colored toilet! And the crappy laminated counter!" He dashed back out and ran laps through the kitchen nook. "So tight and quaint. I can clean my freshly caught fish here. And look at these cheap dark-brown cabinets!" He swung one of the doors open and closed on wobbly hinges.

"I need to inform you," said Gretchen. "That dishwasher is broken."

"Even better!" Serge bounded on the balls of his feet. "I'll use it for pantry storage. I just love the simple morning routine, getting the coffee going, reading the paper and hand-washing dishes that have been soaking overnight." He flung open a sliding glass door and ran onto the balcony. "Mangroves! Ocean! More coral boulders preventing the private beach from washing away!"

Coleman joined him with a tall can of Miller and a chair.

"What do you think of our balcony?" asked Serge.

"If you're sitting down, nobody can see you," said Coleman. "It's the perfect place to get high . . ."

Serge pointed various directions with both arms. "Kayakers!

Skiffs! Kiteboarders! Deep-sea boats threading the channel markers in the limestone cuts! I'm going to do it all!"

He ran back inside. "I'll take it! Where do I sign?"

"You really want it?" asked Gretchen.

"More than anything. At least at this specific point in my life."

"Then let's go back to the office and make it official . . ."

A half hour later, Serge sprinted out of the real estate office in Key Largo, frantically flapping a lease over his head. "Woo-hoo! Now, this is what I call slowing down! Coleman, hurry!"

"Where are we going?"

"To celebrate! This will be the best celebration ever!"

The Galaxie skidded out of the parking lot and sped off down the Overseas Highway.

"How are we going to celebrate?" asked Coleman.

"There's only one proper way to celebrate when you're slowing down and just landed a dream pad," said Serge. "First, a righteous Keys dinner, and for dessert, we'll take ecstasy to the mountaintop by shopping for pot holders, soap dishes, and vacuum cleaner robots."

Chapter 8

CHEZ BENZ

The automated gates buzzed open at a property on Millionaires Row. A high-mileage Nissan with a noisy muffler rolled up the gravel road, past a derelict tennis court before arriving at a circular driveway near the shore.

Mercado trotted down coquina steps from the front door. "Glad to see you changed your mind."

"No, hold up," said Julie. "That's not what I told you on the phone about your proposition from back at the bar. I just wanted to give the situation a look-see."

"Sure, sure, whatever you like."

Mercado turned back toward the door, but Julie stood rigid, still trying to process the immensity and architecture of the mansion. "Fuck."

"Oh, the house," said Mercado. "Yeah, it does have that effect."

Then she glanced around. "Who the hell are all these guys milling around? It's like a convention."

"Business associates," said Mercado.

"They look a little too muscular for office work."

"They have gyms," said Mercado. "Since my dad's health turned and he couldn't keep hands on the day-to-day, we've had to hold more and more meetings here at the house."

"Then why are they *outside* the house?"

"Smoke break."

"They're not smoking."

Mercado glanced back. "You coming or not?"

Julie snapped out of it and followed him. "It looks even bigger from the inside." There was a massive built-in oak cabinet with a pair of floor-to-ceiling glass doors and a digital temperature control. "How many bottles of wine are in there?"

"Never counted."

She pointed in another direction. "You have an elevator?"

"For my dad." He resumed walking.

"What kind of a staircase is this?" asked Julie.

"The architect said it's a floating one."

He led her to the doorway of the master bedroom, and Julie had to recalibrate again: They could fit *two* Airstreams in here.

The old man's eyes were closed, and Mercado faced a woman on the other side of the bed. "Sleeping or resting?"

"He's been doing both."

Mercado turned the other way. "Julie, this is Belinda, one of his nurses . . . Belinda, this is Julie. She's going to be spending a lot of time with my father from now on."

"Mercado!"

"Sorry, I know. Just a look-see." He headed for the door.

"Where are you going?" asked Julie.

"Business." And down the stairs he went.

Then a soft, cracking voice from behind. "Julie?" A cough.

She turned to find Raffy Benz awake, and trying not so well to push himself up on the pillows.

"Let me help you with that." And Julie did what she had done so many times back at her trailer.

"Julie's a nice name," said Raffy. "So you're a friend of Sonny's?"

"More like an acquaintance."

"Don't pull this old fart's leg," said Raffy. "He's told me so much about you, like he's known you your whole life." He tried to lean forward the best he could. "And of course you know he's single. That boy could use some ballast. Family's everything."

"We really just met."

"He says you know all there is and more about offshore fishing. Learned it from your dad. Is that true?"

"I had a great childhood. He took me out every time he could, and if there weren't many customers, he'd let me throw a line in the water, too. Except, with all his coaching, I got a little too good."

"Too good isn't in my vocabulary."

"It wasn't in ours, either, until the day I made my first big catch," said Julie. "It's not positive for a charter boat business if the captain's little girl catches something much bigger than any of the paying customers do."

Raffy nodded and repeated himself. "Family's everything. What did you catch?"

"What?"

"On your dad's boat."

"Just about everything."

"Pull up a chair and don't be a stranger," said Raffy. "What was this big first catch you landed that pissed off the customers?"

She took a seat. "It was this bull dolphin. I mean dolphin the fish, not the bottlenose mammal."

"I know the difference," said Raffy. "That's why restaurants have to call it mahi-mahi on the menu, or these fools say, 'You killed Flipper!' . . . I'm babbling. Continue."

"Beautiful creature, bigger than anything I'd ever seen up till then."

"They sure like to jump out of the water and put on a show."

"And how," said Julie. "It was west of the sun, and it lit up all glistening green and yellow, splashing and hurtling into the air. I can still see it vividly right now as I tell you. Took me way over an hour, and my dad offered to spell me at the rod, but there was no way that was happening. By the time we released him next to the boat, my hands were bleeding all over the place."

The old man winked. "But it was more than worth it, eh?"

She broke into a broad smile at the memory. "Totally. But after that, whenever I caught a fish, I'd tell one of the regular customers that it was beginner's luck, and hand the rod to them."

Raffy's head fell back on the pillow with his own smile. "Reminds me of when I was fishing as a boy. Of course the whole neighborhood was so poor that nobody had a boat, so it was shore fishing. But it was more dangerous than any boat at sea."

"Why?" asked Julie.

"Because us little kids were called the *runts* where I come from, known as local bandits and viewed like an infestation of rats. Even if you weren't involved, you always had to watch out for the squads employed by businesses to sweep us from the streets."

"Did they hurt you?"

"If we were lucky," said Raffy. "They shot us like vermin and piled the bodies in trucks to take out to the countryside. As I said, rats."

"Jesus, they killed children?"

"Aggressively. Do you want to hear a fishing story or not?" Raffy asked with another wink. "Usually just caught a bunch of tiny junk fish, and I was happy with that. But then one day— *Bam!*—something hit my line . . ."

Julie leaned forward, eagerly awaiting the rest of the story . . . and waiting . . . "Mr. Benz?"

"Yes?"

"What did you hook?"

"What hook? What are you talking about?" asked the old man. "Who are you?"

Suddenly, the house shook from a roaring sound down on the beach. Julie rushed to the window in alarm and watched Mercado ducking under the blades and into the Sikorsky.

The helicopter took off from the private pad and soared away over the coconut palms.

ISLAMORADA

The Galaxie crossed the bridge at Snake Creek. The occupants wore matching Coral Shores High School T-shirts and flapped green-and-gold felt pennants out the window.

"Serge," said Coleman, "why did we buy all this crap at the convenience store?"

"To show we're down with the community," said Serge. "I'm always ten moves ahead on the cultural chessboard. We're in a tourist destination, after all. Sure, everything seems chill on the surface: all smiles as visitors spend freely on umbrella drinks and Hemingway snow globes. But we're just one power-grid collapse away from a complete breakdown of the social order. Once credit card machines become paperweights, the tourists will be rounded up in the camps or find themselves carrying suitcases over their heads, wading through swamps back to the mainland."

"We had to do that once."

"That was just a misunderstanding," said Serge. "Weddings on the beach are supposed to be happy occasions. I was only trying to increase their fun."

Coleman nodded. "It was just a few water balloons from the balcony."

"And some paint balloons," said Serge. "The point is you need to meet your neighbors more than halfway, and if you're going to drop anchor in a neighborhood, the social fabric depends on T-shirts and pennants."

"But why the high school?"

"Because I'm taking it to the next level. Owning property is one thing, but if you're our age with these shirts, it means you're raising teenagers, and everyone else takes a step back and thinks: 'Yikes, they're flying right into the thickest shit cloud.' And out of sympathy they give you extra slack for behavior that colors outside the lines."

"What if they ask about our children?"

Serge shook his head. "They never do. All you have to know is how the football team is doing. Then you form lasting friendships based on love of family and hatred for the other schools."

Serge crossed a final bridge onto Upper Matecumbe. The Galaxie pulled off the south side of the road and rolled past a row of huge charter fishing boats. "There it is," said Serge. "Whale Harbor, home of the famous seafood buffet."

"Buffet!" said Coleman.

"I know." Serge sighed. "You need to burn another joint for value . . ."

They walked inside. Two other men passed by with toothpicks. And Coral Shores T-shirts. "Go 'Canes!"

"Damn straight!" said Serge. "Green and gold forever!"

"So how many kids do you have going there?"

"What?" said Serge. "Uh, hey! How about that quarterback?"

"Having a lousy year," said the man. "So how many kids? My daughter's class president and probably knows them."

"Ha, ha, ha," forced Serge. "Don't you just hate those other schools?"

"I was only curious how many children you have there."

Simultaneously:

Serge: "Two."

Coleman: "One."

They glanced at each other.

Serge: "One."

Coleman: "Two."

"What? You don't know how many kids you have at Coral Shores?"

"Ha, ha, ha, ha—" Serge suddenly pointed at the floor. "Spider!"

They ran away.

Moments later, the pair collapsed against the metal counter at the beginning of the buffet line by the oysters on half shells.

"Whew!" said Serge. "That was a close one."

"When you're high, parents are worse than police," said Coleman.

They grabbed plates and began working down the food line. Serge spooned octopus salad onto his plate.

"Man!" said Coleman. "They've got everything. And I don't know what most of it is."

"But it's all good or this place wouldn't be so packed," said Serge. "Approach it like your drug use: Try a little of everything."

Coleman loaded up his plate with mussels, smoked something, fried shrimp, shrimp crepes, peel-and-eat shrimp.

They found a table and grabbed nutcrackers for the snow crab legs. Serge jotted on a clipboard.

A large piece of Coleman's crab shell hit someone at the next table.

"Hey, watch it!"

"Sorry." Coleman leaned toward the clipboard. "What's coming up?"

"I am so jazzed!" said Serge, cracking open a crab leg of his own.

Coleman popped a shrimp in his mouth. "Because we got the condo?"

"That in general, but specifically we're about to immerse ourselves in the 'moving-in experience,'" said Serge. "Don't get me wrong: Up until now, we've led a lifestyle that others can only dream about, living the ultimate freedom of the road and charting a course wherever our moods led us each day."

"So what's this 'moving-in' deal?"

"I've only heard the rumors," said Serge. "But it's something that millions of our fellow citizens go through over and over."

"And that gets you excited?"

"Coleman, I'm required to explore all aspects of the Great American Experiment, and this is a major segment of our culture that's been missing from my life, like Shakespeare in the Park, or collecting yams shaped like presidents."

"So how does this experience work?"

"The word out on the street is that it involves cleaning products."

"What are those?" asked Coleman.

"Who knows, but I heard it has something to do with dusting and scrubbing toilets." Serge noshed a bit of crab cake. "This is going to be the best supply run ever!"

"Toilets?" said Coleman. "Ick!"

"They're not going to bite," said Serge. "And you've seen a lot of toilets close up in your day."

"They aren't the problem," said Coleman. "It's just that cleaning them takes up too much time. Chicks are, like, cleaning toilets nonstop."

"I know what you mean," said Serge. "Life happens for them in short bursts between grabbing the bowl cleaner. Men, on the other hand, have these things in perspective. We clean toilets on a sane schedule."

"But when will we know it's time to clean them?"

"When we need a chisel," said Serge. "Any more is overkill."

"But why do any of that at all?" asked Coleman with a mouth full of snapper. "Why can't we just go on as we always have?"

"Because this isn't a dive motel, and we're not housebroken." Serge sampled the conch chowder. "We can't just keep setting curtains on fire and driving away."

Coleman put an oyster on a cracker. "My friends who've just gotten married always complain about being housebroken."

"That's because they have a supervisor hovering over them with the power to ration sex. There's too much riding on the lemon Pledge." Serge tossed a mollusk in his mouth.

"It sounds like I'm a dog that can no longer poop wherever I want," said Coleman. "That's a lot of pressure."

"Take one for the team," said Serge. "Plus it's not just about cleaning. There's decorating, too!"

Coleman looked up in sudden terror. "Jesus! The Pottery Barn!"

"Good heavens, no!" said Serge. "That's my home-decorating motto: Not a speck of guest towels. I plan to unleash a whole new school of interior decorating that's guaranteed to land us a seven-figure deal for coffee table books."

Coleman squirted snow crab juice in his eyes. "So what's your plan?"

Serge tapped his clipboard. "If I ever settled down, my dream pad was always a fishing cabin. But in the Keys, that's just begging for disaster. You saw what that hurricane did to my favorite cottage at the Old Wooden Bridge."

"I didn't see anything," said Coleman. "All that debris fell on me, and you had to pull me out. Remember?"

"Well, our new unit is safely up on the fourth floor, and so weathered and outdated that it's perfect!" said Serge. "Like I told Gretchen, it'll be our dream fishing cabin in the sky."

"Where do we start?" asked Coleman.

"First, all the wall hangings in there have to go. The condo's great, but the owner has no taste, like that faded wooden plank over the TV painted in tropical colors with palm trees and a margarita glass: *It's Five o'Clock Somewhere.*' You know me; I'm all about Florida kitsch, but occasionally it drifts over to the dark side."

"Won't the owner get mad if you just start throwing his stuff out?"

"I'll store it instead because it might have sentimental value, like he takes it down and has his dominatrix spank him with it."

"Can't he get another plank?"

"I'm not taking the risk," said Serge. "Until YouTube came along, I didn't realize how complex God constructed the blue-print for human reproduction, with an infinite array of narrow sexual trenches."

"Trenches?"

Serge got out his cell phone. "Eventually a dark van will come along and pluck me off the street, never to be heard from again, for watching all this sexual gibberish. And it won't be the government, but Google or Facebook, because I clicked terms of agreement without reading . . . Back to the trenches. Observe these videos I've bookmarked."

"What am I watching?"

"A stiletto heel breaking a light bulb . . . This is a compilation of sexy elbows . . . People wearing smelly socks . . . And this one is bondage, except it's only the big toes tied together with string . . . This other chick is blowing up balloons."

"She's not even making balloon animals," said Coleman.

"And in a subcategory of that fetish community, this woman is popping bubble wrap . . . But it gets weirder. Check this one out."

Coleman pointed at the tiny screen. "A woman is just reading a book?"

"There's a huge book-reading fetish community out there," said Serge. "And it also has subcategories: out loud, silent, whispering."

"So where is this book-reading video going? When does the sex start?"

"This is it, for an hour and six minutes. As the saying goes,

'Life is short, but it's also pretty wide—'" Serge's head slowly swiveled.

Coleman continued munching shrimp after shrimp. It took a while before he noticed his buddy was uncommonly quiet. "Serge, what's the matter?"

Serge tilted his head toward a pair of nearby tables. Eight men who looked like football players in black suits. The men ate in silence. "Those guys who just came in."

Coleman turned. "Jesus, they're huge. And their plates are piled like mountains."

"I've seen the phenomenon before at a buffet near a weight-lifting gym," said Serge. "They're bulking up. Probably make three more trips to the food line before hitting the exercise equipment."

Coleman shrugged and popped another shrimp in his mouth. "The Keys get all kinds of strange visitors."

"Something tells me they're not tourists."

"Okay, not tourists. But why are you watching like that so long?"

"Studying," said Serge. "I've got this weird feeling we might run into them again. Islamorada is a small place."

Coleman picked a crab shell from his hair. "You're imagining shit."

"Probably right." Serge took a deep breath and threw in the towel, actually a napkin. "I can't eat another bite. Let's bounce. Shopping spree!"

Coleman staggered out the door to the parking lot. "Man, am I stuffed." *Burp.* "That was way better than you told me." He glanced down and patted his bulging stomach. "I think I have a food baby."

"Looks like twins."

Chapter 9

Deep-drafting fishing boats headed in from the Straits of Florida until they saw land, then back to the marina, down the winding mangrove creek, past the channel-side Habanos shack-restaurant where the pelicans watch you eat conch fritters.

Above the channel was the landmark serpentine stretch of U.S. Highway 1 that the locals all know and love, from the east end of Plantation Key, snaking over Tavernier Creek, and down onto the far shore of Key Largo.

A 1973 Galaxie raced through a stretch of the Keys where everyone was racing to get somewhere else: past a modest movie house, a barbershop with an actual barber pole, the Mariners Hospital, and a pastel-green hardware store advertising crab traps and a tent sale for fiberglass fish replicas. The Ford's windows were down, and a salty balm swept through the car. Serge tapped the wheel, hummed and smiled with penetrating ice-blue eyes of focus.

Coleman popped a Schlitz, chugged, and farted with anti-focus. "Serge, why are you so happy?"

"You know how we go on supply runs?"

"Yeah, all the time. Ammunition and snacks."

Serge slapped the outside of his driver's door. "Hot damn! I can't take the anticipation! This is going to be the biggest supply run ever!"

"Jesus," said Coleman. "How many dudes are you planning to wax?"

"Did you already forget? It's for our condo," said Serge. "Up until now we've been living exclusively in dive motels, or on someone's couch, where redecorating is met with ungratefulness."

The car continued up the highway, through the more wooded and sparsely populated span of central Key Largo. Coleman watched as they passed the wild bird rehabilitation center, imagining vultures with drug problems. "This does sound like a lot of fun. I've always wanted to fix a place up exactly the way we want."

"And therein lies the rub," said Serge. "The fishing-cabin-in-the-sky theme will be a cinch. Lots of nautical souvenirs, sepia-tone photos of lighthouses, antique barometers and maybe some of those fiberglass fish from the hardware store. After that it gets dicey."

"How so?"

"It ain't a dive motel anymore," said Serge. "When it's your own place, people just expect you to entertain."

"Like what? We'll have to ride unicycles?"

"That could work," said Serge. "But I think what polite society has in mind is sitting around and talking. I've also heard rumors they expect food and alcohol."

"But we've entertained in motel rooms."

"I'm talking about voluntary entertainment," said Serge. "This might require us getting in touch with our feminine side."

"That's the side that touches me all the time," said Coleman. "It helps to close your eyes and pretend."

"I could have gone all day without hearing that," said Serge. "Anyway, it's going to be a steep learning curve to becoming more civilized, which is why we must force ourselves to think how babes do."

"How in God's name do we do that?"

"Ask the babes."

"Chicks are more civilized?"

"Ever live with a woman?" asked Serge.

"No."

"I did briefly."

"That's right," said Coleman. "Molly, your ex."

"I got just a whiff of the phenomenon," said Serge. "Not enough data to extrapolate my own dynamic model within the margin of error. So I called a bunch of my married friends. The results were terrifying."

"What did they say?"

"Initially after the wedding, things were pretty much fair, with roughly equal amounts of possessions visible in the house."

"So far, so good," said Coleman.

"Then the wives meticulously mapped out military maneuvers, slowly acquiring territory like the German army," said Serge. "The guys' stuff was systematically squeezed out into the garage, storage or attic. My married friends said that before they knew what was happening, there was so little evidence of their shit that they thought they'd walked into the wrong house."

"That's fucked up."

"No kidding," said Serge. "But here's the worst part: All the guys said their wives were right. That the houses looked more fantastic than they could ever have imagined."

"Don't you hate that?"

"Seriously," said Serge. "And as a consolation prize, the husbands were rewarded with 'man caves.'"

"Man caves rule!" said Coleman.

"No argument here," said Serge. "Except it's all a trick. The term 'man cave' sounds so empowering: 'Why yes, I am master of my domain down here in a dank corner of the basement, where all my shit has been quarantined in a bad-taste ghetto: bear rug, *Playboy* pinball machine, old refrigerator with a beer tap in the door, Rolling Stones tongue poster, autographed baseballs, moose heads, samurai swords, shelves of *Star Wars* figures, dartboards, neon beer signs, drum sets, Nerf basketball hoops, comic books and a nude female mannequin in a leather Marlon Brando motorcycle hat.'"

"What's the problem?" asked Coleman. "Sounds like great stuff to decorate the entire home."

"Unless you want to entertain," said Serge. "If you invite any couples over to dinner in a place like that, right after they leave, the wives will place you on their husbands' no-fly list."

"Why?"

"Because women selflessly dedicate countless hours to civilizing us," said Serge. "And now, on the drive home from your place, a wife can see that look on her husband's face: 'Yeah, what *is* all my shit doing in the basement?' And then you're suddenly cut out of his life like his unmarried cousin who brought him home drunk one night from the cock fights."

"What about a woman cave?" asked Coleman.

"That's the rest of the house."

"Oh, yeah."

"Here's where we start . . ." The car re-entered population on the east end of Key Largo near the Pennekamp underwater park and pulled into a shopping center.

"Kmart?" asked Coleman. "I thought you liked Walmart."

"I *love* Walmart," said Serge. "Especially when I'm not shopping. It's a human terrarium better than any zoo. Like the news story last year from their Citrus County store: Florida woman arrested while riding a motorized cart, drinking a half bottle of wine and eating sushi and a rotisserie chicken."

"I wouldn't even notice something like that," said Coleman.

"Who would have thought that Kmart is now the upscale experience?" Serge parked near the entrance, and they soon were pushing shopping carts.

Coleman glanced around curiously. "There's not a whole lot of people in here."

"The entire chain took a wallop after spokesperson Martha Stewart started signing prison autographs for packs of smokes."

"Where are we heading?"

Serge stopped the cart and pointed up at a sign over an aisle: "Linen."

"What's that?"

"We'll find out."

Wobbling cart wheels traveled twenty feet.

"Well, I'll be," said Coleman. "Towels. Do you think we need them?"

"That's the talk in the county jail," said Serge. "I think we're supposed to have a set. Grab one of every different color . . ."

A few minutes later, the cart made a left turn. Coleman looked around with a hanging-open mouth. "What is this aisle?"

"The household cleaning products."

"We've never been here before."

"I have," said Serge. "But only for stuff to make explosives."

"What do we do?"

"Start reading labels to find out what these products are actually intended for."

"Here's some bleach," said Coleman. "And ammonia. Here's something that says it makes things sparkly."

"Grab a few bottles of each." Serge pushed his cart. "If it doesn't work, it'll come in handy later."

Farther up the aisle, Coleman grabbed a spray can. "Hey, Serge. I found something I think I've heard of from TV. It's called Febreze."

"You may have just hit the jackpot." Serge examined a can of his own. "Babes are like the only people who buy this junk, so it has to work wonders. We may not even need all these other products."

Coleman nodded. "Just spray Febreze on everything."

"That could be our perfect new strategy," said Serge. "If we fall short in other domestic areas, simply douse the whole place with Febreze like we're bug bombing."

"We can even spray it on our visitors," said Coleman. "That should impress them. How many do we buy?"

"Hold on," said Serge, scanning the array of different-colored cans. "They come in all these weird smell-flavors. We need to ask an expert."

"Like who?"

"Any woman on the planet," said Serge. "There's one right now."

They wheeled the cart up the aisle. Coleman pointed as they passed the toilet scrubbers. "Do we need those?"

"No. It's nothing Febreze can't handle." Serge stopped the cart next to another shopper and held up a can. "Ma'am? Excuse me. I don't mean to interrupt, but I need your advice. Should we hoard this stuff for social Armageddon?"

"What?"

"I understand it's huge with the babes, so it must be great."

A scowl. "Did you just say 'babes'?"

"Not my fault," said Serge. "My entire gender is primitive. Women will lead us to the light. You've just been nominated to help us." He pointed at the cans in the cart. "There are so many confusing scents that I don't know what to pick: forest, bamboo, something called 'Whispering Woods,' lilac, jasmine, bramble—whatever that is—apple, pumpkin, ocean, aqua, cedar, cranberry and Bora Bora. What do you suggest in the event some chicks visit?"

"Did you just say 'chicks'?"

"I'm innocent again," said Serge. "Please refer to previous comment. So anyway, my favorite scent would be 'neutral,' but they don't seem to carry that. On the other hand, they stock 'Hawaiian,' so I was hoping for 'Florida,' except that's probably a dumpster smell that was rejected by the focus groups— Hey, where are you going? . . ."

Serge heard giggling and turned around. "Is something funny?"

"Yes," said the woman in a Bud n' Mary's Marina tank top. "You."

Serge, sincerely clueless: "Did I make a joke?"

She stifled her giggles. "Are those the best pickup lines you could think of?"

"What? I'm not picking anyone up."

More laughter. "Don't bullshit a bullshitter. You were so obvious it was comical."

"I was?"

She nodded. "When you're in a grocery store, or a place like this, pickups are so common that women have to put up force fields. We learn to see it coming."

"I had no idea this was going on," said Serge. "What's the tip-off?"

"Whenever a guy approaches you asking advice and acting helpless."

"That really works?" asked Serge.

"Almost never, but it doesn't stop men from trying." She set a box of detergent down and took off her reading glasses. "Your eyes are uncommonly ice blue."

"And yours are green, like those tinted streaks in your hair," said Serge. "So what kind of pickup lines actually work?"

"You never know until one does," said the shopper, shaking her head with another chuckle. "Everyone's an eccentric down here in the islands. Okay, I believe you now: You were sincerely seeking product advice."

"Thanks," said Serge. "Because if I'm trying to pick someone up, I always use the direct approach to establish trust." He leaned forward and whispered something in her ear . . .

Moments later, Coleman stood at the far end of the Kmart parking lot, a few feet into the woods. He finished peeing and zipped his pants. Then he picked a can of beer up off the ground and finished that, too. He had taken a few cans with him to the woods, but that was the last. Oh well, there were more in the car.

Coleman walked over and knocked on one of the windows. No answer. He knocked again.

Finally, Serge looked back over his shoulder as the car continued squeaking up and down on the suspension. "What!"

"Can I open the door and get more beer?"

"Of course not! Don't you see what's going on here?" *Squeak, squeak, squeak.* "Show some respect for the lady!"

Coleman went back to sitting on the curb near the woods and biting his fingernails. He was bored. He found a rock on the ground and began tapping it against his forehead until he decided that it hurt and tossed the rock clanging down a storm drain. He then decided it would be a better idea to start hitting himself in the head with a smaller rock.

The car finally stopped squeaking, and Serge stepped out of the back seat like someone who had just completed a life-affirming swim in the open ocean. He was followed by a woman with tinted hair stuck to the sweat on her face. An errant bra strap down over her shoulder. She staggered a step sideways before reacquiring a straight line.

"Coleman!" yelled Serge. "Stop with the rock and get over here! I'd like you to meet someone!"

"I saw her in the store," said Coleman.

"A proper introduction. I hadn't gotten her name yet," said Serge. "This is Tanya. She's going to come over to the new pad and save us from our Paleolithic homemaking instincts."

Tanya quickly scribbled on a scrap of paper. "I hope you aren't just saying that to get rid of me."

"Of course not!" Serge pointed back at the Kmart sign. "We have history."

"Okay, here's my number," said Tanya. "Swear to me you'll call?"

"Even better!" said Serge. "Cleaning aisle, same time tomorrow? I have the feeling that becoming housebroken is going to be a steep upward curve with lots more trips here, and I'll need professional help."

"Okay then," said Tanya. "Nice meeting you guys."

"Right-o!"

They climbed back in the car and headed west down U.S. Highway 1.

Coleman threw a rock out the window. "Are you really going to see her again?"

"It's another crapshoot."

Part Two

Chapter 10

1,700 MILES AWAY

The remote road through the leafless trees was dark and snow-covered. In fact, it was still snowing. The nearest farmhouse was five miles. There were no streetlights or moon, and it would have been completely dark except for the Oldsmobile sitting on the center line, engulfed in flames. The motto on the license plate: LIVE FREE OR DIE.

The police would arrive when the car was down to a smoldering chassis. They found the body of the driver inside, except it was in the back seat.

The New Hampshire State Police alerted the Royal Canadian Mounted Police, because the car was discovered near frozen-over Lake Derby, north of the White Mountains and, more germanely, just south of the Canadian border.

It was standard procedure.

Whenever some brainless crime happened and decades in prison loomed, or even the death penalty, perpetrators this close to the border made a break for it. The main roads with the U.S. Customs checkpoints were the obvious entry points. So obvious, in fact, that fugitives never took them. They instead chose a run on foot, through the woods. Except at this time of year, when it was so cold and the snow so deep, those on the lam didn't want to stray too far into the elements and instead tried to sneak around the outside of the customs buildings, and were easily captured. Or they were shivering so bad, they banged on the frosty windows begging to come inside.

Others, however, had access to proper winter clothes and equipment.

That's where the microphones came in.

New Hampshire has always had a fierce independent streak. Hence the license plates. During Prohibition, the state was notorious for bootlegging and rum-running down from Quebec. More recently, they've helped Massachusetts residents sneak liquor back home to avoid taxes. It's true: New Hampshire police would pull over and detain Massachusetts authorities whose cars had been sitting in NH package store parking lots in an attempt to surveil their residents when they came out of the stores, follow them south and fine them when they crossed the border. New England is quaint.

Other smuggling continues to this day, especially in the summer, when hikers carry eighty pounds or more of ultra-potent weed across the Canadian border in overloaded backpacks.

Here's what the United States did. Instead of a wall, feds installed a grid of camouflaged, battery-powered microphones so sensitive they could hear a rabbit fart. The backpackers never realized it, but for hours, their every step was tracked through the woods until they needed to cross a back road and found ten police cars waiting with smiling officers leaning against fenders.

This particular night, just after the burned car was found, it was all hands on deck, and it didn't take long. The microphones west of the lake picked it up first. It almost deafened the officers listening on the headphones.

A pair of snowmobiles crashed through the snow and bounded over moguls. Helmets, ski masks, goggles, full speed ahead. Anyone else would have slammed into five trees by now and been killed. But this crew knew the route by heart. The terrain opened up into treeless tundra.

The police agreed: Too much of a coincidence that they'd just found a homicide victim in a torched car, and now a textbook race for the Great White North. They confidently dispatched teams to intercept. Headquarters diligently tracked the drama. The roar of the engines continued streaming in from the microphones, and monitoring screens lit up as they traced their quarry to within a mile of the international border. It was almost too easy.

"Where are they now?" asked a sergeant parked roadside in the snow.

"Coming right at you," said headquarters. "A minute . . . forty-five seconds . . ."

"Okay, boys," yelled the sergeant, racking a shotgun. "This is it."

"Thirty seconds," said headquarters.

"We can hear them now. And see their headlights," said the sergeant. "They're almost here."

"Ten seconds . . ."

"Why aren't they slowing down?" said the sergeant. "They've got to see the road—"

And suddenly, all the officers scattered as the snowmobiles, still at top speed, hit a slope of snow at the edge of the woods, went airborne, and crashed—window high—into a pair of police cars.

All officers drew their weapons and ran to make arrests, except they were pretty sure their targets wouldn't be walking away from this one.

Then: *What the hell? Where are they? . . .*

If you know anything at all about snowmobiles, you'll know there's a safety feature. A kill switch, similar to those in boats. If the person piloting the craft gets thrown and releases the hand grips, the switch shuts it down.

The officers inspected the debris and discovered that the kill switches had been hot-wired to stay open.

The sergeant turned and fumed as he stared up into the icicle-draped woods. "Sons of bitches jumped off!"

"Sarge," said a corporal. "I think they used the roar of the motors to cover the sound of their escape from the microphones."

"Shut up!"

TWO HOURS EARLIER

A lonesome fishing cabin glowed on the shore of Lake Derby. The kerosene lanterns were lit and a propane stove grilled steaks, filling the single room with that rib eye glory. The meat had been doused with bourbon. So had the cabin's occupants.

Two snowmobiles sat outside, along with a husky guard dog.

A man with a shaved head and full beard poked a Colt .44 Magnum out the door, then his head. The coast was clear. He let the dog in and fed it the gristle and fat that he'd just cut off the meat. The bone would come later. The dog's name was Bongo. The man's beard was a rich Irish shade of red, so they called him Blue.

Also in the cabin were three other men of various builds: Duke, Mulch and Weezer. Their necks tattooed from the state prison in Concord. The last occupant was a woman called Vix. More details to come on her name. Blue jeans and a tank top, with additional layered clothing that was finally covered with an army fatigue jacket. Her hair was an untamed black mop, and she said maybe two words an hour. She decided to exceed her quota. "Where is that fucker?"

"He's late," said Blue. "As usual."

They were the north end of a contraband pipeline down to Manchester, then Nashua and Boston. The cabin, as fishing cabins tend to be, was rustic, with pitch and tar between the boards, trying to keep out the cold with foolish results. The day had been a steady gray, so the guys spent it doing coke. It evened out the H.

The last steaks were about ready, so they snorted a few more lines off the table, to perk their appetites, which was drug logic. They heard a car outside, and headlights hit the window. Knocking at the door. Two spaced raps of knuckles, then a third. They didn't really need the code, because nobody else would be so far out in this weather. And if it were the cops, they wouldn't knock.

Blue opened the door and glared. "You're late again."

A man in a jacket with a fur-lined hood blew into his cupped fists and stomped his feet on the doorstep for warmth. "Come on! Let me in!" He went by Twitch.

"Give me the backpack and shake the snow off first."

He swatted flakes and frost from the fur hoodie. "Jesus, you want a *Good Housekeeping* seal?"

Blue turned around. "Guys!"

The cocaine and steaks would have to wait. The gang tore apart the backpack, pulling out five-pound bags of compressed primo buds, and stacked them on the table.

"Did you stick to the route by the river?" asked Blue.

"Of course, like every other time." Twitch pulled a deceptively small battery-powered stereo from a jacket pocket. "And I played the recording of wind and rustling leaves like you told me, in case they put in new microphones." He turned it on, and it was as if a tornado had entered the room.

"Jesus!" Blue snatched it and killed the power.

Normally the gang took a bathroom scale and placed a tall kitchen waste basket on it, filled it with the pot, then subtracted the weight of the basket.

Blue reached under the sink and set something new on the table next to the drugs.

"What the hell's that?" asked Twitch.

"A vacuum cleaner," Blue snapped sarcastically. "It's a digital scale, you idiot."

"You've never used one before."

"Is that a problem?"

"Why would it be?"

As the gang weighed each bag and tallied the numbers, Twitch began to live up to his nickname.

"Getting nervous?" said Blue, tabulating the final digits.

"No."

"You should be." Blue stood up. "Do we not pay you enough?"

"Plenty. Appreciate it."

"Then why have you been ripping us off?"

"What are you talking about? I swear I haven't."

"We couldn't be sure, because the bathroom scale isn't accurate enough," said Blue. "So this time we had our friends in Quebec weigh it down to the gram, just as we did here. You're almost a pound short, like we suspected on the other runs." He got up and grabbed the handle of the Colt on the counter next to the sink. "If we go outside and tear apart your Oldsmobile, we're not going to find it?"

"Okay, okay, look, yes, I did it," said Twitch. "I didn't mean to!"

"You're babbling," said Blue. "You didn't *mean* to steal from us?"

"I mean I got jammed up with these other guys and was desperate!"

Blue pulled the gun off the counter and let it hang by his side. "You're more afraid of them than us?"

Twitch heard the hammer cock. And he already knew everyone was seriously coked up. "I can fix this! I can make you rich!"

"Now you're really babbling."

"No, seriously. I've been setting up a score," said Twitch. "It was too big for me, and I was waiting for the right people to go in with."

It was time for Blue to remain silent and let Twitch freak out some more. Build motivation to get the money or the drugs back.

"It's huge," said Twitch. "You won't regret it." He sat at the table and grabbed the piece of paper they'd used to add up the weight. "Here's the address, and here's the floor plan . . ." Then he spit out the rest of the details like an auctioneer.

It was so specific it drew interest.

"How much are we talking about?" asked Blue.

"A least a couple million, but probably a lot more."

The other people in the room glanced at each other.

Vix stepped forward. "Can't you see he's bullshitting? We need our weight returned!"

"Just a second," said Blue. He set the Colt back on the counter and took a seat at the table to study the diagram. "How did you hear about this?"

"Cellmate last year," said Twitch. "It was all he ever talked about. Big plans for when he got out."

"Do you trust him?"

"Not at first, but yeah, definitely," said Twitch. "He knew so much about it that I've forgotten more than I remember."

"What's this X?"

"The stash is either under the building or in the floor or the backyard. That might be a patio."

"Your cellmate wasn't clear?"

"He kept drawing that map over and over, and the X kept moving."

"That didn't make you suspicious?"

"It made me *less* suspicious," said Twitch. "The truest stories are the ones that change slightly, like they haven't been rehearsed and memorized . . ."

And as Blue was studying the drawing, Twitch slipped a hand into his jacket and jumped backward toward the door.

"He's got a gun!" yelled Vix.

"That I do," said Twitch, slowly aiming the pistol back and forth at all the other occupants. "Now here's how this is going to play out. We're calling this one a draw. Step away from the counter. Then you're going to take your shoes off and follow me outside and wait until you can't see my taillights anymore—"

The husky named Bongo didn't like a gun pointed at his owner. Twitch never saw the jaws coming. They began shredding his arm, the one not holding the gun. Twitch screamed and blasted away wildly until Bongo whimpered and collapsed.

"*Ahhhhhhhhhhhhh!*" screamed Vix. She lunged for the gun on the counter. *Bam! Bam! Bam!* "Motherfucker!" *Bam! Bam!* "You killed my dog!" *Bam!*

The power of the .44 slugs was like getting shot and hit by a linebacker at the same time. They sent Twitch stumbling backward until he hit the door. For what seemed like the longest time, he stood there silently with surprised eyes before slowly sliding down to the floor, leaving a long red streak. Nothing left of his life but the burnt smell of gunpowder and a faint layer of smoke in the upper half of the room.

"Okay, this is a fuckup," said Blue.

"He killed my Bongo!" screamed Vix. "I just wish I had more bullets!"

Blue sat back down at the table. "What's done is done. We need to focus on a serious exit strategy."

"What are you talking about?" asked Vix.

"I'm talking about not going to death row."

"But it was self-defense," said Vix.

"Doesn't matter. It was in the commission of a drug deal. And I have priors." Blue got up and grabbed a duffel bag. "Pack your shit."

"What about him?" Vix pointed with the empty gun still in her hand.

"Grab everything he's got, wallet, cell phone, then we burn the body. In the car," said Blue. "It'll give us a head start. Let's go!"

They all got busy in a crazy hurry and were finished in minutes, hoisting straps over shoulders.

"Listen up," said Blue. "Here's the plan. One person each. The snowmobiles, and his car. Vix will ride with me in our vehicle to pick everyone up at the meeting points we discussed in case something like this happened. After we regroup, we'll drop off the pot and figure out where to go from there."

They each grabbed one of Twitch's limbs, dragging him through the snow and into the back seat of the Oldsmobile.

"Blue, are you sure we should chance making the drug drop with the cops looking for us?" asked Vix.

"We don't need those guys from Manchester after us, too," said Blue. "Besides, they'll all be expecting us at the Canadian border."

"So we head south?"

"Exactly." Blue trotted back toward the cabin.

"Where are you going?" asked Vix.

"Forgot something."

He ran back inside, grabbed a piece of paper off the table and stuck it in his pocket.

Chapter 11

Serge screeched back into the condominium parking lot.

"That sure was a crazy shopping spree," said Coleman. "The back seat is full of stuff I've never used before. Broom."

"Because the maids at the dive motels did it for us." Serge popped the trunk and pulled out a folded metal contraption with wheels. He flipped it open. "Ta-da! My mandatory personal condo shopping cart. Condos are a different universe that most people never glimpse without a telescope. But personal shopping carts are in the DNA of the condo tribe, because you can't shlep a million shopping bags across the parking lot and up elevators, like you can if you just park in your own driveway at a regular ranch house. Let's fill up my Shopping Cart of Ecstasy, shall we?"

They finished topping it off with the contents of the back seat. "This cart rocks my world. Maybe I can motorize this thing and add headlights."

"And pimp it out with a sound system."

"Good thinking."

Coleman upended a pint of Wild Turkey. "I better get moving before I can't."

"Another salient thought. You're on a roll."

They took the elevator and went inside unit 413. Serge became a blur of movement. "Coleman, give me a hand. Pull all this junk off the walls, starting with this ridiculous painted plank over the TV."

"What will we do with it all?"

"Stow it in our outdoor storage locker."

"Where's that?"

"An alcove around the corner from the elevators."

They loaded up the cart again and wheeled it out the door. Then into a tiny room as Serge switched on the lights.

"Cool," said Coleman. "There's like all these narrow closet doors with a unit number on each."

"I know! It's like an extra mini auxiliary condo for our condo. If I ever can't find you, I'll look in here." Serge stuck a key in a padlock and began tossing stuff inside the door with abandon. He was wheeling the empty cart back out when he suddenly froze and Coleman crashed into him.

"Why'd you stop like that?"

"Look!" Serge pointed with a trembling finger at the wall. There was a stainless steel hatch with a swing handle.

"What's that?"

"Our condo has a trash chute!" He slipped a hand into a pocket in his shorts. "This just keeps getting better and better! Observe . . ."

Serge held a Lincoln penny to Coleman's face, then opened the hatch and threw the coin inside, pressing his ear to the opening.

Clang, clang, clang, clang.

"Serge, why'd you just throw that penny down the trash chute?"

"Because I'm pretending I'm on top of the Citrus Tower. You know how there's a little slot up on the observation deck, and children stick pennies in it and listen to them clang all the way down? But now we have that joy right here! Instead of being forced to drive hundreds of miles, I can just walk out my door." He resumed wheeling the cart. "The savings in gas money alone will pay for this place."

They went back inside their new unit.

Almost as soon as Serge closed the door:

Knock, knock, knock.

Serge jumped back. "Holy shit! Who can that be? Who knows we're here? Cops? Fans?"

"Maybe the sweepstakes people," said Coleman. "That would be nice."

Serge tiptoed to the front door and looked through the peep-hole. There was a parabolic image of an older woman with some kind of covered dish.

Serge tentatively opened the main door, then the screen door with a wire sculpture of an egret. "Yes? Can I help you?"

A big smile in return. "I'm Maggie. Maggie Crenshaw. And you're our new neighbors! I'm right next door. Can I come in?"

A puzzled Serge stepped aside. "Be my guest."

The woman entered the kitchen and placed the dish on a counter. "Hope you have a sweet tooth because I baked you brownies."

"Sure, I like brownies." He shook her hand. "I'm Serge."

"You're going to love this place!" said Maggie. "All the neighbors are so close, really tight-knit, except for the vacation renters. But some of them have been coming for years, so they count, too. The newer ones, we'll just have to see. Me and my husband, Bert, retired here from Sheboygan seven years ago and haven't regretted a day. Let me give you an introduction to Pelican Bay. Know where the trash chute is?"

"I just threw a penny down it."

Maggie looked curiously at a pyramid of Febreze on the counter. "Do you fish?"

"When I find the time."

"Fishing's great here, especially out on Meditation Point," said Maggie. "Just be careful, but I know you will."

"Careful? Why?" asked Serge. "Sharks? Piranhas?"

"No," said Maggie. "When I mentioned the vacation renters, I didn't want to be negative since you just moved in, because for the most part this really is a lovely slice of paradise . . ." She lowered her voice like a conspiracy. ". . . But between you and me, there's an all-out condo culture war down here in the Keys. Half the owners are investors who lease their units most of the year, and they rent to young people who party all hours in a perpetual spring break and tear the place up like it's a budget motel in Key West. Completely ignoring the rules, dripping chlorinated swimming pool water through the lobby and elevators, throwing liquor bottles in the trash chute that shatter and wake you up at three in the morning, disposing of fish parts in the laundry room garbage cans causing a wicked smell and leaving a trail of fish juice leading right up to their doors, and you knock, and they say, 'Wasn't us,' and then passing out on the lobby sofas, usually in wet swim trunks again, not to mention all the burnt food and smoke alarms that perturb us."

"I read about it in the minutes of the meeting."

"Now about your neighbors," said Maggie, grabbing one of the brownies. "There's me and Bert, of course. And Gary the bachelor, always trying to get a tequila party going, not to be confused with Zack, the other bachelor, who's always winking when he leaves a party with a new date but nobody thinks he's getting any, and Sonya, who's divorced and threatened Gary and Zack with restraining orders. Trevor and Judy have been here the longest, and put up all the signs you see not to play music, wash clothes or use the trash chute after ten o'clock. It was Judy's idea to add 'No Exceptions!' Personally, I would have put a smiley face, you know, honey instead of vinegar. Joey was some kind of sports star at Florida State who got expelled under hazy circumstances after being caught in the middle of the night going through a chemistry lab with a flashlight, but we're under strict instructions not to talk about it because they're still trying to track him down to pay back the scholarship. Alfred and Hazel from Saskatoon use assumed names over their mail slots for similar reasons that didn't involve a flashlight but we don't know what. And Jen-Jen, also known as Queen of the Board . . ."

"Because she's president of the condo board?" asked Serge.

"No, she travels the country for board game tournaments and has like a million trophies for Monopoly, Scrabble and Battleship crowding her out of her unit. Old Man Sweeney fought in the first Gulf War and has PTSD, except the VA says it's from his last marriage. Mr. Kelley now has to wear a neck brace all the time because insurance investigators are staking out his place with zoom cameras. And if you ever hear really loud Allman Brothers and Grateful Dead at night, that's retired Lieutenant McCloud from Milwaukee, the most conservative cop you'd ever meet who went hog-wild six months ago with the medical marijuana and is probably illegally sharing because now music is coming from all the units around him. And Professor Fontaine from Cornell, who nobody has laid eyes on in almost a year."

"That's odd," said Serge. "Is something wrong?"

Maggie shook her head. "Just hasn't stepped foot outside. Lieutenant McCloud, who lives below him, can hear stomping around and the occasional screams."

"Sure sounds like something's wrong," said Serge.

She shook her head again. "It's all part of a big college grant he received. Something to do with modern culture. You know all those boxes you've seen stacked up on those tables in the lobby?"

Serge nodded. "Pretty big piles."

"Thank Amazon," said Maggie. "Ever since they got big, it's more and more packages, but everyone's honest around here and there weren't any issues until a shipment of Gary's margarita glasses went missing, and they turned up in a bag of smelly fish parts stuck in the trash chute or we never would have found them, so if you could help us keep an eye on the renters."

"You were saying about the professor?" asked Serge.

"Oh, right. Sooner or later you'll notice a ridiculous amount of Amazon boxes addressed to Professor Fontaine."

"Science equipment?" said Serge.

"No, the grant money is to see how long he can survive without leaving his unit purely through apps on his phone. Between Amazon and Grubhub and the private shopping services, he's made it ten months."

"Just one thing," said Serge. "If he never sets foot out of his place, how do the Amazon boxes get to his unit from the lobby?"

"There's an app for that, too," said Maggie. "And he cuts his own hair. The phone takes a photo of his head and downloads instructions."

"So his unit is like that closed-ecosystem biodome in the Arizona desert?"

"Except his grant specifies that his domicile must be integrated into a regular neighborhood," said Maggie. "For potential practical applications."

Serge squinted. "What could possibly be practical about seeing how long you can stay inside your own house?"

She shrugged. "Who knows what the future will bring?"

"My money's on a decline in intelligence," said Serge.

"Almost forgot." Maggie grabbed another of her own brownies. "I mentioned earlier about fishing from Meditation Point. You know how all those giant coral boulders line our little beach like a seawall to keep sand from escaping? At the very end near the mangroves, the rocks come to a narrow point, barely wide enough for the single beach chair that's always there. It's only minutes from everyone's door, and anytime you want to let your head unwind, just sit out there and stare at the sea like you're on the bow of a ship. My advice? Go at night when there's a moon and incoming tide, and you'll come back inside totally recharged.

Anyway, great meeting you and welcome to the neighborhood!" She pointed at the door. "Need to check on the unit for damage."

"Damage in your own unit?"

"No, my other unit," said Maggie. "Few years ago we bought a second one here as an investment, and the rent pretty much pays for everything. It's also caused a conflict because I'm now the only full-time resident *and* vacation renter. It's like not belonging to a political party: Both sides talk crap behind your back. Let me know about the brownies. Later."

Chapter 12

A FEW DAYS LATER

It was the end of February, which meant the annual Nautical Flea Market was underway at Founders Park in Islamorada, which meant traffic was fucked. All manner of antique fishing rods and lures, harpoons, blown-glass floats and nets, beach paintings, wood carvings of turtles, brass compasses and bells. It kicked off with all-you-can-eat pancakes. The Rotary Club was in charge.

Crowds squeezed through the tents. Someone contemplated the wisdom of purchasing an anchor as police directed the crawling traffic out on the highway. A large shadow suddenly zipped over the roofs of the cars. The Sikorsky helicopter flew a couple more miles before hovering for a gentle touchdown near the shore.

Mercado Benz trotted inside and up the floating staircase to the master bedroom. Julie was standing with hands on her hips.

Benz held out his palms. "What?"

"You know what! Where have you been?"

"I told you, business."

"And no way to contact you!" said Julie. "No word how long you'd be gone!"

"You seem upset."

"Upset? All I've been doing the last few days is running back and forth between my trailer and here. You know the level of attention our fathers need?"

"Quiet down! I can't hear Andy Griffith!"

"In a moment, Papa."

"I haven't been getting sleep!" said Julie. "If I had known you were going to cut the head nurse loose . . ."

"I figured it would be better to get to know my father if you had privacy. Plus I know how good you are with all the years at the care facility. Figured the situation here could use a fresh set of eyes, you know, to tweak the program."

"You planned this?" said Julie. "You ditched me, knowing I wouldn't shirk my responsibility?"

"I apologize," said Mercado. "It's my business style. Let me make it up to you." He began peeling cash from his scorpion money clip again.

"You think you can just buy me?"

"No, I think you can let me make it up to you. For your father again." He continued pulling bills loose.

It wasn't in Julie's nature to get mad, let alone *stay* mad. In fact, it took a tremendous amount of energy, and now she was spent. "Okay, look, I know you love your dad and would do anything. Of all people, I get that. I found a bottle of hot sauce under his sheets."

"I couldn't say no on that one."

"But this simply isn't going to work. I'm stretched too thin. I need to think of my own father first."

"And of all people, *I* get that," said Mercado. "Fair enough, you gave it your best shot. Did the guys pick you up in the limo as I instructed?"

"Just like every other time."

"All right, let's drive you back home . . ."

The limo fought against the flea market traffic until it pulled up to a silver Airstream. One of the crew opened the back door to let Julie out. She turned to say goodbye. Instead: "What are you getting out for?"

Mercado stood next to her. "Do you suppose we could go inside and talk?"

"If you still think you can convince me . . ."

He shook his head. "It's not that. Just my dad . . . This is new territory for me. Can we talk, only for a little bit? What do you say?"

"You realize there are support groups for this kind of thing."

"And you probably realize that I'm not a group kind of guy. Almost all my conversations are one-on-one."

"What exactly is it that your family does again? You were fuzzy the first time."

Mercado paused. "I know a lot about the Keys, the particular strain of people. Much is tolerated down here that doesn't fly in other parts. The conchs definitely don't mind their own business, because everyone knows everybody's business. But they also don't care, and don't tell outsiders. You can throw a rock down here and it will bounce off three people keeping secrets from the mainland. Hiding from the past, reinventing a future. It's what makes the Keys the Keys."

"Where are you going with this?"

"Your father was a fishing captain, right? And I'm guessing by his age he was around in the seventies, and his crowd at the docks was pretty tight-knit . . ."

"Now I get where you're going. I won't ask about your business." She unlocked the trailer. "How do you take your coffee?"

"Black."

She got the pot going in the kitchen nook. "Hope you don't mind, but it's the cheap stuff . . ."

"Julie? Is that you out there?"

"Coming, Dad."

Soon, three people crammed the back bedroom. Two on chairs sipping coffee.

Captain Ralph adjusted the pillow under his head. "I don't believe I've met you before."

"Dad, this is Mercado."

Benz got up to shake the wrinkled but ruddy hand. "Pleasure to meet you, Mr. Cootehill. Julie here has told me all about you."

"Are you seeing my daughter?"

"Dad! It's not like that."

"It could be," said the captain. "He takes pride in how he dresses, says a lot about a man. And no wedding ring." He turned to Mercado. "She thinks I'm helpless, but I can take care of myself. What I'm worried about is my daughter. Doesn't get out much on account of me. A woman loses her people skills, and one day she's pushing a shopping cart of trash."

"Dad! It isn't like I'm not sitting right here in the room."

Ralph leaned toward him. "But that girl has the biggest heart I've ever seen."

"Mr. Cootehill, you needn't worry at all about your daughter," said Mercado.

"Mercado, what does your family do exactly?"

"Import-export."

"Anything more specific?"

"We got started in the seventies."

"I see." The captain rested his head back. "Ah, the seventies, when the sixties went into exile in the Keys. What a time, what a *great* time. If you were here, you'll never forget it."

"I was just a boy," said Mercado. "But I remember."

"Hate to be one of those guys who waxes nostalgic," said Ralph. "Things aren't like they were in the old days. We didn't know all this greed and development was just around the corner waiting to pounce in the eighties. Plus it started getting seriously dangerous, spilling over from Miami, different breed of cats. Go-fast boats."

"Julie told me you had all kinds of stories from those times," said Mercado.

"Oh, I could tell you a million!" said Ralph. "But I'm sure you have better things to do."

"Yes, I'm sure he does," Julie said nervously.

"Not presently. And I like stories," said Mercado. "Pick one."

"If you say so," said the captain. "It was one of the earliest. It all started with the Taco Man."

"Taco Man?"

"I still call him the Taco Man to this day," said Ralph. "He was stationed at the Navy base at Key West, where he was discharged. He loved the place so much that after he got out, he stayed and bought a taco cart and became a regular fixture on Duval Street. Everyone ate his tacos. But he was a go-getter and soon was running the finest leather goods shop on the island. Knew everybody, friends always crashing on his couch. What was his name? Tom something or other."

"Daddy, it was Corcoran."

"That's right, another Irishman," said Ralph. "It was February of 1977. And I remember the date because of this song."

"Song?"

"You know how sometimes you hear a song, and it involuntarily triggers memories of exactly what you were doing at the time in your life when the song first got big on the radio? In this case, the song is history. The Taco Man told me the whole thing. One of his friends that used to sleep on his couch had this sailboat, a thirty-three-foot Cheoy ketch, and he asks Taco if he wants to sail to the Bahamas, and Taco says absolutely. So they set sail from Key West to Exuma."

"Exuma?" asked Mercado. "A lot of hidden coves out there. They weren't going to—"

"No, no, nothing shady like that," said the captain. "This was strictly pleasure. Anyway, communications wasn't like it is today with first graders on cell phones. So they're sailing a few days with no contact from land, and arrive at Staniel Cay. They furled the main and mizzen and motored to the dock, where they tied off. And his friend—this crazy-looking young guy with bushy blond hair and a Wild West mustache—says he needs to find a phone and call to see if he still has a job. So they walk in sandals through this empty, hot town and find a place called the Bahamas Telecommunication Company. But it was just this tiny, dusty concrete-block building with absolutely nothing inside except a phone on the wall with no dial."

"Then how did you place a call?" asked Mercado.

"Just pick up the receiver and an operator came on, and you made a collect call back to the States. So the guy calls his office, and immediately there's some kind of disagreement, because the guy says something like: 'You weren't supposed to use that one. You were supposed to release the other . . . Oh, oh, it is? Really? Well then, I guess you know what you're doing. Bye.' . . . The guy hangs up and Taco Man is waiting, and his friend says, 'I guess I still have a job.'"

"So what was the call about?" asked Mercado.

"It was out to Los Angeles. The offices of ABC Records, to be exact. The guy was an unknown singer-songwriter who had toiled for years without any real notice. The executives at the record label told him that after its release on Valentine's Day, his first hit single was smashing the charts in America."

"What was the song?" asked Mercado.

"'Margaritaville,'" said the captain. "After nearly a decade of hard work, Jimmy Buffett had just broken through back home as *the* Jimmy Buffett, and for days at sea he didn't even know it."

"Wow," said Mercado. "That's some story."

"Actually, when I said the song was the story, it was just half the story, marking in time the rest of the tale," said Ralph. "When they got back, Taco Man says to me, 'Have I got a story to tell you,' and I said, 'So do I,' and we compared notes and realized it was too much of a coincidence to be a coincidence."

"Don't leave me hanging," said Mercado. "What was the rest?"

"I size you up as a worldly man," said Ralph, "so I guess this won't surprise you. Plus the statute of limitations has long since run out . . ." And the good captain regaled Mercado with the tale of a seaplane crash and the day all his customers got to fish for free. ". . . 'Margaritaville.'" Captain Ralph stared at the ceiling. "Every time I hear that song, it's as vivid as yesterday . . ."

"Wow," said Benz. "That was quite a story. But what's the co-incidence with the Taco Man?"

"Like I mentioned, we later compared notes and realized it was the same day," said Ralph. "Exuma isn't that big of a place, but they still have an airstrip like many other cays in the Baha-mas. While Jimmy was inside making that phone call to the rec-ord label, Taco Man remembers hearing a plane take off, except it wasn't from the airstrip. It was a seaplane skimming across the waves until it got airborne. Before it took off, he recalled seeing an inflatable Zodiac boat loading large square packages into the plane, and decided not to stare too long. And after it crashed, it made big news, with photos of the wreckage being pulled out of the water. Taco Man recognized it as the same plane."

"The story just gets better," said Mercado. "How much was in the envelope?"

"Envelope?"

"The one the guys in the van gave you."

"Oh, two grand."

"That was a lot back then," said Mercado. "Weren't you scared?"

"The first time," said Ralph.

"First time?" asked Mercado. "There were others?"

"By the tenth exchange, it's about as stressful as eating a doughnut."

"But these were clearly criminals," said Mercado. "What if

they pulled guns and tried to rip you off? I've seen stories in the papers all the time about drug deals gone bad and, well, it doesn't end pretty."

"Not these deals," said Ralph. "They were definitely the frightening types, but they were also businessmen. What was two grand when they were going to sell it for twenty? To them, it was found money. Plus, they knew that the charter captains were a small community. Rip one of them off, and the phones stop ringing about stuff floating off the Keys. They weren't about to kill the golden goose. Everyone made out."

Mercado shook his head. "Can't believe there were that many bales floating around."

"More than you'd think," said Ralph. "Pilots or guys in cigarette boats were always dumping evidence if they ended up in a pursuit from the law. Other times, planes would miss a drop zone, or the guys waiting below couldn't corral all the shit. Casually written off as the price of doing business."

"It seems hard to imagine now," said Benz.

"You have to think of the times," said Ralph. "The Keys have always been a smuggler's paradise. A very long history of which few are aware dates back centuries to galleons sailing gold and silver and gems back from the New World."

"How is that smuggling?" asked Mercado.

"The royal families taxed the loads, so the crews were always smuggling extra secret stashes, I mean hundreds of pounds. To this day, treasure salvagers are still hauling up far more than was on the ships' original manifests. The tradition continued through various forms of contraband until the eighties, when cocaine screwed everything up, and we captains said, 'Whoa, these new dudes are way too crazy and dangerous,' and we shut everything down. But back in the seventies, it was still an innocent time when even the most upstanding, religious family men were in on it because suddenly the children of charter boat captains were going to college pre-paid."

Mercado turned. "Julie?"

"I knew about it. But my dad didn't realize I did."

"You did?" said Ralph.

"Sure," said Julie. "Remember that first time when the seaplane crashed? And you told me to go below? I watched the whole thing through the slits in the louvered door. Of course, as I got older and they were finding more and more, it just became too obvious."

Ralph rolled his eyes at the ceiling. "Life never stops surprising you."

"I even knew what 'square grouper' meant. Fishermen's code for the bales."

The captain just shook his head. "I thought I was being discreet."

"Are you kidding?" She turned to Mercado. "There was so much being brought ashore sometimes that one boat wasn't enough, so the captains would let their friends in on the action by getting on the radio: 'The square grouper are biting today out here.' And the next time, that captain would repay the favor. But the slang spread so quickly that it became a joke, and they had to switch codes. Heck, today there's even a couple restaurants down here called the Square Grouper . . ."

Eventually, Captain Ralph nodded off, and Julie knew it would be for the night. Mercado joined her in the kitchen nook at her invitation for cinnamon Danish.

"Julie, um, I have a proposition."

"I told you no." She set her Danish down. "Please don't tell me you were cynically being nice to my dad in there so I would soften."

"Nothing like that," said Benz. "Another proposition. I really wanted to get to know him. He's had a fascinating life."

She sat back and folded her arms. "Okay, I'm sufficiently ready. Lay this proposal on me."

And he did. "What do you think?"

She remained quiet for the longest time. Then: "You have got to be kidding me!"

"What's the problem? Everybody wins."

"No, not the proposition," said Julie. "You weren't in there chatting with my dad to soften me up. You were *auditioning* him?"

Mercado shrugged. "It needed to be the right fit."

"I'm angry with you now."

"I can see that. I'll be going." He got up and stopped just before closing the door. "I know you're set against it at this moment, but the offer's open. As time passes, you'll realize it's the best for your father. And you'll benefit, too."

The door closed and she heard a limo drive off.

Chapter 13

JUST OFF THE OVERSEAS HIGHWAY

A '73 muscle car parked behind Pelican Bay after another whirlwind shopping spree, this time among the unnaturally high concentration of galleries and antiques shops in the Keys.

Hammer, nails and a carpenter's level lay on the kitchen counter. Serge hung a framed, numbered-edition lithograph on the wall. He squinted and nudged it slightly to the left and stepped back. "Perfect."

Pop. A beer was guzzled. "What's that painting?"

"Watercolor of the Honeymoon Cottage out on Pigeon Key under the Seven Mile Bridge," said Serge. "By Carol Garvin, called *Paradise on a Dollar a Year.*"

He grabbed hooks and a tape measure, working his way clockwise around the living room. Another nail was hammered.

"And that?" asked Coleman.

"My favorite artist, Winslow Homer," said Serge. "Palm trees blowing in a hurricane, painted in the late 1800s."

More nailing.

"And that?"

Serge sighed and lowered the frame. "Coleman, this is intricate work. Some of these need two hooks and if it's not perfectly level, I'll have bad dreams."

"Sorry." *Glug, glug, glug.*

Serge raised the frame again. "Just wait until I'm finished and I'll give you the complete tour."

"I can do that." *Pop.*

Serge moved along with his tools, hammering and hanging. Eventually, he was done. "Here's another Homer of a small child at a whitewashed wall in the Bahamas, also from the nineteenth century. This is an archival print of the Sand Key lighthouse off Key West, back when there was still sand. Another old photo of a barracuda in the Straits of Florida. A framed *National Geographic* from 1927 with an article on the Dry Tortugas, before the great Labor Day Hurricane submerged Bird Key. A stark black-and-white photo of the southernmost point marker at sunrise. And finally the giant centerpiece over the couch, a framed nautical chart of the Keys from the National Oceanic and Atmospheric Administration with the fathoms listed so we always know what the deal is."

"What about this other stuff?"

"Less is more," said Serge. "So I tastefully spaced it out. An antique black world globe, an antique ship's clock, a string of faded crab-trap floats, and on the pass-through counter to the kitchen nook, giant souvenir ceramic drink mugs from the Mai-Kai and Bahi Hut."

Serge walked over to the TV and looked up at the large blank space on the wall where the kitschy wooden plank had been. "Less is more, but this is too much less. It needs a great piece, the *perfect* piece, because it's over the TV and we'll be looking at it so much that if it isn't stratospheric, we'll unknowingly become bloated." Serge snapped his fingers, then grabbed his car keys. "Wait here!"

Coleman continued through the beer until it made him horizontal. An hour later, Serge returned. He had to push open the door with his foot because of the awkward load in his arms. Then more hammering, and a thick wire was guided across three nails over the TV.

Serge reached down and shook a shoulder. "Coleman, wake up!"

"Ooo! Huh? Where am I?"

"Under the coffee table," said Serge. "Get out here and tell me what you think."

Coleman crawled. "About what?"

"The perfect piece!"

Coleman finally stood. "Damn! That's righteous!"

They both smiled and stared up at a magnificent fiberglass sailfish from a hardware store.

"Our fishing cabin in the sky is complete!" Serge began merrily pirouetting in place. It was only seven hundred square feet but not tight. A floor plan of essentially two rooms: the living room and the bedroom. The kitchen nook sat just inside the front door, but it was mostly open, providing broad lines of sight for that extra sense of space. The canary-yellow walls might seem ridiculous at first, until the sunlight from the balcony hit them, spraying rays of cheer and turning the fiberglass fish's sail iridescent.

"This is what it's all about!" Serge strolled to the bedroom door. "Coleman, we haven't discussed the permanent sleeping arrangements yet. I figured we'd take turns, alternating between the bed and the couch, but you usually end up sleeping in whatever spot you've taken a landing for the night."

"I'm cool with that."

"Then it's settled. On the nights you're not under the coffee table, you can have the bed." Serge had another expanding smile as he cut open the top of a tall cardboard box and extracted the contents. "This just keeps getting better and better. I never thought in a million years I'd extract raptured joy from something like this!"

Coleman hit an onyx pipe. "What the hell is that?"

"I can't believe the march of technology." Serge flipped through an instruction manual. "Vacuum cleaners have become so advanced that they look like some special instrument from the space station. Plus these new, portable recharging models are game changers. And you know what that means? It officially qualifies as a gadget. I must probe every aspect."

Serge got it all put together, studied the controls and plugged it in. "We are ready for launch. T-minus ten, nine, eight, guidance is internal, five, four . . ."

He flicked the power switch, and the motor roared to life.

Coleman ran into the bathroom and locked himself inside.

Serge sulked and killed the power. He went to the bathroom and talked through the door. "Coleman, it's just a vacuum. We've discussed this before."

Coleman tentatively stuck his head outside. "What's that other noise?"

"Someone's knocking on our door again." Serge headed across the unit. "Except the knocking is much louder than usual. Never a good sign."

Out the peephole was Maggie. He opened up. "If it isn't my favorite new neighbor."

"Serge, I need your help!" Her face was a mask of desperation. "I don't know if I should call the police!"

"Good thinking," said Serge. "Never call the police unless you check with me first. Now, what seems to be the problem?"

"It's my vacation renter." Maggie took a seat on the couch, practically in tears. "I checked the unit and it was empty but looked okay. Then one of my neighbors knocked on my door and said that my renter was stomping around Meditation Point acting all weird, like he was on drugs. And right then another neighbor arrived and said the renter was running around the swimming pool asking people for a gun."

"I won't lie to you," said Serge. "Asking a bunch of strangers for a gun is generally a red flag."

"What should I do?"

"Make that call to the police . . ."

Two officers arrived promptly at Serge's door and came in. "We received a report that there's a problem over in unit 415? Which one of you called us?"

Maggie raised her hand.

"And you are?"

"The owner. I'm worried. I don't know what's going on!"

"Florida's going on," said Serge.

"Excuse me?" said one of the officers.

"Just stating the obvious," said Serge.

The officers exchanged confused glances, then looked back at Maggie. "We were at that unit earlier today."

"Why?" asked Maggie.

"Because we received another call a couple hours ago about that unit . . . Uh, I'm not quite sure we understand. You say you're the owner, and yet you don't know what's going on in your own unit?"

"It's a vacation rental," said Maggie. "I live in my other unit."

"Oh, that makes more sense," said the second officer.

"Excuse me," said Serge. "You mentioned two calls, but she only called once. Who was the other one from?"

"The young guy renting there," said the officer. "We just assumed it was the owner's son."

"That's weird," said Serge. "He called the police on himself?"

"Told us some people were after him and had been following him for days in a blue car," said the officer. "Apparently a dispute over a woman. I think he was on drugs. Most likely bath salts."

"Then you can get him out of there, right?" said Maggie.

The other officer shook his head. "Our hands are tied. We didn't see any drugs or paraphernalia, and he wasn't acting threatening, just jittery. We told him we'd sweep the area for a blue car, and suggested he try to get some rest."

"You have to get rid of him!" said Maggie. "He was asking people at the pool for a gun!"

"Do you know if he got one?" said the first officer.

She shook her head.

"If he has a gun, that would change things," said the second officer. "Unfortunately we can't eject him because this is a civil matter."

"What do you mean?" asked Maggie. "Hotels can throw undesirables out."

"He also mentioned he's been staying there six weeks," said the officer. "Is that true?"

Maggie nodded.

"I hate to be the one to break the bad news, but Florida's landlord laws broadly protect renters," said the other officer. "They're designed to prevent unscrupulous slumlords from exploiting tenants, not like in your case."

"But I'm not a landlord," said Maggie. "I just manage a vacation unit."

"You're a landlord now," said the officer. "He established residency at a month. Prior to that, you can eject someone for any or no reason. And if they refuse to leave, it's criminal trespassing and we can arrest them. That's why most motels won't allow guests to stay thirty consecutive days, or the person in the room becomes just like someone with a lease on a house, and then the motel has to file in court and go through lengthy eviction proceedings. Meanwhile, the person's living there free."

"But what am I supposed to do?"

"I suggest you hire an attorney," said the officer.

They heard someone run by outside: *"Blue car! Blue car! Ahhhh! Blue car!..."* The screaming trailed off and a door slammed.

"Did you hear that?" said Maggie, pointing with a shaking hand. "And this person is trying to get a gun!"

"Call us if he finds one." The officers headed out of the unit. "We're very sorry."

Maggie's face fell toward her chest, sobbing. "What am I going to do?"

Serge placed a reassuring hand on her shoulder. "What you're going to do is go back to your unit, relax and forget any of this ever happened."

"How can you say that?"

"Because this is right in my wheelhouse," Serge replied. "Trust me."

A MILE AWAY

Mercado had told Julie to just let some time pass. It only took a day.

Over on the Row, the guards opened the gate and let the high-mileage car pass through, as they had been instructed.

Julie pulled into the circular drive to find Mercado waiting with a smile. Her mouth was firm. "How is this supposed to work? . . ."

The next day, the post-modern mansion on the sea was a furnace of activity. One moving truck took stuff out, another brought more stuff in. Then the other trucks making store deliveries arrived from Miami.

Mercado led Julie up the floating stairs and made a right turn toward a door on the opposite side of the hall from his father's. He opened it and gestured inside with an outstretched arm.

"What's all this?" asked Julie.

"Your new bedroom."

Her mouth hung open at the sight of a space big enough to train elephants. And the furniture! An entire top-of-the-line midcentury modern suite. "How much did this all cost?"

"That's not important," said Mercado. "And if it's not to your taste, you switch it out. Won't hurt my feelings. I don't know what women like, so I had the decorator pick it out."

"Decorator?"

"Follow me," said Mercado.

She did, entering what seemed to be an endless walk-in closet. He handed her a piece of paper with three numbers.

"What's this?"

Mercado walked to an abstract painting hanging on the back wall. He grabbed the left side of the frame, and it swung open. "That's the combination to your wall safe. Go ahead . . ."

She was practically dizzy as she dialed up the numbers and opened the round door. It was crammed full of stacks of hundred-dollar bills.

"What's all the money for?"

"To fill up this closet," said Mercado. "You expect me to shop for you? I don't even know your size." He heard the elevator doors open down the hall. "That must be the medical staff from the ambulance service."

Out wheeled a stretcher with Captain Ralph. He had wide eyes. "Fuck me! So this is how the other half lives? I'm expecting angels and harps."

Julie ran over. "Dad, are you okay? How was the trip?"

"They're treating me like the president," said the captain. "Do I get to see my new room now?"

"Right in there," said Mercado.

The medics wheeled him into the master bedroom, where a new king bed had been placed next to the older one.

"On three," said one of the health staff. "One, two . . ."

They gently lifted the captain into the bed.

"You must be Ralph," said Mercado's father.

"That would make you Raffy," said the captain.

"I'd shake your hand," said Raffy, "but I can't reach."

"Me neither. Another time. What are you watching?"

Raffy pointed with the remote control. *Gunsmoke.*

"I love *Gunsmoke*," said Ralph. "What about *Andy Griffith*?"

"Now you're talking!"

"What's the food like around here?"

"Shit. Got any hot sauce?"

Mercado smiled and turned to Julie. "Let's go downstairs and allow them to get acquainted. It's looking like the beginning of a beautiful friendship."

They took seats on an arctic-white leather sofa near the glass wine closet. "You really didn't have to do this," said Julie.

"You're the one doing me the favor," said Mercado. "This works out nicely for everyone. You mentioned the auditioning before? The nurse had told me that it would help my father's condition if he had someone to talk to, and not just anyone, but a person with common interests and memories. My dad now has the perfect roommate to keep his mind sharp, and moving your father here frees up your schedule to run things. You'll be on salary."

Julie's forehead tensed with ripples of skin, and she opened her mouth. Then closed it.

"What is it?" asked Mercado.

"Okay, here goes nothing," said Julie. "I know what you do for a living. At least I'm pretty sure."

"I knew you were smart," said Benz. "Does that bother you?"

"Yes. Actually quite a lot," said Julie. "Doing what was best for my father drove the whole decision . . ."

"And?"

Her chest inflated. "Still, your family business . . ."

"I figured you figured that out a while ago," said Benz. "Except now you're having second thoughts because of that? You're scared?"

She nodded.

"Here's the deal." He took her hands in his, not flirtatiously. "My family—as well as all the others—have always lived by a solid code since I was in short pants. Family is everything, and if you're family and not in the business, you're a civilian. That's strict with us. Nothing will ever happen to you or your father. I've given instructions to all my guys. In fact, you'll be safer here than if you were still living back in that trailer. You have my word. You're family now."

"For some stupid reason, I trust you," said Julie. "But I'm also worried about something else. My father's always been independent, even cantankerous. Sure, he and Raffy were polite on the introduction, but what if they don't hit it off?—"

The pair suddenly jumped when raucous laughter echoed down the stairs.

Mercado looked up at the ceiling and shouted: "What are you two crazy kids up to?"

"You wouldn't believe what Barney Fife just did."

Benz turned to Julie. "I think you have your answer."

Chapter 14

MEDITATION POINT

S erge was slowing down again.

    He sat in a chair and, for a rare moment, did absolutely nothing.

Coral boulders formed a semicircle around him, and ahead, nothing but an incoming tide from the Atlantic Ocean. Three pelicans glided by. A kayaker set out for the tiny mangrove Kalteux Key, near the intersection of two boating channels featuring more of those ubiquitous green and orange markers topped with frigate birds and white poop.

"Maggie was right about Meditation Point. It puts your head in a whole new space. That's enough sitting."

Serge jumped up and grabbed some of the cardboard boxes he'd hauled down to the beach from the trash room. He began cutting with large scissors.

"What are you making?" asked Coleman.

"Remember *Romper Room*?" *Snip, snip, snip.*

"And how! I loved that show!" said Coleman. "Except the woman never called out my name when she'd look at the screen and say, 'I see Tommy and Sally and Mikey.'"

"Know what you mean. I waited and waited, except never a Serge." *Snip, snip, snip.* "But it's time to let that go and just fondly remember the good parts."

"So what does *Romper Room* have to do with your project?"

Serge told him while tearing off strips of duct tape.

"Oh, man, that was the coolest." Coleman leaned toward the cardboard. "Can I get in on that shit?"

Serge rattled a can of spray paint. "Already figured your dimensions into the equation."

Finally Serge was done. "Let's give this baby a test run. The paint is still wet, so just use the handles."

"Cool."

One by one, people around the pool curiously sat up and watched Serge and Coleman trotting across the beach. Then more staring from residents in the lobby. The pair took the elevator back up to their unit, and Serge placed his project out on the balcony. "I'll let it finish drying there or the fumes will give us headaches."

Serge's head turned as a long scream went by the outside of the unit with Doppler Effect. *"Blue carrrrrr!..."*

"Drying will have to wait," said Serge. "That's our cue."

"Cue?"

"We're on, Tonto."

The pair went onto the balcony, preparing to launch Operation Romper Room. They came back inside and opened the front door.

"I don't hear anything now," said Coleman.

Serge looked down over the railing to the parking lot. "There he is."

"Where?"

"Pacing manically and jerking his head around down by the back entrance at the swimming pool," said Serge. "To the elevators!"

They got off in the lobby just as the jumpy young renter came inside near the table stacked with Amazon boxes.

"Yo! Homes!" yelled Serge. "Beep! Beep!"

The renter looked up. *"Ahhhhh!"* And dashed back out the door.

"Coleman! After him!"

The pair ran across the parking lot. But it was slow going because they were both inside taped-together cardboard boxes that wrapped around their waists to form a cute little *Romper Room* car. It was painted blue.

Coleman panted. "I don't mean to question you, but this doesn't look anything like a real car. I can't understand how your plan is working."

"If he was freaking out from an *invisible* blue car, this must be the deathmobile," said Serge. "He's on drugs."

"Oh, right."

"Ahhhhhhhh!"

"Beep! Beep! Beep! Beep!"

The terrified renter kept running, screaming and glancing back. *"Ahhhhhhh!"* On the front of the cardboard car, Serge had painted headlights that looked like tiger's eyes. The grille of the vehicle featured fangs dripping blood.

The renter ran at freakout speed for the back gate to the swimming pool, but the sunbathers saw him coming—"There's that jerk from the other day!"—and formed a human wall on the other side of the fence, gripping the gate hard.

The renter kept glancing over his shoulder, grabbing the pool gate's handle, but it wouldn't budge.

Serge and Coleman trotted toward him, holding the cardboard box up around their stomachs. "Beep! Beep!"

He turned around. *"Ahhhhhhh!"* And jiggled the gate frantically to no avail.

"Get lost!" said one of the sunbathers. "You're not coming in here!" said another. "What the hell are you on?" said a third.

"But I need to come in!" The renter looked back again as the cardboard was closing fast. "I need a gun!"

"Hey, asshole!" said the first sunbather. "We got a nice place here! We don't need your kind!"

Serge stopped right behind him. "Beep! Beep!"

"Ahhhhhhh!" The renter took off sprinting again. He ran up to his old parked Caprice and grabbed another handle, but it was locked. *"Ahhhhhh!"*—dashing down the sidewalk along the community room with the Ping-Pong tables. He made it to the elevators, and the doors opened just as the blue cardboard entered the lobby. He jumped inside and the doors closed.

The *Romper Room* car stopped. "What now?" asked Coleman.

"Quick run up to our pad for more supplies, then over to Maggie's place." Serge pressed the elevator button. "We've just entered the knockout round of my plan . . ."

Maggie opened her front door when she heard the knock. Then looked Serge and Coleman over. "What the heck?"

"No time to explain," said Serge. "Do you happen to know the owners of the unit directly above your vacation rental?"

"Yes, great friends," said Maggie. "Bradley and Trish, who live for *America's Got Talent,* make puzzles and ride recumbent bicycles."

"I'll have to hear it later," said Serge. "Right now, we need a favor from them . . ."

They were all soon standing in the living room of a two-bedroom unit on the fifth floor around a coffee table scattered with five hundred puzzle pieces of the 1968 Chicago Democratic convention riot. "What on earth is going on?" asked Bradley.

"Remember my problems with the vacation renter I told you about?" said Maggie.

The couple nodded. "I can't believe the police couldn't do anything," said Trish.

Bradley pointed toward the carpet. "And the noises coming up from the floor! It sounds like he's strangling parakeets!"

Maggie gestured at the cardboard car. "These are my new neighbors, Serge and Coleman. They've agreed to help."

Bradley scratched his head. "A *Romper Room* car?"

"Please stand back," said Serge. "I'm a professional."

He set the car on the floor and the pair climbed out. "I'll need access to your balcony."

This, everyone in the unit had to see. The sunbathers had become irresistibly curious at a level of strangeness that was unprecedented even for the Keys. They gathered in the driveway, sipping tropical drinks and shielding their eyes as they stared up at the balconies.

Serge opened a pouch that he had fetched from his unit on his way over to Maggie's. Out came a rope fire-escape ladder. He attached the hooks to the balcony's railing and climbed over the edge, carefully getting a foothold on the first rung. The sunbathers began to cheer.

After several more rungs, he was even with the top of the balcony railing one floor below. He began swinging the ladder back and forth until finally letting go and tumbling onto the lower balcony. More cheers.

Serge stuck his head back over the railing and looked up. "Coleman, pass me down the cardboard."

"Here you go . . ."

It dangled and Serge snatched. He climbed inside it again and pulled the ersatz vehicle up to hip level. Then he grabbed the handle on one of the balcony's sliding glass doors. As expected on an upper floor, it was unlocked. "Perfect."

Serge slid it open and crept inside.

The vacation renter wasn't hard to find, curled up in a quivering ball on the sofa, hiding his head under a blanket and making non-verbal noises of distress, masking the sound of Serge's entrance.

"Beep! Beep!"

The blanket flew off the renter's head with another scream, but there wasn't much room to run. Serge chased him, circle after circle, through the living room and kitchen nook.

"Beep! Beep!"

The renter repeatedly glanced back. "What do you want from me!"

"I'm your Uber driver. Please get in."

Then Serge slowed up to give his target some separation, which the renter used to dash for the front door. He flung it open and made a beeline for the elevators.

Serge casually strolled back onto the balcony as cheering began gathering steam from the crowd below. He looked over the railing as the renter never broke stride, running the gauntlet of sunbathers, who splashed him with drinks and pelted him with plastic cups. "We never want to see you again!" "Don't come back!"

"*Ahhhhhhhh!*" And he hightailed it down the street until he was out of sight.

Serge smiled to himself as he headed back upstairs. Everyone was already waiting outside the unit, breaking into applause.

"I can't thank you enough," said Maggie. "How will I ever repay you?"

"The 'thank you' is enough thanks," said Serge, lifting his gaze wistfully upward toward the clouds. "I'm just a rambling kind of guy, moving from town to town, helping the helpless, and thinning out the jerks— Let's leave it at that for now. But currently I'm in my pump-the-brakes phase, so I'll be hanging around for a while, at your service if any more condo hiccups arise."

"Then at least let me invite you to dinner," said Maggie.

Serge looked at Coleman and began to nod. "We can do that. But one more thing: Don't thank me yet."

"Why not?"

"Because this was just batting practice," said Serge. "My work isn't done with him."

"But he looked so terrified," said Maggie. "He's got to be gone for good."

"Except we're dealing with drugs," said Serge. "He'll be back."

"And then what?"

Serge grinned at Coleman. "The bonus round."

Chapter 15

U.S. HIGHWAY 1

A Pinto with a defective muffler cruised along the Connecti-cut shore, from New London to Madison and finally Green-wich, before crossing the state line into New York. Then Jersey, Pennsylvania, onward, Virginia, the dirty roadside crusts of snow getting thinner . . .

Four men and a woman were running on fumes, far beyond normal hunger and fatigue. They pushed south with the help of cocaine, which had a way of pushing back.

In the rear seat, a raven-haired woman named Vix took a long snort off her arm, then howled like a coyote.

Blue usually drove, because he was the leader, and Vix usually rode up front in the passenger seat, because she was his girl. The three other guys made do bunched in the back seat. Unless Vix was into the coke and making Blue grit his teeth from her virulent snake tongue. Then Blue forced her to trade places with one of the guys in back, often at gunpoint. Like now. It was an unstable isotope of an alliance, with an adhesive of sex.

Weezer turned around from his new spot in the front passenger seat. "So what kind of name is Vix anyway? Where did *that* come from?"

The rest of the car reflexively seized up as Vix screamed and grabbed his hair and repeatedly banged his melon against his headrest. Then a pistol came out. "Don't you ever ask me that again or your brains will be on the windshield!"

A sore spot? You think? The others would discreetly explain to Weezer later: Her parents were more than a little unhinged, the kind of people who, during the Christmas season, put up such an insane tonnage of yard decorations that it made the local news. What separated her parents from the others was that they left the lights up all year. They were kind of into the spirit, and all their children were named after reindeer. Vixen had gotten off easier than her brothers, Prancer, Comet and Cupid. Schoolyard beatings started early and ended late. Mocking chants of "reindeer games." Vix finally began fighting back, growing increasingly vicious until she developed a taste for it, smashing faces into lockers and lunch tables with shuddering aftermath that made even the toughest football players wince. She became one of the first foot soldiers in the War on Christmas.

But back to the car . . .

Vix tapped out more coke for another damaging snort and wiped blood from her nose. "Son of a bitch, I am so sick of this shit . . ." Then a profanity-heavy tirade, followed by another slap fight with everyone else in the car. The gang was used to it, and had to let it slide. Because she was Blue's girl.

But then her errant palm smacked the side of the driver's head.

The Pinto veered into the oncoming lane, headlights and honking horns, before Blue regained control of the wheel and got their act back together between the stripes.

"Jesus Christ!" yelled Blue, swinging his Colt toward the back seat. "So help me I will shoot you in the fucking face right now! We might as well simply turn ourselves in. What if the Highway Patrol just saw that?"

The woman firmed her mouth and exhaled hard through flared nostrils.

The pistol remained pointed as the driver glanced back and forth from the road to Vix. "Are you going to shut the hell up? They're probably still searching Canada, so we're home free unless we self-destruct!"

"I'm tired of all this driving," said Vix. "Trying to sleep sitting up back here, and only a bag of pretzels."

"Who's *doing* the driving?" said Blue. "The first days are the most important. We have to put as many miles as possible between us and your fuckup back at the cabin."

"Thought you said they were looking for us up north."

"Concentrating their search, but probably bulletins everywhere across the northeast," said Blue. "Now will you keep your shit together?"

She nodded and Blue stowed the gun.

"I have to pee."

Blue clenched his teeth again in exasperation. He checked his watch. Getting up on midnight. "Okay, all right. I'll find a place, but we're up early tomorrow and no bitching . . ."

It was one of those motels where you could imagine the buzzing sound of the flickering neon sign before you could hear it. The rest of the nearby joints were full at this hour, but this one still had vacancy because other guests didn't want to stay with the kind of people now arriving in a Pinto.

The snowplows had shoved frozen drifts up to the sidewalk. Five people climbed over them with paper bags of tacos and practically crashed into the room. They fell onto the beds without even turning down the stained spreads. Weezer drew the short straw for a spot on the floor. A bottle of Jack made the rounds.

Vix grabbed a remote off the nightstand. *Click, click, click.* "This asshole TV doesn't work!"

"Screw the TV," said Blue. "And keep your voice down. I'm tired of warning you!"

"Or what?"

Blue just muttered, because he was trying to concentrate. Sitting at a scuffed little desk with the folded piece of paper he had snatched before leaving the fishing cabin, he grabbed the motel room's twenty-nine-cent ballpoint pen and made vigorous circles on the page to get the ink flowing.

Vix walked over. "I'm calm now."

"I'll throw a parade."

She took a long slug of whiskey. "Do you think that guy was telling the truth?"

"I was fifty-fifty back in the cabin, because a person will say anything in his situation." Blue made notations on the page. "But now I'm almost certain it's legit."

More coke on the back of her hand. *Snort.* "What makes you think so?"

"He was too specific. Of course he could have just been jabbering." Blue tapped a spot in the middle of the page. "So I looked it up at last night's motel, and the address checks out, along with everything else I could verify. The type of home, the neighborhood he described."

"Do you think this guy is as rich as he said he was?" Coke *and* whiskey.

"It's certainly beginning to look that way," said Blue. He tapped another spot. "We even have a diagram to his stash of money and whatever else."

"I didn't see Twitch draw anything."

"Because you were too busy being a pain in the ass."

"I told you not to talk to me that way!" said Vix.

"I don't want to get into it again," said Blue. "And I'm working. Think of the dollar signs."

She did. And more whiskey. "But if the dude is this big in the drug business, he must have guards. We're supposed to just waltz in and say pretty please?"

The sound of her voice was getting on Blue's last nerve. "I know this is an alien concept to you, but that's what planning is for." And then he said it on purpose: "Enough of these reindeer games."

"*Reindeer* games! I know how to plan," said Vix. "Like a makeshift silencer. Go straight to hell!"

What was she talking about? Blue turned around to see Vix holding a pillow. It went directly to his face, followed by the muzzle of a gun.

Poof!

The red mess hit the wall with a splat.

The three other guys sprang up. "*Holy shit!*" "*What did you do that for?*"

"He said 'reindeer games.'" She waved the pistol around the room. "I'm in charge now! Any objections?"

Back on their heels. The remaining trio shook their heads.

"Good," said Vix, grabbing a taco and the whiskey bottle. "Let's start winding it down. We've got a lot of driving to do tomorrow." *Snort.*

Chapter 16

SOUTH FLORIDA

A late-morning sun sparkled brightly off fifty and sixty stories of glass and metal.

The hegemony of the downtown Miami skyline had shifted in recent decades from office towers to high-rise condos. Some newly constructed penthouses sold above thirty million.

The lobbies reflected the price tags. Vaulted ceilings hosted two-story sculptures, ivory waterfalls, arching green-tinted glass over atriums. Staff in white gloves stood like statues, alertly awaiting desires. Valets swarmed the Ferraris and Bentleys as they pulled under the cantilevered canopy at the entrance.

Why not? South Florida is the undisputed condominium capital of America. From the gleaming towers on Singer Island to West Palm Beach, Boca Raton, Fort Lauderdale and points south, thousands of residents enjoy a sanitized lifestyle of ocean views, bright marble, indoor fountains and rarefied lawn-free luxury. But there are exceptions.

Down in the Keys, a different breed of buildings: low-slung, casual curving affairs erected in the early 1970s and looking every bit of it, in both age and period architecture. If condos were shoes, these would be flip-flops. Their tiny lobbies decidedly more laid-back and bare-bones functional. Stacks of free shopper newspapers, grids of mailboxes, wicker tables with avocado lamps and plastic daisies in flower pots. Next to the dented elevators: taped-up notices announcing the next board meeting, fishing boats for sale, lost cats.

Then something that would cause the Miami condo crowd to perform a triple-Lutz shit fit: the sharing shelves. At Pelican Bay, a wooden bookcase ran all the way along the south wall. The honor system. Borrow what you wanted, donate what you could. The top shelves featured dog-eared paperbacks about romance and military heroes, followed by torn-dust-jacket hardcovers of *Jaws, The Towering Inferno,* and three-pound volumes by James Michener involving Hawaii and Texas. Next, activity equipment. Chess sets, dominoes, playing cards and a deflated beach ball. Finally, the bottom shelves, stacks of vintage board games from across the generations. Monopoly, Trouble, Risk, Life, Clue. None would be recognized by today's kids. Everything was sun-faded.

A key turned in the lock of one of the mailboxes. Someone bent down and peered inside the flush-mounted metal slot. "Please, please, please . . ." A hand pulled out the contents. Serge mumbled to himself as he flipped through the envelopes of possibility: Paradise Dry Cleaning, Tropical Transmission, Keys Tax Preparation, DUI? NO PROBLEM!, window tinting, septic tanks, seawall repair . . . He reached the last envelope—"Coupons for smoothies? Fuck that nonsense!"—and slammed it all down into the garbage can. He turned and bumped into a cheerfully short woman. "Oh, I'm sorry . . ."

"No, it was me. I wasn't paying attention and stepped up behind you."

"I mean about my blue language," said Serge. "I need to learn how to accept life's daily micro-disappointments, like the all-too-frequent Mailbox of Disappointment. I'm just into the power of positive thinking. Before I open a mailbox, all options are on the table. Something in the slot could change my life, and by next week I'm wearing a special radiation suit with a revolving red light on top of my helmet while studying quarks in an apprenticeship at the CERN supercollider in Switzerland, but that piece of mail never seems to come no matter how many years I wait. I've begun to suspect that the mail carriers are stealing them because you know how you always seem to get a new carrier every few months, and if I ever visit Switzerland they'll all be there with revolving red lights. I just drank coffee." He stared glumly down into the trash can. "I wish they'd instead steal the flyers for thrifty toilet snaking."

"Don't worry about your language." The woman smiled warmly. "It's a relaxed community. And I do mean community." She unlocked her own mail slot. "Everybody keeps to themselves in the big Miami condos and doesn't even say hello. But here, we're family, always looking out for each other, always more than enough helping souls."

"I'm getting that vibe." He held out a hand. "My name's Serge."

"Nice to meet you. I'm Jen-Jen, but my friends call me the Queen of the Board. Humbling story, but I'll take it." The woman flipped through her own mail. "So you must be one of the new guys they're talking about."

"New guys?"

"Yeah, everyone knows everything around here"—tossing envelope after envelope in the trash—"I met your roommate yesterday out by the pool. He was a bit wobbly . . . actually, more than a bit. Knocked over our table of cocktails and fell facedown in my patooty."

"Lord!" Serge covered his face. "I'm so embarrassed about that first impression."

"Why?" asked his neighbor. "That's *everyone's* first impression."

"What do you mean?"

"It's inevitable." An envelope for a credit-repair scam was tossed in the garbage. "People first come to the Keys, and it's so postcard-paradise that they lose their minds for a while. We all went through that initial partying phase. It'll pass."

"Coleman? I don't know if you're a betting woman—"

"Anyway, I just wanted you to know that everyone in the whole condo is totally supportive of your lifestyle."

"You *are*?" asked Serge.

The woman nodded and tossed more envelopes in the trash. "The rest of the country is so uptight that they'll hemorrhage if they don't watch out. But 'tolerance' is the Florida Keys middle name. You and your partner are more than welcome here."

"Wow, that is tolerant," said Serge. "So you really know about our lifestyle?"

"Of course. It's obvious."

"And you're completely cool with it?" said Serge.

"The whole package."

Serge whistled. "I was worried the Keys wouldn't live up to my outrageous expectations, but this is even better than I'd ever imagined. We've been on the run practically our whole lives."

"Well, you can stop. Whatever makes you happy is nobody else's business. That's how we all roll down here at Pelican Bay."

"Damn!" said Serge. "The tolerance just keeps on giving."

Jen-Jen checked a last envelope for a free pedicure and trashed it—"Fuck"—then headed for the sharing bookcase and crouched.

Serge followed and idly grabbed a book-club edition off a shelf. *Portnoy's Complaint.* He put it back and glanced down. "What are you looking for?"

"A game." She pulled out a tattered cardboard box. "It's board game night up in my unit on Wednesday."

"Oooo! Games!" said Serge. "Can I come?"

"The more the merrier." Jen-Jen tucked the box under her arm. "The only rule is nothing digital."

"Someone has to tend the flame of the old school."

"No joke." She headed for the elevator.

"Where are you going?" asked Serge.

"To set up. I know it's still a couple of days away, but I'm anal that way."

"Can I help?"

"Okay." She checked her watch. "But there's not a ton of time. It's spaghetti night up at Maggie and Bert's—" She suddenly covered her mouth. "Oops, that was incredibly impolite if you weren't invited."

"Resume relaxing," said Serge. "We were."

They took the elevator to the fifth floor and entered a condo unit dominated by trophy cases. Huge golden cups on wooden stands and silver statues of Olympianesque people raising board-game playing pieces in the air. Then countless rows of ribbons and medals. Serge felt like he was at the home of Martina Navratilova. He walked along the cases, reading more engraving. "These are from cities all over the country."

"Of course," said Jen-Jen. "Most people don't know it, but there's a huge tournament circuit out there. I spend a few months a year on the road."

Serge pressed his nose to the glass. "This biggest one with the wheelbarrow on top is from Vegas."

"The World Series of Monopoly is the most intense," said Jen-Jen. "Guys with dark sunglasses and black cowboy hats."

"Did you hear that Hasbro recently retired the thimble playing piece?" said Serge. "I couldn't take solid food for days. Why not just piss in church?"

"Sounds like you're really into it," she said, removing a board from the flat box. "You play?"

"Like a fiend," said Serge. "So intense I need to keep a blood pressure thing on my arm."

"Most people just roll the dice," said Jen-Jen. "They don't realize there are complex strategies. You have one?"

"Not unless you count balls-to-the-wall," said Serge. "The other players have favorite colors for properties, or they dig certain names like Marvin Gardens. Not me! The first few laps around the board, I buy absolutely everything I land on until there's nothing left. Then I go on a construction binge that would shame Levittown after World War Two, building houses around the board clockwise as fast as I can, subsidizing the development frenzy by flipping deeds over for bank mortgages. Sure, I fall way behind in the beginning because I'm the one collecting the least rent. But once all the deeds are faceup again with red hotels everywhere, who's their daddy?"

"And you've never played on the circuit?" asked Jen-Jen.

"Not unless it was in a fever dream," said Serge. "Why do you ask?"

"Because you've just described the fundamental strategy that separates tournament champions from amateurs," said Jen-Jen. "Monopoly is my absolute favorite!"

Serge looked down at the table. "Then we'll be breaking out Monopoly on Wednesday?"

"Nobody will play with me anymore," said Jen-Jen, opening a tattered box on the dining table. "The last night got particularly ugly. I don't want to talk about it."

"Well, you picked a close second." Serge picked up a playing piece. "Clue is the bomb. Or it's the shit, depending on the day's lexicon."

"Any strategy with this game?" asked Jen-Jen.

"Actually I do have one, and it's totally legit!" said Serge. "I came up with it after reading the rulebook five times, and it hit me: 'Hold . . . on . . . just . . . a . . . second! This is too good to be true!' So I looked again, and sure enough, completely in bounds. Except every time I win with the tactic, the board gets knocked over in the middle of the screaming, and I say, 'You're only being jerks because I've read the rules and you haven't,' but by then I'm alone again."

Jen-Jen unpacked more of the frayed box. "So what's this strategy? . . ."

Chapter 17

ISLAMORADA

You know how sometimes there will be a bunch of dogs lying around resting with their chins on the floor, and suddenly, all at once, they raise their heads and look around like they've noticed something important has just occurred that they don't understand?

That's what happened to most of the humans in the vicinity of Plantation Key. It was afternoon on a Monday.

People in the groceries and hardware stores and diners stopped talking and glanced back and forth. So did the drivers of sports cars and sedans and pickup trucks, crossing the grated bridges on U.S. 1. They couldn't put their fingers on it, just felt it in their bones.

Because at their range, it was subsonic . . .

In the Upper Keys, the development is mostly concentrated around the bridges between the islands, because it is a boating culture. The channels under the bridges provide easy access to the seas on both sides of the archipelago. Resorts with massive docks, waterfront restaurants and subdivisions laced with finger canals.

In the middles of these ribbon-thin islands, the population stretches out and the commercial enterprises become more modest, right up against the highway. Appliance repair, outboard engine repair, fishing bait.

One such building on Upper Matecumbe Key was a short, single-story concrete-block deal with a flat roof. The left side of the building used to host a contractor who built boat davits on seawalls, and the other side had been a Sherwin-Williams with red paint spilling over a globe.

Now the whole front featured a pale sky blue. It was decorated with a mural of clouds, balloons, tropical fish and mermaids. The paint for the mural had been bought at the going-out-of-business sale when the Sherwin-Williams moved away.

A Datsun pulled into a parking space and Julie got out. She approached the front door under a driftwood sign: HAPPY SEAS LONG-TERM CARE AND HOSPICE.

Small children sat at equally small tables with construction paper, safety scissors and library paste. Some went over to a wall for more supplies. The wall of cubbyholes. Each child had one with their own nameplate, and several were decorated with shiny stars, glitter, and decals from Disney movies. The staff had cubbyholes, too, on the top row.

The word *bittersweet* was invented for the Happy Seas. Because space in the Keys is at a premium, some of the long-term kids went home at night; the others did not. Julie always stopped and took a steadying breath each time she stepped inside the front door. It was early afternoon, and the cushioned mats had been laid out for naptime.

Julie studied them. Apparently the person who had set them out hadn't gotten the word. Julie bent down and rolled one of them up, and stuck it in a closet. Then she went to the cubbyholes and removed one of the nameplates. BETH. She reached up into her own cubbyhole, pulled down a cigar box, dropped the nameplate inside, among dozens of other nameplates, and put the box back, followed by her purse.

"Julie . . ."

She turned around. "Yolanda, what's up?"

"Did you hear that thing about an hour ago?"

"What thing?"

"Just about everyone felt it," said Yolanda. "But if you were close enough, you also heard it. I was getting out of my car, and there was this deep pop."

"Pop?" asked Julie.

Yolanda shrugged. "Maybe an accident. Sounded like something not so bad happened nearby, or something very bad happened in the distance. This sounded far away."

"Now that you mention it," said Julie, "I do remember something. I was getting mail from my trailer and noticed a dull thud. The water in my goldfish bowl rippled. Anybody have a clue?"

"No, but if it was important, we'll eventually find out."

"People are chatty down here," said Julie, heading over to one of the small tables to assist in some kind of project involving Popsicle sticks.

The sun tracked across the sky, baking the roof. Toward the end of the afternoon, Julie was enjoying a fruit cup. She was in the break room of the Happy Seas. The TV was on. Julie liked the chunks of cantaloupe the best. She worked her fork around the bowl, selectively spearing grapes, strawberries and melon so there would be more cantaloupe at the end. The walls were decorated with seahorses.

She looked at the TV when the local news came on with a giant red banner across the screen: BREAKING NEWS! MYSTERIOUS LOUD SOUND!

Julie walked over and turned up the volume.

"*. . . There has been a major development in the mysterious loud sound this afternoon in the Upper Keys that caused residents to flood* *police phone lines with calls. Authorities at this hour are reporting a major boating accident on the bay side of Plantation Key south of the Cowpens Channel in an unnamed area affectionately known as Toilet Seat Cut, across from the Pelican Bay condominium. At least one person is presumed dead. A fuel explosion is suspected at the moment, but authorities say a final determination will be made in the coming days . . ."*

Julie stood momentarily with a strawberry on the end of a fork, then stuck it in her mouth. She turned the volume down on the TV and sat back at the table . . .

Ten minutes later, she was standing again, cranking the volume back up on the set. The newscast had entered the international segment of the coverage. Julie had missed the front end of a story, but a certain last name had caught her ear.

". . . There has been a major development in the mysterious explosion two days ago in a quaint American fast-food restaurant outside the capital of Bogotá, Colombia. Dozens have been injured, and five are confirmed dead, including three members of the infamous Millan cartel. It appears that the other two fatalities were innocent bystanders. Nothing has been confirmed, but speculation is that the bombing is another salvo in a growing wave of violence between the cartel and the Benzappa family. Just last week, two lieutenants in the Benzappa organization were killed by masked gunmen on mopeds as the victims stepped out of a butcher shop . . ."

Julie lost her taste for cantaloupe.

"The attacks appear to be a turf war created by a power vacuum surrounding the head of the family, Rafael 'Raffy' Benzappa, who is reported to be in failing health and resting at an undisclosed location out of the country, presumably the United States." An outdated photo filled the screen. *"It is not known whether Rafael is still in control, but local law enforcement believe the day-to-day operations are being handled by these two men"*—a pair of new pictures came on the screen—*"A.J. Benzappa, on the left, is the muscle of the family and the Sonny Corleone heir apparent. The figure on the right is*

his younger brother, Mercado Benzappa, also known as Mercedes Benz, who is reputed to be the nonviolent handler of the financial side of the family business . . . Hold on, we've just received word of another large blast in the coastal town of Barranquilla, sister city of Tampa, Florida—"

Julie turned off the set and tossed her cup in the trash. She arrived at the desk of the shift supervisor. A purse strap hitched over her shoulder. "Yolanda, I need to leave early today."

"Is everything okay with your father?"

"He's fine," said Julie. "I'm just not feeling so well. I'm sorry."

"Julie, you're a volunteer," said Yolanda. "You don't have to *ask* to leave early."

She simply nodded and left the building.

When she reached the post-modern home on Millionaires Row, the whole compound was on high alert. All the guards patrolled the grounds. It was the first time she'd seen them openly carrying weapons. And so many more guards than usual. Two were already urgently awaiting her at the gate by the street. They let her in and quickly closed it.

One of them then opened her passenger door.

"What are you doing?" asked Julie.

"Riding with you to the house." He held his weapon against his shoulder in the ready position, in case he had to shoot at something through the car's glass. "Once you're inside the house, I suggest you stay away from the windows."

"Is this about what was on the news?"

"It's better we not sit still in the car."

"Are me and my father safe?"

"We have everything under control."

"It doesn't look that way from this seat."

Another guard quickly ran from the front door when the car stopped in the driveway, and they hustled her inside.

"Where's Mercado?" asked Julie.

"Had some business that suddenly came up."

"Geez, you think?"

When Julie entered the master bedroom, the curtains were uncharacteristically drawn shut. Another guard stood at the back wall, cradling an insane battlefield weapon with a mortar launcher. Raffy and her father were both asleep. Julie pulled up a chair and sat quietly, listening to the freight train of thoughts in her head.

Chapter 18

Knock, knock, knock.
 The neighbors began arriving at dusk. Dinner was almost ready.

Another knock. Jen-Jen came in. "Something sure smells good around here."

Maggie and Bert were at the stove. "Hope everyone likes spaghetti and meatballs."

The sun had set, and the day grew dim. The last kayakers paddled back to Meditation Point.

Pelicans flew over the coconut palms, rustling from the breeze on the incoming tide. A timer went off somewhere, switching on all the yellow balcony lamps and showcasing the condo's gently sweeping art deco curves.

More knuckles knocked on wood.

"Be right there! . . ." Maggie opened the door and smiled at Serge and Coleman. "Come in! Come in! Glad you could make it!"

Serge smiled back and held up a white box from a bakery. "I didn't know what to bring, so I brought cupcakes."

Coleman wiped frosting from the corner of his mouth. "I kind of ate one already. Sorry."

The woman took the box and headed for the kitchen. "I hope you also brought your appetites."

Serge patted his grumbling stomach. "I've been fasting all day. I always do that when I'm invited to dinner because if it's something I don't like I'll still eat it. That's just good manners."

"Well, I make a walloping spaghetti and meatballs."

"Spaghetti and meatballs!" said Serge. "My absolute favorite! Did you know that Sparta used meatballs to turn the tide of the Peloponnesian War? I just made that up. I think something's wrong with me."

Maggie smiled. "What would you like to drink? Wine? Sparkling water?"

Serge eyed an appliance on one of the counters. "Oooo, is that coffee?"

"Uh, yeah," said Maggie. "But it's yucky cold from this morning."

Serge's hands made a drum roll on the edge of the table. "Hit me! Tallest cup you've got."

"If you say so . . ."

Serge sat and chugged, and soon Maggie turned around from the stove.

"It's ready." She slipped hands into pot-holder gloves and set a giant dish on the table. "Everyone have a seat and serve yourselves." Then she walked over to a large piece of teak furniture that housed an old RCA stereo. "I thought I would play some music." She slipped a vinyl album from its sleeve and set it on the turntable.

Serge and Coleman joined neighbors at the table. The plates and silverware were all there, along with a large bowl of tossed salad and a loaf of Italian bread that bookended the casserole dish in the middle. "Dig in and don't be shy . . ."

Serge grabbed salad tongs. "I still can't get over how friendly everyone is here. Especially considering how the rest of the country is in jerk mode."

"I guess we've just lived long enough to know what's important." Maggie spooned a giant meatball. "Life's too short to get angry about silly stuff, and it's all silly stuff."

Serge turned toward Coleman and pointed across the table with the tongs. "This is what I'm talking about! These are my people! Not like those other assholes." He covered his mouth. "Oops, my bad."

"Don't worry about it," said Maggie. "Parmesan? It's freshly grated."

Serge accepted the bowl and sprinkled liberally. Lively jazz filled the condo. "Hey, I remember that song, 'A Taste of Honey.'"

"You really know your Tijuana Brass," said Maggie. "Most people today wouldn't even recognize it, but back when it was big, it was everywhere."

"You're not kidding about everywhere," said Serge. "The malls, pizza parlors, barbershops, all day every day. It was the soundtrack to my childhood. You know how when you hear a huge song years later, you flash back to everything in your life when it was a hit? Now when I hear that album, I think of beach hot dog joints, the jai alai fronton, lifeguard stands, plaid swim trunks, Tom Collins highballs, the old chevron signs at Publix, suntan lotion that *accelerated* skin damage, S&H Green Stamps, running through sprinklers under palm trees, and sex."

"Sex?" asked Maggie. "How old were you?"

"I was only four, but it was my earliest sexual memory. My folks also had this record, *Whipped Cream & Other Delights*." Serge got up and grabbed the album cover. "They didn't realize what they were leaving lying around the living room, and I didn't, either. At first it looked like a woman in a wedding dress. But after a while I realized she was naked and covered in whipped cream *sculpted* into a dress. I must have stared at that album for hours, because at four years old, where else can you get that?"

"The album cover was a huge controversy at the time," said Maggie.

"I can see why," said Serge. "Sigmund Freud was a regular freak, but I think he had a point about peculiar events in our formative years that create bizarre sexual wiring, which lies dormant for decades. In my case it was Wonder Bread."

"Wonder Bread?" asked Maggie.

"Freud was big on potty training gone awry," said Serge. "I don't remember how old I was, but my feet still couldn't reach the floor when I sat on the toilet. And sit I did! My mother was always making me sit on the toilet for what seemed like hours. 'But, Mom, I don't have to go!' 'Yes, you do. It's all in your head.' 'I really don't have to go. I want to watch *Combat!* on TV.' 'No, stay there . . .' And she'd leave the bathroom and come back with a plastic sack. 'Here, eat this.' The first time she did it, I stared at her and said, 'Bread?' And she goes, 'It will help push it out.' Some time later, I realized it was all an attempt at psychological trickery, like I was deliberately constipating myself, which, back in the 1960s, was my personal breakdown of trust between the generations. Anyway, thirty years later I'm in bed with a woman, at a point when you *think* you're comfortable in the relationship, and I ask her to eat Wonder Bread, and I remember the word 'sicko' and her car screeching away. Was that just me?"

Maggie and Bert were still processing the last few paragraphs.

Serge snapped his fingers. "Topic!"

"Topic?"

Serge nodded hard. "The key to a fantastic evening celebrating dinner with close friends. Choosing the right conversation topic is absolutely critical to bonding. Pick the wrong topic and it's screeching tires again."

"Why don't you decide?" said Maggie.

"Okay then." Serge unfolded a napkin in his lap. "That little tree growing out of the western side of the old Seven Mile Bridge. I've been watching it for years. First it was just a little sprig, but it's grown bigger and bigger against all odds out of a rusty crack in the span. No soil or anything. How does it do it?"

"Oh," said Maggie, "you mean Fred the Tree."

"Fred?" said Coleman.

"All the locals know about Fred the Tree," said Maggie.

"Dang," said Serge. "The stuff I'm learning from Operation Pump the Brakes."

"We all love Fred," said Maggie. "Out there alone, valiantly thriving. We thought for sure that Hurricane Irma would take him out, sitting up high and all exposed as he is. But nope, not Fred. He puts a smile on all our faces and gives us hope."

"Please!" said Serge. "More data!"

"A few years back, in the winter, the locals started hiking out on the old bridge to string Fred with battery-powered Christmas lights. He even has his own Facebook page."

Serge set his fork down. "Knock me over with a feather . . ."

A pair of black armored vans with their lights off slowly rolled down a side street toward the sea. Just before reaching the water, they parked out of sight around the end of the Pelican Bay condominium. A team in black helmets and Kevlar vests quickly jumped out, grabbing shields.

Soon, red laser beams crisscrossed the parking lot as the platoon silently raced toward the sidewalk and up a spiral staircase . . .

F red is now my role model," said Serge. "Next topic: How long have you two been married?"

Maggie smiled at her husband. "It will be fifty years in August."

"A half century!" Serge whistled. "Now *that's* against all odds. You must have a secret, because humans aren't hard-wired for monogamy. We think we are, but that's only because society has thrust it upon us to prop up the housing industry. Another reason for the illusion of monogamy is simply lack of options in the middle class. If you doubt that, read any celebrity movie star magazine, where the sex lives are like musical chairs."

"Actually," said Maggie, "we do have a secret—"

"Stop right there!" said Serge. "Before you say anything else, I need to warn you about something. Since people aren't built for monogamy, that's where imagination comes in. And this is where it gets slippery: role-playing in the bedroom. Good God, the lengths we go to to make a marriage last. I wouldn't know because I was only married a year, but there were a few cringeworthy moments . . ."

"I remember," said Coleman. "That time when I came into your apartment and you were tied up to a chair, and luckily I was able to free you in time."

"In the *wrong* time," said Serge. "Just before my wife came out of the bathroom in her own costume. Then there was the time I asked her to eat Wonder Bread *and* whipped cream. You'd think I'd learned my lesson . . ."

Maggie and Bert glanced at each other.

". . . The next few days were unreal," said Serge. "The stamina that woman had for slamming doors. Where was I going with this? Right. I had a friend whose father told him that the main reason he was able to stay married to his wife so long was that she was crazy about role-playing in the bedroom. And my friend is like, 'Dad, Jesus, I could have gone to my grave without hearing that.' So, Maggie, if your secret to a long marriage is that Bert here enjoys dressing up like a Power Ranger, I'd prefer to move on to the next topic."

"No," replied Maggie. "I was going to say that our secret is we listen to each other."

"Whew," said Serge. "Another close one—"

Bam! Bam! Bam!

It wasn't knocking.

The dead bolt lock splintered through the door frame. Black helmets and shields charged in. Red laser dots hit the chests of everyone at the dining table.

"Down! Down! Down!" "Everyone get on the floor!" "Let me see your hands!"

The dinner guests didn't need to be told twice. They dove from their chairs and flattened on the ground.

"Don't move! Don't move!" "Spread your arms and legs!" "Keep those palms flat on the floor!"

Coleman turned his face on the tiles. "Serge, there are too many instructions for me to keep up with."

"I can't understand this!" said Serge.

"I know," said Coleman. "One order after another. Hands, legs, floor. It's like Twister. I hope they're not keeping score."

"No, not that," said Serge, suddenly grimacing with a wince. "How on earth did they find me? I take every precaution! A snitch? No, not these people. Conspiracy? I blame the media . . ."

The pair watched as black combat boots paced past their faces.

"So what's your plan to escape?" asked Coleman.

"Don't have one."

"Stop joking around," said Coleman. "You always come up with something."

Serge shook his head. "Not this time. There are too many of them, too trained and ready, in a small space with civilians. I'm sorry."

"It's been a good ride," said Coleman.

"I just can't believe that this is how it all ends," said Serge. "Seriously? Spaghetti dinner in an old condo? I was expecting a final showdown in a hollowed-out volcano with a James Bond villain—"

"You two! Shut up!" "No talking!"

The dinner party remained silent and prostrate, with pumping hearts and heads full of questions.

The tactical team continued swarming as Serge raised his head from the floor. "Officers, I can explain. All these other people are innocent and don't know anything. I promise I won't resist—"

"Didn't I tell you to shut up?"

Semi-crouched officers spread out, darting from room to room, pointing tactical weapons. After a few seconds: *"Clear!"* *"Clear here, too!"* *"Bathroom's clear."*

The squad leader radioed headquarters. Then down to the people on the floor: "Where's the gunman?"

The flattened neighbors glanced at each other quizzically. "What gunman?" asked Maggie.

"The crazed prison escapee threatening to shoot all of you."

"What are you talking about?" said Maggie. "We were eating spaghetti, which is cold now."

Three of the tactical officers huddled to whisper. Nodding around their small circle.

"Okay," said the first officer. "Stay where you are, and we're going to check a few more things." He got out a cell phone while the others conducted a last, slower sweep.

Finally, the platoon leader returned to the dining room and removed his helmet. "Okay, you can all get up now. Why don't you have a seat at the table?"

Maggie eased herself into a chair. "What's going on?"

"I'm sorry you had to be put through this," said the leader. "Do you have any enemies?"

"I still don't know what just happened," said Maggie.

"It's called 'swatting,' as in SWAT team. You can look it up on the Internet," said the leader. "A nefarious form of revenge, but one far more deadly than keying your car doors."

"Still not following."

"An unfortunate sign of our times," said the leader. "An outgrowth of the polarized culture. People used to just receive empty threats or a dead rat in the mailbox. It started with crazies lashing out at others over politics, and now it's spread to all sorts of personal disputes. If someone has a serious bone to pick, they call 911 on an untraceable phone and say something like they're hiding in a locked bathroom because a gunman has broken into the house and is insane or high on drugs, taking them hostage and threatening to shoot everyone. The caller gives the address before finally saying something like 'Oh my God, he's trying to break down the door!' and screams and hangs up."

"Wow, that's some revenge-reach," said Serge. "An enemy can attack you from blocks away."

"You're thinking too small," said the tactical leader. "In one of the most famous cases, a guy in Los Angeles swatted someone in Kansas City, fourteen hundred miles away. Over a ridiculous online video game feud, not that there's any good reason."

"This all sounds so terrible," said Maggie.

"Whether it's revenge or a brainless prank, it puts everyone in danger," said the leader. "When it first began, SWAT teams were bursting in to find stunned families saying grace before dinner with their kids at the table and even babies in high chairs. After the phenomenon started trending, word went out to departments across the nation."

"I get it," said Serge. "And then you guys begin responding with a slight hesitation, because now in the back of your minds, it might be a hoax with innocent people inside the place, putting your whole tactical team at higher risk. Has anyone gotten hurt yet?"

"Remember the video feud I mentioned?" said the lieutenant. "The guy called and said he'd already shot one person and had a bunch of gasoline to burn the place down with the others inside. Except it ended up being the wrong address, some guy who had nothing to do with the feud."

"What happened?" asked Maggie.

"The poor guy who lived there behaved like any utterly con-fused person and made some kind of benign move that appeared threatening. Shot dead."

"Tell me you're joking," said Serge.

"Look it up." He placed a business card on the table. "We take this extremely seriously. If you have any idea, no matter how doubtful, who might have wanted to do this, please call us imme-diately."

Chapter 19

THE NEXT DAY

A post-modern mansion sat still and quiet in the middle of Islamorada's Millionaires Row, but it was different.

The already unusually large number of guards had been tripled, and they were no longer even attempting to be subtle about brandishing military-grade firearms previously concealed under their coats. A helicopter landed and Mercado rushed out.

Inside, everyone standing around the largest flat-screen. Local news on high volume.

"... *Breaking news at this hour with more developments from the boating explosion that rocked the waters off Plantation Key yesterday afternoon. A local fishing guide escaped injury after jumping in the water shortly before the blast to retrieve a hooked tarpon in our delightfully quirky and beloved Toilet Seat Cut. However, his customer wasn't nearly so lucky. Authorities have since identified the victim as one A.J. Benzappa. Confidential sources say the deceased is reputed to be in operational command of the Benzappa family in*

Colombia while his father recovers from an undisclosed illness. The same sources also indicate that while the fatal mishap was initially classified as a simple mechanical failure with the fuel system, the victim's identity has raised suspicions of foul play, and federal agents are en route to investigate what might be a latter-day assassination in the so-called Cocaine Cowboy Wars that rocked South Florida in the 1980s. Back to you, Chet..."

Mercado turned the set off. "Does Julie know?"

"You definitely could say that," replied a lieutenant. "She's been seeing the same TV reports."

"Where is she?"

"At the care center."

"Guard?"

A nod. "But he's staying out front in the parking lot. They're a little funny about guns inside that place."

"We need to get organized," said Mercado, taking a seat at the head of the dining table. The others followed his lead and pulled out their own chairs.

Benz looked around the table. "When did you know?"

Silence.

Bam.

A fist pounded the table. *"When did you know!"*

"Sir, we didn't until yesterday evening, just before we told you," said a lieutenant to his left.

A fist banged the table again. "Am I employing only imbeciles?" His head swung. "Goose?"

A head lowered. "We started to get worried yesterday, but we weren't sure."

"You had an idea? You didn't come to me?" screamed Mercado.

Someone else at the table cleared his throat: "We didn't even know A.J. had gone fishing. We thought he was already on his way home."

Mercado stood up and grabbed his chair. It flew into something that broke glass. "So I have to find out my brother's dead from TV? Reporters were joking about something called Toilet Seat Cut?"

All faces around the table looked back and forth at each other with guilty expressions.

"What is it?!" yelled Mercado. "What does everyone in this room seem to know but me?"

"Uh, sir," said Goose. "We needed to confirm something first. And get certain things lined up back home."

Mercado's face became blood red, an exasperated noise held in behind tightened lips. His hands searched for something else to break. He forced himself to settle down in order to form intelligible words. "How does any of that prevent you from telling me what you're hiding?"

"Because we were ordered not to," said Goose.

Now Mercado's rage swirled with confusion. "Ordered?"

A nod. "Very strict."

Mercado's head pulled back. "By who?"

"Your brother, A.J."

Mercado sat back down in grief-filled thought, and the rest of the men at the table began to uncoil. The one sitting closest to him was named Cinco.

Cinco was Mercado's oldest, most trusted lieutenant, and they went back since before the beginning. Cinco was actually his nickname, and it sounded cool in America, but back home it was simply the number five, from his soccer jersey when he and Mercado played as boys in the dusty streets outside Medellín. The third in command at the mansion was Goose, who also played ball with them as a boy. His number was seven, but they called him Goose instead.

The men around the table stared at fingernails, the ceiling, anything. Cinco used the prolonged pause to address the crew. "Guys, can you give us the room?"

They didn't need to be asked again. The place cleared out like there was a bomb threat, which, in a way, there was.

Goose stood respectfully by the table and raised his eyebrows.

Cinco looked up. "You can go, too. No offense."

"None taken." He left.

After the door was closed, when it was just the two of them, Mercado's demeanor changed as it would with someone he had been kicking old soccer balls around with since they were waist-high.

Cinco placed a hand on his friend's shoulder.

Mercado, totally vulnerable: "Does my father know yet?"

Cinco just shook his head.

Then Mercado shook his in kind. "What's going on? I just lost my only brother; what happened to him? What is the deal with these orders?"

"It's your father."

"My father gave the orders?" asked Mercado. "But the guys said it was A.J."

"A.J. delivered the orders to the crew, but they originally came from your father."

Mercado looked up toward the second-floor bedroom. "Now I'm totally baffled."

"It was a long time ago," said Cinco. "Actually, a really long time ago."

Mercado listened through his puzzlement.

"You were only a teenager . . ."

"Teenager?" said Mercado. "What could anything back then have to do with this?"

"It was the one and only time that you ever got your hands dirty."

Mercado solemnly lowered his head. "I remember that. Not a day goes by without regret."

"Your father and your older brother were really mad."

"But I did what I had to do. I was protecting the family."

"Not mad at you," said Cinco. "At our people who put you in that position."

"I keep telling myself I had no choice."

"You didn't," said Cinco. "And despite their anger, your father and brother were secretly very proud of you."

"I didn't know that." Mercado raised his face with a wisp of nostalgia. "A.J. was so much older, twenty-five when I was still in high school. All our sisters were born between us. I so looked up to him . . . But how are that thing back then and what happened yesterday . . . ?"

"You and A.J. were brothers, a lot alike in so many ways, but also so very different," said Cinco. "Everyone could tell right away that A.J. definitely was going to command the family one day, even take it bigger than your father. They also knew you just weren't cut out for it."

Mercado suddenly had a stung look.

"That didn't come out right," said Cinco. "It's just that everyone saw you were meant for even higher things. Your brother and father talked about it all the time. A.J. admired you. They had plans. College was obvious. So was having no connection to the business. You would carry the family name, become a kingmaker back home."

"But I dug in my heels and demanded to work in the family until they relented?"

"They were disappointed, but also not at the same time," said Cinco. "With your degree, you would stay on the financial side, legitimate investments. You had the mind for it."

"In other words, no getting my hands dirty."

"Very strict orders were given," said Cinco. "Nothing was to happen to you, nothing to be spoken in your presence about the wet side."

"Orders again?"

"Your brother also knew there was the possibility that this day would come," said Cinco. "Contingency plans were put in place. Before you could be told and maybe do something out of character—"

"You mean revenge?"

"—arrangements would be made and you would be kept safe. And I was chosen to have this specific talk that I prayed I'd never need to make," said Cinco. "But that day is here. The whole top echelon back home has already made their moves and, well, now we're in one of those discreet areas. You understand."

"I do," said Mercado. "And I'm glad it was you they chose."

The door creaked. One of the crew stuck his head inside. "Mr. Benz, intercom from the front gate . . ."

Mercado checked his watch. "Open it. And tell the guys to get their weapons out of sight."

Cinco searched Mercado's eyes. "You sure you're okay?"

"I've got this." Mercado smiled the smile reserved for old friends in times like this.

They both stood up from the table. "I'm here," said Cinco. "Anything you need."

"There is one thing," said Mercado. "The next time you go up to Key Largo I want you to get something."

"Name it."

"Pick up a football. Not American. A real football."

"Why?"

"I'd like to kick it around with you."

Chapter 20

THE NEXT DAY

Knock, knock, knock.

The neighbors began arriving at dusk. Dinner was almost ready on the stove. Another in an unending series of cordial dinners in tight-knit Pelican Bay. Except this evening had a theme.

Another knock. Maggie and Bert came in. "Something sure smells good around here."

Serge looked at the various pots and pans, then Jen-Jen. "Spaghetti and meatballs? Excellent!"

"It's very popular around here, the one thing everyone likes that won't start a fight." She circled the table, placing forks and spoons. "We're still trying to forget the California pizza night that was pizza in name only. We had no idea what kind of toppings they're using three time zones over. Chickpeas?" Jen-Jen smiled back over her shoulder. "Serge, I heard you like coffee even at night. I made a pot—"

A chair fell over as Serge sprang toward the counter.

Jen-Jen glanced while he hoisted a mug in front of his mouth. "Why don't you bring that to the table to have with your meal."

Serge held up a finger to give him a moment. His head went all the way back with the cup pointed at the ceiling and rivulets of brown fluid running down his chin. Then a supremely satisfied *"Ahhhh"* before slamming the mug down on the counter. "Let's rock!"

Everyone dug in.

Serge athletically twirled pasta onto a fork—"Some prefer a heavier utensil, but the technique is like a home-run swing, all in the wrist speed"—and stuck it in his mouth. "Damn, this is great! Both the food and the company. Another feast with my fantastic new friends! Two words: dinner conversation! The key to breaking bread is a fabulous confab! But you have to put severe thought into choosing the perfect topic. The wrong topic is like a turd in the salad bowl. Sorry, I forgot you're all eating. I've got the topic! I've got the topic!"

"What is it?" asked Maggie.

"Insurance."

"Uh, okay," said Jen-Jen. "That wouldn't have been my first thought, but continue."

Serge nodded emphatically. "Dig! This is my first stable domicile, and word out in the halls was that I needed a condo policy for my contents, so I visited the agent's office and it was easy-peasy. Quite reasonable rates, too, because it's a condo, and you don't have to worry about a bunch of mishaps that apply to regular homes with yards and all, like freak lawnmower accidents where you turn it up on its side, then stand back and throw various objects at the blades for scientific data, because I'm naturally curious that way. I promise I won't do that here. Where was I? Right, the policy. So I'm reading the fine print like I always do or you could be agreeing to work the swing shift on a sex farm. And I swear I'm not making this next part up: I'm skimming down the final page and get to this one codicil and look up at the agent: 'Is this for real?' And she says, 'What?' And I point at the page. '"Trampoline Exclusion"?' And she says, 'Oh yeah, our claims adjusters have detected an explosion in recent years. You wouldn't believe all the injuries from brainless stunts since people started filming themselves for the Internet.' Of course I'm sure they got a lot of pushback from the powerful lobbying interests representing Big Trampoline. But anyway, I say to the agent, 'Do I really need the exclusion? I'm in a condo, and on the fourth floor no less.' She says it doesn't matter, they've seen it. I say, seen what? And she types quickly on her laptop and turns the screen toward me. Sure enough, in living color below the search terms 'trampoline' and 'balcony,' two guys competing in the Darwin Awards world championship. I told her if the insurance company really wanted to cover their bases, they should adopt the 'Coleman Exclusion,' where they aren't liable for anything that happens after someone says, 'Hold my beer and watch this.'" Serge smiled and looked around the table at sets of eyes staring back.

An hour later, everyone was stuffed and into the red wine. Serge helped Jen-Jen clear the table and prepare the evening's theme: setting up the board game.

Maggie stood at a shelf. "You got another trophy."

Jen-Jen shuffled the game cards. "Chutes and Ladders in Atlantic City. They had to go to instant replay."

Coleman elbowed Serge. "How do you play Clue?"

"It's a mystery game." Serge eyed the various playing pieces. "Like being in *Murder on the Orient Express,* except it takes place in a creepy old mansion. To give you the *Reader's Digest* version: three solution cards—suspect, weapon, and room—are randomly removed from the deck facedown and placed in an envelope. Then the players slink around the mansion, throwing out theories that cause other players to slowly reveal their cards in a protracted process of elimination that takes hours until someone figures out the three cards nobody is holding and wins."

"Sounds boring."

"That's the beauty of board games," said Serge. "They're *designed* to be boring. Especially Clue. I just told you the official rules, but the real playing action is what happens off the board, among the neighbors gathered around the table, cooped up as the tension mounts. People getting drunk and irritable, embarrassing stories told, marriages dissolving, affairs sparked during trips to the kitchen for fresh ice cubes, layers of civility peeled back, true feelings bubbling to the surface after simmering for years: 'Fred, when are you going to paint your goddamn fence?' 'When you start picking up your dog's shit.' 'I do so pick it up!' 'Yeah? The Baxters agree with me, right, Jerry?' 'Phil, you could do a little better cleaning up after the beagle.' 'Jerry, you've been talking to Fred behind my back? Well, at the last barbecue, I fucked your wife!' 'Debbie, you actually fucked Phil?' Then Debbie runs off crying, and everyone peels away in their cars and puts out for-sale signs. And that's how you play Clue. It's loads of fun!"

Everyone got their snacks and drinks ready. The three solution cards were placed in a secret envelope in the middle of the game board, and the battle began. Actually, it began *before* it began.

"Coleman, give me that playing piece," said Serge. "You know I'm always Colonel Mustard."

"I'm keeping it," said Coleman. "I saw it first."

"What are you, in second grade?"

"You can be Professor Plum."

Serge picked up the tiny dagger playing piece. "Don't make me use this."

Coleman grabbed the tiny revolver. "Stay back or else."

Serge lunged for the colonel. "Give it."

Coleman jerked it back. "No . . . Ow! My hair!"

"Then open your hand," said Serge. "Ow! My little finger! . . ."

Moments later, Serge and Coleman sat on the couch with arms folded, glaring at each other.

The rest of the guests finished collecting the playing cards off the floor and set the upended game board back on the table. Jen-Jen smiled toward the couch. "We're ready again."

Everyone retook seats.

"I want to apologize to the room," said Serge. "I'm so embarrassed."

"Don't worry about it." Jen-Jen replaced the envelope of solution cards. "I play at the tournament level and see much worse. Once, in Reno, Scrabble spilled into the parking lot and someone went over the hood of a Trans Am."

The competition resumed and this time proceeded without incident. Players asking each other questions, jotting notes.

"Coleman," Serge whispered sideways. "Hope you're happy. Now neither of us gets to be Colonel Mustard."

"At least you don't have to be Mrs. Peacock."

"Ahem!" said Jen-Jen. "Serge, it's your turn. Ask your question."

"Oh, right." He fanned out his cards and held them close to his nose like it was the Wild West. Only his eyes visible, peeking over the tops of the cards, suspiciously shifting his pupils back and forth at the other players.

"Serge," said Jen-Jen. "We're waiting . . ."

"Okay, I'm ready." He laid the cards facedown in front of him. "Maggie, did you know that in the early versions of Clue, the lead pipe playing piece was actually made of real lead, and had to be replaced because of poisoning possibilities? This is a pretty old game, and who knows about that lead pipe on the table. I say we roll dice and the loser has to taste it."

"Serge—" said Jen-Jen.

"What?" said Serge. "There's no rule against trying to spice up the game."

"An actual question?"

"*Allll* right," said Serge. "Is it Miss Scarlet in the library with the candlestick?"

"Nope," said Bert.

Everyone scribbled notes. And so the evening went, eight

o'clock, nine, ten. Ice cubes dwindled; an empty bottle of Smirnoff hit the trash can. Eleven o'clock, midnight . . .

Zack jotted a final note. "I've got the solution! Mr. Green in the conservatory with the wrench." He sat back with a big smile, waiting for the cards to confirm his prowess.

Jen-Jen peeked inside the envelope. "Nope, you're wrong."

A shocked expression. "That can't be," said Zack. "I could have sworn . . ." He checked his notes again. "I *am* right. There's no other possibility!"

Jen-Jen shook her head. "You lose. You're out."

The same expressions of surprise began to round the table as the kitchen clock ticked toward one.

"But I don't understand it . . ."

"You're out," said Jen-Jen.

"How could I have been wrong? . . ."

"You're out."

"What the hell's happening here? . . ."

"You're out."

The players continued falling one by one to elimination until only a single person was left . . .

S erge grinned as only someone on the verge of a massive and decisive conquest can. He finally cleared his throat. "It was Colonel Mustard in the billiards room with the rope."

The other vanquished players checked their notes. Sarcastically: "Yeah, right." "No way." "He's out, too."

Jen-Jen opened the envelope again and laid the cards on the table. "Serge is correct. He wins."

"But how . . ."

"It can't be . . ."

"Something's not kosher . . ."

Then Gary read back through all his notes for the evening. "Wait . . . just . . . a second."

"What is it?" asked Maggie.

"He cheated." Gary held up his notepad. "During the first two rounds, Serge asked the rest of us about cards that he himself was holding."

"I'm offended." Serge placed a hand over his heart. "That's not cheating."

"It totally is."

Serge shook his head. "It's my patented secret tortoise-and-hare Clue strategy. Sure, I waste my first two rounds asking about my own cards, but I'm betting on nobody else reading the rules, and everyone is thrown off track the rest of the night until I slowly overtake the table and win."

"It's dishonest!"

"Cheater!"

"I'm with Serge," said Jen-Jen. "It's right there in the rules in black and white. He's actually quite clever."

"He's an asshole."

"Hey!" said Jen-Jen, looking down at her chest. "Don't throw the lead pipe at me." She picked up a playing piece and flung it back.

"For fuck's sake!"

"This is bullshit!"

Drinks were knocked over, and more stuff flew. Playing cards, the game board again. Serge jumped up and spread his arms. "Brothers and sisters, cool out . . . Ow!" He grabbed his right eye. "Who threw that?"

Someone else grabbed a cold pot off the stove . . .

Residents in nearby units slowly began to emerge onto the balconies in their nightclothes. "What's all that racket in there?"

Then they looked down the hall toward the elevators— "Uh-oh"—and ran back inside.

Serge was still in the middle of the dining room, vainly trying to make peace. "Let's sing: *'I'd like to buy the world a Coke—'*"

Suddenly there was a loud banging on the front door that got everyone's attention. The room went silent. Serge began to trot: "I'll get that."

He opened the door to find a team in black. "Good evening, officer. How can I help you tonight?"

"Sorry for the intrusion," said the leader of the SWAT team. "We believe you've been the victims of another hoax, but regulations require that we come check it out in full gear just in case. It's left to my discretion whether to bash down the door or knock."

"Thanks for knocking," said Serge.

"Hold on," said the supervisor. "What's that red blotch on your face?"

"Spaghetti sauce," said Serge. "Next question."

The leader stuck his head in the door. "There's more sauce on the walls. And playing cards and stuff all over the floor. Is everything okay in there?"

"Couldn't be better," said Serge. "We just played the most excellent game of Clue."

"Mind if we come in and check things out?"

"Sure thing," said Serge. "Watch out for the broken glass . . ."

The tactical team made the rounds, checking closets and under beds again, then regrouped with their "all clear" reports.

The puzzled leader approached the dining room, looking at all the neighbors now sitting demurely around the table, hair and shirts damp with splashed drinks and sauce. "Are you sure you were all just playing Clue?"

They slowly nodded.

"And nothing else is amiss?"

They shook their heads.

"Okay then." The SWAT leader took a deep breath. "Here's what it's beginning to look like. We've now gotten two hoax calls to the same condo building. We confirmed the first was from an untraceable throw-away phone with prepaid minutes, and I'm guessing we're going to find the same thing here."

"What can be going on?" asked Maggie.

"It appears that one of you has a serious enemy," said the leader. "Who among you was at the last unit we stormed?"

The neighbors glanced back and forth. "Almost all of us were," said Maggie.

"That makes it tougher," said the leader. "If you all could discuss it and see if any of you has experienced any vandalism lately, maybe a flat tire you didn't think anything of at the time. Hang-up calls or missing packages."

"Anything to cooperate," said Jen-Jen. "But then what do we do?"

The leader waved his team toward the door. "Compare notes in a process of elimination and try to figure out which one of you it is."

Serge jumped to his feet. "Did you hear that, everyone? A real-life game of Clue!"

Chapter 21

1980

The commercial airliner banked over the stone lighthouse on Boca Chita Key and the remaining pioneer homes out in the waters of Biscayne Bay called Stiltsville. It swung west over the cruise ships near Government Cut, bleeding off altitude and lining up the landing.

The control tower gave clearance and the jet touched down at Miami International Airport. It pulled to a gate for international arrivals. After clearing U.S. Customs, two of the passengers headed for baggage claim and found a chauffeur holding a sign. BENZAPPA.

The pair climbed into the back of a limo that pulled away from the airport and onto the Dolphin Expressway. It was a short drive until they were into that gleaming downtown skyline. They passed Freedom Tower and the site of the future basketball arena, southbound, before leaving the tallest buildings behind. The new buildings up ahead may not have cast the biggest physical shadows, but they loomed large in other ways.

The Brickell financial district.

One of the passengers looked out the window at a bulldozed construction site. Few knew at the time that the project would become a Miami architectural landmark called the Atlantis Condominium, with a trademark five-story square cut out of the middle high above the road, growing palm trees. Its image would be featured in the opening credits of a very popular TV show. The limo drove another minute before arriving at the entrance of a bank that was heavily leveraged in the Southern Hemisphere. As they say, Miami is the capital of Latin America.

The two passengers exited the vehicle and strolled through the sparsely furnished marble lobby that echoed footsteps. They took no notice of the guard station before entering the elevator.

On the tenth floor, closed to the public, the receptionist didn't request identification or the reason for their business. Just a big smile. "He's in there waiting for you."

The two men wore blank expressions the whole time, never acknowledging the receptionist's existence as they strode with purpose toward a pair of oversize maple doors that opened before they reached them.

A shorter man in a suit directly from Rome gave them another smile. A yellow handkerchief peeked from a breast pocket. "Come in! Come in!" They shook hands perfunctorily and took seats overlooking the bay and Star Island, home of the mansion from the upcoming movie *Scarface*.

More pleasantries, one-sided, from the man in the suit, the bank president. "Imagine how happy I was to know I'd be in town when I heard about your visit. I hope our service has been up to your standards. Call me personally if not."

"Everything's fine," said the older of the two men, named Caprio.

The banker turned toward the younger of the two, actually barely older than a boy.

"And this must be Mercado," said the president. "I've been hearing so much about you. How are things in school?"

"Graduating next month," said Mercado.

"That's good! That's fantastic!" said the obsequious president. "I understand you'll be going into finance. Excellent choice."

"His father is very interested in his future," said Caprio. "Very interested in him handling the financial side of the business."

The president turned again to the young Mercado. "Your father is a great man. The word was passed to us that you're looking for an internship. You are being groomed for big things, which you obviously deserve."

"So everything's set," said Caprio. It wasn't a question. "After he finishes school, you will begin dealing with Mercado concerning the family business, until you are only dealing with him."

"And I am very much looking forward to it," said the president.

Caprio stood without words or ceremony, and Mercado took the cue and stood as well. They curtly departed the office, leaving the bank president with an outstretched hand.

The limo headed south, out of Miami and into Florida City, then through the barren mangrove flats at the bottom tip of the mainland before crossing the bridge to Key Largo. The trip to Florida had been purposed to make the Mercado introduction, but there was other business. They left Key Largo behind, crossing the bridges at Tavernier and Snake Creeks and the span at Whale Harbor.

It was after dark when the limo pulled into a corrugated metal building the size of an airline hangar. One of the many high-and-dry marina boat storages with vessels stacked to the ceiling.

A windowless van sat in the middle. "Wait here," Caprio told Mercado before disappearing into an office in the back. Almost as soon as he went in, he came out, followed by others.

They opened the doors to the van, and Caprio turned to Mercado. "Get in back."

"He's coming with us?" the driver asked Caprio.

"He stays glued to my hip," said Caprio. "I promised I wouldn't let anything happen to him."

The van pulled out of the covered dry storage.

T he docks along charter boat row were deserted, save for two people hosing down boats after sportsmen had dragged off their bloody catches. One vessel had been christened BONANZA. The name across the stern of the other was covered by a tarp from earlier when they were dumping fish guts.

"Bobby, how's your dad doing these days?" said Gil, the captain of the *Bonanza*. "We keep missing each other pulling in and out of here."

"He's fine," said Bobby. "Would like to cut back on the hours and enjoy the work a bit more."

"Hard to do when you're self-employed."

"That's what he keeps telling me," said the youth.

They were still spraying the decks with pressure hoses when headlights appeared at the end of the darkened dock. The captain looked at his hand and the number he had written on it from the phone booth. "Say, Bobby. Why don't you go down below in your boat for a bit."

Bobby tilted his head to see the approaching van. "I understand." He made himself scarce in the cabin.

Here's the deal if you have a fishing boat that sails the open seas, and you're in the charter business. Or even if you aren't. You are always armed. Heavily. The most pleasant pleasure craft cruising offshore is a maritime beauty on the outside and a floating arsenal down in the hold. To this day, the Keys still have pirates. A smaller boat pulls alongside to ask directions, or how the fishing is going, whatever. If the people in the other vessel are novice and don't know the waters, they may not fare nicely. Every now and then people still go missing, and the Coast Guard finds an empty yacht floating halfway between Miami and Bimini. Any seasoned charter captain won't let another vessel remotely near; all required communications are conducted over megaphones or the radio. Most have pistols or rifles, but some of the captains prefer shotguns, because the sound of the pump racking will change a pirate's mind before he knows it.

As headlights approached, the captain looked down at a toolbox and pulled something out of it. The vehicle stopped and cut the lights next to the *Bonanza*. Caprio turned toward Mercado: "No matter what, stay in here until we're done."

The others got out and approached the stern, stopping at the dock cleats. They glared without words, as they were known to do.

Something about their glare made the captain tremble as he reached for a duffel bag. Another reason for the tremors was that the bag was too small for pot bales, but plenty big enough for kilo bricks of cocaine.

It was taking longer than usual for a transaction of this sort. The captain was freezing up. He had conducted many a sale of square grouper, as had the other fishermen, without the slightest change in blood pressure. After all, marijuana was benign. What was the big deal gaff-hooking weed out of the sea? Practically everyone sold bales down at the docks with no further thought than if they were selling bait to the tourists.

But this cocaine business was different. A scarier breed of cat was coming around in the vans. The charter captains had talked about it at length over draft beer. It was so much more money. But the vibe wasn't right. Neither was the risk. Almost all the captains decided to let the bricks of coke float on by in the Gulf Stream. They concluded it was just a matter of time until a deal went sideways.

Captain Gil was one of those on the cautious side of the debate. But business had been slow, and dollar signs flashed in his eyes when he saw the few bricks bobbing in the swells eight miles south of the Alligator Reef Lighthouse. What the heck? Just one deal and he'd be set for the season.

Now, however, with his knees knocking in the stern of the boat, he wished he'd never seen the tightly wrapped packages in the water.

The buyers became more than impatient. It was always a lightning-quick, in-and-out operation to minimize exposure. Almost never a word spoken. This time became an exception.

"What's your fucking problem!" shouted Caprio.

Which only made the problem worse. Captain Gil became like the rusting-up Tin Man in *The Wizard of Oz*.

"For the love of God!" yelled Caprio. He turned to one of his crew. "Sal, board the boat and grab that goddamn duffel bag."

Captain Gil had already made one mistake, and was about to make a bigger one. First, as the van approached, his nerves had skewed his judgment and he'd decided to fetch a nine-millimeter pistol from the toolbox and set it near one of the livewells, like if things didn't turn out all peachy, he could take on everyone.

Second, as Sal put a foot atop the stern, Captain Gil's left hand began to shake even more and involuntarily move toward the location of the pistol, and it was none too subtle. Sal saw it and jumped back on the dock. "Gun!"

Just like that, an instant standoff, everyone with weapons drawn, including Gil. Third mistake.

Caprio began repeating himself: "What's your fucking problem?"

Gil was too shaken to speak or shoot. The buyers didn't want to shoot, either, because business was good. Caprio knew the captain just had a nervous first-timer on his hands. He calmed his voice: "Relax and set the gun down. We have your money. Let's just wrap this up. Nobody gets hurt, and everybody gets rich . . ."

On the next boat, eyes peered through the slats of the door leading below. Captain Gil was like a second father to Bobby. The youth had already grabbed the pistol stowed in the berth of his own boat. He muttered to himself: "*Come on, Gil, put the gun down.*"

That was exactly what Gil intended to do. But the pistol was a semi-automatic with a round in the chamber and a light trigger pull. And a sweaty index finger in charge. As he reached to set it down, Gil was as surprised as anyone when it went off. Wasn't aimed or anything, but it still lodged in one of the van's fenders.

Hell broke loose. Everyone opened up on Captain Gil.

All attention was on the *Bonanza,* firing away. Nobody noticed the teenager on the next boat, climbing up from below, aiming his own gun at Caprio.

Nobody except Mercado.

He jumped out of the van with one of the many weapons just lying around inside.

Bobby's first shot hit Caprio in the left shoulder.

Mercado had better aim. He put a tight grouping of bullets in the chest, and Bobby fell backward down the steps to the cabin.

Caprio's mind swirled. There was too much going on. He felt the pain in his shoulder and saw the blood. Then he saw the lifeless feet in the next boat, and finally Mercado with a recently fired weapon.

"I thought I told you to stay in the van!" yelled Caprio.

"That guy was going to shoot you."

"He *did* shoot me."

"Well, he was going to shoot you again," said Mercado.

"Okay, you did good. We'll discuss this later." Caprio kicked the ground. "I was supposed to keep you safe!"

"I am safe." Mercado started throwing up.

"How did this get so fucked!" Caprio shouted at nobody in particular. "Sal! Grab that duffel bag and clear out of this shit show!"

The van sped off without headlights . . .

In the days and weeks to follow, police classified the homicides as a botched robbery, probably committed by out-of-town idiots who thought they'd found easy targets alone on the dark dock and didn't realize charter boats have arsenals. Drugs never came up.

Back in South America, there was a lot of shouting. Strict orders that Mercado was to be kept as far away from the heavy-lifting side of the business as scientifically possible. The youth was assigned permanent desk duty with the ledger books. And for the rest of Mercado's life, that ugly night down at the dock would be his one and only personal kill.

Chapter 22

ISLAMORADA

Well after midnight, Serge was relaxing with a book. It was spread across the steering wheel of a 1973 Galaxie speeding east up the Overseas Highway after a dinner party.

Coleman leaned over from the passenger seat. "What are you reading?"

"Coleman! Will you watch the road!" Serge snapped as he turned a page. "I can't do everything."

"I was only curious."

"But I told you to keep an eye out for other vehicles and stationary objects," said Serge. "It's irresponsible to drive distracted."

Coleman sat back.

His silent pouting finally got to Serge. He sighed toward the roof. "Look, I'm sorry I yelled at you. I was just getting to a good part." He closed the book to display the front cover.

Coleman read the title and scratched his head. *"A Purple Place for Dying?"*

Serge opened the book again on the steering wheel. "By the godfather of Florida fiction, John D. MacDonald. Installment number three of the iconic twenty-one-volume Travis McGee series. Each novel had a color in the title."

"What's this 'Purple Place' got to do with the book?"

"Nothing at all."

"That doesn't make sense," said Coleman. "It's in the title."

"Pure genius," said Serge. "In most of his books, MacDonald would simply drop in a random line containing the title, and that was it. Onto the cover it went."

"You can actually make up titles like that?"

"Sure." Serge turned another page. "Just have one of your characters blurt something out."

"Like what?"

"I don't know. Just whatever randomness hits you at the moment."

"Give me an example."

"Okay, let me think a second." Serge tapped his chin. The famous waterfront Lorelei Restaurant was coming up on the left. He looked out his open driver's window at a giant plywood roadside sign: the landmark mermaid advertising the eatery to passing traffic. Serge snapped his fingers. "I've got it. *Mermaid Confidential.*"

"That's it?" said Coleman.

"More than enough." Serge sipped a cup of cold coffee. "For whatever reason, just have one of the characters in your book blurt out *Mermaid Confidential,* and you've got your title."

"Sounds shaky," said Coleman.

"I don't make the rules." Serge set the book on the seat between them. His mouth became firm.

"Serge, why are you making that expression? What's the matter?"

"Don't get me wrong, it's been a fabulous evening: a fantastic dinner party with close friends, intimate conversation, fun game of Clue! I mean, sure, the playing board got upended, guests throwing pieces at each other and wrestling, spaghetti sauce on the walls, and the SWAT team arrives. But every dinner party has its little hiccups."

"Then why that serious look on your face?"

"It's been bothering me ever since we left," said Serge. "Who's making the swatting calls? Who among our group is being targeted?"

Coleman pointed. "There's our condo."

Serge pulled in the driveway. "Screw it. I'm wide awake from the coffee . . ." He began slowly circling the parking lot. Near the end of the first lap, he rolled to a full stop. "I know that car. But it can't be . . ."

Serge got out his cell phone and dialed. After eight rings, on the other end: "Mmm, uh, hullo . . ."

"Hey, Maggie, it's Serge. Sorry about the late hour. Did I wake you?"

"No, insomnia," said Maggie. "Still upstairs with some neighbors watching TV. Did you realize there's actually a movie called *Clue*?"

"Yes," said Serge. "But right now I'm on security detail. You wouldn't happen to have heard anything about your old renter, would you?"

"Oh, yeah, he's back in the unit. He returned and still had a key and let himself in," said Maggie. "I called the police and they said he had remaining time on his rental agreement that he'd already paid for, and he hadn't broken any laws."

"Why didn't you tell me?"

"Because he seems to have calmed down and we haven't heard a peep," said Maggie. "I didn't want to upset you after everything you've done for us."

"I understand. Enjoy the film." *Click*.

"What is it?" asked Coleman.

Serge parked the car. "Follow me . . ."

They crept toward an old Caprice. "Whose is this?" asked Coleman.

"That asshole renter."

"How do you know?"

"Because it's the car he tried to get into the other day when we were chasing him across the lot in our *Romper Room* car." Serge peeked in a window and spotted something on the passenger seat. "Unbelievable. What an idiot!"

"What?"

"He never disposed of the disposable cell phone. It's sitting right there. That defeats the whole purpose."

"Disposable?"

"The jury's not back yet, but I believe we just found our swatting culprit. And now I know who his revenge target was: me—" They heard distant footsteps in the after-midnight quietness of a peaceful condominium. "Quick! Coleman, crouch down with me in front of the bumper."

They waited in stillness as the footsteps grew louder, and the driver's door of the Caprice opened. Then some rummaging around until the door slammed, and the footsteps headed away. Serge tentatively poked his head up over the hood. "Shit!"

"What is it?"

"He *did* eventually find a gun."

Coleman's head rose next to Serge's. "What's he doing?"

"Taking that spiral staircase, probably up to our unit to give us what-for."

"Why is he pasting himself like that against the wall of the staircase and taking super-slow steps?"

"Paranoid. Still on drugs," said Serge. "This is our chance. To the elevators!"

They dashed across the parking lot and rode up to the fourth floor. "Coleman, wait around the corner. I'll run inside and get our blue car and join you. Then, when he comes to our front door, we'll ambush him from behind . . ."

The pair waited until they heard the footsteps again. They saw traces of the renter through architectural slits in the outside of the staircase. "Get ready . . ."

They waited. And waited.

"What's taking so long?" asked Coleman.

Serge watched through the staircase slits and saw shoes pass by their floor. "I was wrong. I wasn't the target. Maggie and Bert are. To the elevators!"

They got out on the next floor just as the renter was about to exit the staircase. "Coleman, quick! We'll circle around and head him off before he can get to their unit!"

It was a close footrace in opposite directions, but the cardboard car came around the corner and arrived first. The alarmed renter yelped and raised his gun.

"Coleman, duck!"

The trigger was pulled. *Click*.

"Our luck continues," said Serge. "It's a semi-automatic and he forgot to chamber a round."

"Drugs," said Coleman.

The renter dashed off with a panicked squeaking sound, followed by Serge and Coleman. "Beep! Beep!"

The young man took the staircase, and a blue car beat him to the ground floor on the elevator. It was waiting. "Beep! Beep!"

"*Ahhhhhhh!*" Back up the staircase, as Serge and Coleman followed, round and round up the spiral steps until they were on the seventh-floor penthouse level. Serge stopped.

"Why'd you do that?" asked Coleman.

"He's heading down the hall to the penthouse, which is a dead end. He'll be coming back."

"Then what?"

Serge just smiled and gazed at the rest of the building in the opposite direction.

"Oh, I get it."

It didn't take long. Running feet slapped back down the hallway toward them. Just as they were about to head down the staircase, Serge and Coleman popped out of hiding a few steps ahead. "Beep! Beep!"

The renter sprinted in the other direction, hopping a short wall onto the gravel-and-tar roof covering the remainder of the complex. "Coleman, wait here. Getting over this wall is above your pay grade."

The foot chase continued, threading through all the giant, whirring air-conditioning condensers pumping cool goodness to the units below. The renter repeatedly spun around to fire an impotent unchambered pistol.

"Beep! Beep!"

Serge had expected some kind of difficult final confrontation, but all ended with more whimper than bang as the renter actually seemed relieved to reach the end of the roof and disappear into the blackness.

"Where'd he go?"

A few seconds later: *thud.*

Serge winced and walked back to Coleman.

"What happened?"

"Couldn't have gone better. He tied a gift bow on this whole affair," said Serge. "The police will discover a disposable cell phone in his car with two suspiciously timed 911 calls in the memory, a body with drug-choked arteries next to an automatic pistol, and no signs of struggle in the gravel on the edge of the rooftop." He inhaled the crisp night air. "The end of a perfect day."

Part Three

Chapter 23

CENTRAL GEORGIA

The green ink of the tattoo started at a sharp point just above the bikini line at the butt crack, also known as the coin slot. From there, the ink slithered up her spine. The snake was so large that it took several sittings to complete. The final session had finished off the part where the reptile coiled around her neck, and its head stared out with a forked tongue in whatever direction the woman was gazing. It created the creepy impression, upon first meeting her, that you were staring at two faces. The snake's tail had rattles.

The woman lay on her stomach poolside with the back of her bikini top undone for tanning strategy. Just over a weed-choked chain-link fence, semi-trucks roared by on Interstate 75. Passing motorists looked over the fence at the scarce people on loungers desperately trying to catch some sun under belched black clouds of diesel smoke, and they became depressed by proxy. It was the tiny town of Forsyth on a long, vacant stretch of the highway north of Macon. Exit 187. That would be the number of miles to the Florida state line.

If you didn't know that the actual country town of Forsyth was a short drive away through the woods, you would have thought this was it. Just the typical cluster of businesses around an anonymous interstate exit ramp designed for brief stops by long-haul truckers and family vacationers. Convenience store, fast food, gas. The fruit stands changed with the geography. Peaches and boiled peanuts would soon give way to oranges and grapefruit. But even as interstate exits go, this one was a dog with fleas. And there literally *were* dogs with fleas, roaming vacant lots. Most motorists seeking a break to stretch their legs and resupply on snacks pulled off the highway, took one look, and kept on driving. The two things it did have going for it were an auto repair shop and a discount motel. If you broke down on the highway in the vicinity, this is where you got towed. If it was a Sunday, and the auto shop was closed, there was the motel.

It was a Sunday.

A few hours earlier, much drama and screaming on the side of the highway next to a column of steam pouring out from under the hood. The yelling came from the woman with the diamond-back tattoo. The breakdown hadn't been anyone's fault, and none of them even knew the cause. But whenever there was a pothole in the woman's life, she needed someone to kick like she needed oxygen. Her wild mane of jet-black hair blew in the wind as she verbally unloaded on her male travel companions, standing along the shoulder waiting for the towing service. Passing truckers honked, and she gave them the finger.

She had since cooled down in the pool. And now she sat up on the lounger, tying off her bikini top. Truckers honked.

It had been a draining drive without air-conditioning. Made even worse by the detour. The day before, they had been southbound on another interstate, I-95 . . .

Like even the most loosely organized criminal gang, they had a group dynamic, whether the members knew it or not. Blue had been the undisputed leader, and Vix had been his girl, until she Swiss-cheesed him back in Richmond. During the highway miles since, Vix had been on an inverted roller coaster of coke, whiskey, meth, and oxy, and she slightly began to wonder if she might have been a tad rash shooting up her boyfriend like that. After all, in the various roles among the gang, she really wasn't bringing much to the table to earn her keep, except screwing the leader's brains out. Blue had been falling in love, and Vix had been conducting a transaction. Now he was gone, and her social footing was on vapors. Vix glanced around at the other occupants of the car and performed calculus. Blue had been the unquestioned alpha male of the group. With Duke, Mulch and Weezer, though, there was rough parity. She knew whoever she chose would become the dominant leader, because he would be the only one getting laid, which carries unspoken currency in male circles. She glanced at Duke, with a slight edge in strength and the likely selection. But Weezer and Mulch were brothers, which could mean a voting bloc. She decided to split the siblings.

They'd pulled into a truck stop near the North Carolina line, and Vix surprised Mulch by following him into the men's room and giving him a hummer in one of the stalls. Mulch was delighted, and Vix had resumed control.

Then it was back on the highway. The guys chugged Coors, and Vix was in the back seat snorting more marching dust. And snorting, and snorting. The only intermissions were shots of Jim Beam in an attempt to keep the road to disaster between the guardrails.

Vix inhaled again like a feral hog and turned around to Duke, sitting beside her. "What the fuck do you think you're doing?"

He was pressing buttons on a cell phone. "Seeing if there's anything interesting in here."

"You stupid motherfucker!"

Duke never saw the punch coming, and his brain momentarily floated from its moorings. He rubbed his jaw. "Christ! What did you do that for?"

"You turned the dead guy's phone on."

"So?"

"So until now, they thought we were headed to Canada," said Vix, grabbing the cell off the floorboards and shutting it down. "By turning that thing on with the GPS, you just told them we're heading south! You've burned us!"

"I think you're overreacting."

Another sock in the jaw. Then Vix slapped the headrest in front of her.

"What the hell?" yelled the driver. "I'm in traffic here."

"Take the next exit! Head west!"

"That's not where we're going."

Another jolt to the headrest. "We are now! Just do it!"

If this were a classic old movie, a map would have appeared on the screen, with a red line moving left, explaining to the audience that the hapless crew had departed Interstate 95 and was jumping across the back roads from Raleigh to Charlotte until they reached Lookout Mountain south of Chattanooga.

"I don't know why we keep circling," said Mulch. "And don't you dare hit my headrest again!"

Vix withdrew her fist. "I've counted three trailheads up the mountain, each with a single car parked in the dirt. I'm waiting for dark. We need to switch cars because they know what we're driving, which wasn't that important until fuck-stick Duke bird-dogged them to us by turning on the phone."

"Why not just grab one of the cars now?"

"First, it's still light out," said Vix. "Second, some of these vehicles belong to day hikers. I want one from overnight campers. That way the car won't be reported stolen until at least tomorrow, if not days . . ."

The sun finally set, and darkness fell early as it does in the mountainous woods. The gang continued on, rolling slowly over the hills.

"There!" Vix pointed at a Tahoe backed into a small gravel parking area out of view from the winding road. Mulch hit the brakes. The Tahoe had decals from a university.

Criminals possess a certain skill set that dumbfounds the general public. All innately seem to be able to access vehicles without the keys. Mulch instantly opened the driver's door and disabled the blaring alarm. Out came a screwdriver, and the ignition roared to life. Then he found spare keys over the visor.

They had just finished transferring all their belongings to the sports vehicle. "Wait!" said Vix. "Quiet!"

"What is it?" asked Mulch.

"Someone's coming . . ."

The gang went silent as distant chatter could be heard through the trees. The voices grew louder until a pair of college guys with flannel shirts and backpacks rounded the final incline down into the trailhead's parking patch. *"How did you misjudge our hiking time?" "You're the one with the map." "Another hour and we'd have been stranded without a tent for the night . . ."*

Then the Tahoe came into view and they suddenly stopped. Their logical reaction: "What the hell are you doing with our car?"

"We noticed it was unlocked," said Vix. "Just securing it. You need to be more careful."

"No you weren't!" The guys ran the final yards despite the weight of their packs. "You were stealing it!"

One of the things higher education doesn't teach is how to read certain people who were never cut out for dorm life. Vix's brain worked like a computer, and the binary data had been tabulated before the hikers even came into view.

The students dropped their packs. "You're in trouble now!" The other pulled out a cell phone, just in time for its screen to be splattered with blood as Vix opened up with a fusillade from a nine-millimeter. The rest of the gang jumped back, startled again at her casual leap to maximum violence.

Vix ejected the gun's empty clip and slammed home a new one, racking the slide to chamber a live round. She calmly strolled to where the hikers had fallen. One stared up at the forest canopy with empty eyes. The other was mortally wounded but still gasping.

"Still think you're smarter than me, college boy?"

Blam! Blam! Blam! Blam! Blam!

The body jolted as each slug slammed the torso, until the second hiker had the same eternally confused look in his eyes as his friend. Vix stared down through the gun smoke. "Mother*fuckers*!"

She looked back toward the Tahoe and three guys with no words.

"Hey, you stupids!" yelled Vix. "Are you just going to stand there or help get these lumps of shit off the trail?"

They swung into service, grabbing ankles. Soon the bodies were far enough into the brush.

"Should we cover them with something?" asked Mulch.

"No, they won't be found until people notice the vultures." Then Vix pointed at a wrist. "Duke, get that watch. It's worth something."

He bent down, and Vix unceremoniously put two bullets in the back of his head.

Now the other guys couldn't even be coy about their reactions.

"Jesus!" said Weezer.

"What did you do that for?" said Mulch.

"Playing with cell phones." She opened the Tahoe's passenger door. "Let's get a move on."

They headed west, Vix sitting up front with Mulch in the Tahoe, and Weezer following in their own car. Across the river near Jasper, Tennessee, the woods grew thick, and Vix spotted an abandoned logging road with an unlocked gate. She told Mulch to stop.

Weezer had his instructions. He drove their car a short distance up the road until taking a turnoff that dwindled until there was no road at all and the car got stuck. It took him a half hour to hike back to the main road.

The Tahoe was gone.

That was the plan.

Vix couldn't just sit on the side of the street where they were ditching an evidence vehicle, out in the vulnerable open, waiting for the police to come by and question them about their intentions. So they circled around, repeatedly passing the unlocked gate until Weezer finally reappeared. He climbed in the back seat.

Vix pointed. "Head west."

"But that's the wrong way."

"Just head west!"

When Vix's rage wasn't acting against her own self-interests, she was actually quite cunning. A few miles after driving away from the logging road and merging onto a proper state highway, she grabbed the cell phone that had gotten Duke killed. She turned it on.

Mulch glanced over from the driver's seat. "What are you doing that for?"

"Fixing Duke's fuckup."

"But I thought you didn't want the cops to know our position."

Vix allowed the phone to sit on her lap as the GPS pinged. "That was before they knew we were heading south. Now I want them to know . . ." She allowed it to remain on until it had pinged off at least three microwave towers, establishing their fresh vector. She popped the battery from the phone and slung it out the window, scattering smartphone pieces on the pavement.

"Why did you just turn it on and ditch it out in the woods back there?" asked Mulch.

"Because I needed to create a new pattern of movement. When they eventually find the old car, they'll know we switched vehicles. This way, the final signals from the phone will put us where we want them to search, heading west. We're on a long-haul high-way, and they'll be looking for us from Nashville to Memphis . . . Turn around . . ."

The Tahoe left the highway and backtracked east across isolated country roads until they eventually heard the rumble and saw the headlights of trucks crossing the overpass of an upcoming interstate.

"What now?" asked Mulch.

"Take the first ramp."

The Tahoe accelerated and merged with evening traffic, flowing southeast, away from their former swath of brainlessness.

They put up for the night on the south side of Atlanta, in the landing pattern of Hartsfield. The next morning, the first red-eyes arriving from L.A. awoke the guys before six. Vix was already up. In more than one way. She inhaled and capped a coke tooter. "Let's hit the road!"

Weezer covered his head with a pillow. "Why so early?"

"Because we have to make up for lost time."

"We're now on some kind of schedule?"

Vix spun. "Mulch!"

Mulch understood his new role: "Weezer, for God's sake, just do whatever she says."

They opened the Tahoe's doors. "Now, no more delays!" said Vix, taking a last toot for the road. "Or I swear to fucking God—"

That's why the guys were more than a little unnerved less than an hour later as they stood on the shoulder of southbound I-75 next to a steaming radiator.

Weezer whispered out the side of his mouth. "Does she have the gun on her?"

"It's safest to assume that she does."

Vix continued stomping up and down the edge of the highway until the tow truck arrived. She sat on Mulch's lap as they crammed in the cab and drove to an auto repair shop.

"It's closed!" said Vix.

"It's Sunday," said the tow driver.

"What are we supposed to do?"

"There are shops open back in Atlanta, but you don't want to know how much that tow will cost." The driver nodded toward the neighboring budget motel. "That place is cheaper. The mechanics will be open bright and early tomorrow morning."

A Tennessee State Trooper was the first on the scene.

It was a general welfare check, called in by the families of the two backpackers.

The hikers were experienced and cautious, using the buddy system and always leaving detailed itineraries with their relatives. So when the guys hadn't arrived home as scheduled the previous night—and weren't answering their phones—their folks knew exactly where to send the authorities.

The trooper had arrived at the appointed trailhead. He radioed back to the station that there was no Tahoe. Which was good news and bad. It meant the students had probably made it down out of the mountains and weren't in some kind of jam up on a ridge. But where had they driven off to?

Twenty-four hours had passed, but they were college kids, after all. If the pair had been missing female students, it would have drawn more concern. But these were guys. Police constantly received such calls, and the students usually turned up at a friend's house where they had slept it off, or made a spontaneous beeline to the Redneck Riviera to funnel beers.

Twenty-four hours became forty-eight, and the police performed the standard due diligence of tracking their digital footprints. No ATM withdrawals, no texting, no motel receipts from Panama City, nothing . . .

As the saying goes, when you plan a crime, fifty things can go wrong, and if you can think of twenty-five, you're a genius.

And Vix was the one doing the thinking.

The authorities wouldn't have to wait for the vultures. Vix had been so obsessed with Duke activating that stupid cell, she never thought to search the hikers for *their* phones, and the batteries had lasted another six hours after the shooting.

The second night, the authorities were back at the trailhead that the families had reported. Thanks to help from the cell phone company, they triangulated the hikers' last position to an area the size of a living room. A search team began bushwhacking off the trail with huge flashlights that split an eerie fog. They quickly found the unfortunate pair slumped over each other. Then a weird thing: There was an extra body.

Fingerprints were taken, as well as photos for facial recognition. It got an immediate hit for one Duke Dupuis, freshly wanted in connection with a murder in New Hampshire. The Tennessee Bureau of Investigation was already on-site, but now it was a multi-state affair, which brought in the FBI.

The lead agent on the case, by the name of Branch, arrived with his team in the rain. Luckily the local sheriff had been able to make cast impressions of the Tahoe's tracks before the clouds cut loose.

The various jurisdictions shook hands.

"What are you thinking?" asked the ranking sheriff's deputy.

"We were looking for five people trying to cross into Canada," said Branch. "That was before the first victim's phone was activated down here. Which means they're not too smart."

"What about the hikers?"

"Targets of opportunity when the gang was trying to change vehicles because they knew we had their plates," said Branch. "Which means they're desperate . . . and dangerous."

"Where do you think they are?" asked the deputy.

The rain let up, and Branch checked a notepad. "They turned the initial victim's phone back on a second time about twenty miles west of here, I'm guessing in the Tahoe, somewhere on the highway near a place called Jasper."

"That would put them toward Memphis," said a lieutenant with the highway patrol.

Branch stood in thought.

"You don't seem too sure," said the lieutenant.

"I'd definitely be watching the roads toward Memphis, but they already backtracked on us once near the Canadian line. And when they activated that victim's phone the first time, it was only for a few seconds. They must have realized their mistake."

"So when they turned it on the second time outside Jasper?" asked the lieutenant.

"Unless they're really stupid, that was intentional." Branch turned around and stared toward a reddish moon that had just risen over the dark road. "I'd put my money on Atlanta and Seventy-Five south."

"Why not Eighty-Five toward Mobile?" said the deputy.

"Seriously doubt it," said Branch. "I've seen enough of these wild fugitive runs that hurtle toward a bad ending."

"Which means?"

"For some reason, they always head to Florida."

Chapter 24

PELICAN BAY

A purple curtain of sky shrouded the horizon as a typical afternoon storm approached from the south. The dark backdrop brightened the almost fluorescent turquoise water in the foreground, where the sun still shined until it soon wouldn't.

A telephoto lens aimed off a fourth-floor balcony toward the incoming fishing boats with the tall, shiny tuna towers trying to beat the weather back to safe harbor.

Click, click, click.

Serge heard the sliding glass door open behind him with some commotion.

"Coleman, what kind of misadventure now?"

"I was trying to get this thing onto the balcony when it just came alive."

Serge observed his buddy wrestling with an orange collapsible canvas chair that soccer moms use. Coleman had somehow uncollapsed it as he tried to exit the living room, and he now struggled with the chair as if trying to pull an open umbrella out of a telephone booth.

"Here," said Serge. "Let me help you with that before we no longer have a chair or glass doors."

He casually guided his pal onto the balcony with room to spare. "There you go." Coleman promptly tumbled backward and rolled, tangled in the chair again, fighting it, bonking his head on the concrete balcony wall.

Serge calmly watched the fiasco from his own folding chair. Coleman finally freed a stuck arm and threw the chair off him in a tangled pile. Serge grabbed it and set it back up in its intended configuration. "Ready to sit?"

"Not yet."

Coleman ran back inside and returned with a giant tumbler of rum mixed with pineapple and banana juice. "These chairs have drink holders!"

The beverage sloshed, and Serge quickly turned to shield his camera. "Watch it! I've got technology here!"

"Sorry." Coleman sucked through a straw.

"Just don't move for a while." *Click, click, click.* He set down the camera and picked up binoculars. "This is the first chance I've had to truly immerse myself in the Art of Slowing Down. Until now we've been dealing with drug addicts and SWAT teams, which is your basic background noise in Florida. But here we finally are, home sweet home."

"You sure love this balcony. I've never seen you stay still for so long."

"Balconies are key to the mission." Binoculars scanned the horizon. "We couldn't be more embedded in nature, and I've been up since before sunrise picking out the rhythms since the tide changed. See that flock of pelicans flying right to left a quarter mile away?"

"Is that what those are?"

"They're about to turn straight toward us and fly directly over our balcony."

"How do you know?"

"I learned their flight pattern this morning." Serge lowered the binoculars. "They follow the shore and for some reason enjoy the updraft against our building."

Coleman fired up a fatty and raised his head toward the flock. "Far out. You were right."

"See that other bird with a white breast coming at us? That's an osprey."

"How do you know this far away?"

"Because it came off a special platform on top of that telephone pole in the distance that was constructed by conservationists. There's a mating pair on top. They've been swooping down over the mangroves to snatch sprigs for their nest."

Coleman chugged his drink. "Now he's flying offshore."

"Must be lunchtime. Dig! He'll pull up into a stall, then dive-bomb the water."

They stopped to watch. *Splash.*

"Damn," said Coleman. "He caught a fish!"

"You see those bumps rippling through the water near the mangrove roots?" asked Serge. "Crocodile, immature one about four feet, which means mama croc is nearby."

Coleman nodded. "Alligators are cool!"

"No, those are freshwater. This is salt," said Serge. "The Upper Keys are one of the country's only habitats for the American crocodile."

"I'm really high now."

"Keep those flash-sector reports rolling in." Serge raised the binoculars again and narrated as he turned the focus knob, drawing the view from the far edge of the horizon to the water's edge: "Cruise ships, cargo ships, military ships, shrimp boats with all the riggings extended, yachts, bow riders, skiffs, canoes, kayaks, paddleboards, healthy-sized fish leaping from the water, meaning even bigger fish are just behind, herons and egrets stalking the shallows, iguanas sunning themselves on coral boulders. With this balcony, nature has come to us! . . ."

"I need more rum." Coleman headed inside.

". . . Not to mention at night! Out here in the remote Keys, the lack of light pollution is legendary. I've been able to see more stars than I'd ever dreamed, plus the bands of the Milky Way and the elusive Southern Cross constellation. The other evening a harvest moon rose in glory over Meditation Point. And if that wasn't enough, I saw four meteors last night, including a fiery red one that flamed out just a few hundred yards off our railing here. Isn't that swell? . . . Coleman? . . ."

Coleman waddled back out the sliding door. "I'm here."

"Were you listening to what I said?"

"Sure, every word."

Serge stopped. "You've been walking around with that chair stuck to your butt?"

"Yeah? So?"

"Why not just pull it off?"

Coleman and the chair sat back down in unison. "Less work. Can we go to the liquor store?"

"Right after the storm. It'll be here soon, but won't last long."

They settled into respective tasks. Serge continued burning through his camera's memory card, and Coleman plowed into his substance supply. Such was their decades-long division of labor.

A half hour passed, and the wind picked up from the approaching gale.

Coleman sat amid pot ashes. "I'm now even higher. And a little drunk."

"Roger," said Serge. "The flash-sector readiness level has been elevated to hammered."

Suddenly, something gigantic, moving fast, flew right in front of the balcony. A large arc of green, blue and yellow nylon.

"Ahhh!" yelled Coleman, tipping over backward in his chair. "What the fuck was that?"

"A kite."

"I've never seen a kite like that before."

"Because it's for kiteboarding." Serge leaned over the balcony railing and pointed down. "There's a guy at the other end of the sail."

Coleman, chair still attached, bent over the rail. "It's like surfing."

"Except the ecstasy doesn't stop when the waves end," said Serge. "You just keep riding the wind as far as you want."

"That dude's really zooming!" Coleman stretched out an arm with a fortified tropical drink. "Look! He was just off our balcony, and now he's almost to the boat channel! . . ."

"Notice how his knees are bent like shock absorbers, skipping across the crests of the swells?"

"But isn't he worried about that storm coming in?" asked Coleman, his hair beginning to whip.

"He'd be more worried if there wasn't a storm," said Serge. "More wind. On a calm day, they just skim merrily along. But on an afternoon like this, anything's possible."

"Like what?"

"I've been studying this guy," said Serge. "I'll bet I know what's coming up."

"What?"

"Just watch."

The pair leaned intently. The distant surfer in a black-and-lime wetsuit deftly worked the twin controls in his hands, bringing the sail around strong, directly in line with the wind. After picking up serious velocity, he bent his knees more deeply than before. Then, at the precise moment, he raised the sail and pushed off.

"Holy cow!" said Coleman. "Look at him fly!"

"Amazing, isn't it?" said Serge. "He's catching some radical air."

"He's coming down now," said Coleman. "Perfect landing . . . But how's he going to get back?"

"That's the beauty of it," said Serge. "The really good guys and gals can expertly maneuver their kites and tack back against the wind."

"Wow! He's doing it," said Coleman. "But how did you know he was going to make that jump in the first place?"

"Like I said, I've been studying him."

"I don't follow."

"Another dividend from slowing down, with all the hours I've been spending on this balcony. Before you realize it, you're flowing to the rhythms of nature, as well as nature *lovers*, noticing a bunch of stuff you're not even trying to." He gestured at water splashing into the mangroves. "Some visitors have given renters a bad name, but I looked it up on the Internet last night. This particular place is all over the bulletin boards of nature athletes, one of their hidden little gems that they want to keep secret from the tiki-hut crowd. Something about how the deep crescent of the curved shoreline forms a cove with the thick jungle of vegetation toward the creek, creating the perfect air currents for windsurfers and these kite guys, not to mention the kayakers and paddleboarders who like to make their way out to our little mangrove Kalteux Key a few hundred yards offshore. Word's definitely out on their coconut telegraph that this is the perfect spot to drop anchor for a week, and I've been noticing more and more lugging their gear in from the parking lot to launch off of our coral point. I'm beginning to feel the whole electricity of this place tingling through my bones."

Coleman looked left toward their tiny, boulder-protected private beach. "Others are joining them with their sail things."

"Must have seen the storm from their balconies. They couldn't resist." Serge turned and opened the sliding door. "Neither can I."

Coleman followed him inside. "What are you going to do?"

"Take up kiteboarding."

"Do you know how?"

"Not yet." Serge left the unit and pressed a button in the elevator. "But how hard can it be? . . ."

Minutes later, they trudged across the white sand under a darkening sky.

A few of the more experienced surfers climbed into the water and pushed off from the point. Some of the others who had come down from their balconies looked out at the wind-raked waves and decided discretion was the better part of valor.

"Serge," said a panting Coleman, "it's looking pretty savage out there. You sure this is a good time for your first try?"

"The *best* time."

"What about taking lessons?"

"Lessons are a wise move for the general public," Serge said as he approached the nearest group of enthusiasts. "But for someone who wants to take it to the next level, it'll only force me to unlearn bad habits. With my binoculars from the balcony, I now know all the secret wrist moves from the finest . . ."

A lean young man stood in the sand near the point, holding his board and staring out to sea with indecision. Then he shook his head and turned around.

"Excuse me," said Serge. "Nice board."

"Thanks."

"How much?"

"It's not for sale," said the student from Arkansas.

Serge pulled out his wallet. "I don't want to buy it. I want to rent it. How much?"

"Not for rent, either."

"Good opening gambit." Serge began removing twenties. "There's a theoretical monetary tipping point where everything's negotiable. And you don't look like a communist. How much?"

A shake of the head. "Have a nice day."

"You're an admirable opponent." The wallet started producing hundreds. "How much?"

The sight of all the currency began itching at the young man. "Do you even know how to sail?"

Coleman drained a beer. "He doesn't."

"Then that settles it," said the man. "It's way too wild out there today for someone who doesn't know how."

"What?" Serge glanced over at the waves. "That's a walk in the park for me."

"But your friend said you can't sail."

"Him?" said Serge. "Ha! Ha! Ha! Ha! Coleman is an idiomatic fiend with the lexicon. By saying I don't know how, he really means I'm super bad on the waves, or I've got some righteously sick moves. See how that works? The opposite is the truth. Get it? I'm not literally sick. I don't have a fever. Actually, I do have a fever, and the only prescription is renting your shit." Even more money appeared. "I'm a Christopher Walken fan. How much?"

They reached the tipping point.

"Okay, I guess . . . But what if you fuck up my board?"

"Here, hold this while I'm out there." Serge handed him the billfold. "Go ahead and look. There's a lot more money in there than any new board could cost. If anything happens, you'll be upgrading."

"You're going to just trust me with your wallet?"

"And I'll have your board," said Serge. "What other endgame do you envision except a benevolent prisoner exchange?"

The man opened the thick wallet and his eyes bugged. He quickly looked up. "What exactly do you do?"

"A little of this and that, which I can't disclose for your own legal protection. But I've had my eye on a more steady position now that I'm slowing down: non-attorney spokesperson. I watch a lot of TV, and it's a burgeoning field. Plus I'm a cinch to nail the interview: 'Have you ever been to law school?' 'Not a day. Which one of those is my new desk?'"

The man just stared.

Serge tapped a foot and swept an impatient arm at the waves. "Come on, it's now or never. We got a deal? . . ."

Moments later, Coleman and the young college students stood next to each other on the tip of Meditation Point, watching Serge paddle out into the daunting storm and prepare to raise the kite sail. The sky was almost completely black three hours before sunset, and three miles out, a wall of stinging rain could be seen moving in fast.

The student turned to Coleman. "You know your friend's crazy."

"You have no idea."

"I meant taking crazy risks."

"No, he really is insane," said Coleman.

"But he's your friend."

"He'll admit it to you himself." Coleman stuck his head inside the neck of his shirt to light a joint, then popped his head back out—"Shit"—and watched the joint fly away. "He's actually proud of it. Says it gives him an edge on the others. The police want to ask him about it."

The student looked at Coleman again without speaking.

Other boarding enthusiasts on the beach began to join them on the point.

"Is he nuts?" asked a Vanderbilt sophomore.

"Yep," said Coleman.

"I knew this was a bad idea," said the Razorback senior.

"Look!" said someone on the right side of the group. "He's got the kite up! He's killing it!"

"He'd better lean back and keep it low."

"He is!"

"Damn! How fast do you think he's going?"

"Faster than any of us on this trip!"

"That's one sick run!"

"Wait . . . He's heading straight toward that mangrove islet out by Tavernier Channel . . ."

"Kalteux Key! . . ."

"Why isn't he turning? He's got a stout starboard wind . . ."

"He will. Give him time. He's too good to have gotten this far in this weather just to blow it now . . ."

"He's still not turning! What's he waiting for? . . ."

"Look at his wrists on the controls! He's doing something else instead! . . ."

"He's not about to try what I think he is . . ."

"Of course not. That would be sure suicide . . ."

They all watched in a group, collectively holding their breath.

"Oh my God! He *is* trying it!"

The gang went silent. Serge rocketed east in a low crouch, spraying an atomized mist behind the board, before finally springing up at the last moment just before the first sandbar.

Jaws went slack on the beach as Serge, the board and the kite sailed high up into the bruising sky—*"Yabba-dabba-doooooo!"*—and kept on going.

"Look at all that air he's catching! . . ."

"He's trying to jump the whole island! . . ."

"He'll never make it! . . ."

"He's making it! . . ."

"Nobody would ever believe it! . . ."

"I hope somebody's filming this! . . ."

"I'm getting it all! Streaming live on our channel! . . ."

They continued watching the improbable, triumphant leap. The onshore wind carried a tiny voice from the sky in the distance—*"Oops. Fuck."*—before three things went three different directions: the board, the kite and Serge.

The gang covered their eyes in a chorus of painful groans.

Finally, hands came down. "Did he hit the island or the water?"

"Doesn't matter. The sea's only a foot or two deep around Kalteux."

"Do we call an ambulance or the morgue?"

Another student with binoculars. "Unbelievable! He's okay! He must have fallen into the boating channel behind the island! ..."

An hour later, Serge's shoulders were red from all the slaps on the back from the students. A slashing rain had commenced, and they were all gathered below an overhang near the lobby.

"I will never forget that jump! ..."

"It's the stuff of legend! ..."

"You're already going viral on the net! ..."

Serge stared down. "But I didn't make it."

"Some of the best gigs are failures."

Serge just shook his head. "I still feel like that skier who pinwheels off the side of the ramp during the intro of ABC's *Wide World of Sports*."

"What?"

"Before your time ..." Serge finished counting out hundreds and placing them in a young man's hands. "Sorry about your board and kite. We square?"

"More than good. It was worth it just to see that," said the student. "What's next for you?"

"Something much more calm," said Serge. "Like the Snake River Canyon. Later ..."

Chapter 25

A FEW WEEKS EARLIER

A hazy red sun was about to set as the fishing boats cruised back in from the Straits of Florida. A visitor from South America stared out an upstairs bedroom window, watching the fleet as a formation of birds skimmed over the water. He finally turned away.

Another visitor in the room looked him over. "Cinco, why is your arm all scratched up?"

"Oh, this?" He twisted his forearm upward. "I went to a marina a few miles from here."

"What?" asked Mercado.

"It's Robbie's Marina, the famous local attraction," said Cinco. "If you're staying around here, you're supposed to go, like a law or something."

"For what?"

"The big thing at Robbie's is to buy a bucket of little fish to feed to much bigger fish called tarpon."

"You mean like to catch them? With a fishing pole?"

"No, you just give them away," said Cinco. "There's a big pen of tarpon by the dock. You feed them by hand. Everyone says it's fun."

"So the tarpon scratched up your arm?"

"No, that was the pelicans."

Mercado just stared.

"Apparently the local pelicans have figured out the program," said Cinco. "As soon as you're about to feed the tarpon, all these pelicans swarm out of nowhere. One of them swallowed my arm up to the elbow."

"What did you do?"

"What else? Gave him the fish," said Cinco. "If you've ever felt the back of a pelican's throat, you'll do anything to make it stop. And that's when my bucket of fish flew in the air and all hell broke loose."

"And that's supposed to be fun?"

Cinco shook his head. "I didn't realize that the man with the stick was on break."

Mercado closed his eyes momentarily, then opened them. "I know I will regret continuing this conversation, but . . . the man with the stick?"

"I was wondering why all the other customers were waiting in back with their buckets, and I was the only one walking out to the pen with a fish in my hand," said Cinco. "Then after I pulled my arm out of the pelican, the man with the stick came back and started banging it around."

"What for?"

"To keep the pelicans away while the other tourists fed the tarpon."

Mercado chuckled. "So you wasted money on a whole bucket of fish and didn't get to feed a single tarpon?"

"No, I went back and bought another bucket and finally got to feed them," said Cinco. "Those fish are gigantic and fast! Their heads explode out of the water and snatch the little fish from your hand before you realize it. Got the end of one of my fingertips. Scared the living shit out of me."

"Everyone says this is a good thing?"

Cinco nodded. "I wanted to learn about America."

"What did you learn?"

"That a guy fighting off pelicans with a stick while you hand-feed scary fish is their best idea around here of a great time."

"And this makes sense to you?"

"No, it was one of the craziest things I've ever seen," said Cinco. "But the Americans seem to know what they're doing, so it must be me. I think I'll go back tomorrow."

The sound of snoring.

Cinco walked over to join Mercado on the side of a bed. "How is your father?"

"Sleeping," said Mercado.

"I did that thing you said."

"And?"

Cinco tilted his head. "Other room."

They went into a smaller, empty bedroom, and Cinco pulled out a notepad. "The father is quite old now, former charter boat captain."

"I'm assuming his boat was moored at that old dock we used to visit," said Mercado. "Are you sure it's him?"

"Correct."

"What was the significance of the boat's name on the stern?" asked Mercado. "*Julie*?"

"I'm getting to that." Cinco flipped a page. "It's his daughter . . ."

Cinco read through the rest of the notes, ending with an address.

"Let's take a ride," said Mercado.

They arrived in a parking lot on Upper Matecumbe Key.

"What's with all the mermaids painted on the front of the building?" asked Mercado.

"It's a hospice," said Cinco. "Long-term care, too. Kids, mainly."

"She works here?"

"Volunteers."

"What is she, like some kind of saint?"

"Some kind," said Cinco, handing him a black-and-white surveillance photo. "At least that's the word around town. I've gotten to chat with a few of her colleagues at a nearby lunch counter. Something called Mangrove Mike's, whatever that is."

"She looks so innocent," said Mercado. "Did you find out what she does in her spare time?"

Cinco flipped a page in his notebook. "Almost nothing. Just takes care of her sick dad and leaves only to volunteer here and grocery shop."

"That doesn't leave much room to set up a chance meeting," said Mercado.

"Still working on that."

Mercado lowered his head. "Can this make me feel any worse?"

"I know what you must be going through about this."

"It's simply something that has to be done."

"I know, I know," said Cinco. "Just give me the orders."

Mercado leaned toward the windshield. The door on the front of the building had opened. "Is that her?"

"That's Julie," said Cinco.

"Home address?" asked Mercado.

"Getting close," said Cinco. "Tried following her after work, but this traffic."

"Okay, take me back to the house," said Mercado. "Keep doing what I said, and let me know if you find out that thing . . ."

THE NEXT DAY

Cinco climbed a floating staircase. He walked over to Mercado and whispered in his ear.

Mercado slowly began to nod and pointed toward an empty room. They went inside and closed the door.

Cinco flipped open his notepad. "From the public records, it looks like she's her father's only relative. At least the only one in the picture."

"Mother?"

Cinco shook his head.

"Address?"

"Just the father's. I got it from the county property appraiser, not too far from here."

"That would make sense," said Mercado. "Being a fisherman with a boat docked at Upper Matecumbe. You said Julie takes care of him. Maybe we could find her there?"

Cinco shook his head again. "Drove by a few times, but it looks empty. A pile of junk mail on the porch. I think it's a rental— between renters."

"Julie has to live *somewhere*," said Mercado.

"I was thinking an apartment, but that would have shown up in public utility records," said Cinco. "Sorry I couldn't have been more help."

"It's not your fault," said Mercado. "Let me know if you find out any more."

Cinco nodded and flipped his pad closed. But he stayed in place.

Mercado looked up. "What?"

"No disrespect, but this seems like a lot of work," said Cinco. "I don't see the payoff."

"From time to time in life, the most important things have no obvious payoff," said Mercado. "You'll understand shortly."

Cinco nodded again. "You've always been the smartest person in any room. I guess I just don't see bigger pictures the way you do."

Mercado had shifted his attention to the international news section of the *Herald*. "Get back with me when you have more."

Cinco nodded respectfully and left the room . . .

A few days later, Mercado arrived by helicopter. Before seeing his father, he ducked in a guest bedroom for another private meeting.

"Get ready to be happy." Cinco opened his notepad. "Her dad moved. I didn't catch it at first for a couple reasons. One, it's in the name of a local attorney, heaven knows why, which clouds it from a public records search."

"What's the second reason?"

"It's an Airstream trailer," said Cinco. "Who downsizes like that? He had a nice stucco stilt house near the ocean."

"Then how'd you find it?"

"I followed Julie one evening last week and she turned down a narrow row of mobile homes, and I thought, 'This can't be it. Must be visiting friends.' Then I got blocked by someone pulling out a boat. But last night she went down the same tiny street and went inside an Airstream and stayed all night."

Mercado stood up. "That's great. Let's go."

"I have more good news," said Cinco.

Mercado sat back down. "I'm all ears."

"The trailers are packed like sardines. Too many prying eyes," said Cinco. "And her defenses will go up if you just knock on her door."

"But we can't just forget about this."

"I have a better idea," said Cinco. "Remember you asking me about her habits and if we might be able to arrange a chance meeting?"

"I'd almost forgotten about that."

"Well, I have your chance meeting," said Cinco. "Pure luck. I was back at that lunch counter today, and her colleagues were talking about their weekly night out where they're all in public."

"That is lucky."

"No." Cinco shook his head. "I already knew about the night out. I hear them talking about it every other time they're there. Loud too. The thing is, they're frustrated they can almost never drag Julie out with them, because she has to get home to her dad. They're worried about her social life. So one of them offered to stay with the father."

Mercado's eyebrows tightened. "What's all this mean?"

"Julie will be joining them in an excellent place for a chance meeting," said Cinco. "I've already checked it out. Totally casual beach bar, except it's dockside. Mostly stools, and other people wandering with drinks behind the stools. The perfect spot for strangers to strike up conversations all night and nobody would think twice. And stone crabs for three bucks."

"What's the name of this place?"

"The Mar Bar." Cinco extended an arm east. "Just up the Old Road. We don't even have to get back on the highway."

Mercado smiled and patted Cinco on the back. "Okay, here's the plan: None of the other guys can *know* there's a plan. When the time comes, I'll start acting stressed, and pound a table and say I need a drink, and then you say, 'I know exactly where to go.'"

"Good plan," said Cinco. He didn't move.

"I see that look in your eyes again."

"What look?"

"That knowing look," said Mercado. "I always assumed you knew the story."

"I heard rumors, but nobody was supposed to talk about it."

Mercado turned his gaze down the stairs. "What about the other guys?"

Cinco shook his head again. "It was so long ago, and there's a lot of turnover in this business. I'm absolutely sure none of them has any idea."

"Keep it that way." Mercado headed for the stairs. "Now I have to prepare to accidentally bump into someone."

Chapter 26

BACK TO THE PRESENT

A Ford Galaxie crested the modest bridge at Whale Harbor.

"Coleman, stop scratching your arm. You're only going to make it worse."

Coleman kept scratching. "Where did all those fucking pelicans come from? I touched the back of one of their throats. That's not good when you're high."

"I told you to wait for the guy with the stick."

"Why did we have to feed those big fish by hand anyway?"

"Because it's loads of fun," said Serge. "I know what I'm doing."

The Galaxie crossed the Snake Creek Bridge onto Plantation Key.

"Serge, what's that piece of paper on the steering wheel?"

"My Pump the Brakes to-do list." A pen made a mark in a square. "Buy sailfish in hardware store: check! Get five rolls of pennies from bank for trash chute: check! Off-road mag wheels for my personal condo shopping cart: check! . . . What am I missing?" He glanced at the needle on the gas gauge. "Yikes, we're below empty. Time to tank up."

"Food," said Coleman.

Serge angled the car off the highway. "Don't get your hopes up. This is one of those barely functional gas stations that doesn't look like it has a convenience store or even room to walk around. No garish Budweiser sign in the window. Probably just a rack of windshield wiper blades and expired pork rinds. And do you know how hard it is to expire those fuckers? It's nearly impossible, but off-brand Florida gas stations have perfected the improbable."

As soon as Serge stepped inside, he froze like he was seeing a burning bush.

"What is it?" asked Coleman.

"I am so going to love this neighborhood! We've found our emergency go-to spot," said Serge. "I had zero expectations out there at the pumps. That's why I never would have seen this coming."

"What?"

"Check it out: an authentic Cuban lunch counter! And just around the corner from our new pad. That increases property value!"

"Look at all the people crammed in here," said Coleman. "And only three tiny tables wedged in between the motor oil and fishing lures. Guess most are ordering to-go stuff."

"Word's gotten out, but not among the tourists because all they see is a generic gas station," said Serge. "We need to keep it that way or the waiting lines will make me act inappropriate." He looked around. "You've got local families, construction workers, high school kids, a sheriff's deputy, an electrician." He ran over to peer into a glass display case. "And it's not just any lunch counter, but the full Monty . . ."—pointing at the various shelves—"They have everything: *croquetas de pescado y pollo, empanadas de carne, tequeños de queso, papa rellena . . .*"

"Looks like a crab cake."

"It does, but it's a potato ball with a ground beef core. And *pandebono,* more empanadas, Colombian and chorizo. And for beverage, a full line of Jarritos Latin sodas, from mandarin to pineapple, bottled the old way." He grabbed a postcard menu off the counter. "This doesn't list everything on the big wall menu. I'll need photos to remember the selection so I can make my decisions at home before coming here, or I'll end up in front of this case paralyzed by choice shock." *Click, click, click.* "Coleman . . . Coleman? . . ."

"Right here." He waddled back from the coolers with a beer suitcase. "What's the name of this place anyway?"

"From the signage, it looks like it has two names: Islamorada Latin Café, and Café 90, which I'm guessing is from the mile marker across the street, just like the Marker 88 seafood restaurant two miles down the road." Serge turned with his camera. "And I haven't even gotten to the chalk menu board of specials up on that other wall . . ." *Click, click, click . . .*

"Serge." Coleman pointed on top of the far end of the counter. "What's that?"

"Oh my God! I didn't notice because I was riveted on the food." He stepped back to widen the camera frame. "They're not simply phoning in the cultural experience with just food. That's a metallic sculpture of a rooster, like they'd decorate these family joints back in the old country!" *Click.* "The rooster's still not in the frame." He backed up farther, bumping into a table. "Sorry." *Click . . .*

Coleman paid for the beer. "So what are you going to get?"

"We're leaving."

"But you were so excited about the food."

"*Too* excited." Serge pocketed his phone. "We need to regroup, so I can graph a grid of their cuisine on an X-Y plane to plot the perfect dinner combo. Come on . . ."

They climbed back in the Galaxie, and Serge left the door

open as he got out a protractor and began to work on his graph. Engrossed in thought—

Bam!

The protractor went flying. "What the fuck was that!"

Coleman took the unlit joint out of his mouth. "Sounded like someone slammed their fist down on our trunk."

Serge checked the rearview. "Shit!" A large, muscular Monroe County sheriff's deputy in a dark green uniform walked up along the side of the car. "We're screwed!"

Serge's eyes flickered as his mind spun through a film reel of everything in the last few minutes that could have gotten him caught. "I can't believe it ends like this! And right after the Rooster of Happiness. Yet I can't think of anything that I overlooked that would have attracted the law? Maybe it was something Coleman did . . ." He turned. "Ahhhh! Coleman, eat the joint! A deputy is almost at my door."

Coleman shoved it in his mouth as the deputy leaned down toward the driver.

"Good afternoon," said Serge.

"Sir, if I may ask. What was your business taking all those photos in the café?"

"Was that wrong?" asked Serge. "Was my behavior coloring outside the lines again?"

"Technically, they are open for business to the public, so it's legal to take photos during regular hours," said the deputy. "But you were taking so many that I'd be remiss not to ask why."

"I wanted photos of the menu, so I could make charts and decide what to order next time I came in."

"Photographing the menu would be understandable, but if that were the case, you'd just stand at the counter and take a picture. You were backing way up, bumping into tables and taking way too many photos and too far away than a menu would explain."

Serge stared down at his lap. In a sheepish voice: "I wanted the rooster in the photo."

"The roost— What?"

Serge looked up with a glint in his eye. "You see, I just moved down here and I'm so jazzed to join you good people! My third eye is so centered! The Old Road, this café, the Nautical Flea Market, the tiny Ace Hardware up the street with crab traps and mounted fish, and they have a photo from *Miami Vice* on the wall . . ." He pulled out his camera to display a photo. "See? The whole cast signed it. Where else can you find that next to the hex wrenches?"

"Oh." The deputy's demeanor began to swing. "So you're not just passing through. You live in Islamorada now?"

Serge nodded gleefully. "And we're going to the Coral Shores High School football game tonight."

"You know students or families there?"

"Not yet," said Serge. "That's why we're getting tickets. You have to support the community. Go Hurricanes!"

"Where are you living?"

"We're going condo. That place around the corner called Pelican Bay." Serge held a hand discreetly to the side of his mouth and lowered his voice. "I'm guessing nobody told them that that's the name of a supermax prison in California."

The deputy grinned in return. "I had the same thought . . . Is your friend all right? He's hacking on something and drooling."

"Accept what you can't change, right?"

"Anyway . . ." The deputy extended a hand to shake. "I'm Deke. Welcome to the neighborhood. Probably be seeing you around."

"Probably."

The deputy walked away, and Serge fell back with relief in the driver's seat. "Jesus, was that close."

Coleman spit the contents of his mouth into his hands. "Give me more warning next time. What now?"

"Shop for the condo! . . ."

Fifteen minutes later, Serge and Coleman left an auto supply store carrying fog lights for their personal shopping cart, and put them in the shopping cart.

Serge's eyes bore down like lasers. His fingers manically tapped the countertop.

The woman on the other side waited with the smile of eternal patience. Wearing a pink Café 90 shirt. "Have you decided what you want to order?"

"Yes," said Serge, "but I can't buy everything. That's the crisis. Heck with it. People are waiting behind me. I'll design my own sampler plate: one of each meat turnover in the glass case."

"Will this be to go?"

"Nope," said Serge. "Today I'm going to take root at one of your three tiny tables and enjoy the eclectic parade of humanity patronizing this fine slice of the old ways. Did I tell you how much the metallic rooster puts me over the moon?"

"A few times."

"There's no such thing as too much positive reinforcement." Serge stepped back. "I'll wait over here . . ."

They finally called his name, and Serge skipped to the counter. He grabbed his Styrofoam lunch container and turned around. "Come on, Coleman!"

"But, Serge, all the tables are taken."

"That they are. I guess it will be takeout after all—"

Suddenly: "Serge!" A muscular arm was waving them over.

"Deputy Deke!" said Serge. "I didn't recognize you in your civvies."

"Day off." Deke was finishing a thimble-size cup of Cuban espresso. "So how are you liking our little island community?"

"The opposite of buyer's remorse!" said Serge. "It gets better every minute. I went through a whole roll of pennies this morning at the trash chute."

The deputy smiled and stood. "I was just leaving, so you can have my table."

"But someone else is still sitting at it."

"Doesn't matter down here. If chairs are available, you sit. That's how we get to know our neighbors." Deke smiled again. "I'd like to introduce you to someone . . . Serge, this is my old friend Julie. Julie, this is my new friend Serge."

Serge nodded respectfully. "Pleasure to meet . . . Are you sure we won't be bothering you?"

"It's a great day," said Julie. "What could you do to bother me?"

Crash.

Coleman knocked over a chair, then rolled over the top of it and into the legs of other customers waiting in line, taking two of them down like bowling pins.

Serge sighed. "You may want to reconsider your answer."

Julie chewed a bite of sweet plantains and pulled out the chair next to hers. "Have a seat before your stuff gets cold."

"That's mighty neighborly," said Serge. He stopped to take stock of the new acquaintance. No makeup, straight black hair, loose blue jeans and a shirt with a cartoon design of children dancing. Below the kids was the name of an establishment.

"Couldn't help but notice your T-shirt," said Serge. "You work at a hospice and long-term-care place?"

"Used to, full-time," said the woman. "Technically I just volunteer now."

"What stopped you, I mean, if I'm not being nosy, which I am."

"No sweat," said the woman. "My dad's health. I split my time now between him and the kids."

"That's awfully noble." He extended a hand. "My name's Serge."

"Deke just told me."

"If I may probe further," said Serge. "Hospice is tough enough, but children—that's got to be difficult."

"There's a saying," said Julie. "The words 'pediatric' and 'oncology' should never go together, but it's life. I'm just lucky I found what I want to do. Wish I could do more."

"Specifically?"

"Resources," said Julie. "The care facility I work at is strapped.

We like to do things for the kids to make them happy, take them out places for field trips, but it's money we don't have."

"What about those foundations that make children's dreams come true?" asked Serge.

"We've gotten some in the past, but it's few and far between. There are a lot of worthy outfits vying for the same money," said Julie. "Luckily we live in the Keys, where there's a lot of free enjoyment that really lights up those little faces. Snorkeling and fishing off the beach. The trails at the state parks. Climbing the lighthouse in Key West. Those places always waive admission for us. But mainly it's just the walls of the facility for weeks on end. We read books from the library, and do crafts, and have firefighters and police officers visit for show-and-tell."

"Sounds like you're doing your best," said Serge.

Julie nodded. "It's amazing being around these kids. Despite everything they're facing, they remain so relentlessly happy that it touches you. It's beyond bittersweet."

"I know what you mean," said Serge. "Obviously not to the degree you do, but a while back I was on an outing with some kids like that, and I wanted to simultaneously laugh and cry."

She put her fork down. "What was it?"

"I had this young reporter friend at a newspaper," said Serge. "His name was Reevis. You don't know him, not that you'd have any reason to. Anyway, he had this one feature assignment and said I could come along. So we drove down to the Sarasota Bradenton airport, where one of the big airlines had donated some aircraft time. Me and Reevis boarded, and then a bus arrived, carrying all these cute kids with no hair, and they came bounding down the aisle bursting with joy. It amazed me how many had never even been on a plane. The plan was for the jet to taxi around the runways, while the pilot narrated like they were actually flying. Personally I think it's okay to lie in a case like that. The kids buckle in, and we're rolling around the tarmac. *'We've ascended to thirty thousand and the sky looks clear.'* All the children are shrieking and giggling, and total disclosure: I was shrieking and giggling, too. Planes are my weakness. I always like to pretend, and this time I was an aborigine from deepest, darkest Borneo who'd never seen the White Man, let alone a plane, and for some unknown reason I'm in one now—I didn't flesh out that part of the fantasy—and I'm disoriented, jabbering like an idiot: 'What is this strange tube I'm in? Why are the gods making the trees outside go by so fast? And how did the gods get peanuts inside this shiny packet? The lack of legroom is freaking me out! I must call on the gods: Help, Help! My knees are uncomfortable!' The kids got a kick out of it! See, that's one of the things you need to know: People either love flying with me or hate it. No middle ground."

"I'll make a mental note," said Julie.

"I like to err on the side of too much data," said Serge. "You never know, do you? So the jet turns onto one of the bigger runways, and we're picking up speed and the kids are bonkers, and I'm looking out the window thinking, 'We're going way too fast for just some fun, make-believe laps around the airport.' And of all things, we actually take off! It was a surprise the airline had planned all along. The kids are losing their minds! And I'm still in character from Borneo: 'We have turned into the sacred birds! And my people never knew the sacred birds had beverage carts! . . .' What a great day."

"Why are you telling me all this?"

"I have complete admiration that you volunteer for the unfortunate children," said Serge. "You want to give the kids an experience they'll remember? An airplane is a can't-miss if you could swing it. I'd even be happy to come along and enhance the experience."

"I think we could leave that part out."

"I'd like to volunteer, too."

"For what?"

"At the care center. I want to be just like you," said Serge. "What's the point of life if you don't give back? I've tried volunteering before, picking up trash at state parks, handing out laundry detergent at dive motels to people who don't have exact change. But your plan seems more focused. When do I start?"

"I'm not sure it's the best—"

"But I'm great with kids, always making them laugh and I'm not even trying. In fact, I usually don't even know why they're giggling." Serge dabbed his mouth with a napkin. "As I always say, the laughter of children is the nectar of the universe. I have no idea what that means. So, we're good? Right? On the same page? In sync? With the program?"

"What—?"

"Damn!" Serge looked at his plate. "Got to talking so much and completely forgot about my food, and now my empanadas are cold like the other times." He stood. "I'll just get a to-go box and nuke these back at the condo. Maybe I'll see you around town."

"Maybe."

Serge and Coleman left, and Julie looked down at her food, blinking hard a few times. "What the hell was that?"

Chapter 27

TWENTY THOUSAND FEET

Clouds hung low, creating a mist in the mountain jungles of islands formed by dormant volcanoes.

A Learjet continued its flight plan north over the Greater Antilles. A half hour later, the pilot began his descent and touched down at Fernando Luis Ribas Dominicci Airport. A stretch limo was waiting.

Mercado and his guards climbed inside, and the driver began navigating the narrow streets. Benz looked out the windows as blocks went by: strings of ancient attached homes, painted the loudest shades of yellow, green, orange, pink, descending down a steep street like stairs.

Old San Juan is the jewel of Puerto Rico. It sits elevated like a fortress, because that's how it was designed. Sprawling forts still stand on each end of the city, built to protect the harbor from Spain's enemies. Along the northern shore, the forts are connected by a forty-foot-tall city wall. It used to drop down to an empty beach, but centuries back, the poorer inhabitants began to squat and build shanties in the sand outside the protection of the wall, until an entire slum filled the shore. It is called La Perla. To this day, everyone knows that unless you live there, you don't go there.

Along that upper side of the island, past El Morro fort and Santa María cemetery, is Calle Norzagaray. The street threads itself between the colorful buildings and the drop-off at the edge of the city wall. At one quaint spot on top of the wall are a few stone tables and seats, situated among old-growth palm trees, overlooking La Perla and a foamy surf rolling in from the ocean.

The limo stopped at the curb. Mercado and his bodyguards got out, but only Mercado sat down at one of the tables . . .

Things had gotten fucked up.

The head of the Benzappa organization, old man Raffy, was the most respected among the family leaders in Colombia. But in business, especially this one, there is a deep chasm between respect and loyalty. So when Raffy had taken ill, there were condolences. And when Raffy announced that day-to-day operations would be turned over to his oldest son, A.J., the knives came out. Everyone knew A.J. would be more than formidable. But they also knew that next in the line of succession was the younger sibling Mercado, with soft hands and no résumé except his accounting ledgers. The calculation was made in less than a second. A.J. was blown into the sky over Toilet Seat Cut.

It was a *mis*calculation.

Mercado might not have had experience with the bare-knuckle side of the business, except this was family. Someone would have to pay. But, lacking the stomach and experience for that kind of hands-on work, he just gave a vague order. Specific would have been better. His men didn't know when to stop. Yes, someone did pay. And someone else, and a few more, and a lot more. The bombings and drive-bys were so continuous, nobody had time to catch their breath. Everyone's business didn't just suffer but screeched to a halt.

The predictable happened. A meeting was called . . .

The limo backed up into a side street. His team spread out across the road, with heavy artillery under their jackets, in striking distance of the stone tables and chairs on top of the city wall overlooking La Perla.

The reason for the meeting's location: neutral territory.

Mercado sat alone at one of the tables, checking his watch. He hated to wait, but that was part of the game.

Finally, an even larger limo pulled up, and an old man got out with his entourage. They remained standing while the patriarch took a seat on the other side of the table.

"Señor Morales," said Mercado. "Thank you for giving me your time."

Morales stared at the white breakers offshore. He held out a hand, and one of his bodyguards gave him an opened bag of Goldfish crackers. He began tossing them one by one to the pigeons. "You know, me and your father go way back, running the streets as children."

"I've heard the stories," said Mercado.

"That is why the current developments are so troubling to me." The old man turned to face Mercado. "What's been happening recently back home? Very bad for everyone. Draws too much attention."

"Yes, Señor Morales," said Benz. "And I'm sure you realize my own family has suffered losses."

The old man held up a hand. "What met your brother was wrong, stupid. Nobody consulted me. And it needed to be dealt with. But you have crossed lines. Many, many lines."

"But it was my brother. I—"

Morales held up his hand again. "I realize you're from the financial side of the family and don't know the rules. That's been taken into consideration. And you didn't start this. Plus your brother would have been good for stability." He shook his head. "It's this new generation. Too impatient. There is plenty to go around."

"Señor Morales, what can I do for you?"

"You are a lot like your father. I knew you could be reasoned with." He tossed a final Goldfish cracker. "No more moves on the others. I'll go back and straighten them out, and there will be the peace." Then he turned again to the sea, meaning the meeting was adjourned.

A limo emerged from a side street, and Mercado got in.

As soon as the vehicle was gone, Morales made a weak gesture with an index finger. One of his men leaned his head down to Morales's mouth. The old man whispered. The younger man stood back up and nodded.

ISLAMORADA

A finger pressed an elevator button.

Serge grinned at Coleman. "Guess what tonight is?"

"What?"

"Monopoly night!" Serge sipped a mug of coffee. "And you know what that means? I'm sure to lay waste to the competition with my secret scorched-earth strategy!"

"How can you be so sure?"

"Jen-Jen is at a tournament in Atlantic City. That leaves the field wide open."

They rode the elevator up to the appointed floor and knocked on a door.

"It's open. Come in."

Serge stepped inside with a wide smile.

"How have you been?" asked a neighbor named Lilly.

"Fantastic, except I'm out of pennies." He chugged more coffee.

"Pennies?"

Serge aimed an arm east. "The trash chute. Best entertainment value in America, except it's like crack. I went to the ground floor so I could dumpster-dive where the trash comes out, because legally the pennies are still mine until the truck arrives. But it was a fool's errand and I found myself hip-deep in the ejecta of the current human circumstance. I tore through a couple bags and Jesus! What kind of lives are you people living? A half-eaten pair of edible undies? I guess someone had a big dinner. I also found these crazy Polaroid photos that would strain your imagination at the angles the human body can attain, except my lips are sealed because the Garfields deserve their privacy. But that's not the point. I'm standing in a dumpster and am suddenly struck by a profound wave of sadness. Why? The contemporary state of American idiom. Any brainless TV commentator used to say 'train wreck,' but that's been overtaken by 'dumpster fire.'" Serge killed the rest of his coffee. "And I've been wondering, how do the dumpster people feel about this ugly trend? They're hardworking Americans like the rest of us, pillars of the community, coaching softball and taking pride in spot-welding these majestic containers of trash-gathering hope. Then they go in the break room just trying to eat a pimento sandwich in peace. But no, the TV on the wall is tuned to CNN and a story about congressional gridlock, and all the employees involuntary tense up as they nibble slowly with closed eyes—*Please, no, don't, God, I'm begging*—and then the anchorwoman finally gets to it: 'This is yet the latest political dumpster fire . . .' and everyone in the break room slams down utensils—'For fuck's sake!' 'Will it never end?'—containers of yogurt splattering on the wall under the TV. But here's the thing—I've seen a lot of actual dumpster fires in my life, not that I'm admitting anything, and every single one I've ever witnessed: completely contained, no collateral damage. Paper, grease, gasoline, highway flares, doesn't make a difference. No matter how hot, my money is always on the dumpster. So the company needs to steer into the skid and turn the slur on its head with a slick new ad campaign featuring swimsuit models throwing Molotov cocktails: 'Dumpsters: Safely on Fire for Sixty Years.'"

Serge smiled again and patted his stomach. "Let me take a wild stab. Spaghetti and meatballs tonight?" He glanced at the stove. Nothing was cooking. He looked at the empty dining table, then where Lilly's shoulders were bobbing as she silently sobbed. Her husband stood beside her, gently holding her hands.

"Lilly," said Serge. "I didn't know you worked for dumpster."

"It's not that," said her husband, John. "We had to call off Monopoly night, but we couldn't reach you."

"What happened?"

"We just got some medical bills."

"Oh." Serge's mouth firmed with understanding. "I'm so sorry. The cost of doctors today is ridiculous. Bills are frequently a shock, but I'm sure everything will be all right in the long run. As the saying goes, at least you've got your health."

"I don't know," said the husband. "I've never seen any bills like these. I thought there must be some kind of mistake, so I called our insurance company, and they said no, those are the right numbers."

Serge frowned. "Do you mind if I take a look?"

An arm pointed. "They're over on the counter."

Serge cast aside the torn-open envelopes and joined the couple at the table with a stack of paper. As he read down each page, his expression went from concern to alarm. "Holy shit! What did you have, a quadruple bypass?"

John shook his head. "Just an injection."

Serge came to the final total, just north of fifty grand. "I can't bear to look at these any longer." He put them down and faced John. "Start from the beginning and tell me what happened."

"About three weeks ago, I began having this pain in my back that kept getting worse and traveled around to my rib cage until I could only take shallow breaths without practically screaming."

"Sounds terrible," said Serge. "What happened next?"

"My regular doctor in Key Largo examined me and said I had a pinched nerve that must hurt like hell, but was easy to knock out with a steroid injection."

"Did the doctor give you one?"

"No, he said it was a special injection into a nerve root in the vertebrae that was beyond his expertise, but he'd gone to medical school with a specialist who was top-notch at this kind of stuff. He gave me a prescription and a referral to a pain clinic in Miami. So I drove up there, and his school friend gave me the same diagnosis, and since he wasn't that busy, he could do it that afternoon."

"Lucky you," said Serge. "Go on."

"So after lunch I came back and met him again in his office, and he took me in the next room, and there was a special table where you could lie on your stomach and put your face in a padded doughnut. A woman was waiting, who smiled and said she was the anesthesiologist, but since I wasn't getting anesthesia, she was just observing on standby."

"For what?"

"Who knows?" said the husband. "At least that's what I thought at the time. But now I definitely know. Anyway, I got a shot of lidocaine in my back to deaden it, and the doctor had a special machine to take a series of X-rays to guide the bigger needle to the nerve root. It barely took five minutes, and sure enough, a week later, no more problems . . . until the mail came today."

"What exactly did the insurance company say?"

"I had gone 'out of network,'" said the husband. "I explained that couldn't be right. I specifically checked that the doctor took my insurance. The claims woman said that was true, but the clinic itself where I got the shot wasn't in network. I said it was the same damn building where the physician worked, and she replied it didn't matter, that I could leave the network by simply going in the next room, and I told her that's literally what happened."

Serge whistled. "It really drives up your copay, but at least you still have your insurance for most of it."

"Not remotely," said John. "The insurance woman said that because the clinic isn't in their network, they don't have a negotiated schedule of fees. In those cases, she said, and I quote, 'The clinic is free to charge any amount they want, except they're not going to get it.' And I said, 'You mean they're not going to get it from you?' She replied, 'That's right. We'll pay the percentage of the industry-standard reasonable cost for the procedure. The patient is still responsible for the balance.'"

"How much did she say was reasonable?" asked Serge.

"Two thousand, tops," said John. "I tried calling the clinic to negotiate, but the woman in billing practically laughed and threatened to put a lien on the condo."

Serge blinked hard and forced himself to pick up the bills again. "Okay, I'm going to look into this for you. I just need for you to explain to me a few things in here that don't make sense. What's this five thousand for anesthesiologist? I thought you said you didn't have anesthesia."

"I didn't," said John. "That's one of the things the insurance company looked into. Turns out that while I was facedown in the doughnut, the so-called standby anesthesiologist came over and gave me the initial shot of lidocaine. If the doctor gave it, that charge wouldn't have appeared."

"What a racket! That's like charging five grand for Novocain before getting a wisdom tooth pulled." Serge tapped another spot in the bill. "And this ten thousand?"

"Urinalysis," said John. "The state now requires pain clinics to check patients getting opioid prescriptions to make sure they're not getting extra pills elsewhere."

"But you were getting a steroid shot, not drugs," said Serge. "You didn't need your urine checked."

"That's exactly what the insurance woman said. And they also charged extra for a full DNA analysis of the sample. And the facility charge—"

Serge held up both hands. "I've heard enough. I've seen this movie before."

"What are you talking about?"

"It's a burgeoning medical scam," said Serge. "And you absolutely wouldn't believe it unless you got the medical bills yourself, which you now have. But it's becoming so rampant that the phenomenon has spawned the terms 'surprise billing' and 'drive-by doctoring.' Look it up on the Internet. One person had a sliver from his finger removed for twelve grand."

"Drive-by?"

"That term specifically applies to your experience with the anesthesiologist," said Serge. "Someone out of network comes into an operating room to perform a minor service the patient doesn't even know about—often because they're out cold on the table—and charges at an exorbitant rate just because they can."

"Good lord," said John. "Doesn't the hospital know about it?"

"They're the ones behind it," said Serge. "Since patients mostly pick hospitals that are under their insurance plans, those facilities are bound by contracts with the insurance companies as to what they can charge. So to boost their profit margins, they bring in these other cats at a higher percentage, and the patient doesn't realize it until the mail truck arrives."

"But it wasn't a hospital, just this little pain clinic."

"Even worse," said Serge. "It was probably among those that got caught up in all the police raids in the last couple years because they were so brazen: One-stop shopping for all your dope-addict needs, with lines out the door. Doctors and nurses were arrested, and the places boarded up. But because the clinics were incorporated, the owners couldn't be charged, just the companies, which they dissolved, re-formed and put new signs on the building. Some of them went into the more lucrative field of surprise billing. Big-name hospitals are bad enough, but they can only go just so crazy with the numbers because, well, they're hospitals and people in the community will talk. But the sky is the limit with these clinics."

"There's nothing we can do about it?" asked Lilly.

"Nothing at all *you* can do. Me, on the other hand?" He grabbed the stack of bills. "Can I borrow these?"

"Knock yourself out."

Serge got up from the table. "Come on, Coleman. This will be more fun than hotels on Marvin Gardens."

Chapter 28

A late-model Chevy Tahoe crossed the Florida state line and stopped at the official welcome center featuring missing-persons bulletins, human-trafficking bulletins, crime-prevention bulletins, and racks of travel coupon booklets printed on the kind of cheap paper that leaves the ink in your hands. An Army veteran sat at a folding card table outside the restrooms, accepting donations for trucker-style military hats with waving flags, screaming eagles, Vietnam service ribbons and logos to remember POWs. The cocker spaniel at his feet was named Biscuit.

Vix was a rare treat of a travel companion. "You stupid mother-fuckers! Why am I always surrounded by idiots! You all have shit for brains! . . ."

The guy in the Tahoe's driver's seat whispered sideways. "What did we do now?"

"Nothing," said the front passenger. "She's just tweaking again . . ."

Vix's head disappeared from view in the back seat, followed by a violent snort. She reappeared with zooming eyes and blew a snot rocket out the window. "Sons of bitches! I have to pee! Didn't I fucking tell you that?"

Driver: "That's why we're parked in front of the restrooms at the welcome center."

"Oh," said Vix. She marched out of the car, bumping into tourists. "What the fuck are *you* looking at?"

Weezer, in the driver's seat, in general: "This can't end well."

Mulch awoke in the back seat. ". . . What did I miss?"

"It's about Vix," said Weezer. "She's going to get us arrested. We're already too high-profile, even if they think we're in Canada or southbound on Ninety-Five."

"I never agreed to any violence to start with," said Mulch. "Why don't we just speed away while she's in there?"

"Because she's off the rails! Even if she doesn't want to narc, she's liable to say anything to the police in her state. Who's got the gun—"

He cut himself off as children with dripping ice cream cones packed themselves back into an SUV on a thousand-mile road vacation with parents who looked like they'd been subjected to stress positions in preparation for hostage videos.

"Okay, are you in?"

"In for what?"

"We ditch her at the next remote exit."

"Just ditch her?"

"No, I mean the permanent ditch. There are woods all around here. It's a tough call, but it's her or us."

Reluctant nodding. "I can't believe it's gone this far . . ." Weezer made the sign of the cross. "I'll need to go to church and say like a thousand Hail Marys."

"What a pile," said Mulch. "The priests taught that it doesn't count even if you plan to sin, as long as you mop it up afterward with confession."

"That sounds like a loophole."

"You also have to confess to the planning, and the priest's hands are tied."

"This has to be completely solid or nothing," said the driver. "We have to—"

Bam! Bam! Bam!

The guys jumped at the pounding on the windows.

"What the fuck are you cum stains yapping about and not opening the door like gentlemen? . . ."

The car left the welcome center, continuing down Interstate 75, past the exits for Lake City, High Springs, Gainesville, until they pulled off at Wildwood, a long-haul trucker mega-stop because it was at the fork with the Florida Turnpike. Steaming buffets, showers, lounges, garages and a trucker superstore selling chrome pipes, Yosemite Sam mud flaps, CB radios, and mini appliances that plugged into cigarette lighters.

The reason they stopped was the "motel problem." They'd had some luck in the southern states finding mom-and-pop joints that took cash and didn't ask questions. But they'd been rolling snake eyes since the state line.

"Why can't we just show them a license?" asked Mulch.

"Are you fucking stupid?" said Vix. "Because I don't want to go to jail! There are bulletins out for all of us, and a lot of these motels are required to make copies of licenses and turn them over to police, who are looking for people with warrants or APBs out."

"But I'm getting tired," said Mulch.

"That's what stealth camping is for," said Vix.

"What's that?"

"Where you find a spot to sleep in your car without getting hassled," said Vix. "It's a big thing, a whole community of people out there who do it as a lifestyle and post location tips on websites and YouTube. I read where truck stops and twenty-four-hour Walmarts are especially popular. Pull around behind those rigs."

The driver passed several idling semis with rows of orange

lights, until he reached the back edge of the lot. Everyone thinking: *Sleeping in cars is the worst, especially when it involves several people.* The guys resigned themselves and reclined their front seats, leaving Vix the entire back of the car, which was fine with them.

The gang had barely closed their eyes when they were jolted awake by firm knocking on the driver's window. He rolled it down. "Yes?"

"You can't sleep here in your car," said an employee with the name Carl stitched on his uniform.

"But we're really tired." Weezer pointed. "A bunch of other people are sleeping."

Carl shook his head. "It's just for truckers. And they pay for their spots."

"What if we pay the same as them?"

Carl thought a moment. "I guess that might work. Let me see a driver's license . . ."

The car pulled onto the turnpike and began driving diagonally south across the state to pick up I-95 on the east coast. Neither of the guys spoke, lest they trigger a detonation by Vix, repeatedly snorting and chugging and muttering "fuck" under her breath.

Somewhere after two A.M., after Kissimmee, Vix pointed. "Take this exit."

"What's there?" asked the driver.

"How should I know?" said Vix. "But we can't keep doing this. You know how hot it will be if we try to sleep during the day?"

They slowly cruised through a small rural town, rows of old clapboard houses punctuated with churches.

"I don't like the looks of this," said the driver. "We're too conspicuous. I've already seen three police cars sitting with parking lights on."

"Shut up and keep driving!" said Vix. Her head turned. "Stop! Turn around!"

The car pulled off the road, through an ancient stone arch.

"A cemetery?" said Weezer.

"I read it on one of the stealth websites," said Vix. "Drive and pull around behind that mausoleum in back . . ."

The car parked out of sight.

Everyone was so exhausted that they were snoring in no time.

The birds came alive at daybreak, and a beat-up green station wagon pulled through the arch. The caretaker turned on some sprinklers and gathered dead flowers, then a few empty beer cans. "High school kids again . . ."

He approached a trash can next to a mausoleum and saw a bumper. He walked around back.

The gang in the car was jolted again by another knock on the window. The driver rolled it down.

"You can't sleep here," said the caretaker.

"Why not?" said Mulch, looking around at tombstones. "Who are we bothering?"

"You just can't," he said. "If you move along now, no harm, no foul—"

There was a gun on the front seat and small smears of dried blood, not much, but enough not to be normal. The caretaker stopped talking abruptly, and Vix saw him staring at the evidence.

The man slowly began backing away from the car with the kind of frightened eyes that said his next call would be to the police.

"Shit," said Vix, suddenly in motion.

The caretaker was up to the front bumper. Just as he was about to spin and start running:

Bang, bang, bang.

The guys in the front seat ducked and covered their ears. They raised their heads to see the caretaker standing still in front of the car, with even more surprised eyes, before toppling over dead onto the hood. Then they saw the tight pattern of three bullet holes in the middle of the Tahoe's windshield.

"We need to get the hell out of here," said the driver, turning over the ignition and throwing it in reverse.

Vix smacked him in the back of the head. "What do you think you're doing?"

"Escaping."

"With bullet holes in the windshield?" yelled Vix. "How long do you think that will go unnoticed?"

"You couldn't have gotten out of the car before shooting?"

"I didn't know how fast he could run," said Vix. "And I didn't see anyone else wrapping arms around the problem."

"Then what do we do?"

"I'm sure whoever that guy was must have come in a vehicle," said Vix. "Check his pockets for keys."

They stuffed the body in the trunk and wiped down what they could.

Moments later, an old green station wagon pulled out through a stone arch.

Vix studied a hand-drawn map of a house.

Chapter 29

THE DOCKS

A '73 Galaxie drove slowly down the Old Road toward Tavernier Creek, then wound its way through bright gravel to a row of dockside establishments. Food, drink, water sports, straw hats, coconuts carved into non-coconut shapes.

Serge headed toward a rental counter.

"Serge, I thought you swore off of this," said Coleman.

He continued marching with zest. "That was yesterday . . ."

"But you were so mad that I hid under the bed," said Coleman. "Cursing and throwing shit and making me promise to shoot you if you ever tried this again."

"I've since cut back on coffee. For now."

A well-tanned woman with a gold seahorse necklace and element-frizzed brown hair smiled from behind the counter. "How can I help you guys today?"

"I'd like to rent one of your kiteboarding packages."

A gleaming smile. "Then you came to the right place. We have a couple of specials going. Have you sailed before or will you need lessons?"

"Oh, I've sailed before. *Have* I sailed!" said Serge. "In fact, I'm now an Internet phenomenon. But don't watch the videos until after we've left with the rental equipment."

"Why not?"

"Signing autographs only slows me down."

"He can't really sail," said Coleman.

"They say I'm sick," said Serge. "How much? . . ."

A n hour later, the fourth-floor condo unit was filled with in-dustrial noise. Saws, drills, hammering. Coleman wandered into the living room, where a workbench was set up and Serge stood with safety goggles. "Whatcha making?"

Serge drilled another hole and stopped. "A foolproof kite-boarding solution. You're my first customer. I'll bet you're excited!"

"I'm not getting on that thing."

"But I need a test dummy."

"No way."

"Okay, we'll table that topic until I finish my pioneering breakthrough in kiteboarding history . . ."

Coleman glanced at an empty box on the couch. "You bought a drone? And it's all in pieces. The propellers are in the trash can."

"Can you at least let me concentrate? . . ."

After a noisy marathon work session that lasted past dark, Serge finally unplugged the power tools.

Coleman was facedown in his favorite spot under the coffee table. He was dreaming that someone was kicking him in the ribs. He turned his head and opened his eyes. "Serge, your sneaker hurts."

"Get up! I just finished my project! Come take a look!"

Coleman scratched the top of his head like a spider monkey. "I don't get what I'm looking at."

"Pay attention." Serge tapped something with channel-lock pliers. "This part's obvious. I fastened a lawn chair to the center of the board with heavy-gauge roof fittings. It's not going anywhere. I also fashioned a seat belt and a roller-coaster-style shoulder harness from boat straps." He tapped something else on the front of the board. "But this is the pièce de résistance, what makes the whole project hum."

"Still confused," said Coleman.

"It's a remote-controlled kiteboarding navigational system. The lithium batteries are housed inside the rubber gaskets."

"But how does it work?"

"Glad you asked!" Serge picked up a standard pair of kite handles, slid them into a custom brace and snapped it in place with hurricane-window clamps. Then he picked up a box with an antenna.

"Hey," said Coleman. "That's the flying control for the drone."

"And now the kite." Serge flicked a switch and a red light came on. "Observe." He gently pushed a joystick forward. When he did, a whirring sound came from the front of the board.

"Cool," said Coleman. "The handles tilted forward."

Serge then pushed his control stick to the side, and the handles on the board rotated. "It's a triple-axis gimbal stabilizer for large amateur telescopes."

"What's that button on the remote control that says 'Release'?"

"If we're going to live on the water, I needed the perfect device," said Serge. "This is a marine drone, water resistant—to a point. But here's the coolest part! It can carry a small payload. They market it online to fishermen and charter captains who might need a delivery of extra bait, food or drinks. A little camera determines when it's over the boat, then the operator hits the release button, and it's shrimp and beer for all!"

"That's so cool!" said Coleman. "You going to be delivering beer?"

"Not really," said Serge. "That 'Release' button right now is like tits on a bull, but I've got some ideas for when opportunity arises."

Coleman nodded and bent down for a closer view of the assembly. "But I don't understand how that tiny drone remote control has enough power to work those heavy kite controls."

"It doesn't." The joystick and handles rotated north. "It just supplies a tiny RF signal to the drone's components, which I reassembled and hot-wired to actuate the gimbal. Those big lithium batteries then do the heavy lifting. I had to drive up to the mainland and crisscross Miami to gather all the puzzle pieces . . . I need your help to move this. Grab that other end."

"Okay, where are we going?"

"Down to the beach."

"But it's night."

"The perfect time," said Serge, lifting his end of the board off the workbench. "Besides, you know my psychological composition. After completing such a righteous project, there's no way I'll get to sleep without giving this baby a test drive. Plus the moon is rising over Meditation Point in twenty minutes . . . and it's super windy . . ."

A mysteriously modified rental board sat off Meditation Point with its kite in the water.

Coleman cupped a lit joint in his hand. "I can't wait to see how this works."

Serge toggled the remote control. "You'll have a front-row seat."

"What do you mean?"

Serge climbed over the coral boulders with exposed fossils of ancient marine life. Then he walked down a short series of half-submerged concrete steps—nicknamed Stairway to Heaven. He placed the board in the light chop. "Sit down. I'll strap you in."

"Hold . . . on," said Coleman. "You told me I didn't have to."

"I said we'd table the discussion. This is for your own good." Serge grabbed one of the seat belts. "Thank me later . . ."

Coleman took a trembling step backward. "No way!"

"Where are you going?" Serge jumped back over the rocks.

Coleman saw him coming and started running. "Leave me alone! . . ."

There was a reason Pelican Bay was so popular. Besides the condo's intoxicating balcony views and postcard private beach of white sand, there was the unique nightlife. All the visitors worn out from a full day in kayaks and on kiteboards were now winding down in the darkness with beer and cocktails under the BYOB tiki hut hugging the shore. In the city, residents chain bicycles to utility poles; here they chain barbecues to coconut palms, and now smoke and the aroma of steaks wafted out of them. The wind carried laughter and music from a small radio tuned to early Chicago.

"*. . . Make me smile! . . .*"

There was a sudden outburst of commotion, and the other residents all turned and strained their eyes in the dimness.

Serge and Coleman ran in desperate circles in the sand.

"Stop chasing me!"

"Then stop running away!"

"I don't want to kitesurf!"

"Take one for the team!"

Coleman ran behind one of the largest palms and used it as a shield. Serge reached around one side, and Coleman darted around the other, and vice versa, over and over. They began throwing sand at each other.

"Coleman, stop acting like a child!"

"No!"

But with Serge's quicker reflexes, the outcome had never been in doubt, only the dignity of the process. Serge finally got Coleman in a headlock. "Will you come peacefully now? . . . Ouch! You punched me in the dick!" Then a period of rolling around and wrestling on the beach. It ended with Serge grabbing Coleman by an ear and pulling him to his feet.

"Ow! Ow! Ow! Let go!"

"Not until you get in those waves!"

"But it's pretty hairy out there."

"Charlie don't surf!"

All other activity on the beach had come to a stop, everyone staring as Serge led Coleman across the sand and up onto one of the boulders. "In you go!" Shove—*splash!*—and Serge dove in after. Someone resumed flipping steaks.

Moments later, Coleman was strapped in tight. Serge stood waist-deep next to him and worked a remote control. A colorful canopy rose skyward. "Stop squirming."

"But I want to be somewhere else."

"Here comes the moon," said Serge. "It just cleared Kalteux Key. You're about to make history as the first human remote-control toy. Ready?"

"No."

"And . . . takeoff!"

Serge nimbly worked the joystick, sending the nylon canopy higher and higher. The board skimmed forward, slowly at first but dependably picking up speed. It headed out toward a minor boating channel to the south before swinging east, Serge gingerly working the controls as he walked backward in the water.

The board cut around one of the channel markers as a gull took flight. Serge continued backing up until he reached the boulders, and climbed out of the water for a better view from the beach.

"Time to push the envelope!" He yanked the stick all the way back and to the side, bringing the kite around southeast, fully with the wind. The board took off like an Olympic bobsled, its vague image skimming fast across the dark water.

"Ahhhhhhhhh! . . . I'm too high!"

"About to get higher."

Serge slowly moved the stick in lazy loops, while Coleman repeatedly circled their crescent harbor.

"That's enough warming up," Serge said to himself. "Now for the big event. Is he going to be surprised!"

On the next go-round, the kite's angle of attack increased as Coleman gathered steam, banking into a hard turn.

"Whoa!" said Serge. "This is going to look even cooler than I expected . . ."

It is an optical illusion, but you'd swear your eyes are telling the truth: When a full moon rises just above the horizon, it appears vastly larger than when it reaches its zenith in the night sky.

Coleman's water sled was now a *rocket* sled. Serge gleefully continued manipulating the radio controls. "I've always loved the movie *E.T.*!"

As the evening entered that perfect movie moment, Serge timed it precisely, all at once pulling back on the joystick. The whole works leaped from the water to catch serious air.

"Ahhhhh! Ahhhhh!"

And the silhouette of Coleman and his board crossed the massive full moon.

Chapter 30

LATER THAT EVENING

C oleman was out on the balcony. Literally out. Slumped sideways against the railing.

Serge was still at it on the computer, as he had been for hours,
typing search terms and jotting notes. When he was done, Serge
picked up the phone to call in a favor . . .

A few doctors still make house calls these days. Some of those
only take cash. Serious cash. Their practices specialize solely in patients who don't want injuries reported to the police. Call them
Gunshot-Wound Doctors to the Stars. All the shady types living in
gated homes have them on speed dial. Miami has more than most.

A cell phone rang in a condo overlooking Biscayne Bay. Bleary
eyes checked the alarm clock: 3:26 A.M. "Shit." Other people
would have let the phone ring itself out, but the person in bed got
some of his highest-paying clients at such hours, because gunfire
didn't stay on schedule. Also, those clients would have unkind
things to say later if he didn't answer.

The doctor snatched the phone off the nightstand. A groggy voice: "Hullo? . . ."

"Hey, Bones," said the phone. "It's me, Serge. How's it been hanging?"

"Jesus, Serge! Do you have any idea what time it is?"

"Uh, late?"

"Past late!" said Bones. "So late it's early!"

"Then I'll get to the point. I need a favor."

"I figured that. Call me back at a civilized hour, like never."

"Is that any way to talk to your old chum?" said Serge. "Do you recall what time it was when you phoned *me* for a favor?"

The other end of the line remained silent.

"Bones? You still there?"

"I'm here, dammit! What do you need?"

Serge told him.

"Okay, I'll poke around and see what I can find out in the morning."

"No good," said Serge. "It's urgent. I need it like five minutes ago."

"Serge!—"

"Bones, must I remind you that I didn't delay when you needed that beef straightened out with those guys? About that time that you didn't answer your phone promptly when they required your bullet-removal services?"

Another pause. Then: "Okay, okay, I'm getting out of bed." Bones swung pajama legs over the side. "I'll let you know as soon as I find something."

"I'll be waiting by the phone . . ."

THE NEXT DAY

Loud whapping sounds filled the air as the shadow of a helicopter drifted along the Overseas Highway. The black Sikorsky slowed as it hovered above Millionaires Row before making another perfect touchdown on the beach.

Mercado climbed out and ducked under the slowing blades. A woman was usually waiting, looking out a second-floor window, but not now. He went inside. "Cinco, where's Julie?"

"She left you a note . . ."

A limo departed through a pair of security gates on the Old Road and drove all of a mile. The gas station was crammed with sports cars, contractor vans and pickups pulling boats, but far more than could be explained by the need for fuel.

Mercado entered the front door and discovered the reason for the overflowing parking lot.

Lunchtime.

A crowd at the counter, trying to get their orders heard. Above the hubbub:

"Mercado!"

He looked and saw Julie waving him over from one of the tiny tables. He raised his chin and smiled. "I was wondering why you asked to meet at a gas station."

"It's my favorite joint in town, Café 90." She handed him a menu. "Everything's good."

"I never would have found this place otherwise." He scanned the selections. "From the road, there's no clue this is in here." He handed the menu back to her. "Order for both of us."

Soon, food.

"I see why you like this place so much," said Mercado, munching. "What is this? It's like a Cuban sandwich, but a little different."

"*Medianoche,* all the same ingredients except a sweeter bread." Julie was working on her own assortment of meat pastries with a plastic fork. "So how was your trip?"

"Boring." Another bite. "How are our fathers?"

"Great," said Julie. "Binge-watching *Adam-12* now. Somehow

they've been stashing hot sauce. Are you breaking your word that you'd stop that?"

"Me?" said Mercado.

"Okay, you don't have to answer . . ."

"What's that look on your face?" asked Mercado. "It's not a hot sauce look. Is something wrong?"

"No, everything's fine," said Julie. "You've helped my dad so much, and you're paying me way more than I deserve. So I feel weird asking you a favor."

"Name it," said Mercado.

"It's kind of a big favor," said Julie.

"Just spit it out."

So she told him.

"That's it?" said Mercado.

"Except for the part where you say yes."

"It's done," said Mercado. "Does Saturday work for you?"

"Saturday would be perfect—"

"*Julie!*" A sheriff's deputy walked over from the counter. "What a shock seeing you here."

"Oh, hi, Deke." She turned. "I'd like you to meet my new friend Mercado."

"Pleasure." They shook hands.

"Likewise."

The deputy grabbed the spare chair at the table. Normally you'd ask if it was okay to sit in such a situation, but this was the Keys, and Deke's family knew Julie's from way back. Deke downed his tiny espresso and turned. "So, Mercado, are you just passing through?"

"Visiting my father. He has a place down here."

"Really? Where?" asked the deputy.

"A mile south off the Old Road," said Mercado. "I'm here at least every other week."

The deputy's eyebrows involuntarily rose. He thought, but

didn't say: *Wow! That stretch of the Old Road? You must really come from money* . . . Then a change of expression and another thought, this one out loud. "What's your father's name? I might know him."

"I doubt you do because he doesn't get out much now with his health," said Mercado. "Raffy Benzappa."

The deputy definitely knew him, like everyone else in law enforcement down here. This time Deke kept a poker face. "Doesn't ring a bell, but maybe I'll get to meet him sometime." He stood with a smile and an empty espresso thimble. "I'll let you two get back to lunch . . . Nice again to meet you . . ."

The deputy walked away, thinking, *What in the name of God is Julie doing with this guy? I'll have to talk to her later.*

"Seems like a nice guy," said Mercado. "How do you know him?"

"Everybody knows him," said Julie. "His father and mine practically grew up together. Deke followed in his dad's footsteps and is one of the supervisors now, watches out for everyone in this small town like Andy Griffith. Told me a funny story where he recently had to question a suspicious weirdo, but it turns out the guy just wanted to take a photo of that rooster."

"That is a good rooster," said Mercado.

"So listen," said Julie. "Are you sure you're okay with that favor I asked you earlier?"

"Absolutely," said Mercado. "Except now you owe me a favor."

"Here it comes," said Julie. "But I do owe you. What is it?"

"I've come to know you good, yet I really don't know you at all."

"What's that supposed to mean?"

"It means I can read people pretty well and have been around you enough to know what kind of person you are. But I don't know much about what brought you to this point."

"What point?"

"One example: taking care of the kids, devotion to your father," said Mercado. "That's a lot of work, not to mention emotional drain, and you even do it for free. Where'd that come from?"

"I usually don't talk about this." Julie finished a *croqueta* and set down her plastic fork. "But all the girls at work know, and you're helping so much . . . It has to do with Bumbles."

"Bumbles?"

Julie nodded. "I'm the middle of three kids. Older and younger brothers. We called the older Junior. Original, eh?"

"I didn't know you had brothers."

Julie took a deep breath. "They're not here anymore."

"Jesus, I'm so sorry," said Mercado.

"Don't be, long time ago," said Julie. "Anyway, I used to follow Junior around everywhere like a proverbial puppy dog. And you know how some teenagers hate that? But not Junior. We were so close. Dad was teaching Junior everything he knew about fishing, and then Junior would teach me. In his senior year of high school, he passed suddenly."

"So young," said Mercado. "An accident?"

"Pretty much. Real freak thing just up the highway. I would prefer not to get into details," said Julie. "I don't know how my father held up. I was promoted to prime fishing buddy, and he picked up teaching me what he'd been teaching Junior. Bumbles was five when he started coming along with us."

"Excuse me, but that's an unusual name, or nickname I'm guessing."

"Nobody could remember exactly how it started. It was one of those nonsense nicknames that someone just blurts out and it sticks. I think he tried to catch a bee once," said Julie. "Anyway, he was so cute, following me around like déjà vu of me and Junior." Another deep breath. "Something went wrong with his blood, and this time Dad didn't keep it together nearly so well. I can't think of anything sadder than the sight of that tiny coffin."

A long pause. "So that's why you got into helping children."

"Partly," said Julie. "But the rest is really personal. I started because I was trying to find a way to shake the guilt."

"Guilt? From what?"

"You know how parents aren't supposed to have a favorite child, or at least pretend to themselves that they don't? . . . Junior and Bumbles were the greatest, and I loved them so much, but in different ways."

"I'm not seeing the guilt part," said Mercado.

"I knew Junior so long, knew everything that made him tick. But most of the time I knew Bumbles, he was an infant or toddler with no real fleshed-out personality. I was just a kid, too, when we lost them. And I just felt so much more sorrow for Junior. I wasn't trying to. It's just I knew him better. It's logical that my feelings about Bumbles were more abstract. Didn't change how the guilt was killing me. I couldn't escape it, like a big rock on my chest. What did I know at that age?"

"And *that's* how you started with the kids?" said Mercado.

"It began as penance, but then I realized I actually liked it," said Julie. "The guilt went away and it became my calling."

"That's very noble of you." Mercado smiled warmly. "It's amazing how many children you're helping at the center."

"Actually, it's tragic."

"What do you mean?" asked Mercado.

"We could easily help three to four times as many, but not on our budget, plus the tiny building is already at fire marshal capacity," said Julie. "You should see the waiting list. And it's a sad list, because it's unspoken what they're waiting for."

"That is sad."

"Almost as sad as when we have to tell parents why there aren't any spaces available for their son or daughter."

"Why's that?" asked Mercado.

"That their child isn't yet *sick enough*."

Mercado's mouth became solemn as he nodded. "Well, I need to be going. It was nice having lunch and thanks for introducing me to this café." He got up and headed for the door.

"See you Saturday?" said Julie.

"You have my word."

Mercado was true to his word. That Saturday:

The outline of the Florida Keys slowly took shape in the emerald and turquoise waters. A Learjet descended over the Gulf Stream on final approach. It circled west to line up the runway and touched down.

Three vehicles were waiting at the Marathon airport. The first was a black stretch limo, which was to be expected. The other two were not, both white vans, both packed with passengers. The sides of the vans had seahorses, seashells and mermaids.

Julie got out of the first van and greeted Mercado as he came down the stairs.

"Okay," he told her, clapping his hands. "Let's get going."

Julie turned and waved to the cars. Side doors flew open, and a small herd of excited children ran across the runway. Mercado high-fived each of them as they trotted up the stairs, followed by Julie.

The kids oohed and ahhed at the Lear's luxury interior, playing with all the latches and controls. Julie thinking, *This is way better than a commercial airline.*

She smiled at Mercado. "I can't thank you enough for doing this."

"It's no big deal. We're only going to circle the runway."

"I told them that, and they're still out of their minds," said Julie. "They're very good at pretending. Most have never even been on a plane."

Someone pulled up the staircase, and the jet began slowly taxiing around the tarmac without purpose. Children shrieked and laughed, faces up against the windows. Most of them looked too weak to generate all that noise. Some were bald and some had colorful scarves wrapped around their heads. One of the boys wore a safety helmet that his doctors required him to use at all times. The jet turned at the end of the runway for another lap and the delighted screams grew even louder, if that was possible.

The pilot reached the pavement's edge and turned around

again. This time it didn't make an arc, but instead pivoted in place. Then it came to a full stop.

Julie looked over at Mercado. "Is something wrong?"

Mercado just smiled as the private jet began moving again. "Better tell them to put on their seat belts."

The Lear picked up speed, faster and faster, until the tropical landscape out the windows was a blur. Finally, the wheels left the ground and the plane soared skyward in a steep climb. The passengers' reaction was deafening. The pilot first banked over Bahia Honda, then the Spanish Harbor keys. It swung wide above Knockemdown Key to avoid the Navy landing pattern on Boca Chica, then around Key West and all the way out to the Marquesas Atoll.

The children were abuzz, pointing down at tiny loggerhead turtles and a rusty shipwreck sticking out of the water. Then the grand finale, circling the Civil War–era Fort Jefferson in the Dry Tortugas. The kids dug the fort's moat the best.

They finally touched back down at the airport, and the kids who were able to went skipping across the runway. Mercado looked in Julie's direction. "Now don't be getting all sentimental on me."

"I won't."

Then Julie's expression changed. It was something Mercado had never seen before.

"Now what's *that* look?" he asked. But he already knew the answer. He liked Julie, too, but for business reasons that were all too obvious, that was never going to happen. Time to change the subject with a sharp snap of his fingers: "I've got a great idea! Ask me another favor!"

"After all this, I couldn't possibly."

"Okay, then I'll ask and answer it as well: The helicopter? . . . Then the helicopter it is!"

The kids climbed aboard again, in heaven. "Julie, get me the keys to your vans."

"Why?"

"You don't want to leave them here," said Mercado.

"Where are we going?"

"You'll find out soon enough," said Mercado. "I'll have a couple of my guys from the limo drive the vans back."

"I was wondering why the limo was here since you had the helicopter," said Julie. "You planned this all along, didn't you?"

"Huh? Me? . . ."

It would have been a tight fit, but the children were small. The Sikorsky lifted off for the brief seaside trip up the coast to Islamorada. More shrieking and laughing. It touched down on the beach, and Mercado told them all to stay put until the rotors completely stopped.

Then most of them ran around the beach in random trajectories. After they burned off enough energy, Mercado whistled sharply. The children stopped and turned.

"Do you kids like surprises?" said Benz. That got everyone's attention. "Then follow me . . ."

They entered the rear of the largest house they had ever seen, and it was quite a hike for their little legs.

They finally reached the dining room, and another deafening cheer went up.

In front of them, along the wall, stood a row of grimly serious men with weapons hidden inside their black jackets and hands folded obediently in front of them. The dining room table seemed to stretch forever with seating for twenty. Covered with cake, ice cream, candy, soda. Balloons and noisemakers and, topping it off, the donkey piñata.

Frosting soon covered tiny faces, and a donkey exploded.

Julie grabbed one of his hands with no hint of flirtation. "You're a good man, Mercado."

"No, I'm not. But I'm trying to make up for a few things."

Chapter 31

MIAMI

The night sky was electric over the downtown Brickell financial district. Many of the high-rises housed some of the best-capitalized banks in the country, thanks to Latin America. The rest of the skyline jewels were the city's ridiculous concentration of towering condos, the homes of executives running an eclectic economy.

Serge peeked out curtains on a fiftieth floor. "Coleman!" he whispered. "Come here! You've got to see this view when it's lit up! There's the Rickenbacker, and Star Island, and the pink and blue art deco hotels on Ocean Drive, and a cargo ship coming into the port through the jetties at Government Cut."

"Cool."

"Where'd you get that beer?"

"The fridge."

"Didn't I tell you not to touch anything?"

"Just the handle. And some other stuff I don't remember."

Serge let go of the curtain. "We'll just have to wipe what we can down later. It's time to get to work . . ."

The pair crept into the dark master bedroom. Serge knelt next to the bed and smiled at the sound-asleep resident. He prepared to knock on the man's forehead with his knuckles.

Before he could—"Ouch! Shit!"—Coleman stubbed his big toe and tumbled over an ottoman.

The man sprang up in bed. "What the hell?"

Serge pushed him back down on the pillow. "Relax. It's just us."

"Who are you?"

"We're the Wish Fairies," said Serge. "But no wishes for you tonight. These are someone else's wishes. Maybe next time."

"Fuck yourself! I'm calling the police!"

"Damn, you're making this easy," said Serge, slapping a hand reaching for a phone. Then aiming a gun. "First, are you Livingston Nash?"

"Yeah, what about it?"

"Whew," said Serge. "That's a relief. We're finally in the right unit. On the way out, we'll have to untie the guy on the next floor, and really, really, really apologize."

"Like I said, what do you want?"

"I'm afraid there's been a terrible misunderstanding," said Serge. "I've got this friend who visited your clinic for a very brief procedure, but after he got home, your office staff must have sent him someone else's bill, because the total can't be understood even in the weirdest parts of the galaxies where all mathematics is bent by black holes."

"You'll need to take this up with my office manager," said Nash.

"No, I'm sure you're the one I need to talk to."

Nash's hand again went for the bedside table and his cell phone. "Choice is yours. Either get the fuck out before the cops arrive, or stick around and explain all this to them."

Serge skull-cracked him with the alarm clock . . .

Moments later, a bloodied pain clinic owner sat in front of his home computer and looked around.

Serge pulled an aerosol can from his pocket and blasted him in the eyes.

"...*Ahhhhh!* What did you spray me with!"

"Febreze," said Serge. "It's supposed to treat all manner of unpleasantness."

"You asshole!"

Serge looked at the can. "I'm asking for a refund."

"What the hell do you want from me!"

"I can't think of how I could have been plainer," said Serge. "I want you to refund the money you swindled from my friends."

"I didn't swindle anyone!" protested Livingston. "I didn't do anything illegal! I swear!"

"There's illegal and then there's immoral, and yours is a serious circle in hell."

"Even if I agree, it's pointless anyway," said the owner. "I can't access the business computer system from home."

"This gun says otherwise." Serge pointed the barrel at the computer. "I'll bet if you click that icon on your home screen that says 'Clinic,' magic doors will open. If you don't click it, I'm going to click you."

"Okay, okay, I'm clicking, I'm clicking!"

Livingston navigated through his clinic's financial records until he came to the nerve injection for Serge's neighbor. "Tell you what I'll do. I can knock off ten percent. That's more than I should, but if you're saying these friends are having a hard time, then I'm just too nice a guy." He clicked a tenth off the bill.

Another bash with the alarm clock. "What's wrong with my business presentation?" asked Serge. "What part of this looks like I'm fucking negotiating?"

"Okay, okay! How much were you looking for me to take off?"

"The insurance company said the customary cost is closer to two thousand."

"Are you insane?" said Livingston. "You want me to knock off almost fifty grand? I'll be losing money."

"Coleman, is it me? Am I speaking gibberish to this guy?"

Coleman chugged a Heineken. "You're coming in clear over here."

Serge turned back to the clinic owner. "I would never think of asking you to drop the bill to two grand."

"That's better," said the owner. "Now you're being reasonable."

"I want you to take it all off," said Serge. "Give them a freebie. For the inconvenience."

"What!—"

. . . The letter *k* typed repeatedly across the computer screen. Livingston awoke moments later and raised his head from the keyboard. The letter *k* stopped.

"That pain throbbing in your temple would be from the butt of my gun," said Serge. "You have another temple, and I have a lot of time. Erase their bill."

Blood-soaked fingers tapped urgently on the delete button. "You have no idea who you're dealing with."

"Just keep going," said Serge.

The tapping continued until all the numbers were gone from the screen.

"Now, that wasn't so hard, was it?" asked Serge.

"Not for me, but life is about to become a nightmare for your friends," said Livingston.

"I doubt that," said Serge. "In fact, I expect the morning will be full of songbirds and dandelions when I deliver the good news."

"You still don't get it," said Livingston. "You think I'm just some local slimeball who figured out how to game the system in a tiny clinic."

"Uh, yeah, that about sums it up," said Serge.

"Well okay, you're right," said Livingston. "But I have some friends."

"Bullshit," said Serge. "You don't have friends."

"Okay, I don't have friends," said Livingston. "But I have connections. These guys work for me. The kind of guys you don't fuck with, and you just did. One phone call from me—"

Serge raised the pistol to give Livingston a backhand across the face.

"You better kill me," said the owner. "My connections. People have been planted all over the swamp just for giving me a bad look."

Serge relaxed the arm with the gun and stood in thought, rubbing his chin with the barrel. Finally, a single nod to himself. "All right, here's what you're going to do. Take down the whole system. Shitcan the works. And don't say it's not possible, because anyone running a shady operation like yours would definitely have a remote data-destruct back door in case the indictments are about to come down."

Livingston began tapping the keyboard. "Man, you have a serious death wish."

"I certainly do," said Serge. "It's to die facedown in my hundredth birthday cake. Now hit that last button."

Livingston did, and the whole screen zapped to black. He swiveled toward Serge in his office chair. "Hope you're happy now."

"Silly happy."

"Enjoy it while it lasts," said Livingston. "Because when I place my phone call, I'm going to make sure my connections know your friends' names, and I'm going to enjoy it!"

Serge began rubbing his chin again with the gun barrel. "Change of plans. Get up."

"Why?"

"Ever watch game shows?" asked Serge. "You've just earned the bonus round!"

Midnight had approached and gone when the Galaxie arrived back at Pelican Bay. It kept driving past the entrance and instead backed into the no-parking zone out of view from the balconies.

Serge walked around to the trunk, near a narrow path and a sign: PRIVATE BEACH. NO TRESPASSING. He popped the hood.

"*Mmmm! Mmmm! . . .*"

Serge raised a tire iron.

"*Mmmm—*"

Crack.

Silence.

Serge grabbed a travel tool kit from the trunk and slammed the lid. "Coleman, come on! This is going to be a blast."

His sidekick got out of the passenger side of the Galaxie, and it was indeed a blast. The wind hit Coleman so hard, he smacked his forehead on the open door. "Ouch! Is a storm coming?"

"No, just a typical windy night on the shore of the Keys, where there's nothing to block the gale. Let's roll!"

They both leaned hard into the wind and trudged through the sand half as fast as normal. Waves slammed the shoreline, spraying over the boulders and sending a briny mist across the beach.

"Jesus, Serge! Look how high the water is!"

"It's called a king tide," said Serge. "Because of the seasons. The perfect night!"

Coleman stopped and stared out at the incoming waves sparkling in the light of the rising moon. "Here we are again."

"Meditation Point will never get old." Serge walked over to where the residents had chained up their kayaks and paddleboards. "Plus the moon is still below the horizon, giving the perfect cover of full darkness from any prying eyes up on those balconies, except it's so late they're almost all in bed. But we'll still have to hurry to be safe from someone taking an insomniac stroll." He used the light from his cell phone to work a combination lock until it snapped open. "Coleman, help me drag this thing."

They got their board over to a spot in the sand near the row of coral boulders. Serge unfolded his travel kit, removing pliers and a socket wrench. Then he handed Coleman his phone. "Aim that here to give me some light . . ."

Serge diligently seized the task at hand, adjusting one fitting after another.

"I have no idea what you're doing," said Coleman.

"It will be that much more of a surprise . . ."

A half hour later, Serge retrieved his kite from the condo unit and took the elevator back down to the car. He glanced around at emptiness before popping the trunk.

"Mmmm! Mmmm!"

"Dr. Livingston, I presume?" Serge doubled over with laughter. "I've been waiting to use that line my whole life." He leaned into the trunk. "I know you want me to remove the duct tape, but you're a screamer. I can always tell. There are a lot of people asleep around here, and it would be so inconsiderate of me to disturb them with a noisy hostage at this hour."

Serge began marching the captive at gunpoint across the dark beach.

"Mmmm! Mmmm!"

"Damn!" said Serge. "You've got curiosity nibbling on my noodle. I'm dying to hear what's going through your mind. Promise not to scream? Be like a mouse?"

Desperate nodding.

"Yeah?" Serge scratched his stomach with the butt of the gun. "There's still the chance you'll yell, but it will be ultra-brief, and you won't dig the reason why. Here goes . . ."

Serge grabbed a corner of the duct tape and ripped it off.

"Owww!"

Serge mildly conked a forehead with the gun barrel. "You said you'd be like a mouse."

"Okay, I'll lower my voice. What are you going to do to me?"

"That will only make you scream," said Serge. "Next topic?"

"But why? What have I ever done to you?"

"Not to me." Serge poked him in the ribs. "To my friends. I thought we went over the whole deal with surprise medical billing. Weren't you listening?"

"Yes, but that's just money," said Livingston. "Your reaction is so out of proportion."

"Definitely," said Serge. "What's your point?"

Livingston began to quiver, and the water ran down his leg. "It's just not fair!"

"Whoa, chief! Stop right there!" Serge walked around to face the captive, waving the gun absentmindedly in front of his face. "Don't tell me you're one of those!"

"One of what?"

"The rich who claim they're the victims. Whining all the time: 'Life's not fair!'"

"It's not!" said the hostage. "Look at what you're doing!"

The duct tape quickly went back over a mouth, and Serge grabbed his own head with both hands. "Am I the only sane person on the planet? Jesus! Nothing but complaints!" He turned to Coleman. "You know how much I hate people who do nothing but complain all the time?"

Coleman nodded. "You're always complaining about them."

Serge just shook his head in disgust and got out tools. Coleman stuck his head inside the neck of his T-shirt to light a joint in the wind.

Livingston was in a state of terrified bewilderment, finding himself strapped to a lawn chair that was attached to some kind of wide surfboard. Serge latched a final safety belt around the captive's waist, then bent over so they were face-to-face at a range of three inches.

"I've said this so many times that I'm bored, like a cop reading Miranda rights, or a flight attendant explaining how to put on a flimsy oxygen mask. So let's get it over with: Because of your sins you've won a spot as a contestant in my game show, blah, blah, blah. The game changes week to week, but not the premise, blah,

blah. This time you're on a kiteboard, and it doesn't look good. But my contests always have a bonus round—"

Coleman began dancing a drunken jig and singing. *"The bonus round! The bonus round! Will he sink or will he swim? Will his body ever be found? The answer's in the bonus round!"* Burp.

The hostage began whining under his mouth tape.

"And here's your big chance, so listen up," said Serge. "Ever ride one of those stupid Segway things, like walking is beneath your dignity? It's all about shifting your weight. Any experienced kiteboarder could get out of this. I'm your opponent"—he held up a remote control—"trying to foil your every move with brilliant kite maneuvers. And by working your center of gravity, you'll be trying to foil mine. If you're successful enough and can sail out of range of this remote's radio signal, you win. It's all about the boat channels. Please familiarize yourself with the exits. Jesus, I sound like I work for Delta."

Serge dragged the board and captive to the water's edge and the protective rocks. "Coleman, come give me another hand getting this thing over the coral boulders."

They grunted and heaved, and the fiberglass board tipped upward over the rocks with a nasty scraping sound.

"Serge, I think we're tearing the shit out of the bottom of this thing."

"If my plan works, that's the last thing anyone will notice," said Serge. The contraption teetered on boulders halfway under the board. "Lean into it for one last big push. On three: One, two . . ."

A final pair of grunts, and the board pitched forward and nose-splashed into the ocean. Serge vaulted the seawall, landing hip-deep in the water. Livingston's hysterics were louder than ever under the tape.

Serge made a painful sigh. "I guess you want to say something. Okay, okay, I know I'm going to regret this . . ." He removed the tape.

"It's not fair!"

"Tautological motherfucker!" Serge reapplied the tape. "The regret came sooner than I imagined."

The wind increased to a howl, the surf breaching some of the lower boulders onto the beach.

"Coleman, hand me that remote control . . . Thanks. Now, jump in the water and walk out to the kite."

Coleman looked at Serge, then the dark water where the kite presumably was. "You're joking, right?"

"Don't be a weenie. It stays shallow for a couple hundred yards," said Serge. "The quicker you do this, the sooner I'll drive you to the liquor store."

An immediate splash as Coleman tripped over the boulders and belly-flopped into the sea.

"The East German judges give you a ten." Serge rotated a joystick on the remote. "Grab the lines on the front of the board and follow them out until you get to the kite."

Coleman was timid at first, but the water indeed stayed shallow as Serge had promised. He trudged. After a couple minutes, a muffled voice drifted back with the wind. "I've got it. What now?"

"You're going to hold it up, and the gusts and my remote control will do the rest. But not until I give you the word."

"Why not?"

"Look behind you."

Coleman turned around as a thin ribbon of harvest-yellow light appeared on the rim of the horizon next to Kalteux Key. "The moon?"

"We needed full darkness to prep the patient on the beach, or our deeds would have been too obvious and misunderstood." Serge flicked all the switches back and forth on his remote, activating a grid of red, yellow and green lights. "But now that he's off in the water, I need the moon to control the action."

They both waited and watched as the horizon finally released the bottom of the moon.

"Now!" yelled Serge.

As soon as Coleman raised the kite, the wind snatched it out of his hands. Serge pulled the joystick all the way back as the sail caught more wind and altitude. The board took off like a toboggan.

Coleman waded back to shore and crawled over the rocks on his stomach until he flipped into the sand. "What did I miss?"

Serge looped the kite left and right. "Just warming up, getting a feel for the weather."

Coleman looked at the ground near Serge's feet. "Why do you have a second remote control?"

"Remember those added modifications I made after you flew? There are now two extra deluxe features, one involving the chair and the other concerning the yoke maneuvering the kite." He nodded toward the ground. "That second remote controls them."

Coleman pulled a flask from a pocket in his cargo shorts. "This took way more work than most of your other projects."

"And worth every second." Serge angled the kite in a tacking maneuver against the wind. "Forget the pain clinic. I want to make him a contestant just for that whimpering about 'This isn't fair!'"

"Is this fair?"

"Fuck no." The joystick went the other way, and the board slalomed back across the moonlit silhouette of a distant mangrove islet. "It's a deep theme I've been hammering for years: Life's not fair."

"Doesn't sound that deep."

"It is if you run into me on the wrong day." The kite swung west. "If you're alive and in good health, you've won the galactic lottery. Any fairness at all after that is gravy."

The flask emptied. "I can dig it."

"I'll tell you what's really unfair. All the souls waiting to beam down to Earth, sitting in some kind of fifth-dimension holding room watching potential future parents on their first date. 'Come on, Dad! Come on! Don't screw this up! No, the salad fork is the other one!' But today it gets extra tricky. There's now a new form of contraception that we never envisioned. And all the souls in the holding room are gathered around this one guy, 'Trevor, you lucky bastard, he just picked her up in a bar!' 'You're almost home free!' 'Your parents are in the bedroom taking off their clothes!' 'You're about to beam down for sure!' '. . . Wait, what is your mother doing at his dresser?' 'She's picking up an envelope and pulling out a bumper sticker.' 'She's asking him if he's really a Democrat.' 'He says, "Yeah, don't tell me you're a Republican."' The other souls wince as they watch the rest, while Trevor bangs his forehead against the glass: 'For fuck's sake, you've got to be kidding me!'" Serge nodded hard. "Now *that's* unfair."

Coleman pointed toward a kite crossing the moon. "How's the contestant doing?"

"Not so well." Serge brought the joystick all the way around. "He's thrashing so much that his center of gravity is all over the matrix. He better figure it out fast because I'm getting ready to line him up."

The board made one last half loop until its course straightened out on dead reckoning to the east, picking up more and more velocity as it sliced the heavy chops.

Thunder rumbled in from the distant Gulf Stream, and the line of clouds pulsed with heat lightning. The gusts approached the bottom threshold of a tropical depression.

Coleman's hair was straight back in the increased wind, and he leaned forward for balance. "So what were those new features you added to the board?"

"The first was electronic release brackets on the legs of the lawn chair." He was now fighting hard against the kite as it began taking on a mind of its own. "And the second was another mechanical release, this time, where the kite's cords attach to the steering yoke. When that release lets go, there's an extra cord attaching the sail to something else . . ."

Coleman staggered to keep his footing. "I can barely see him anymore."

"Because the island is blocking the view from the light of the moon. You will soon . . . Hand me the second remote." Serge slowly but steadily worked the joystick back. "He'll be at top speed in ten seconds."

"Then what?"

"Unfairness."

Serge dropped the first remote control and threw a switch on the second, releasing the kite cords from the yoke. Then immediately hit a second switch, blowing the board's fasteners to the lawn chair.

Liftoff.

"I see him now," said Coleman. "Man, is he way up there."

Moonlight lit up the captive, still in the chair, as the whole works cleared the highest mangroves on Kalteux Key.

Serge tossed the second remote in the sand. "We've crossed the Rubicon, no turning back."

"He's not coming down from his jump," said Coleman. "He's still going higher."

"The kite has now essentially become one of those parachutes that tourist boats pull to fly visitors around."

Coleman squinted into the wind and the first tiny drops of stinging rain. "I can't make out what the kite is now attached to."

"Oh, that would be the noose around his neck."

"He disappeared," said Coleman.

Serge gathered up the remotes. "Show's over."

"Can we go to the liquor store now?"

"Sounds fair."

Chapter 32

The shrieking was high-pitched and emotional, coming from all directions.

It was the good kind.

Small children ran in circles, for reasons known only to them. Others sat in miniature furniture. The short round tables were covered with paste, construction paper, crayons, finger paint, safety scissors and pipe cleaners.

A little girl named Carla ran up to Julie. "I have a boo-boo."

"Oh, let's fix that up." She applied a Band-Aid. "Better?"

The child nodded with a smile and took off, giggling. Julie resumed restocking groceries.

Just another day at the Happy Seas care center.

The front door opened, letting in bright noon sunlight. Two people walked in.

One of the staff approached them. "Can I help you?"

It wasn't a sincere question. It meant: *I think you're at the wrong place.*

"Can you help me?" said Serge. "No. I'm here to help *you.*"

"I think you're at the wrong place."

"Relax, we're professionals." Serge walked around her.

She ran after him. "Sir, you can't go in there. You're not authorized."

"We're friends of Julie."

"You know Julie?"

Julie heard her name and looked over from the pantry. "Oh, no."

"Hey, Julie!"

"What are you doing here?"

"Volunteering. What else?"

"You can't just show up to volunteer. There are state requirements."

"You didn't say that back at the café when I told you I was coming."

"Because I never expected that you'd actually—"

The noise of childhood excitement suddenly jumped to a new decibel level.

Serge and Julie looked over at a pile of laughing children crawling all over Coleman, who was on his hands and knees on one of the foam play mats. They wrestled with his arms and legs—"I'm getting you! I'm getting you!"—and another straddled his back like a cowboy.

"See?" said Serge. "He's a natural. They love him."

"There are insurance issues . . . and other issues," said Julie. "Please ask him to stop."

"I understand. Wouldn't want to be disruptive." Serge cupped his hands around his mouth. "Coleman, get up and come over here."

"I can't," said Coleman. "They're winning."

Serge grinned at Julie. "See how dedicated he is to the art of playing pretend with children?"

The pair walked over to Coleman and began removing the tykes. "It's lunchtime," said Julie, and they trotted off.

Other staff members had cleared the craft supplies off the tables and began serving beanie-weenies, mac and cheese, fruit cups and tiny cartons of milk.

Serge smiled at the sight and turned to Julie. "So, where do you want me to start? Actually, I have a few ideas of my own to improve this place. I could begin teaching a self-defense class. Of course, we'd need helmets with face masks, and those fighting sticks with the padded ends."

"Serge—"

"What? If you think they were having a blast with Coleman, the padded fighting sticks will put it over the top."

"Serge, we need to talk about you being here. There are rules on who can volunteer—"

Coleman staggered over. "Whew, that was a close one."

Julie cleared her throat. "What I was saying is that I know you mean well, but it's just not appropriate for you to—... Serge, are you listening to me?"

Serge was staring again at one of the lunch tables.

"Serge, can you please pay attention to me? This is important..."

He continued staring at the table. It was abuzz, except for one girl sitting straight up and staring ahead. Nobody but Serge had noticed that her little milk carton was tipped over, dripping off the table.

"Serge! Listen to me!"

He didn't. Instead, he took off running and snatched the girl out of her chair. Then Serge placed her on her back on one of the foam mats. He crouched by her feet, locking his hands together and placing the heel of a palm on her upper stomach just under the ribs.

A quick, short thrust. Then another and another. "Come on, come on. Help me out here . . ." Another pair of thrusts. Finally, a slice of hot dog jettisoned from her mouth, and Serge sat the coughing girl up.

He hung his head with a massive relief sigh. Then Serge looked around at all the wordless people staring back at him. "What?"

A pproaching sneakers slapped the waxed floor of the break room. "Hey, Julie."

She looked up from a cucumber sandwich. "Serge . . . I—I don't know what to say."

Serge sat down with a Styrofoam to-go box. "About what?"

"About *what*?" Julie repeated, extending an arm. "Out there."

Serge turned around to the doorway. "That?"

"Yes, that," said Julie. "And how did you know the alternate Heimlich maneuver for a small child?"

"Doesn't everyone?"

"No."

"Really? I just thought if you're part of society, it's one of the mandatory things to look up."

"And do you have eyes in the back of your head?"

"Again, if you're down with the village, a top priority is remaining aware at all times of what's going on with every child in sight."

Julie just took a large breath and blinked a few times.

"How is she, anyway?"

"The paramedics took her to the hospital, but just for observation," said Julie. "They told us she'll be fine."

"That's a load off."

"Listen, after what we saw out there, you can volunteer here. You have more parental instincts than a lot of parents."

"What about the rules?"

"It's the Keys. We make our own slack," said Julie. "And I'm sorry about my cold reception. I just had a first impression."

"Why? Because I was kind of spazzing out when we met at Café 90?"

"Precisely."

Serge winced. "First impressions have always been ticklish for me. It's basically a roll of the dice. I could be pensive, effervescent, melancholy, introspective, extroverted, free-associating, obsessive and/or compulsive, randomly zany, or trying to get a jarring amount of blood out of my shirt. That last impression is hard to bounce back from."

"What's in the Styrofoam box?"

"Oh, this?" He opened the lid. "A monster Cuban sandwich from the café. That place is evil, I tell you. They get their hooks in, and you can't quit. I had three espressos while waiting."

"The food *is* pretty darn good. Family cooking," said Julie. "Been going for years . . . So where do you live?"

"Oh, the big payoff from Operation Pump the Brakes!"

"Pump—?"

"We scored this righteous pad at Pelican Bay," said Serge. "Everything the real estate agent showed us was so beautiful and bright and full of cheer. But then we got super lucky and found a shithole. I call it my fishing cabin in the sky."

"I know that condo," said Julie. "It's right up the street from me."

"Up the street? Where's your place?"

"Off the Old Road," said Julie. "You know all those mysteriously overgrown gates leading into the woods?"

"Intimately," said Serge. "Which one is yours?"

"The verdigris with the herons and vines, and that big gumbo-limbo just inside."

"I know it!" said Serge. "I take morning walks all the time through there and have worked out an understanding with the local peacocks. They've got an attitude that is unnerving, like they own the road, not moving for any person or vehicle until they're good and ready. They got wise to my peacock prison-yard vibe, so the next day I drove down the Old Road in my *Romper Room* car, and it was total bird confusion: 'Hey, Clyde, what the fuck is wrong with this picture?' Since then, we give each other a wide berth. Anyway, what's with those haunted-house security gates?

I've wanted to jump them a few times out of curiosity, but I have a moral code. Not the kind of code most people would think because of my bonus rounds, especially if you ask those crime scene cleanup companies. But jumping private fences is just inexcusable. I review my moral code each year to account for shifting cultural mores, and next summer I might be jumping gates left and right. I make no promises. Did I mention the espresso?—"

There was a crash at the entrance to the break room. Coleman bounced off the door frame and staggered until he collapsed in a chair at their table.

Julie placed a hand on his arm. "Are you all right?"

"Those kids!"

Julie laughed. "They can definitely wear you out if you don't watch it," she said. "Are you as good with children as your friend Serge?"

"What do you mean?" asked Coleman.

"Getting down and wrestling with them. That's one of their favorites."

"I didn't get down on the floor to wrestle," said Coleman. "A few times a day, gravity has a mind of its own."

"Well, you're already starting to be a favorite."

Coleman tugged Serge's sleeve. "I've got to talk to you. In the corner."

Serge shrugged at Julie. "I'll just be a minute."

He joined Coleman in the corner. "What's up?"

"What the hell is she talking about, good with the kids?"

"Yeah, you were fantastic," said Serge. "The children loved you."

"Loved me?" said Coleman. "They were terrifying! Especially the one trying to ride me like a horse."

Serge inspected his pal's eyes. "Are you tripping?"

"Way too much shrooms." Coleman grabbed the sides of his head. "That's bad when gangs of small children attack."

"Okay, I thought I had rectified our first impression with Julie, but your condition could create a setback. Why don't you sit out front in the car until this shit wears off?"

Coleman pointed at the break room door in horror. "You mean go back through the playroom?"

"I can see this requires dope supervision." Serge turned and waved to Julie. "We need to tend to something out in the car . . ." He grabbed Coleman from behind by the shoulders and carefully aimed him through the doorway like he was delivering an over-size refrigerator . . .

J ulie had wondered about that first day with the choking in-cident, but Serge indeed came back to volunteer on a regular basis, serving lunch, helping to glue glitter on crafts projects, and even sweeping up the back room.

Julie listened to the laughter. This time it was Serge who was wrestling. He finished the particularly strenuous match, and the kids climbed off. He walked over to Julie. "Changed your mind yet about the padded fighting sticks?"

She smiled. "Not yet."

"Just checking." He went back to wrestling.

Chapter 33

THE OLD ROAD

I t was one of those warm and silent days in the Keys.

The silence is not to be underestimated. If you aren't familiar with it, there is a comfortable oddness that you can't quite put your finger on. A flat, bright sea, not enough breeze to even rustle the palm fronds. No nearby roads or restaurants, or the chorus of morning birds now quieted by the noon heat. It takes effort not to relax.

Julie was at an upstairs window, facing the Gulf Stream. She opened the window.

Hot, still air.

She checked her watch and turned around. "Is he late?"

The guard standing by the door just shrugged and smiled.

But then the wait was over. She heard it first, then saw it.

The still palm fronds began to whip and bend as the black Sikorsky hovered down onto its pad on the beach. As usual, the first thing Mercado did was head up to pay a visit to the master bedroom.

Julie was waiting in the doorway. "How was your business trip?"

"Boring." Mercado turned to where both of their fathers were sleeping. "Nothing to talk about. How about here at the house?"

"Also boring. Except the hot sauce intrigue."

Mercado just smirked. "What about the care center?"

"That's a different story," said Julie. "I met the strangest guys at the café, and they've started volunteering."

"What's so strange about that?"

"It would take too much time." She was staring out the window again at the beach. "Why are your guys loading more luggage?"

"This is only a quick stopover," said Mercado. "Just needed to pick up a few things and say hi."

"Say hi? I thought you were going to be home for a few days. Your dad's been wanting to talk to you. So have I."

"This just came up. I'm sorry, I should have called," said Mercado. "What did you want to talk about? You need anything?"

"No, nothing important," said Julie, still looking at the shore. "Just wanted to talk. You're taking a lot of business trips. This doesn't have anything to do with your brother, does it?"

"No, nothing like that," said Mercado.

"Then what?"

"You know I can't get into business," said Mercado. "If I told you anything at all, you'd worry when you have no need."

She nodded. "When will I hear from you?"

"After I land, I'll call and we'll talk tonight." He trotted down the stairs and out to the helicopter.

Julie remained at the window as the chopper's blades began to rotate. Mercado ducked under them, and was back aboard.

The helicopter lifted off and rose slowly to a hundred feet. Mercado was waving down at her from one of the windows.

She waved back.

Bang.

The house shook as the helicopter exploded, shooting twin fireballs out both sides. The blades wobbled as the burning chopper started to spin and tilt, and began falling sideways. Straight toward the house. Toward the master bedroom.

It was happening so fast, there was no time to do anything but have a heart attack. The doomed helicopter filled the entire window when there was a deafening crack. One of the blades broke off, sailing over the roof. It destabilized the already unstable aircraft, and the Sikorsky banked the other way, back toward the ocean, where it crashed just offshore.

A steam cloud rose from the sea like a mushroom.

Chapter 34

ISLAMORADA

Dozens of red and blue lights lit up a post-modern mansion off the Old Road. The news trucks were held back outside the gates.

All night long, statements taken and retaken, photographs snapped. Boats were out in the water behind the house from various agencies. Some collecting evidence, others recovering bodies, still more trying to quarantine aviation fuel and hydraulic fluid with inflatable berms before it could harm the ecosystem.

Julie sat downstairs on a white leather sofa, finishing up a third round of questions and cocktails. She drank with shaking hands. She was beyond conflicted. Of course Mercado knew the business he was in. For all she knew, he deserved it. Still . . .

Cinco walked over to Julie. "May I have a seat?"

"Sure," she said, barely audible. She slid over to make more room.

"I know a lot is going on in your mind right now, but Mercado gave me instructions," said Cinco. "So to take at least one thing off your plate, you and your father can stay here as long as you want, forever if necessary."

"What? He planned for this?" said Julie. "Those were his instructions?"

"Strict instructions," said Cinco. "We're trained to carry out his intentions, and he didn't want you to worry. I'll have more to say after a few days."

"Why not now?"

"Because someone else will be coming around to talk to you."

"Who?"

"That's all I'm supposed to say."

"First you don't want me to worry, and now with the mystery."

"Trust me," said Cinco. "It will all work out."

"I can give you one answer now," said Julie. "Me and my father will be leaving soon. I just need time to make some arrangements."

"Take as much time as you want," said Cinco. Then, to his surprise, Julie grabbed his right hand in both of hers and squeezed and wouldn't let go. Cinco knew it was time to stop talking and just let Julie do her own thing in her own way.

A sheriff's car turned off the Old Road and through the gates. Other deputies guarding the gates waved it through. The patrol car raced up the winding driveway and skidded to a stop in the circle outside the front steps. A deputy jumped out and sprinted through several layers of security because everyone knew him. He dashed inside the front door and stopped, urgently glancing left and right, then shouted in general: "Where's Julie?"

An FBI agent turned from a witness and pointed toward a white sofa. The deputy rushed over to where Julie was still holding Cinco's hand, not exactly distraught or in shock—more like emotionally trying to catch up with an overload of new data.

"Julie! Thank God you're okay! I got here as fast as I could!"

"Deke!" She jumped up for an extended hug.

"I feel so guilty," said Deke. "I was going to tell you about Mercado when I saw you two at the café, but I was still awaiting confirmation reports from other agencies to be absolutely sure before I said something like that."

"No need to apologize," said Julie. "I know all about Mercado. He told me—"

"Stop right there! Don't say another word!" said Deke. "Don't speak to anyone without an attorney!"

"Am I in some kind of trouble?"

"Not at all," said the deputy. "But you can get there real fast by talking about anything you heard here at this house, or anywhere else with Mercado."

"Your family and mine have been friends our whole lives," said Julie. "You're one of the people I trust the most at a time like this. I can't talk to you?"

"*Especially* not me," said Deke. "I'm in a difficult position here. Even if you tell me something you think is innocent, it could open a can of worms if I'm ever on the witness stand. So it's better if only I talk and you listen. First thing is to get you a lawyer, and then anything you need, have them call me. Anytime, day or night."

"I'll be fine."

"We need to get you out of here!"

"I can't leave, at least right now."

"But Julie—"

"My father's here."

The deputy caught himself. "Okay, I understand. It's been a rough day. But you *will* be leaving. In the meantime, I'm going to start regular patrols . . . I'm just so glad you're all right."

Deke released the hug to appraise her. She smiled the smile of strength. Then the deputy happened to look at Cinco. He took a moment to size him up.

Cinco stared back solemnly. Then he gave a single, subtle nod, indicating respect. "I will tell my staff at the gate to be looking for you. All your men will have total access to the property at all times, no questions asked. And if any are asked, you come find me. I'm Cinco."

They shook hands, not friendly, but out of a common interest. "I'm Deke."

"Deke, do not worry. Right now, Julie couldn't be at a safer place."

"We'll argue about that later. Starting tonight, I want to permanently post of couple of my men to patrol the grounds." He raised his eyebrows for a response.

"Done."

Deke waved Cinco over to a corner for privacy. "And since there's no warrant, I don't want there to be any misunderstanding," said the deputy. "My men will also be watching your men. I know your business, and at least one of the guards is probably on someone else's payroll."

"Not this family," said Cinco.

"Be that as it may . . ."

Cinco nodded curtly. "Your men can watch whatever you like."

"Fine." Deke gave Cinco a business card. "We'll talk again." Then the deputy gave Julie a final hug and down the stairs he went.

Julie took a seat and looked up at Cinco. "What now?"

"Like I said earlier, someone will visit in a couple of days, and then I can speak more freely . . ."

S ure enough, two days later, just as Cinco had said, Julie got a visitor.

She was up in the bedroom with her dad when her presence was requested downstairs. She found a man in the dining room who did not look like the rest of the gang. And had a southern accent.

"Julie," said Cinco, "this is the man I said you would be meeting with. I will leave you two alone now."

"My name's Buford Grange." He handed her a business card.

She read it and looked up. "Attorney at law? *You* are a lawyer for the Benzappa family?"

"Let's just say that I've been retained. May I call you Julie?"

"Knock yourself out." She looked at the business card again. "Your office is on Cudjoe Key?"

"Just up the road from the radar blimp," said Buford. "For the last thirty years, since moving down from Macon."

"How did you hook up with Mercado?"

"He had a little local issue. The rest is privileged." Buford placed a briefcase on the dining room table and flipped the latches. "What's important right now is *our* business."

"But I didn't hire you."

"That's why I'll need you to sign some forms, but that comes at the end." Buford pulled out a stack of legal-size folders. "If you could hold your questions till later, because I have a lot to go over, and I'm guessing if you're like most people, this will be much to absorb."

"The floor is yours," said Julie, thinking, *Mysteries abound in this place.*

"First is the quitclaim deed," said the lawyer. "I have durable power of attorney and already signed in Mercado's stead." He slid some paperwork across the table. "Sign those, and I'll notarize them before filing with the clerk this afternoon."

She looked at the papers with a question mark on her face. "What am I signing?"

"Julie, you now own this house. Or you will after I go by the clerk."

Her mouth opened but nothing came out.

"Look," said the attorney, "if you're worried about taxes and utilities—"

"My mind is so far from reaching that train station."

"Julie, do you want me to handle this matter for you?" said Buford. "If you say yes, we have confidentiality, and I may speak more freely."

"Yes."

"Okay then, the big picture." More pages came out of folders. "We both generally know about the Benzappa family, and recently circumstances arose south of here that made business less predictable than usual. Bottom line is that Mercado came to see me in case of an eventuality such as this. He spoke highly of you, and didn't want you and your father to have to move back to your trailer." This time Buford slid an entire folder across the table. "You'll see several bank accounts to be transferred to your name. There's plenty in there for maintenance, taxes, et cetera, including your own personal expenses. You won't want for anything the rest of your life. He also made a donation to your care center. Not a small one."

Julie became flushed. "This is a fortune! How can they, I—"

"From my understanding of the family's finances, this amount isn't much at all to them," said Buford. "They write off more than this all the time without even thinking about it."

"You mean when they lose planes and shipments."

Buford simply smiled.

Julie read down the list of offshore accounts. "The hospice really could use the money. But it won't do anyone any good if we face forfeiture, let alone go to jail."

"Don't worry, the money's all clean," said Buford. "You're not exposing yourself to criminality because it all came from legitimate spinoff ventures, plus the cash has made at least six stops in banks all over the world, from Brussels to Dubai and Zurich and back again. I should travel so well."

Julie inhaled slow and deep. "There's got to be a catch."

"There is."

"I knew it." Julie reclined in her chair. "Okay, lay it on me."

"Mercado had me draw all this up with provisions in case he pre-deceased his father, which he now has." The attorney flipped to a page of caveats. "The main conditions are that Raffy remain here the rest of his life as well, and you'll oversee his care."

"Now it makes a lot more sense," said Julie.

"It's a good deal for everyone involved. A *great* deal for you," said the lawyer. "Mercado was always saying there were some things he was trying to make up for."

"Told me the same."

"I think this here does it."

"But . . . the family, the helicopter," said Julie. "That's the exposure I'm really worried about. My nerves weren't cut out for the last few days. I can't be living in fear, wondering what day shit will finally show up on my doorstep."

"Understandable," said Buford. "Don't ask me how I know this, but I do. It all ended with Mercado. Everyone knows Raffy is in no condition to run anything, and members of the family are already . . . Let me put it this way: It was settled by a truce. Others have moved on and couldn't care less about the old man or this place."

"Are you absolutely sure?"

"This I *really* shouldn't tell you, but the powers that be south of here were expecting Mercado to be handled back in their own country. A.J. and the fishing skiff matter was one thing, but add on a giant helicopter that people saw all up and down U.S. 1. A lot of blowback from our government. Some of their people have already gone missing for the decision to bring their problems up here to our shores . . . The bottom line is that with all the political fallout, plus those guards assigned to protect Raffy for the rest of his life, you'll probably be living in the safest place in all of Florida."

Julie watched the attorney leave, then stared down at where her hands were gripping her knees. "That sure gave me a lot to think about." She looked up as Cinco returned. "What?"

He pulled up a chair and faced her. "Now I can speak candidly."

Julie looked back at the empty doorway, then at Cinco again. "Because the attorney visited?"

"He's also representing me," said Cinco. "I don't know how it works. It's some kind of legal arrangement where I can tell you more stuff. Are you relaxed?"

"As much as I can be with all this suspense," said Julie.

"It was Mercado's wish," said Cinco. "In the event that something like this happened, he made me swear to tell you everything."

"This is getting insanely complex," said Julie. "Whatever you're beating around the bush about, why couldn't Mercado just have told me himself?"

Cinco shook his head. "He never wanted you to know while he was still alive. You'll understand when you hear it."

"Okay, okay," said Julie, rolling her eyes at the ceiling. "So tell me already."

"Remember when you first met Mercado?"

"Definitely. We bumped into each other at that dockside bar."

"That was not a chance meeting."

"Of course it was," said Julie. "I went there with my girl-friends."

Cinco shook his head. "I'd had you under surveillance for two weeks: the care center, the trailer with your father."

"Okay, now this is beginning to get creepy."

"And I eavesdropped several times when your friends would eat lunch at their regular diner, the one with those shark jaws out front that tourists pose next to for photos."

"Creepy is becoming scary."

"You recall when your older brother died?"

"You don't forget something like that."

"Did you read about it in the papers?"

"Yeah, a random botched robbery," said Julie. "They suspected some ex-cons from Miami but could never prove anything."

"It wasn't a random robbery," said Cinco. "It was in your father's boat, down at the sport fishing pier. There was a drug deal. Cocaine, to be precise."

"No way!" said Julie. "Now I know you're bullshitting because my brother would never—"

"Not your brother. One of your dad's friends, the captain of the boat in the next slip. It was after midnight, and the deal soured in a hurry. Your brother just happened to be there, cleaning your father's bilge or something, and he tried to protect the captain. He was shot."

"Who shot him?"

A long pause. "Mercado."

Julie opened her mouth, but only voiceless air came out. Everything froze, and the recognition of truth slammed home with dizziness and nausea, her head beginning to spin on one axis after another. Julie's memory rampaged back through the last several weeks; it was as if she was sitting in a room with a thousand jigsaw pieces scattered everywhere, and suddenly they all levitated and flew together in an instant to form the big picture. She pitched forward and threw up . . .

. . . Cinco was waiting with a glass of water when she opened her eyes.

"What happened?" asked Julie, back of her hand against her forehead.

"You passed out, but I caught you and put you in bed. Here, drink some of this."

She sipped.

"I know you're damning Mercado's soul right now. Mine too," said Cinco. "Except he made me swear to him to tell you."

"Yeah, both of you burn in hell!" said Julie. "But after all these years, what the fuck? I could have gotten along fine the rest of my days without knowing. Why?"

"Mercado was just a boy, too, barely seventeen," said Cinco. "Regardless of the front he's had to put on, he was never a tough guy. It's been torturing him all these years."

"*Him* tortured? So you fix that by torturing me?"

"This is probably the worst time to be blunt," said Cinco, "but you need to get a grip and focus on your father. You have a lot of decisions that need to be made soon. There's the deed to this place, the bank accounts to keep it running for generations, your whole staff—"

"My staff?"

"Again, Mercado was very specific," said Cinco. "You're in charge. Whatever you tell any of the men, they have to do it without disagreement. And if there is any problem, you tell me, and then I'll make them do it."

"And what about you?"

"No exception for me, either," said Cinco. "Whatever order you give, I have to carry it out."

"So are you saying that I'm, like, your boss?"

"When it comes to everything within the perimeter of this property, that's exactly what you are."

Another guard appeared in the doorway.

"Julie, this is Goose, my most trusted associate. He'll handle whatever you need on a day-to-day basis. Anything, ask him."

"Why do they call you Goose?"

"At some point a goose did something. I was really young. Don't remember the rest."

"Do you like the name?"

"Not really."

Cinco cleared his throat. "Goose has it from here. Don't be shy about what you'll require."

"Okay," said Julie, getting out a pen and paper. "I need to make a list."

Cinco nodded. "Give it to Goose."

Chapter 35

ISLAMORADA

Cartoon mermaids waved from a mural on the front of the modest cement-block building.

A woman stepped inside the Happy Seas care center. "Yolanda . . ."

Another woman, sitting behind a desk, looked up, then was on her feet. "Julie! Dear lord! Are you all right?"

"I'm fine."

"It's all everyone has been talking about. So terrible," said Yolanda. "We figured you were busy with the police and all, but we were still worried."

"Well, you can stop now," said Julie. "And I have some good news."

"We sure could use a little of that around here."

"Then get ready for a lot." Julie took a seat. "I have a proposition. You know our waiting list? I think I can help with that."

"The whole thing?" asked Yolanda.

"Hold on to your hat," said Julie. "Also the waiting list for that other place in the Lower Keys."

Yolanda's head pulled back. "What did you do, win the lottery?"

"Yes." She pulled a list from her purse . . .

. . . Three days later, the delivery trucks began arriving at a post-modern mansion on Millionaires Row.

The guards didn't know what to make of it, but they had their marching orders: Julie's word was the law.

The guard named Goose directed the traffic like a general contractor. "Those go in the living room."

The painters were already inside, filling the walls with bright tropical fish and staghorn coral. Workers carried heavy crates through the front door and broke open the boxes and assembled rows of bunk beds along the walls. The giant dining room table and chairs had been trucked away to make room, and a grid of tiny tables and chairs soon filled the space. More workers unrolled the thick foam safety mats.

The efforts took less than a week, and now the previously wide-open floor plan was one big, happy barracks.

THE CARIBBEAN

Bony, varicose fingers reached into a pouch. They pulled out Goldfish crackers and tossed them to the pigeons strutting around under the palm trees. The old man was sitting at a familiar table atop the city wall in Old San Juan overlooking La Perla. The wall was made of sandstone.

Three bodyguards escorted a younger man to the table. He timidly took a seat as the guards stepped back and folded their hands at their waists.

The old man didn't acknowledge his guest. He continued tossing crackers until he was finished. Then he noticed a small boy squatting at the base of a palm tree near the birds. The man removed a shiny coin—a Colombian fifty-pesos piece—and held it out to sparkle in the sun. The child's eyes lit up, and the man tossed it, the coin clattering on the flat stonework until the boy grabbed it and ran off.

The old man's head eventually turned. The younger guest hadn't spoken because you never spoke first. Especially since he had no idea what the meeting was about. He had simply been summoned. It would go like this: A large car pulled up and silent men opened the back door. There wasn't a question or a choice. You simply got in for good or ill, wondering.

The younger man was still wondering with sweaty palms as he waited. Finally, after a dignified pause, the old man cleared his throat.

"Deuce, I gave you an important responsibility. I allowed you to make the decisions. I put my faith in you."

"And I thank you," said Deuce. "I didn't understand about Florida. I would have taken down the helicopter off the coast of Barranquilla if I had known about the Americans. It won't happen again. I swear!"

"Deuce, when you speak so much, you let the other person know you are nervous."

"Yes, sir."

"Now, I am not speaking of the United States thing. I am speaking of our country. I am not hearing what makes me relax."

"It's all under control, but a change like this takes time," said the young man. "Don't listen to whoever is saying such things."

"Deuce, the Benzappa family was in disarray. Command and control had been eliminated." The old man looked down and picked at a piece of chipped paint on the concrete table. "The smart thing to do, the *business* thing to do, would have been to recruit their remnants into our operation. Instead I hear of ambulances and morgues and newspaper headlines."

"It was Mercado," said Deuce. "He was supposed to be the

business side of the family. But who knew that would work against us? He didn't have the stomach to get involved, so he gave his men too much rein after his brother—"

"Please don't tell me what I already know." The old man reached back into his bag of crackers. "Mercado was too emotional. Business has no room for emotion."

"I understand," said Deuce. "So you see why we had to take care of Mercado. His men were out of control. We even got hit at a wedding."

"You have no reason to apologize for Mercado," said the old man. "Unless you keep talking about him."

Deuce lowered his head. "I understand. I will go back and see who I can recruit."

One of the bony hands was raised. "I have heard you are already attempting that."

"Yes, sir."

"And how is it going?"

Deuce's head stayed lowered, this time silent.

"Do not be concerned," said the old man. "I have heard what is happening. Our competition is being unreasonable with our offers. Apparently this Mercado was very popular with his men." A venerable fist suddenly pounded the stone table. "There is also no such thing as *popularity* in our business! What were we supposed to do? . . ." He was now talking more to himself than to Deuce. "We took care of A.J., and then this weak successor Mercado, and all that is left is Raffy, who watches reruns all day and barely remembers his own name. How hard can this be? But no, the longer Raffy goes unseen in Florida, the more his mythology looms over the landscape of the mountains of our homeland. His people are fighting more fervently than ever in his name."

"He's watching TV reruns? In the Keys?" asked Deuce. "Is one of their guards on our payroll?"

A glare wilted Deuce's neck, and his head hung again. "Sorry."

"Raffy Benzappa might be too frail to run the family, but he still is a symbol to these people. I would have preferred a return to peace, but now this thing cannot end like that. I am not pleased."

"Then I will please you," said Deuce.

"You let us take care of what is back home," said the old man.

"And I will go and take care of the myth," said Deuce.

The old man turned to face the pigeons again, which told Deuce two things: It was time for him to leave. And he would have only one chance at this.

The younger man walked away, and the older man dumped the rest of the crackers atop the city wall.

Pigeons swarmed.

Chapter 36

BACK IN THE USA

A green station wagon exited the Florida Turnpike at the only place where there was no other option, because there was no more turnpike.

The toll road's southern terminus dumped meekly into Florida City, the last crumbs of mankind at the bottom of the Florida mainland before more than a hundred miles of islands and bridges to Key West. Vix was sleeping in the back seat.

A Buick was in front of them as they approached the first traffic light. It turned yellow, plenty of time for two cars to get through, but the Buick got cold feet. The driver of the station wagon had big eyes as he slammed the brakes. Vix was pitched forward into a headrest and came alive all at once.

"What the fuck was that?"

"Some idiot stopped on a yellow," said Mulch.

She looked at the vehicle's clock. Midnight. "Where are we?"

"Florida City. I have to go to the bathroom."

Vix looked out the windows as they waited for the light to change. It wasn't raining but she could tell that it had been. Ahead, U.S. 1 was a perfectly straight drag strip about a mile to the mangroves. The street glowed with the lights of convenience stores and fast food and motels with free Wi-Fi. There was a pirate ship.

"How did we get here so fast?" asked Vix.

Mulch eased onto the gas at the sight of green. "The turnpike was practically clear at this hour. We really flew."

Vix slapped him, as they say, upside the head.

"Ow! What the hell was that for?"

"I told you to stay off the turnpike!" screamed Vix. "People are looking for us!"

"But it was taking so long," said Mulch. "Plus, there were police cars on the other roads, too. If I watched my speed on the turnpike, what's the difference except getting here sooner?"

Another slap. "The difference is that it's a toll road."

"I didn't see any toll booths."

"Because everything's electronic now," said Vix. "Every ten miles they take photos of all the license plates to send monthly bills. The computers also run plate numbers against lists of warrants and stolen cars."

"I don't see any cops after us." He instinctively ducked, and her third slap found only air.

"We've lucked out for now," said Vix. "That just means they haven't found the guy at the cemetery yet, or there's some kind of delay in the system. But it's a sure bet they'll soon know our exact route here, thanks to your brainlessness!"

"What do we do?"

"This car's too hot," said Vix. "We need to get it off the road until I think of something. Turn around . . ."

The station wagon headed back under the turnpike's overpass. Mulch looked over at Vix. "You and that map again."

"It's why we're here." She snorted off the back of her hand and studied the diagram of the large house. To herself: "What does this X mean? A safe? Trapdoor in the floor under a carpet? Buried beneath the place? We killed that asshole too soon."

"Do we have enough people?" asked Weezer.

"The three of us can carry anything we find," said Vix.

"No, I mean this guy is supposed to be some sort of big drug kingpin, right? So he's bound to have armed guards and a security system, and probably a big gate and fence. We're going to just waltz right in?"

She folded the map. "No, we're not going to waltz in," Vix said in a mocking voice. Another snort. "We're going to take the fucking place! That money is ours now!"

The guys glanced at each other: *This reeks of doom.*

Vix pointed at the windshield. "Up there, take that road." The vehicle turned, and she directed the driver into a sprawling parking lot that was surprisingly jumping at this hour. Vehicles stretching hundreds of yards all the way to the woods.

"What's with these people?" asked Weezer.

"See that sign? Twenty-four-hour Walmart?"

"Yeah?"

"The other businesses in this plaza are closed, but Walmart's open twenty-four hours, which helps if you're stealth camping . . . Pull down and turn left. It looks like there are some people camping now along the edge of the woods."

The station wagon reached the end of the parking lot, and sure enough, a row of cars sat along the trees with occupants in various stages of trying to sleep.

"Look." Mulch pointed. "I see an empty spot."

"No, keep going and don't speed up."

"But we're tired," said Weezer.

"I have to go to the bathroom," Mulch repeated.

"And I'm watching a police car behind us," said Vix.

Mulch's eyes went to the rearview. "Which one?"

"The one with the police lights on top," said Vix. "Driving slowly and shining a spotlight. Now there's another prowler car."

"They found us?"

"No," said Vix. "They're clearing the parking lot of stealth campers."

"I see what you mean," said Mulch. "The cars are starting to pull out one by one."

"Just the break we need," said Vix.

"What do you mean?" said Mulch.

"Circle around to let the police cars go, then drive to that exit at the back of the lot. I'll explain the rest . . ."

The driver did as told, and soon they were at a traffic light, sitting side by side with a Volkswagen microbus. The driver wore a knit Jamaican cap and a concert T-shirt for some band's fifth farewell tour.

Vix rolled down her window. "Cops kick you out, too?"

"Bummer," said the driver. "Two years ago this place was no hassle. You stealth camp, too?"

"All the time," said Vix. "I know this backup spot down the way if you want to follow."

"Where is it?"

"Not too far," said Vix. "Just up this road before it merges with Old Dixie Highway near the Coral Castle."

"Cool . . ."

. . . The station wagon headed north up the desolate street through Homestead. A mixture of unkempt ranch houses and malnourished industrial businesses. They passed places with roll-down metal doors and signs for guard dogs that may or may not exist. Scrap metal, oil drums, septic repair.

"Take a left," said Vix.

The station wagon drove down another long, dark street. This one with signs of life at the end. A mile in the distance, the tiny headlights of traffic speeding by on Old Dixie. Vix watched the scenery pass.

"Where is this place?" asked Mulch.

"I'll know when I see it," said Vix. "Just keep driving . . . Wait, slow down, stop!"

They pulled over to the side of the road.

Mulch squinted. "It's just an old muffler place. And it's got a fence with barbed wire all around."

Vix opened her door and got out. "I'll take care of it."

She walked back to the Scooby-Doo van. The driver already had his window down, and Vix rested her arms on the ledge. "Here we are! Home sweet home!"

"Yeah, uh, but—" said the driver.

"Who else do we have in here?" She stuck her head closer to see three other people in back eating tacos. "What are you guys, a band or something?"

"Actually, we are," said the driver, brightening. "All original material."

"Where are your instruments?" asked Vix.

"We're still working on that. And we're also working on a name."

Vix grinned. "How about 'Give Us Instruments'? . . . What is that I smell, you naughty kids?"

A sucking sound. A hand extended toward the window. "Want a hit?"

"Sure," said Vix, taking a deep toke and holding it in.

"Listen," said the driver. "I don't know about this place—"

Vix held up a finger for him to give her a second. She exhaled. "I'm sorry. What were you saying?"

"This place," said the driver. "We appreciate the favor, but it's just too sketchy. Doesn't seem very safe—"

Vix held up a finger again as she took another hit . . .

. . . A mile away, midnight traffic roared by on the Old Dixie Highway. A rainless wind bent trees, and country music blared out the open door of a nameless roadhouse. One of the patrons staggered out the door for a reason he had forgotten about since he got off his barstool. He stared across the highway and down a long black street in the general direction of the Air Force base.

The man tilted his head curiously. He watched a series of four distant and silent flashes of light. He stumbled back inside.

Chapter 37

SOUTH FLORIDA

Weary people filed through an accordion arm and into the arrival gate. The info board said the plane had been on time from Milwaukee. Then the next gates: Dallas, Memphis, Salt Lake City. Travelers waiting to board a delayed Pittsburgh flight read books in chairs, lay on the floor for power naps, plugged cell phones into charging outlets.

The midday peak, main terminal, Miami International Airport.

Rivers of people briskly flowed toward baggage claim and ground transport. Pink and yellow jackets, white pants, Panama hats, duty-free bags. Every ten yards, ten different languages.

One young man in a tropical shirt cleared customs at international arrivals and took an escalator. The shirt had tree frogs with big eyes and suction-cup fingers. Five men were waiting at the bottom of the escalator. They led him to a limo at the curb across from the Flamingo Garage.

The black stretch took the Dolphin Expressway east, past the demolition site of the Orange Bowl, into downtown. They parked on Flagler Street and joined more foot traffic, employees from the government buildings out for lunch. Some sat on benches, eating fish sandwiches or reading newspapers. Others shopped in the narrow storefronts. Not a speck of chain franchises, most of the signs in Spanish. For some reason there was an unnatural concentration of places that sold luggage. The man in the tropical shirt entered one, and the rest followed.

A short older man with olive skin and a brown guayabera was helping someone at the counter. He looked up and immediately forgot the customer existed and walked away. *"Hey, what about me? . . ."* The old man reached the back room and waved the new arrivals in. Seconds later, the tropical shirt led his men out. They were wheeling a matching set of the finest hard-shell luggage.

The luggage wasn't empty.

Five men heaved to load the suitcases into the limo's trunk.

The old man from the store stepped onto the sidewalk and extended a hand. "Gracias, Señor Deuce."

The young man in the tropical shirt glared at the sound of his name being spoken aloud, and the old man retreated grimly back inside.

They drove to Little Havana and stopped at a relaxed public park on Calle Ocho. The only other people were more old, olive-skinned men playing dominos. The limo guys went to the trunk and opened the luggage for inspection. They all nodded at Deuce and closed everything up.

They loved America.

If you were in certain lines of business, with certain tasks at hand, you didn't have to worry about smuggling in your equipment. You could just roll up to any of a dozen storefronts in Miami and pick up a set of luggage that came complete with enough military weaponry to take over a small police station, and maybe some bigger ones. Expense was no object, and the guns would soon be tossed into the Miami River like spent Bic lighters. The luggage stores bought it all legally at gun shows.

The limo continued on until it reached the turnpike, then cut south . . .

. . . An hour later, the stretch limo reached Key Largo and pulled around a pile of barnacle-crusted crab traps that was larger than the unlikely shack sitting behind it with all the paint baked off the clapboards. A seasoned local came out of the marina office wiping motor oil from his hands on his overalls. His fishing cap advertised spark plugs. It also had been used to wipe oil.

"She's all set, tuned and fueled," said the owner. "Just took her out for a spin this morning."

Deuce wouldn't have to ask which one. There were only three boats in the slips behind the office, and two didn't look like they could make it out of the channel. The third was a sleek cabin cruiser overpowered by four Yamaha 350s that could get you to Cuba and back in an afternoon. Marinas like this were the Keys version of Miami luggage stores.

The owner tightened questioning eyes. "Is everything okay? Isn't this what you wanted?"

"What I want is to take her for a spin myself," said Deuce.

"I guarantee she's running perfectly, but suit yourself."

The men climbed aboard as the owner untied the bow line from a dock cleat and tossed it. The cruiser took off without nautical etiquette, throttling up in the no-wake zone and smashing smaller boats against seawalls.

A half hour later, the vessel returned, and the owner tied her off again to the pier. By the time he was done, Deuce's men were wheeling luggage down the pier and loading it into the boat's cabin. The owner didn't want to know.

Deuce approached the overalls. "I want tight security until we come back tomorrow afternoon."

"But we're only open until six." He pointed back at a plastic clock-sign in the window.

Deuce pulled out a money clip and began peeling off Ben Franklins. "You've just become an all-night operation."

"Yes I have." The owner counted the currency as the limo's taillights wound their way back through the mangroves toward the highway.

Deuce looked out the back passenger window at long intervals of wild tropical vegetation punctuated here and there by tiny family-owned diners. There seemed to be a lot of cars parked at each. Mrs. Mac's, Harriette's, Chad's, Sunrise Cuban Market.

"I'm getting hungry," Deuce announced.

"And we need gas," said the driver. "Do you know where you want to go?"

"I know precisely," said Deuce. "Keep going until you cross the Tavernier Creek bridge."

The limo continued west through the sparse midsection of Key Largo, where the royal poinciana would soon bloom in the median strip. A cell phone rang, and an assistant answered. He offered the phone to Deuce.

"Who is it?"

"Our guy on the inside."

Deuce put the cell to his head. "Speak. . . . Yes, we're still on. . . . Yes, time is still the same. . . . What about Raffy? . . . That's very good. . . . Don't deviate from the plan and don't call again."

Click.

The limo twisted its way over the creek and down Plantation Key. Deuce pointed. "There it is."

"Where? Captain Craig's Seafood?"

"No, before it."

"There's nothing before it."

"Right here!" said Deuce. "Turn now!"

The driver complied with a slight skidding sensation. "But it's just a gas station."

"From the outside, it *looks* like it's just a gas station."

"What about all the sheriff's cars?" asked the driver. "You sure we want to be around them?"

"Cops have to eat, too," said Deuce. "That means it's good."

They pulled up to one of the pumps. Deuce got out first, and the rest followed, not wanting to betray their doubts. The driver stayed behind. "I'll fill her up."

Deuce opened the door to a small, aromatic space packed with customers. There were two counters. One to pay for gas. The other had a tall metallic sculpture of a rooster.

Chapter 38

A camera flashed.

Serge checked the viewfinder.

Deputy Deke laughed. "Don't you already have enough photos of that rooster?"

"No." Serge stowed the camera and stuck a fork in a *croqueta de jamón*.

Deke waved at the counter. "Guys, come over here. I'd like you to meet someone . . ."

Three other deputies arrived, and Serge stood to shake hands.

"This is one of our best new neighbors," said Deke. "Just got one of the condos across the street. He and his friend have started volunteering with Julie at the care center. We need their kind of community devotion around here."

"Pleasure." "Nice to meet." "Serge, was it?"

The green uniforms returned to the counter, and Serge returned to Deke. "You've now introduced me to half the department."

"Not yet, but we'll get there." Deke finished a guava pastry. "This is a tiny town, and we take care of our own. If you ever need anything."

"You say that as often as I photograph that rooster."

The door kept opening, and most of the new customers waved at the deputy sitting at the small table with Serge. Because everyone in town knew Deputy Deke. More importantly, Deke knew everyone, whether they wanted to be known or not.

"So what have you been doing lately?" he asked Serge.

"Accidentally cornering the market on Febreze," said Serge. "I'm up to my neck in the stuff. You wouldn't happen to know anyone—"

But Deputy Deke wasn't paying attention. The front door had just opened again.

Serge picked up on the vibe and stopped talking. He turned around, first noticing the stretch limo at the pumps, then the five new guys in line at the lunch counter.

Cops and robbers are often flip sides of the same coin, with the same street instincts. Serge and Deke continued staring at the counter: *Something's not right about these guys.* First, they weren't talking to each other. Take any five dudes in line anywhere, and somebody's going to be talking to somebody. Then the rigid body language, like they were escorting a prisoner. Finally—they both noticed it at the same time—Deuce, out of unconscious habit around law enforcement, was staring into the glass of the countertop pastry carousel, the empty one. The five left the store and drove off in the limo.

Deputy Deke stood quickly. "Have to run. Just remembered something." And he was out the door.

"Coleman, get up!"

He raised his head from the table. "What? . . ."

It was a jet-black night on the Old Road, surrounded by thick trees and no street lamps. The only illumination was red taillights that brightened and dimmed as brakes were pressed. First was the limo, then a few hundred yards back, a sheriff's cruiser, and finally, just turning onto the road back at Coral Shores High School, a '73 Ford Galaxie.

Coleman stuck his eye in the pouring hole of an empty flask. "I still don't know what's going on."

"We're riding backup." Serge's focus was screwed tight on the taillights ahead.

"For who?"

"Deputy Deke," said Serge. "He picked up on these five cats back at the café. One was staring into the empty pastry case."

"So what?"

"Classic counterespionage training. If you want to check if someone is surveilling you from behind, you don't turn around but instead look at the reflection in any glass: store window, car, pastry case."

"Why would the guy do that?"

"Instinct. Probably from seeing all the cops in there—"

Brake lights came on at the front of the loose procession. The limo stopped at one of the privacy gates leading toward the sea, then the patrol car's lights came on. The limo began rolling again.

"What's *that* about?" asked Coleman.

"He's looking for something, and I hope it's not what I think."

They encountered no other traffic as the pattern repeated: another gate, another set of brake lights, then onward, again and again. Until the pattern was broken. The limo's brake lights came on again at another gate, but this time it didn't just slow down. It stopped. So did the two trailing vehicles. Then a camera flash, and the limo sped up again, faster than before, and didn't stop at the other gates. Deputy Deke followed.

"Shit," said Serge.

He hit the gas and screeched up to the gate in question.

Two guards with weapons. One shined a light in Serge's face. "Turn around!"

"We have to come in!" said Serge. "We have to talk to Julie!"

"I told you to turn around!"

The intercom at the security gate box came alive with a woman's voice. "What's going on out there?"

"Nothing, Miss Julie," said one of the guards. "Just a lost tourist."

"Julie!" yelled a voice from the Galaxie. "It's me, Serge! I have to see you!"

"Serge?" said the intercom. "What are you doing here?"

"I'll explain inside . . ."

F arther up the Old Road, a black stretch limo was about to turn back onto U.S. Highway 1.

Deputy Deke suddenly lit them up with all his roof lights and hit the siren. They pulled over and the deputy walked up to the driver's window. "License and registration, please."

Deuce rolled down his back window. "Is there a problem, officer?"

"Deputy."

"I'm sorry. Deputy."

Deke examined a license. "May I ask what is your business in Islamorada?"

Deuce smiled. "Why, the same as everyone else's. To admire and enjoy your beautiful islands. Maybe try our hand at some of the famous fishing."

The deputy finished with the registration and handed it back to the driver. "Were you looking for an address back there?"

"No."

"You were slowing at each private gate. And you stopped at the last one."

"Admiring again," said Deuce. "Magnificent verdigris gate with a heron."

"You took a picture of it," said Deke.

"Thinking of getting one for my place."

"Let me see some identification."

Deke was handed a passport, and took a picture of it with his phone, then more photos of the last visa stamps to the United States.

"Is everything in order?" asked Deuce.

Deke returned the passport through the limo's back window. "I don't know what you're really up to, but we have a peaceful place here and don't take kindly to our neighbors being bothered. I suggest you keep moving. There are plenty of other islands up ahead to admire. Pick one of them."

"But we like these," said Deuce. "I think we'll stay here."

"Now it's no longer a suggestion," said Deke. "Life is comfortable here for those not looking for trouble. It can also get uncomfortable."

"Have we broken any laws?"

Deke got on his radio for a moment—"Yes, it's urgent." Then he shined his baton flashlight as he walked to the back of the stretch and, without hesitation, smashed one of the taillights. Deuce closed his eyes in annoyance.

Two other patrol cars with flashing lights pulled up behind the limo. Deke held up a finger, and the other deputies remained inside with their engines running.

Deke returned to the back window. "Don't stop until mile seventy." He slapped the roof of the limo and stepped back. Deuce rolled up his window, and the two other patrol cars followed him onto the highway, across the four main islands of Islamorada, and cut them loose at the Channel Five Bridge, where police at the other end on Long Key would cite them for faulty equipment.

B ack at the ranch:
     Serge and Coleman sat on a couch of snow-white leather. "Julie, we saw them in the café, then on the Old Road. If you don't believe us, ask Deputy Deke."

Julie was bunched up on the other end of the sofa, arms around her knees that were bent to her chest. "You're scaring me."

"Gentlemen," said Cinco, standing over them. "May I have a word?"

They regrouped in the kitchen. "I know you are friends of Julie and mean well," said Cinco, "but she isn't designed for this kind of worry. All of us here are fond of her, too. And protective. We have the best security outside of the U.S. Secret Service. If you have any concerns about her safety or anything else, we definitely want to know about it. But please, Julie doesn't need the stress." He snapped his fingers and two guards arrived. He whispered in their ears. They nodded and took off.

"What just happened?"

"They're already on their way to find this limo of yours," said Cinco. "It shouldn't be too hard with just one highway—"

He was interrupted by a squawking intercom from the front gate. "Miss Julie, we have a Deputy Deke here who wants to see you."

"Let him in," said Julie.

Cinco nodded at Serge and Coleman in the kitchen. "If you could please wait here a moment."

One of the other guards let the deputy in. "Julie, I have to talk to you."

She clenched her knees tighter. "What is it?"

Cinco politely stepped in front of the deputy and lowered his voice. "A moment in the kitchen?"

"Okay."

They rounded the corner from the living room, and the deputy's feet hit the brakes. "Serge! Coleman! What are you doing here?"

"I'm guessing same as you," said Serge. "We picked up on those dudes back at the café and followed them up until they took a photo of the front gate. Something wasn't right. And you know how I am about taking photos. Nobody could be bigger—"

Cinco cleared his throat. "Please, quieter. You're all making Julie a wreck."

Deke peeked around the corner and saw her rocking back and forth on the couch. "Oh, geez, sorry."

"Deputy," said Cinco, "I know you know everything around here, so I won't insult you. I can't say much, but what is certain is that this place is locked down as tight as if you were protecting her at the sheriff's office. And with her father and the kids, I'm sure she'd rather be here."

Deke reluctantly nodded.

"May I impose for a favor?"

"Name it," said the deputy.

"Could you all reassure her?"

Moments later, they left the kitchen and arrived at the couch.

Julie, still rocking with clutched knees. "What were you guys talking about in there that I wasn't allowed to hear?"

"Nothing like that," said Deke. "We were just comparing notes. And I am so sorry, but there has been a huge misunderstanding."

"That's right," said Serge. "A big oopsie-doodle."

"We were only watching out for you," said Deke. "And some suspicious guys caught our attention."

"They were making false moves," said Serge. "But as I've told people a million times, there's no such thing as a false move. A move is still a move, right? Maybe an *unappreciated* move, but false—?"

Deke elbowed him. "The point is that it just turned out to be some new guys reporting to Cinco. I jumped to the wrong conclusion simply because I hadn't seen them around here before. So there's nothing to worry about."

Julie turned to Cinco. "Is that true?"

He nodded. "Even less to worry about. We're beefing up security, because of all your kids staying here now. Promise us you'll not give it another thought."

She got off the couch. "After a glass of wine . . ."

Before leaving, the visitors all clustered with Cinco inside the front door.

Deke leaned. "Call me if your guys find out anything about those new people. You can trust me to be discreet where I need to. It's about Julie."

"Thank you," said Cinco. "And please let me know if your people hear of anything that raises the threat level."

"You'll be the first."

The door opened, and they left through a phalanx of armed guards pacing circles around the fountain at the edge of the driveway.

Chapter 39

The morning sky was weird.

The horizon remained a deep purple curtain from unseen clouds stretching in the direction of Cuba and all the way east toward Bimini in the Bahamas. The visibility ceiling above was blanketed by gauzy stratus clouds that diffused the sunlight like umbrella filters in a photo portrait studio. Combined with the purple backdrop, it created an entire sea of fluorescent jade.

Serge stepped onto the balcony. He stretched his back and blew steam off his first cup of coffee. It was in a souvenir mug from the 2010 Miami Book Fair. The mug's design was the city's skyline composed of books made to look like buildings. He kicked something below.

Coleman was still out on the balcony, from the night before. He grabbed his side. "What kicked me?"

"Arise, Spanky."

Coleman sat up and rubbed his neck. "Why am I so stiff?"

Serge pointed beneath Coleman. "Concrete."

"Oh, right. I keep forgetting that." He reached in his pocket for a joint bent into a U and straightened it out. "Why does the sky look so weird?"

"Atmospherics," said Serge. "I've seen that sky before. And almost every time, the day goes sideways."

"Ow!" said Coleman. "Why'd you kick me again?"

"Get up. We have work to do," said Serge, heading inside. "Who knows how long we'll have to prepare?"

Coleman followed. "Prepare for what?"

"Sideways." Serge slapped a small cardboard box against his pal's stomach and opened a kitchen cupboard. "Load up all that stuff."

As Coleman filled the box, Serge grabbed his wallet and keys.

Coleman hefted the container upward against his chest. "Where are we going?"

"To the nearest fireworks store."

"Is there one down here?"

"We're in Florida," said Serge, opening the door. "You must always be minutes away from fireworks. It's a zoning ordinance."

The '73 Galaxie headed east over the Tavernier Creek bridge to Key Largo. Passing them in the other direction was a psychedelic Volkswagen microbus.

"I'm exhausted," said Mulch, slowing down at the first stoplight. "And all scraped up. Why did we have to carry those bodies so far into the mangroves last night? Why couldn't we have just left them back at the muffler shop?"

"You don't even know that you're stupid," said Vix, face down toward a crumpled hand-drawn map. "We needed to change vehicles. So we grabbed this van. And as soon as they identify the bodies, they know what we're driving now. But they can't ID them if they can't find them."

"Oh."

"Turn here."

The VW left the Overseas Highway and began a slower drive down Plantation Key on the Old Road.

Mulch stared curiously out the windshield. "This can't be the right place. Just a bunch of scraggly trees."

"It's definitely right," said Vix, looking out the window as a mysterious gate into the woods went by. "When I was back at that convenience store checking directions, the woman at the counter said the locals call this Millionaires Row. Lots of dirt roads leading back through the woods to big honkin' seaside mansions. Keep going."

Vix checked the address on her tattered map against the numbers on the gates. The 8900s, 8800s, 8700s. This kind of analytical investigative work required whiskey and coke. *Chug, snort.*

"How much farther?" asked Mulch.

Slap! "What are you, fucking eight years old? You'll stop when I say to!"

They continued on, number after gate after number. Then things changed. The gates and the woods trailed off. More modest houses near the road, industrial lots that welded boat trailers and lifts, a metal building advertising glass repair. On the other side, the trees disappeared, an off-brand convenience store came into view, then the noise from U.S. Highway 1.

Another chug. "What the fuck? We've left the Row, and the number is still coming up."

The men chose not to offer thoughts. Vix decided another line on the back of her hand would lock in her thinking. *Snort.* "Slow down."

The Day-Glo microbus rolled quietly with no other traffic. Vix saw a mailbox coming up. "Stop! This is it!"

They all looked at the house, set back in gravel, relatively near the sea. A decent four-bedroom affair set up on stuccoed concrete stilts. It was painted peach.

"This doesn't look like a kingpin's mansion," said Mulch, forgetting.

Slap! "Do you know what homes sell for down here? And a lot

of kingpins try to keep a low profile. This is definitely our place."
She held up her crumpled page. "It matches what the guy drew."

"He drew a square."

Vix pointed. "That's a square. Couldn't be any other place.
Let's hit it."

They jumped out of the van and walked under the empty stilt
space, where a car or two would normally be parked. Weeds were
free to rise through the gravel.

"I think the place is empty," said Weezer, pointing back over
his shoulder. "The mailbox was stuffed with junk flyers."

"Let's take a look around."

The gang circled the backyard, subconsciously checking the
ground for a place to start treasure digging.

Suddenly, from over the fence next door: "What the hell are
you doing there? Answer or I'm calling the police!"

Normally, people who are where they shouldn't be, confronted
with accusation, will retreat. But cocaine recalibrates the equation. Vix advanced on the fence and counterattacked. "You have
some nerve talking to me that way! Were we impolite to you? No,
but your best foot forward is being a shit!"

Off balance: "Well, uh, what are you doing there?"

She remembered the name from the map. "We're old friends
of Ralph. Ralph Cootehill."

"Oh, the charter fishing captain," said the fence voice.

Inside Vix's head: *Charter fishing captain?* "Yeah, that's him."

"Well, you mustn't have been too good a friend."

"Why do you say that?"

"Because he moved out of this place a few years ago."

"He used to take us out offshore," said Vix. "Only captain we
would ever use. The years got by us. But since we were down here
again, we thought it only polite to drop in and say hello. You're telling us it's no longer his house?"

"No, he still owns it, but he rents it out long-term to fishing
tourists," said the neighbor. "Except it's off-season right now." The

neighbor saw where they were standing in the gravel, and chose not to mention all the times he saw Ralph digging after midnight, back in the day when charter boat captains called a number in a phone booth at the docks and loaded wet containers into windowless vans.

"Do you know where he lives now?" asked Vix.

"Yes, with his daughter, on Upper Matecumbe."

"You wouldn't happen to have the address?"

"Matter of fact I do. Got something to write with? . . ."

. . . The gang climbed back into the van.

"A fishing captain?" said Weezer. "What do you make of that?"

"A wild-goose chase is what," said Mulch. "From New Hampshire to the Keys. What a fucking joke."

Vix was now guzzling the Wild Turkey 101, and snorting from her palm . . . *Slap!*

"Ouch!"

"Just drive."

The Scooby-Doo van rolled on, west down U.S. 1 over the islands of Islamorada, toward a new address.

A Technicolor VW microbus drove onto Upper Matecumbe Key, past the diving museum and a giant mermaid sign for the crowd-favorite Lorelei. It slowed and carefully turned right, threading a tight lane flanked with rows of Airstreams, teardrops and other vintage trailers.

"Stop," said Vix, grabbing a hammer and chisel. "Here we are."

The surviving guys glanced at each other, then at the curved silver mobile home again. They followed Vix as she stepped up on a tiny porch. Another stuffed mailbox. The door was locked but rattling, no match for a single swing of Vix's hammer against the chisel. The door flew open and hit a wall. "Mulch, grab that mail."

They went inside to the smell of an old person. "Fan out," said Vix. "Check everything." She began going through the mail at the kitchen counter, discarding piece after piece.

Minutes later, the guys returned timidly. "We're sorry, but we tore the place apart," said Mulch. "Nothing."

Weezer cleared his throat. "And the trailer's sitting tight on a slab, no room to bury anything . . . Vix? Vix? Why are you so happy?"

"Because we just hit pay dirt!" She held up a government flyer from the pile of mail.

"What's that?" asked Mulch.

"Change of address notice from the post office." Vix flapped it over her head like a developing Polaroid. "They always mail one to the old address in case there's been a mistake or scam."

"So how does that make you so happy?"

"Because the new address is in the heart of the Old Road, right where we were. Our source up in New Hampshire was just going off old info." She waved the piece of mail over her head again. "Now, *this* is the address of a kingpin!"

. . . It was teeth-grinding tedium as the VW van cruised down the Old Road on Plantation Key.

Vix looked up from the post office form to passing mailboxes outside eerie gates. "It's coming up. Slow down! There it is!"

The van was at a crawl as it passed a verdigris gate with a heron and a gumbo-limbo. "That's it for sure!" said Vix. "Did you see the guard inside?"

"Yeah, carrying a MAC-10," said Weezer. "And not too discreetly."

"That means it's definitely on the money," said Vix. "Imagine the score!"

Mulch rolled a few more feet and stopped on the shoulder. "Vix, please don't take this the wrong way, but that's just the one guard we *saw*, and the security system must be impenetrable. You've heard of a suicide mission?"

"Don't be a pussy," said Vix. "We'll come back at night, see what security looks like then and think of something. Let's go get a pizza."

Chapter 40

PLANTATION KEY

A particularly humorless lot of humanity rolled into a gravel parking lot.

Because it was the government center. Driver's licenses, taxes, fines for all occasions.

In the sheriff's substation, a deputy leaned over a functional metal desk toward a computer monitor. In the old days, he would have been going through a mug book. Now it was all digital. Plus, the search was abbreviated because he already had the photos in his phone that he had taken of a passport during the traffic stop. He looked at the name next to the mug shot on the front page, and inputted it.

Cesar Chavez Gutierrez. Aka Deuce.

Deke ran the name through every system. A lot of bad stuff from South America, but not even a parking ticket in the States. He navigated through his phone to the most recent U.S. entry stamps in the passport. Last month, the third and the twenty-fifth.

The deputy didn't need to check through the files on his desk to refresh his memory, because it was still fresh. The two dates came just before the boat explosion in Toilet Seat Cut and the helicopter going down off Plantation Key.

He stood by the printer, impatiently waiting for it to finish spitting out the whole workup on Deuce, then grabbed the stack and ran out the door . . .

. . . The sheriff's cruiser remained parked on the side of the Old Road, where it had been for hours. Deputy Deke going through the files over and over while he sat on Julie's place, racked with self-doubts and second guesses: *What more could I have done last night?* He started burning up his cell phone, calling every agency he could think of, but everyone said the same. There were no warrants, persons of interest, State Department flags or anything else to hold him. *If he does something, then call us back.*

Deputy Deke uncapped a thermos of coffee. His gut had never been stronger. The limo was obviously coming back. But where the hell was it now?

KEY LARGO

A '73 Galaxie made a wild U-turn on U.S. 1, throwing Coleman into the passenger door and spraying Schlitz.

"Serge, why'd you do that?"

"Hold on. I just spotted the limo from last night."

"Beer went up my nose."

"Is that good or bad?"

"I haven't decided yet."

The Galaxie sped east in the dense tourist traffic, but no way they could lose that giant black stretch. A few miles later, the limo made a right turn past a scuba shop. Serge took the same turn, and held back since the road was remote and empty. The tires crept until they reached the end of the mangroves concealing their car. They got out on foot.

"What's going on?" asked Coleman.

"Keep your voice down," said Serge. "They're loading a boat."

The pair watched through mangrove leaves. The limo men were now in black jumpsuits with shoulder and belt harnesses for munitions. They tossed a few last duffels aboard and cast off, motoring down a stagnant canal of tea-colored water.

"Why are they doing that?" asked Coleman.

"Just what I was expecting. They're coming at Julie's place from the sea. It's what I would have done."

They trotted back to the Galaxie and headed west. The pair approached the entrance to an independent pizza parlor, where a Scooby-Doo van pulled out ahead of them.

Vix was still performing on the high wire of whiskey and coke. Weezer had a flat box on his lap. He grabbed the last piece of the pie.

"Hey!" said Mulch. "That's mine! You already had your share of pieces!"

"It doesn't go by number of pieces because they don't always slice it accurately. There are three of us, so I get a hundred and twenty degrees."

"We need a fucking protractor to eat pizza?"

"Ahhhhhh!" screamed Vix. She seized the final slice and flung it out the window. The wind got hold, and it Frisbeed back, splatting on the windshield of a '73 Galaxie.

"I'll take care of it," said Coleman, reaching forward out his window, his fingertips just beyond reach. "Serge, it's too far away. Push it over with the wipers."

Serge briefly hit a switch for a single sweep of the wipers, and Coleman peeled the slice off the glass.

Serge glanced sideways toward the passenger seat. "I hate to ask, but what are you doing?"

Coleman continued chewing. "Free pizza! I love the Keys!"

The sun still had some time above the horizon, but the thick, tall trees already cast long shadows on the darkening Old Road.

Deputy Deke was still there with cold coffee, parked several gates up in draping vines for surveillance coverage. The van was next, parking directly across the street from Julie's gate. Vix somehow still had situational awareness; to avert suspicion, she told the others to get out and stretch while she snapped photos of the foliage like a tourist. The Galaxie arrived and parked a discreet distance on the other side of the gate. Serge grabbed a cardboard box from the back seat, which held the contents of a kitchen cabinet, along with some fireworks and a roll of duct tape. The peacocks showed up.

T he sun was down for good, and powerful search beams split the night over the water. The tunnels of light swept left and right, finding channel markers to guide back the last fishing boats of the day.

One speeding cabin cruiser wasn't using searchlights to find depth markers. It raced parallel to shore a half mile out. It was a long, choppy run west from Key Largo, the hull repeatedly rising up and slapping hard and loud down onto the waves. The mist from the spray made everyone's nostrils salty.

A half hour later, Deuce monitored the GPS. "Slow down. We're a hundred yards out. Turn north." The cruiser came around slowly in the direction of shore . . .

. . . Serge filled a knapsack with the contents of his cardboard box and grabbed bolt cutters. "Coleman, we're on."

They crept up to a gate. "What is this place?" asked Coleman.

"One of Julie's neighbors," said Serge, snapping something with the cutters. "And one of the few places along here with just a gate. No cameras or security alarms." They slipped through and Serge aimed a flashlight. "Follow me."

They found their way to an abandoned tennis court and Serge turned right into the woods.

"Where are we going?" asked Coleman.

Serge cut through a chain-link fence dividing land. "We need to get over a couple of properties until we're next door to Julie." The flashlight led the way.

Soon, they were peeking over a fence as armed guards patrolled the grounds of a post-modern manse. A new guard came out one of the back doors, deliberately leaving it unlocked. He relieved the previous sentry stationed facing the water. Serge and Coleman watched as the new guard glanced around suspiciously before aiming a flashlight out to sea and flashing it three times. Somewhere from the dark water, three flashes came back.

"What's that about?" asked Coleman.

"Two things," said Serge. "They've got someone on the inside, and it's about to go down."

They continued watching as the vague, dark outline took the shape of a cabin cruiser with no running lights. It approached the dock behind the mansion, and one of the crew grabbed the first pier, followed by someone else with a mooring line . . .

Back on the Old Road, more whiskey and cocaine. Two guys increasingly tensed up, knowing what was coming. Vix was about to fall off the high wire. "I am so fucking tired of all this waiting! When was the last time we saw a guard go by the gate?"

Her passengers shrugged.

"I didn't hear an answer!"

"Uh, a l-l-long time," said Weezer.

"That's what I thought!" Vix put the van in gear and turned in reverse, pointing the microbus directly at the driveway. One last gonzo snort, then she upended the whiskey before winging the empty bottle out the window, followed by a distant crash on the pavement. Her pupils were tiny pinholes as she clenched her teeth with the clamping strength of a mako shark.

"W-w-what are you going to do?" asked Mulch.

"I want that money!" She floored the gas, and tires spun before finally grabbing traction, catapulting the VW across the road and smashing through the wrought-iron gates. Alarms went off all over the house.

"Shit!" Deputy Deke said to himself, starting the patrol car and grabbing a microphone. ". . . Request backup . . ." He turned in the driveway and ran over broken pieces of metal.

Down at the dock, the boat crew looked toward the house when they heard all the alarms. "Have they already detected us?" asked a deckhand.

"Not possible," said Deuce. "But something happened. Get running! . . ."

Serge watched them cross the long stretch of lawn as he reached into his knapsack. He lit a fuse and heaved an object overhand.

Boom.

The boat crew hit the ground. "What the hell was that?"

"Keep moving!" yelled Deuce.

Serge lit another and heaved it.

Boom.

They hit the ground again, now crawling for their lives.

"Serge," said Coleman, "why did you tape all those cherry bombs to the cans of Febreze?"

Serge lobbed another. "Shock them with explosions and awe them with lilac."

Boom.

A VW van raced up the driveway. Then a sheriff's cruiser. Inside the house, guards ran every which way as Julie frantically gathered children from bunk beds and herded them upstairs. Men in black jumpsuits continued crawling across the manicured backyard. Serge dashed toward the water.

Boom.

Everyone within sight turned south toward the dock, where Febreze shrapnel had hit the cabin cruiser's fuel line, turning the works into a fireball.

The explosions drew the outdoors security patrol to the rear of the property, but the boat crew had already slipped in the unlocked back door. The house was in a state of madness. Alarms still going off, guards running into each other, children screaming. Julie had one more group of kids to shepherd to safety but . . .

The front door flew open, and the occupants of a psychedelic van ran inside. They raised pistols. "Nobody move!" yelled Vix. "Drop your weapons!"

From behind, Deputy Deke rushed in. "No, you drop your weapons!"

From a back door, the boat crew charged into the room. "Everyone! Hands up!"

From a side door, Serge arrived smiling with Coleman. "What did we miss?"

It wasn't a Mexican standoff; it was a United Nations standoff. There were so many opponents that nobody knew which way to aim their weapons. Barrels with laser sights kept crisscrossing the house in the violent geometry of a Pink Floyd concert.

One person had rehearsed for the moment. Barely audible, Deuce: "Now."

Gunfire erupted from the black jumpsuits. Several of the house guards immediately went down, and everyone else leaped for cover. Others got off shots from the floor, taking out two of Deuce's men. Serge pulled his pistol and dove toward the remaining children on the first floor, balled up against a wall with Coleman. He found himself skidding across the marble into Deputy Deke. They were soon joined by Cinco, all returning fire.

More people went down. Loose guns clattering across the floor. Julie was at the foot of the floating staircase, crouched with two children, then made a run for it and got them into a bedroom. On her way back down the stairs, she was hit in the leg and tumbled the last few steps before landing on the floor. One of the house guards took three in the chest and fell backward on top of

Julie, pinning her, his submachine gun still clasped in his lifeless hands.

In many battles, there is a time to cease fire and let the smoke clear to take account. That was this point. The fog of war was thick in the giant living room with hazy layers of gun smoke. Motionless bodies and others vainly slithering in blood slicks. A chorus of moaning and groaning. Barely audible distant sirens. Serge, the deputy and Cinco formed a protective wall in front of the children. Deke clutched his bloody shooting hand. "I'm hit. I lost my gun."

Serge checked his pistol. "I'm almost out."

Cinco saw one of the house guards standing next to Deuce: "Raffy's upstairs, door on the left."

"Goose!" yelled Cinco. "How could you?"

"Nothing personal," said one of Raffy's most trusted body-guards. "It's just business."

He and Cinco simultaneously raised their weapons and fired, and both fell dead.

Deuce turned the other way to one of his boat crew. "Enough of this foolishness. Kill them all."

"What about the children?"

"If they're in the way."

That started it again. The guards that had taken cover opened up, along with Deuce's gang and the passengers from the micro-bus. Serge kept firing until: *Click.* "Now I'm definitely out."

A few more bursts of gunfire, until sheer attrition silenced the house again. Those still alive on the floor glanced around. *Who's left?*

The only person still standing and armed marched forward toward the back of the room in bone-throbbing psychosis. Vix raised her pistol with a vibrating arm. "Where's the fucking money?"

"What money?" said Serge.

"The money this kingpin is hiding in this house!" yelled Vix, waving a diagram. "I have a map!"

Serge upturned his palms. "There's no money here."

"Yes, there is!" She took another menacing step forward. "And we've worked hard for it! We deserve it! Driving all the way down the coast and then going to the wrong house of some fishing captain, and then a trailer where we got this address. What a bunch of fuckery!"

Serge's brain fluttered with mental index cards: All those rumors of captains burying money from the bales. Captain Ralph fit the timeline . . . He heard the loud sirens pouring up the driveway. Just stall.

"You've got the wrong idea."

"Last chance!" screamed Vix. "Where's my money?"

Serge stood up and spread his arms. "Please, the children."

The deputy rose to his feet next to him. "Yes, think of the kids."

Vix began to shriek behind her gritted teeth. "I hate children! To hell with all of you!"

The two defenseless men made themselves as wide as possible into a human shield. They squinted and braced. Vix stiffened her shooting arm, and squeezed the trigger.

Bang, bang, bang, bang . . .

Vix almost appeared to dance as she high-stepped sideways.

Julie, still pinned under the guard, continued firing with his machine gun. "Don't . . . fuck . . . with . . . my . . . children!"

Vix finally hit the wall. She stood momentarily with unclenched teeth until her legs gave way, and she slid to the floor.

Serge and Deke just stared with open mouths at Julie, as deputies and peacocks raced in through the front door.

Epilogue

Deputy Deke Fuentes recovered from his wound and was heavily decorated for valor during ceremonies that were reported prominently by all the island papers that advertised boat sales and CBD outlets. During the ensuing investigation, Deke personally took over looking into the backgrounds of everyone at the shootout, and gave Serge and Coleman a clean bill of health without really looking very much.

All the major newspapers in Puerto Rico reported a mysterious explosion on top of the city wall overlooking La Perla. The blast was traced to a bag of Goldfish crackers. Police listed one fatality, an old Colombian named Morales with notorious business connections. Shortly afterward, through back channels, Julie received word that she no longer had to worry about any more threats to her children.

In the confusion after the shootout, Serge found a map on the floor near Vix's body. A few days later, he bought orange vests and hard hats and tiny flags to plant in the ground like the ones that utility companies use. None of Captain Ralph's former neighbors questioned Serge and Coleman as they dug freely behind the fishing captain's old house.

J ulie's private care center on the Old Road became famous, and she received plaques at banquets from Key West to Miami to CNN. A foundation was set up in response to all the inquiries from people asking where they could make donations. Money flooded in, but one curious donation stood out from the rest: several anonymous cardboard boxes full of dusty cash. It arrived the day after she had discovered tiny flags and a giant hole behind her father's old house.

W ord of the wild night on the Old Road swept through the residents of Pelican Bay, and Serge became an even bigger hero than ever. At the next meeting, he was elected president of the condominium board in a landslide. Serge's first official act was to declare massive voting fraud in the rigged election, and he refused to accept the position.

O n his way out of the meeting, Serge smacked himself in the forehead. "I knew I was forgetting something!" He drove up to the Kmart on Key Largo and found an irate Tanya waiting in the aisle for cleaning products. "I've been coming here every day!" Serge profusely apologized and promised to make it up to her. She finally relented and agreed to join the guys for the New Year's Eve celebration in Key West.

As the minutes ticked down toward midnight, thousands of people clogged the end of Duval Street outside Sloppy Joe's saloon. Many were holding up cell phones to video the giant conch shell sitting atop a tower on the roof. It was a long-standing tradition: Soon, the shell would lower down to the bar's roof, just like the giant crystal ball in Times Square.

"Don't get me wrong," said Coleman. "I've had fun and all, but this year kind of sucked."

"I know what you mean," said Serge. "And I feel guilty for even thinking it, because we're blessed just to be alive. But the last twelve months did have a serious layer of crud. On the other hand, things can only go up. I have an uncanny sensation that this coming year is going to be the best ever!"

Tanya clutched Serge's arm and whooped as the conch shell began its descent from the tower. The countdown from the crowd was deafening: "*Six, five, four, three, two, one . . .*"

The shell finally reached the bottom, and giant numbers brightly lit up.

2020.

ABOUT THE AUTHOR

Tim Dorsey was a reporter and editor for the *Tampa Tribune* from 1987 to 1999, and is the author of twenty-four other novels: *Florida Roadkill, Hammerhead Ranch Motel, Orange Crush, Triggerfish Twist, The Stingray Shuffle, Cadillac Beach, Torpedo Juice, The Big Bamboo, Hurricane Punch, Atomic Lobster, Nuclear Jellyfish, Gator A-Go-Go, Electric Barracuda, When Elves Attack, Pineapple Grenade, The Riptide Ultra-Glide, Tiger Shrimp Tango, Shark Skin Suite, Coconut Cowboy, Clownfish Blues, The Pope of Palm Beach, No Sunscreen for the Dead, Naked Came the Florida Man* and *Tropic of Stupid*. He lives in Florida.